Penguins and Panamas

by Jamie Gray

ABOUT THE AUTHOR

Jamie Gray has worked in the theatre industry for over twenty years and was engaged in many different roles from stage hand to stage manager (and pretty much everything else in between) He's even dared to try his hand at acting occasionally and considers himself a half decent performer, however most of his friends think he's just spent far too much time in the dark.
This is his second novel which has been somewhat influenced by a cruise holiday around South America with his wonderfully tolerant wife.

Stephen / a really lovely man / love

ISBN-13: 978 1973798026
ISBN-10: 1973798026

This novel is a work of fiction and although based on a cruise itinerary around South America it is the author's artistic interpretation of the events that took place. Some of the dialogue has been influenced, but not replicated, by occurrences witnessed and conversations overheard. The geographic locations are real, however the named characters are a product of the author's imagination and any resemblance to actual persons, living or dead, is entirely coincidental and unintended.

www.jamiegrayauthor.com

'New Beginnings'

Tuesday 1st January 2013

Hello 2013!

At the start of this new year many of my fellow inmates on this spinning ball of rock we all inhabit will be desperate for a 'New Beginning', an optimistic expectation for things to be, at least, somewhat better than before.

So I imagine that as the masses sang 'Auld Lang Syne' last night there were a fair number of individuals who couldn't wait to rid themselves of an ill-fated 2012. With trembling hands they would have symbolically drawn a line in the sands of time, then stepping over it as the clocks struck twelve they'd have begged for 2013 to be kinder to them.

These same folk might even have woken this morning convinced that the gods will finally recognise it's their turn for a share of some long overdue good fortune...starting with a six figure lottery win maybe, or a more tolerant partner who understands and accepts their strange habits.

For a short while levels of hope will be high, but I reckon there's going to be a lot of very disappointed folk over the coming weeks and months. By Easter some will be wishing their lives away and begging for the prompt arrival of 2014, maybe that will prove to be a better year...or, most probably, not!

For me personally, last year was great, and 2013 already seems perfect as today marks the first official day of my very own 'New Beginning' in the guise of retirement from the overbearing, but essential, shackles of paid employment.

After many long years with my nose to the grindstone, the time has finally come to embark on a long anticipated new adventure. I just hope it's the start of many interesting and happy chapters and not a sad finale with a depressingly short epilogue.

To that end I've pushed the boat out and booked a last-minute cruise holiday.

This isn't just any old cruise though, this is a twelve week vacation of a lifetime, heralded by the travel agent as an 'Epic Voyage of Discovery around South America'.

Considering my only other encounter of this mode of transport was the Isle of Wight ferry, on which I was violently sick, I'm not quite sure if it's the wisest thing I've ever done.

According to my retirement counsellor Jake, I have to seize the opportunity and take some time initially to 'discover myself'. Now I genuinely thought I knew who I was, but according to Jake (a forty year old 'Life Realignment Specialist' who looks like a seventy year old hippie) I don't.

However I do know that my lovely lady is keen to ensure that I don't get bored and she's already 'discovered' a long list of jobs for my attention.

So when I saw the words 'Voyage of Discovery' scrawled on a card in the window of the local travel agent, I took it as an omen, an opportunity to come up with a plan to organise my newly acquired spare time before she does.

Anyway it's done, and there's no turning back as there's a no refund policy for such a late booking, so I have just five days to prepare and pack...oh and tell you know who. That might prove to be a bit of a surprise considering she only sent me out to book a couple of weeks in the Mediterranean to escape the worst of the British winter. But this holiday was cheap, ridiculously cheap in fact, and it has an added bonus as there's a good chance to see penguins. She loves the little critters and has always wanted to see them in their natural habitat, so I'm hoping she'll be happy and forgiving.

There is one of Jake's suggestions that I really like, and that's keeping a diary or journal, a record of any aspirations and dreams I have. He reckons this will provide a focus for the future now that I don't have the regular routine of employment. I've always fancied myself as a bit of a writer and have often penned pieces of nonsense in my desk diary at work, so I'm going to give it a go.

Maybe I'll turn out to be a geriatric Adrian Mole? (probably more like a male menopausal Bridgette Jones)

Anyway, I've got to go and break the news about the imminent 'Voyage of Discovery' to my dear lady, so I'm taking her to our local for supper tonight as she'd never make a scene in a public place, I hope.

Right well, more tomorrow.

Wednesday 2nd January

Five sleeps to go!

Last night ended much better than it'd started.

Initially my dear lady was really happy because of the penguins (wise move to mention them first up)

Then she'd found out how much the cruise had

cost, sparking a debate about how much more cash we'll need to take with us, not to mention all the other 'stuff' we'll have to buy before we even get on the ship.

The ensuing row about how I should be more careful with our money was quite intense, and fairly loud.

The other diners in the pub weren't actually invited to offer an opinion, but they did anyway. Siding with my dear lady's point of view was obviously considered the best way to calm her down and stop her throwing those little packets of sauces at me. Thank goodness health and safety deem it dangerous to have glass bottles of the stuff on the table nowadays, I can now see why.

When the landlady had arrived with our meals she obviously felt the need to add her two pennies worth as well.

"And don't forget you'll be expected to tip the staff," she'd announced a little too sarcastically for my liking.

"Bet you never thought of that did you?" she'd added with a well aimed sneer in my direction.

I'm sure her comment must have been for the benefit of someone else as I always leave a pound coin on the table to show my gratitude.

Silence followed as my dear lady embarked on a vengeful drowning of her scampi in the last two packets of ketchup. I'd kept quiet and hoped she wasn't thinking about doing the same to me.

"And you'll need to get vaccinated."

Thanks go out to 'Mr and Mrs We've Travelled the World on a Cruise Ship' on the next table for that snippet of information.

But they were very positive about cruising and spent the rest of the evening cheering my dear lady up, especially when they guaranteed we'd have a wonderful time.

It turns out that they were right about the vaccinations. The travel agents had failed to inform me that as part of the trip takes us down the mighty Amazon River we have to be in possession of a valid Yellow Fever certificate and malaria tablets.

So I've arranged an appointment for both of us at a private travel clinic in the city tomorrow.

Meanwhile, my dear lady has proceeded to take the house apart in a bid to ascertain what we have in the way of suitable holiday wear. It appears there's nothing of hers which is current and nothing of mine she likes the look of.

Why am I not surprised.

We're off shopping, so more later.

Well 'goodbye' to a thousand pounds of my swiftly dwindling retirement lump sum, and 'hello' a car loaded with carrier bags full of surprises.

"What's in this one?" I'd asked each time she came out of a shop.

"It's a surprise," she'd answered.

She must have bought thirty surprises.

I'd felt it important to inform her that at my time of life I'm not sure I could cope with more than one surprise at a time.

She'd replied 'Oh really?' and disappeared into another boutique, expensive looking.

Will I ever learn?

To be honest I don't mind her treating herself, but I'm not as forgiving of the stuff she's bought for me.

Why would anyone need more than one decent formal suit, and does she really imagine I'm happy to wear a bright pink shirt in this day and age?

Yes, I admit my old dinner jacket is probably not an up to the minute, shiny shawl lapelled example of modern 'haute couture' apparel, but it has a certain style that I like. She says it also has embroidered pockets and wide lapels which apparently went out in the seventies.

Once we we're back home again she made me try on absolutely everything I possess, even the old y-fronts stuffed at the back of the drawer. There are now six bin bags full of cast-offs in the garage and we're going back to the shops after tea.

I think I just heard my wallet whimpering.

At least she's spent most of the day humming 'Happy Feet' so I reckon that overall she's in high spirits.

Thursday 3rd January

Four sleeps to go.

I don't think I've had so many clothes in my entire life, and I've certainly never owned twenty pristine pairs of pants and thirty matched pairs of socks before.

But I really put my foot in it last night while we were re-stocking my entire wardrobe in the men's department. I'd implored my dear lady to curb her enthusiasm.

"After all," I'd declared, "There's a very good launderette and ironing room on board."

It took me almost twenty minutes to find her to apologise.

She was trying to sneak back to the car with yet another 'surprise' which she'd claimed was an advance payment for the washing and ironing service she'd be expected to supply whilst we're away. From the price I could see on the label, I reckon it would have been cheaper to buy a new set of clothing in every port and donate my dirty laundry to a dockyard skip.

Maybe it's best I don't ask if it's too late to take that latest surprise back.

Still, I really like the new batch of cotton shirts she's bought me, and even the shorts she's chosen don't make my legs look too ridiculous.

But I'm not so keen on the rainbow bright Speedos as they're very tight and ridiculously brief. With the overhang of my belly it doesn't look like I'm wearing anything at all from certain angles.

And so to the clinic.

I hate needles, what on earth was I thinking?

Dear Sirs,

It was with some trepidation that I attended your Travel Clinic today for a routine Yellow Fever Immunisation, to comply with the requirements for my imminent trip to South America.

On arrival my wife and I were initially greeted in a courteous manner, but this polite façade soon slipped to reveal some very inconsiderate and uncaring treatment after I clearly explained to a member of your staff that I was in fact petrified of receiving an injection.

Now it's okay for my wife to make fun of my phobia, but I consider that it was inappropriate for the staff to join in and mock me for my apprehension.

I really do appreciate that my fear of needles is irrational, and probably quite childish, but was it really necessary for the attending nurse to not only point this out repeatedly, but also to laugh hysterically whilst giving an overly graphic description of the procedure?

I think not. It's no wonder I passed out!

The final insult came when I was charged an extra fifty pounds for the care I received during my faint, which I may add only happened as a result of the actions of your staff.

As usual the big corporation wins and small individual fools like myself pay the price for being just a little bit normal.

Yours Sincerely.

I wish I had the bottle to send this.

But thanks again go out to Jake for his suggestion to include my moments of anger and grief in this journal, I really do feel a lot better for penning my anguish. But my pride may take a little longer to heal, especially if my dear lady insists on continuing to sing 'Needles and Pins' by The Searchers for the next twenty four hours.

Friday 4th January

Three sleeps to go.

Everything is now piled on the bed in the spare room ready for packing, and although there seems to be an awful lot I'm not sure it would be prudent to mention the on-board launderette again.

Anyway it's my job to get everything neatly tucked away in the cases, supervised of course, and it needs doing before she decides to add any more stuff we won't actually need.

When it comes to packing I'd settle for stuffing several armfuls of apparel straight into a carrier bag.

But for my dear lady the preparation to go on this holiday seems to have been almost as exciting as the event itself. Over the last couple of days I've witnessed a complex set of emotions in her as the routine progressed.

Here are my observations.

Euphoria – the realisation that the holiday is literally just around the corner and she must quickly assemble all the trappings required for the perfect holiday.

Expectation – she has to try everything on. Time for a 'FASHION SHOW'.

Irritation – nothing fits properly.

Hope – she vows to go on a diet immediately, despite there being less than a week to go before departure.

Despair – she realises that her plan to lose the required amount of weight is probably way too ambitious.

Happiness – so there's an immediate need to go shopping.

Excitement – she's going shopping, and that means spending 'his' money.

Indecision – where to start, there are so many nice things in her favourite shops.

Resolve – not to spend too much because the holiday has already cost 'us' a small fortune.

Denial – it's pointless to skimp on looking good, after all it is the holiday of a lifetime.

Guilt – she feels she may have been a little self indulgent so quickly heads for the Men's Department.

Distraction – she has to pass Lingerie on the way

and stops for a quick look.

Exhaustion – this is as a direct result of not asking 'him' to help carry the bags. She daren't!

Confusion – back home she claims to have no knowledge about how she managed to buy so much more stuff than she was planning on? Seems like someone deliberately set out to distract her resolve.

Defiance – it wasn't her fault, she was mugged by shop assistants.

Justification – he needs to see how good you look, time for another 'FASHION SHOW'.

Damage Limitation – she starts with the sexy underwear!

Gratitude – to the shop assistant in Lingerie, red is definitely the way to brighten her man's mood.

Determination – with all her new outfits neatly assembled with the acceptable and wearable old stuff, she needs to be considerably ruthless to get under the weight allowance.

Surprise – the rearranged pile of clothing that equates to the standard weight allowance is dwarfed by three other enormous stacks of stuff she just has to take as well.

Anguish – how on earth is she going to get by with so few possessions?

Hostility – stupid allowances!

Embarrassment – the sudden realisation that the holiday is a cruise. There are no restrictions.

Happiness – she can take everything after all.

Laziness – 'he' can bloody well pack, after all she got everything ready.

Paranoia – she's convinced something will be forgotten if 'he' packs.

Panic – she'll need to supervise to make sure 'he'

doesn't return half her stuff to the wardrobe.

With this last line in mind maybe I should just let her get on with it herself.

Ah well more once it's done.

I knew I should have let her do it.

Anyway, after fourteen repacks and a lot of sulking from me, we have eight bulging cases lined up downstairs, padlocks and luggage labels applied.

My dear lady is happy though. She's in the bathroom singing 'Another suitcase, another hall'.

I daren't tell her yet that I'm fairly certain they won't all fit in the reasonably priced family saloon I've hired to get us down to Southampton.

Saturday 5th January

Two sleeps to go.

I phoned the insurance company this morning because our policy states that we're not insured if we're absent from the property for more than forty two consecutive days.

Their customer service chappie told me we'll have to comply with the following conditions.

Drain the water from all tanks and pipe work on the property.

Leave the central heating on with the thermostat set to twelve degrees centigrade.

Really?

Turn off the electricity, gas and water at the mains.

Leave one or more lights on a timer to come on after dark.

What?

Now I know insurance companies will go to any lengths to avoid a payout but even they can't expect to get away with such blatantly obvious contradictions. Or is this just their way of letting us know that we're not covered whatever we do?

There was more.

All the windows and doors should be locked (oh that's a novel idea)

Empty the fridge and freezer (might be difficult to eat half a pig in a day)

Put small, empty plastic bottles in the toilet pan and cistern.

Ensure pets are not left unsupervised.

Finally we've got to make arrangements for someone to visit the property once a week while we're away. The person or persons in question must be of exemplary character and without any convictions for burglary or receiving stolen goods.

I have to admit that I'm grateful they care enough to remind me of the dangers of letting a convicted felon have a set of keys to my three bed semi, not to mention how heartless it would be to let the dog fend for himself for twelve weeks.

Anyway, with the news that someone will have free range to roam our rooms my dear lady decided the house had to be spotless. It's really not that untidy but she's determined the locals aren't going to be given the slightest opportunity to gossip about us and our slovenly ways.

It's such a shame that all of my old clothes had been thrown out, and my new ones packed away, because I've had to spend the day vacuuming the house in just a pair of pants.

Not a pretty sight.

At least they're new ones with no holes.

Thank goodness my dear lady hasn't insisted I clean the windows as well.

She went to see our neighbour Marjorie, who has kindly agreed to help us out. Now to be honest I didn't have the nerve to go round myself to ask if she has a criminal record, which is probably for the best considering the way I was dressed.

By lunchtime everywhere had been dusted, polished and vacuumed. Beds had been changed and the bathroom literally sparkled.

We decided to follow half the recommendations from the insurance man, the logic being we should at least be able to claim for half the damage caused in the event of a problem. So in the afternoon I'd unplugged everything, set the heating thermostat to twelve degrees and all the windows were locked. The pig agreed to stay in the freezer (did that class as an unsupervised pet I wonder?) and I managed to find four small plastic bottles which were ceremoniously deposited in the required areas.

To finish off I laid out a trail of extension leads, timers and low wattage LED lamps.

I was just surveying my handy work when it started to feel quite chilly.

That's when I'd realised we still had to spend the night here and I was in my underpants.

It took over an hour to switch everything back on, and I managed to spill a cup of coffee all over the immaculately hoovered carpet in the process when I tripped over one of the extension leads.

Then there was the small matter of the bathroom.

My dear lady had decided to take one of her 'indulgent soaks' complete with a bottle of Merlot and scented candles. As I'm driving tomorrow she had the whole bottle to herself, the after effects of which caused quite a commotion.

I heard her scream and bounded up the stairs two at a time.

Thank goodness for new pants and tight elastic.

Now I'm not quite sure what she thought she'd seen down the toilet, but when I got to her she was trying to beat a defenceless plastic bottle to death with a toilet brush. Luckily I'd arrived just in time to stop her from flushing it away and blocking the pan.

It took ages to clean up the mess, not helped by her singing 'Red Red Wine' at the top of her voice for almost an hour.

Ah well, at least she'll sleep well tonight.

Sunday 6th January

One sleep to go.

My dear lady didn't want to run the risk of travelling tomorrow as there's always a chance of breaking down, or getting stuck in traffic. So we've come down to Southampton a day early to allay her worry.

And it turned out to be a very fortuitous decision.

I was up early and headed off to pick up the hire car, only to discover that I was right about the suitcases.

They wouldn't fit in.

However, that didn't stop me from trying.

I'd spent a good hour attempting a 'Krypton Factor' type three dimensional puzzle, but without success. My pride severely dented, I'd had to concede defeat and take the car back.

The only other vehicle they had available was an enormous 4 x 4 truck which cost me an extra £150.

Even worse, it was too big to get on the drive.

Assuming there's a clause somewhere in the home insurance policy about not alerting the local criminals about our imminent departure, I'd hoped to pack the car discretely.

Now I had to ferry all of the cases down to the bottom of the drive instead, lifting them up to head height to load them on the back. The accompanying grunts and groans were loud enough to wake the dead, let alone the local villains.

When I'd finally got everything loaded my dear lady announced that she couldn't find the passports and suspected they'd been accidently packed in the smallest of the cases.

Now if I'd bothered to stop and think for a minute I would have remembered that I'd personally packed and locked all of the cases, and at no point did I touch the passports (way above my level of responsibility) so there was no way they'd even left the house yet.

But I didn't stop to think.

Instead I cursed and sweated as I rummaged through piles of once neatly folded shirts, which were now untidily crumpled.

The passports duly turned up, but nowhere near the cases. Least said about that the sooner my back may feel a little less painful.

Anyway we'd finally got underway around midday, but I found leaving the house a bit emotional.

Suddenly three months away seemed a very long time and I'd started to worry.

Fortunately, manoeuvring a small tank down the motorway soon had my mind concentrating on other things. But I have to say the ride was very comfortable and the four hour drive passed quickly.

All too soon my weak, unmanly body was complaining about the half ton of uncooperative luggage which needed unloading and dragging up to a room on the third floor. This was duly followed by the small matter of dropping off the hired monstrosity and the half mile walk back to the hotel.

Anyway, everything is where it should be now and it's time to get on and enjoy as the holiday starts right here, right now.

We're off down to the restaurant for a bite to eat, and as it's 'Happy Hour' I might treat my dear lady to a glass or two of fizz to get her into the spirit of things.

More later.

I think I've had one too many 'I'm on holiday' beers. I just hope I remember the eight suitcase obstacle course in our room if I get up to pee in the night.

That's a joke, more a question of will I ever get to bed. Every time I leave the bathroom my dear lady finds it amusing to sing 'Drip, drip, drop little April showers', which sends me flying back to use the loo again.

Oh well, at least it gives me some time to finish this.

Monday 7th January

It's 6pm and we're safely on-board our floating

holiday home and on our way at last.

We'll be off for our first evening meal on-board shortly, but there's enough time to try and record the events of the last 24 hours.

Goodness only knows what happened last night, but I woke up this morning with a banging head and a throbbing knee.

Once we'd been seated in the restaurant I remember ordering a glass of Prosecco and a pint. Todd, our young and seemingly enthusiastic waiter, quickly returned with two pints and two glasses of fizz.

When I questioned this his reply was a chirpy, "It's Happy Hour, two for the price of one mate."

Now I thought that meant we'd get the cheapest free, rather than have the order doubled.

Oh well no worries.

By the time the starters arrived we'd already polished off the first round of libation, so with a regal wave of my hand over the table I'd requested 'the same again please, Todd'.

"Starters, drinks or both?" Todd asked.

Through the descending alcohol induced fog it took me a second or two to focus on his face.

"Two more beers and two glasses of bubbly," I said.

I didn't realise the silly mistake I'd made.

Why?

Todd thought I was lining up the drinks as 'Happy Hour' was about to end...he bought four pints and four flutes of Prosecco.

The rest of the evening is considerably vague.

All I really remember was trying to get to bed amid my dear lady's singsong attempts to confine me to the bathroom.

When I woke this morning I was perched on top of the largest case. How I'd ended up there is a complete mystery.

After such a boozy night it was probably a mistake to set an alarm when we didn't need to be at the cruise terminal until 2pm.

Why do they call it a terminal?

Not a very good choice of word for the excited traveller, doesn't it also mean fatal?

We'd called for a taxi after breakfast, taking time to explain about the copious amount of luggage we had and could they send an appropriately large vehicle.

The dispatcher obviously wasn't listening, or had never tried to get eight large suitcases and two passengers into the back of a Toyota Corolla saloon car, which is what turned up.

Despite our protests the enthusiastic driver wasn't going to take no for an answer, or lose the fare. The four smallest cases were quickly crammed into the boot and the lid tied down with a handy piece of rope.

My dear lady was ushered into the back seat, where she was unceremoniously walled in with the two largest cases, one either side of her.

Then I'd helped the driver lift the two remaining cases onto the roof (devoid of a roof rack) and with yet more rope he'd secured them in place.

Finally I jumped into the front seat and he'd piled our remaining bits and pieces on my lap.

After a ten minute drive we were at the port (and I think he went the long way round.)

We'd stopped briefly at the side of the building

where a group of jolly stevedores had taken our eight cases and carried them carefully to the loading area whilst whistling a happy tune, after all luggage football is never played in full sight of the customer.

But in some ways I wish it were, because when I was finally reunited with my cases I would like to have been able to put a face to the bastard who managed to tenderise a brand new Samsonite into something resembling crumpled cardboard.

Anyway, we were then delivered to the main entrance.

We'd checked in and waited to pass through security. This involved a hectic process of suspicious scrutiny by a group of burly men and women well trained in the art of intimidation.

The lady in charge of loading up the x-ray scanner belt we were directed to scowled and sniffed in utter disdain as we approached. We duly deposited all our worldly goods, and dignity, into her grey plastic tray and she watched me intently for any obvious tell tale signs of deceit as I removed my belt and shoes.

"Have you anything else in your pockets?"

"No," I'd replied.

"Are you sure?"

I'd patted my pockets with gusto.

"No, nothing there," I'd announced with a smile.

"No keys?"

"No…there's nothing left in my pockets."

"No loose change?"

"No…there's nothing left in my pockets."

"Phone?"

"As I said there's nothing left in my pockets."

"You've just put a hand in your pocket so I

thought you were checking for something. Are you wearing a belt?" she asked, even though she'd watched me remove it not ten seconds ago.

Maybe next time I should do it to music.

"No my belt's in your tray. That's why I have my hand in my pocket. It stops my jeans falling around my ankles."

"So there's nothing in that pocket?"

"No."

"How about the other one?"

"There's nothing."

"Have you remembered to empty your back pockets? Wallet? Comb?"

"No."

"Is that no you hadn't remembered or what?"

"There's nothing in my pockets."

"Then please proceed through the scanner sir," she'd said with a sarcastic grin.

As I'd started to walk away I'm sure she was still unconvinced about the emptiness of my pockets.

"Just have one final check before you go through please sir," she'd called after me.

"Otherwise you might be delayed getting onto the ship."

I was suddenly aware that ahead of me one poor guy was being led away to a private room by two six foot bruisers intent on discovering the reason he'd somehow managed to make their mystical arch machinery thing beep. He too must have been certain his pockets were empty, so like an idiot I'd stopped and obediently searched through my pockets again, just to be sure.

I'm convinced it won't be long before they have us all stripped down to our underwear to ensure we're not trying to sneak (love that word) anything remotely illicit past them.

But I have to ask how much contraband could be hidden in the framework of a wheel chair or the battery compartment of a mobility scooter?

They meticulously inspect and x-ray the heels of our shoes and yet poor old Ethel, who is unfortunately confined to a wheelchair, is automatically waved through as if it would be deemed highly unprofessional to even consider a lady in her position could be a potential smuggler, or worse.

At least we didn't trigger any alarms so security were happy to let us proceed without any further molestation.

But it felt a little seedy as we stood re-assembling ourselves along with a group of complete strangers, who were obviously checking everyone out for holey socks.

Thank goodness for my dear lady's shopping prowess.

Anyway, moving on.

After a short walk our excited anticipation of the last few days finally became a reality as we stepped aboard.

The ship appears very bright and airy and first impressions are really positive.

Our cabin B94 actually has a balcony, which is a bonus because the travel agent said we only had a porthole. It's roomy and very nice.

After stowing away our stuff (notice I'm really getting into the lingo) we'd headed off to our muster station for a safety drill, and a first proper glimpse of some of the folk we're going to be sharing this tin box with for three months.

Okay, here was the first surprise.

I accept we've been lucky enough to have taken retirement early, but somehow we weren't expecting to be two of the youngest passengers, A quick look around the room suggested we are.

The Captain voiced a welcome to all over the ship's tannoy. He sounded quite friendly as he'd detailed what we should do in the event of an emergency, or if someone fell overboard.

As he delivered a hefty maritime list of 'dos and don'ts' I'd felt my mind drifting, and by the time he'd reached the part about 'what we should do in the unlikely event that we have to 'abandon ship' my attention had been captured by something else.

A large proportion of the assembled appeared to be asleep.

Information that may ultimately be the difference between life and death was being relayed, but no one seemed remotely bothered.

Maybe they thought that things couldn't possibly go so badly wrong, or more likely they didn't care.

Then I heard our skipper say something that I'm now desperately trying to dispel from my already overcrowded imagination. Apparently there is enough food on each lifeboat to last several weeks.

I understand why no one was listening now. That is a scenario that should never have to be considered.

But then it's probably a whole lot better than the alternative.

After muster we'd taken our lifejackets back to the cabin, wrapped up warm and headed outside for what was described as 'The Grand Sail Away', with complementary champagne, a military band and fireworks.

I suppose they have to push the boat out (literally) considering how much money most of the seven hundred expectant passengers have paid.

Talking of which, we've agreed not to discuss the topic of cost with our fellow travellers, considering we've paid less than half the original brochure price for an outside cabin, and been upgraded for free.

It had been an overcast and damp day, not unusual for January, but as our gallant captain slowly manoeuvred us away from the quayside the grey drizzle intensified to a steady downpour.

As the military band played 'We are Sailing' several confetti canons erupted to shower the pristine decks and passengers with thousands of ribbons of multicoloured tissue paper.

Spectacular.

Then the fireworks started, both on land and on the ship.

Those on land were a lot less volatile than the explosive outburst of one lady in a cream trouser suit as she disappeared beneath a falling cloud of the now damp confetti. Her male companion quickly tried to brush away the litter but it was too late. Her cream suit was now blotched with colour, mainly red, just like the ladies face.

A memorable start for all.

For me the whole experience felt very grand and reminiscent of the black and white films I've often seen on the telly showing the Titanic as she sailed from Liverpool.

I'd shouted the same to my dear lady over the noisy rapport of the fireworks, as we'd sipped our complementary glass of 'Sail Away' champagne.

But maybe that wasn't the most prudent topic of conversation on a vessel about to embark on a transatlantic crossing in the winter. The lady in the cream and colour flecked trouser suit certainly didn't appreciate the comparison either and stormed off in a huff.

We'd soon found ourselves alone, peering back at the port as everyone else had headed back inside to warm up.

The band had finished their moving rendition of 'The Bonnie, Bonnie Banks of Loch Lomond' and were joined by a hard-hatted group of Dockers whooping and hollering their hearty goodbyes. I couldn't help but wonder if this was a 'fare thee well and bon voyage' or just a right regal 'good riddance' to a crowd of eccentric individuals?

I'm sure they were thinking the UK will be a much saner place for the next twelve weeks.

"Well that was good," I'd said to my dear lady.

"Yes indeed," she'd replied, giving me a kiss on the cheek.

"And thank you," she'd added with a big smile.

She didn't elaborate so I've no idea what I've done, and I didn't want to ask either just in case I'd misheard her.

So we're off, with 85 nights aboard on this South American Odyssey.

Today marks a new beginning for us both, a chance to embark on this completely different and final age of our lives, starting with this long anticipated holiday. A voyage into the unknown to discover places new and exotic, an adventure, a quest in search of wonders untold, mysterious people and breathtaking scenery (all we need now is a map, a wizard and a handful of dwarves)

But first there's an obstacle to overcome, the small matter of our dining companions.

When we'd arrived back at the cabin we were greeted by a small card announcing we'd been allocated table number one two eight, second sitting.

Eighty five nights with eight complete strangers, hopefully not the lady in the cream suit.

I have to admit I'm a little pensive about this, what if we don't get on?

Quite without thinking I've surprised myself by writing a little ditty.

My tale is of a table
Neatly laid and looking great,
Pristine napkins, candles lit,
It's number one two eight.
With each and every sailing
Fresh faces would appear,
Would they all be happy?
Would they all drink beer?
Would they be a nice crowd?
Up to have some fun,
Or would they all be nutters?
Into fighting - throwing buns.
With first night nerves all tingling
Wondering who we soon would meet,
Me and my dear lady
Set off to find our seat.

I don't think that's too shabby, in fact I'm really starting to enjoy this writing malarkey.

Anyway we're off to meet and eat.

More later.

That was a very interesting evening. It wasn't as

strained or stilted as I'd expected and everyone was very friendly and chatty.

Our fellow travellers are,

Derek and Pat, a couple from Bristol

Ron and Nancy, they're getting off in Rio.

Steve and Louise, from Yorkshire, also debarking Rio.

Jeff and Pru, he's Scottish, she's a vegan.

The food was really good and our wine waiter managed to cajole us into consuming a whole bottle of Merlot! I can see things could become quite indulgent if we're not careful.

The major question has been 'How far is everyone going?' It felt a bit like 'Hello, nice to meet you, when are you leaving?'

Even the wine waiter asked me "Are you going all the way sir?"

"Hopefully," I said with a wink.

My dear lady put her head on my shoulder and started singing.

"You should be so lucky, lucky, lucky, lucky."

After she and Pru had finished laughing she'd added, "Keep drinking sweetie and we'll all get what we want."

I'll need to consider her meaning once the alcohol fog has cleared.

And so to bed, with a wish for no more than a trouble free time over the next three months and a slight hope that we find at least one couple we can get along with.

Oh and penguins, we need to see lots and lots of lovely penguins.

'The adventure begins'

Tuesday 8th January

Day 1 'at Sea' - Go Explore.

For a first night, in a strange place, I slept really well.

My dear lady commented that I'd slept like a walrus with asthma, whatever that means. I think she was just being sarcastic about how much I'd had to drink. I admit I'd felt nicely relaxed, but I definitely wasn't drunk.

We had breakfast in the Conservatory, the self-service restaurant. There was plenty of choice ranging from a full English to kippers, or freshly made omelettes, not to mention the porridge, pancakes, waffles, croissants, pastries, muffins, fresh fruit and pots of yoghurt (I can feel my arteries hardening already)

I didn't sample it all, because I don't like kippers.

Eventually my dear lady managed to drag me away (but not before I'd pledged my undying love for the pastry chef) and we'd spent the rest of the morning exploring the ship (with my dear lady, not the pastry chef)

At lunch the buffet was nicely laid out again and food was good and plentiful (this may become a serious problem) I asked after my friend the pastry chef but apparently he's 'too busy making stuff to come out'.

After a yummy curry, my dear lady went to an

afternoon art class.

Meanwhile I just wandered round the promenade deck for an hour before heading off to one of the many bars for an illicit beer, or three.

We were meeting up for a coffee after art class and on the way to the lounge I had to pass through the reception area.

A lady was loudly voicing a complaint.

I casually took a nearby seat to listen.

She was moaning that the inside cabin she'd booked didn't have a window overlooking the sea, or any window overlooking anything for that matter. When the guest relations manager tried to explain that only outside cabins had windows she got really shirty and asked why a cabin outside would need a window when it was already…well…already outside. It took a while for the manager to explain that the outside cabins weren't actually outside, but rather outside on the inside, whereas the inside cabins were in fact inside the outside cabins. Therefore if the inside cabins were to have a window then they would be looking directly inside at other cabins, and not outside at the sea.

The lady was speechless.

As a gesture of goodwill the manager then offered a complementary upgrade to an outside cabin.

She thanked him for his kind offer but said she'd prefer to have a cabin on the inside which had a window looking outside, rather than being in an outside cabin with a window looking outside, which she considered was, in fact, impossible.

When it was pointed out again that cabin being offered wasn't actually outside but rather inside, just on the outside of the inside one she already had, she asked if she could have one with a sea view instead.

Around 6pm my dear lady headed off for a soak in one of the hot tubs on the top deck singing 'Relax' by Frankie goes to Hollywood, while I took myself off to the gym.

With all the temptations around me I'm determined to keep active and not put on too much weight, but I don't want to overdo it.

Misguided fool that I am.

As I strode out on the treadmill I'd reflected on my first day as a fully fledged cruiser.

More importantly sea sickness hasn't raised its ugly head.

So we're well under way and the adventure continues.

Wednesday 9th January

Day2 'at Sea' - Race Y'all!

One thing has become abundantly clear, some the folk on this cruise are very competitive.

I say individuals but it appeared that some are working in pairs, or even as part of a team in order to subdue and humiliate their unworthy rivals.

It all started around the lido pool this morning with an obligatory show of 'one-upmanship' in the innocent guise of a few souvenir t-shirts, caps and sweat shirts from around the world. These were clearly meant to demonstrate the wearers past travelling prowess and dared all comers to challenge their right to be the 'top dog' on this trip.

I myself had initially sported a t-shirt from the Isle of Wight, thinking it made me look quite cool, but would soon realise that I was in a completely different and, much lower, league.

Within minutes of taking a seat I'd spotted the individual wearing 'I've been to the Seychelles', so I'd quickly covered up.

Even his display wasn't to last long and he soon had to give way to a more experienced pair who removed their coats to reveal 'We trekked across the Atacama Desert'. Their turn to humbly concede and bend the knee came with the swift appearance of the more obscure 'Machu Pichu by Llama' elite.

This posturing continued for an hour or two until the arrival of a group with multiple displays from around the globe.

However, these tactics were merely a feeble attempt to outflank their strutting opponents, who were refusing to yield under any circumnavigation of the world, no sir!

Anything from Europe and Australasia was dismissed without a second glance and even obscure trips to 'The Real Rural China' were considered 'old hat' and relegated to the bottom of the bragging rights league table with 'nil point'.

Whilst initially it was considered that 'Whale Surfing the St Lawrence' was a very strong contender, the wearer was summarily disqualified from the competition and vilified after it was discovered to be a self-printed fake.

After many a taunt and several grunts of intimidation, it came down to a direct, one round, winner takes all face off as 'I've herded penguins by helicopter in the Falklands' met 'We tracked polar bears in Longyearbyen' in the final.

After much parading and swaggering the parties

involved decided to call it a draw and went off together to compare trips.

I was informed by a seasoned cruiser that this was misdirection and in reality they would be attempting to bore each other to death over a gin and tonic in order to decide the true winner.

And I thought 'grown-ups' were beyond all of that.

Obviously not.

Another thing I've noticed is that everything that happens on board a cruise ship is dutifully recorded with an official photograph.

The little bleeders are everywhere and have developed intricate surprise tactics so you don't have time to decline their attention. They hide around corners to leap out and catch you unaware, or one of them dresses up as a pirate or parrot and grabs hold of you while the other one blinds you with multiple flashes.

The photos are then displayed for all to see in the gallery near to the main bar area.

Being quite self-conscious and not wanting to attract any adverse criticism of my appearance, I'm developing a phobia, and earlier today I found myself creeping around the ship hoping to remain anonymous.

I'd even checked in the cubicle of the toilets just in case one was lurking with intent. Unfortunately I don't think the guy in the cubicle was convinced by my reason for disturbing his solitude.

Those tight Speedos and bright pink shirt are definitely out of the question now. Being immortalised wearing those for all to see must be avoided at all costs.

Tonight was the first formal night and everyone looked resplendent in their finery, including my dear lady and I.

The photogs were in their element, and having set up several 'staged scenes' to make the occasion appear special, they were waiting en-mass at the entrance to the dining room.

Fortunately there were many who, on this occasion, were actually keen to be digitally immortalised in their best bib and tucker, so we managed to slip through unscathed.

The meal was really good and table one two eight seems to be livening up. Even Jeff has decided to shelve his dislike of the English, especially with the help of the large single malt I got him.

However, with so many gentlemen wearing white tuxedoes this evening I felt really sorry for the waiters. It must have been difficult to see were the diner ended and the table cloth started.

As I said, my dear lady looked stunning and everyone had smiled in her direction, well maybe it was just the men. I'd felt really proud with her on my arm as we'd left the restaurant, it bought a bit of a lump to my throat.

I was distracted long enough for one of the damn photogs to jump out and capture the moment, the super bright flash causing me to stumble and trip over his tripod.

I bet I looked a right fool.

My dear lady offered little sympathy for my dilemma, in fact she spent all evening singing Manfred Mann's 'Blinded by the light' and giggling.

How rude.

Thursday 10th January

Day 3 'at Sea' - Race Y'all (part 2)

I was right about the difficult task faced by the waiters last night.

As I'd passed through reception this morning there was a gentleman claiming his 'favourite white tuxedo' had been 'gravyfied' and ruined.

Well actually, it was his wife that was doing all the complaining, and yes she really did use the word gravyfied. Her apparently distraught husband stood in the background, silently plaiting his hands as his partner detailed how devastated he was at the destruction meted out to his once pristine, expensive Saville Row pride and joy.

From what I could see his server must have had a terrible night of it, the front of his jacket being liberally smeared with a variety of different substances. One definitely looked like gravy but there were also a ketchup like red smear and a run of English mustard, nothing else edible could be that colour.

Like myself, I suspected the Guest Services lady had reservations about the validity of their claim, but it appeared she had little choice.

"Leave it with us Sir," she'd called over to the gent. "We'll send it down for dry cleaning."

"That won't work," the wife had shouted. "It's ruined I tell you, ruined."

"Well if that's the case...Sir...then we will obviously replace the item."

She'd folded the jacket carefully and placed it on the counter, setting the completed claim form next to it.

"If you could just sign this for me please Sir."

She'd held out a pen.

"I'll do it," the wife snapped, making a grab for it.

"I'm sorry Madam, but the claimant has to sign the form, and the owner is the claimant. Please Sir."

The man shuffled over and reached for the pen. On the third attempt he managed to catch hold of it and signed the counter next to the form.

"That's quite a tremor you have Sir, worst I've seen in a while. You must spill things all the time."

"He's angry about his jacket," I heard the wife yelling, as I'd headed off for breakfast.

I've made a mental note to travel this route to the dining room every morning.

My friend the pastry chef was a no show again this morning as he's being kept busy making croissants, muffins and Danish pastries. I'm not surprised really as they are extremely popular. I noticed several guests walking off with huge plates full of the delightful treats. Well they'll need something to keep them going for the half hour the restaurant shuts between breakfast and lunch.

Can't have them starving and wasting away on the sun-loungers now can we?

After yesterdays displays of 'one-upmanship' and the settling of the matter of the most seasoned cruiser, I thought it would be a little more peaceful around the decks today, especially as the weather has improved and everyone is stuffed full of cake and sun bathing.

But today hails the beginnings of a physical challenge in the form of this morning's 'walk a mile around the decks' activity. Despite the member of staff in charge of the event insisting that the walk would be conducted at 'a gentle pace' and 'just for fun', it transpires that three of the weaker and less ambulant attendees are now receiving treatment in the medical centre for trample injuries, and one poor lady is still missing.

Okay, I admit I may have slightly exaggerated the competitive nature of the situation, but trust me some of the folk here are really 'in it to win it' and it doesn't seem to matter what 'it' is. It could even be the simple matter of how many pastries is it possible to smuggle out of the buffet before the head waiter says something.

To say the least, I'm surprised.

I accept that I've never been very sporty and even in my work life I didn't have to assert myself or contend to prove my ability, so maybe I've become soft. But I never realised this older generation I belong to is still so competitive. It's strange that those who no longer need to 'prove' themselves work so hard to do just that.

Does it all come down to the fact that we the human race still retains so much of our basic animal instincts, each of us desperately needing to prove that we're so much better than the next person.

Maybe I need to get with the programme otherwise I may literally get trampled underfoot.

But at my time of life I really can't be bothered.

Well the first three sea days have come and gone and I've really been surprised at how relaxed I'm feeling. My dear lady is transformed, or maybe it's me who's transformed and she has less to contend with.

I've enjoyed watching the increasingly amusing

antics of our fellow passengers, and in the evening it's been fun getting to know our dining companions, who I may add are a lot less opinionated than some.

There have already been some serious fallings out amongst other tables, mainly over who sits where and when. Fortunately we're all having too much of a good time to be bothered. We've even been heading off to one of the bars together after dinner, and there's talk about us forming a quiz team.

My dear lady, who hasn't picked up so much as a pencil since her schooldays is enjoying art classes and has discovered she's actually quite good at it.

Tomorrow will bring the first of many new destinations for us to explore, the island of Madeira.

The weather promises to be good so all is well, except I think my dear lady has lost the plot. She's been at the wine again and keeps singing some silly ditty about 'Have some Madeira my dear.'

But for the life of me I have no idea where that came from.

Friday 11th January

Day 4 'Madeira' - Fun-Fun-Funchal.

A bright and sunny day greeted our arrival to the fair island of Madeira, apparently famous for its flowers, fortified wine, levadas and mountainous slopes.

But first there's the small matter of breakfast.

The buffet area was awash with people this morning, so much busier than usual, and when we'd arrived there was little left. The only items available were porridge, cereals, fried eggs and a tray full of sliced fruit.

Everything else had been hoovered up.

As we left the ship I was surprised to see many of the passengers struggling down the gangway with seemingly very heavy backpacks. I'm curious to know what they've got in there, especially when they're only going for a walk around the town.

Maybe it their dirty laundry to deposit in a dockyard skip.

It was great to see the sun along with a bright blue sky (we've heard it's snowing back home) so our expectations were high.

Before we can go sightseeing we have a mission. My dear lady's art teacher had charged his budding Picassos with the task of finding an art supplies shop in the town in order to purchase charcoal pencils for a later project. Information led us to believe there were several to be found near to the cathedral, so off we set.

I think it fair to say we covered every inch of the tiny narrow back streets within several hundred yards (like metres but better and easier to understand) of the visually ornate religious centre of the town.

Finally, just as I'd started to melt in the sweltering humidity, we'd stumbled on our required destination.

There was nearly a mishap as my dear lady confused her graphite with her charcoal, but she's claiming it had something to do with English to Portuguese translation issues. But all turned out well, and clutching her three new artists tools, one soft, one medium and one hard, she'd emerged triumphant from the shop (leave the room if you even sniggered then)

During the search we'd discovered the location of the main market. This would be our next stop.

The flowers, the fruit, the fish and just about everything else proved fascinating. There was a veritable smorgasbord for the senses (not necessarily all good) and we spent a good hour sampling Madeira wine, Poncha (an alcoholic fruit punch) pineapple bananas and candied hibiscus flowers, as well as taking lots of pictures.

We'd bought a few bits and pieces and a couple of bottles of the local hooch (it would have been rude not to after all the freebies we'd consumed)

Then we'd headed back to the ship to lighten our load.

Strolling back into town for a mooch, we'd headed toward the chair lift up to Monte.

The trip up the mountain in one of the modern cable cars was spectacular, and it was much cheaper independently than on a ships tour (I love a bargain).

At the top the views were fantastic.

We visited the botanical gardens and then watched as some terrified folk set off for the downward journey in what looked like an armchair.

This extreme sled ride down the hill while sitting in an ordinary small sofa, is guided and steered by a local man and his mate who stand on the back. I just hope they all have very good life insurance policies.

Definitely not for us, so we came back down the way we'd gone up, after all we wanted to live long enough to enjoy the rest of the cruise.

On this trip we're determined to indulge our senses with as many aspects of the local cultures and traditions as possible. It is really important to us to immerse ourselves fully into the experience of each new and exciting destination and attempt to blend in with residents.

To see what they see, feel how they feel, do what they do.

In order to facilitate the start of this intricate process we'd headed straight for a bar.

Not the first one we came to, no that wouldn't be right. Instead we walked to the outskirts of the city and found a street pavement bar full of interesting locals, oh and really cheap beer (see, I told you I love a bargain)

The views over the sea toward the outlying islands were stunning, and sitting there under the trees with the sun on our faces and sipping cold beer, we'd found a little piece of magic to take forward on our journey, a memory, an experience that no camera could do justice to (in other words we forgot to take a picture)

There was a bit of embarrassment when a couple had sat down at an adjoining table and started unloading a backpack.

There were loads of sausage sandwiches, Danish pastries, fresh fruit and pots of yoghurt, and the table was filling up quickly.

The waiter had come over looking puzzled.

"Two beers," the man shouted. He had a very large belly.

"Ah...English," the waiter replied. "You can't eat your own food here."

"Why not?" the man had demanded loudly.

"I've ordered beer."

"You can have the beer, Sir. But we serve food as well, so please pack all this away."

"Just bring the beer."

At this point my dear lady had kicked me under the table and nodded toward the road. A rather large, mean looking policeman was heading our way.

He shouted in perfect English, "Do we have a problem here?"

Bellyman had attempted to turn to face the speaker, probably to give him a mouthful of abuse. But his distended waistline was firmly wedged under the table.

The lady however saw who was coming and had quickly suggested there was somewhere else they needed to be, urgently.

She refilled the backpack in record time and they were gone.

Without any further comment my dear lady and I had just stared out to sea, and the peace returned.

After an hour we'd reluctantly made our way back into the heart of the town, stopping at the cathedral to have a look round inside.

After a bit more strolling around the shops, we'd indulged in several bags of freshly cooked chestnuts.

Delicious.

Then a final stop at another street bar for a taste of the local specialities, a piece of Madeira cake with a glass of Madeira wine.

The ambiance and lifestyle is very relaxing, and if an opportunity presents itself in the future we'll definitely return to this magical place full of friendly locals, it was great.

And did my dear lady have as much fun as I did? Well she's currently singing Lou Reed's Perfect Day, and apparently she's glad she spent it with me.

Could it get any better?

Saturday 12th January

Day 5 'at Sea' - a bright and sunny day.

We now have seven full sea days as we cross the mighty Atlantic Ocean towards our next port of call, Barbados in the Caribbean.

We had a very indulgent day in Funchal and if all our port days are similarly excessive, I'll need to be more conservative during our sea days.

So I've decided to make more of an effort in the 'be a bit healthier department'.To that end I'd planned to have fruit for breakfast, like yesterday, then head for the gym.

Well I did have the fruit, but I couldn't refuse the plate of carbohydrate treats my friend the pastry chef had saved for me. When at first I'd declined his offerings his broad smile disappeared, replaced by a look of total dejection. Then I'd noticed there were several enormous trays of pastries and bread rolls on the counter, not to mention a huge pile of sausage and bacon in the hot section and a market garden of fruit piled high.

The penny dropped at last, (I can be a bit slow on the uptake at times) and that explains the lack of food yesterday and the heavy backpacks. It wasn't just the couple at the bar who'd made a picnic to take ashore, more like everybody.

Assumingly they did it to save paying for anything in the town, which is a shame. The food on the ship is very good, but surely it would be better to try something different whenever the opportunity arises. I certainly will, but then I'm not a regular cruiser and things might change if our spending money starts to dwindle.

Meanwhile, the staff not realising the scale of yesterdays smuggling operation had increased food production today believing their guests were just eating more.

Technically that was true.

When I finally made it to the gym I had it in my head that I needed to address the several hundred calories I'd just consumed (it was forced on me, honest it was) not forgetting all the yummy sugary stuff I got through yesterday.

I've never really been one for 'keeping fit' and the ship's gym is my first experience of proper equipment (the cheap exercise bike and cross trainer we bought with good intentions several years ago seized up through lack of use)

For now I'm just sticking with the treadmill.

I'd set it going at four kilometres an hour on a gentle slope convinced that an hour at that would be enough to 'fight the flab' as Mr Wogan used to say.

This was going to be easy.

Then I'd found the button! The one that was going to tell me how many calories I was burning. With great expectations I pressed it.

It was broken.

It must be broken.

Yes the numbers were going up, just very slowly.

After 10 minutes it read '35 kcals', after 15 minutes '53 kcals' and I was sweating.

There must be some mistake.

At this point a lady in a track suit and wearing a badge had come over.

"Hello," she'd said. "I'm Nadia the personal trainer. You're looking worried, is everything ok?"

Not wanting to appear like a complete novice I'd

replied that I was fine, but a little disappointed in how slowly the calorie counter was moving.

She'd smiled that knowing smile and I knew she was thinking 'idiot'.

"If you'd like, I can draw up a programme to speed things up a bit."

"That would be helpful," I'd replied, sucking my belly in another inch or so and desperately trying not to sound too out of breath.

"I could supervise the programme and sort out a diet sheet as well."

"I don't want to put you to any trouble."

"No trouble at all, Sir, in fact I'm happy to give you a special rate."

Okay, I'd walked straight into that one.

I tried to explain politely that I was just looking to stay as I was rather than aiming to become an Adonis, I didn't have that much money.

"And neither of us have that much time, Sir," she'd replied sounding disgruntled. She reached over to press another button on the machine.

Everything suddenly speeded up, including her departure, and it had taken me a few frantic paces to get close enough to the panel to turn it down again.

Ah well, at least there was no one else there to witness my moment of embarrassment, the gym must be the least populated area of the ship. Apart from me there's been nobody else there.

After a light lunch we'd decided to go and sit out on the lido deck by the pool. The weather has picked up to the point where the sun worshippers are out in force and revealing more than the rest of us want to see.

I've never been one to take off my shirt in public,

as I'm sure the world can live without another flabby, pasty white belly.

But seeing the size and shape of some of our fellow travellers I'd felt brave enough to head back to the cabin to change into a pair of shorts. I even unbuttoned my shirt, but no more than that for now.

It was really good to feel the warmth of the sun on my body as I'd relaxed into sun lounger, my eyes tightly shut. The sound of waves breaking was hypnotic and all the worries of the past seemed to just melt away.

I must have dropped off for a moment or two and was jolted back to reality by my dear lady, asking if I would mind fetching her an ice-cream.

With pleasure.

I'd stood in the queue behind a well tanned elderly couple in their swimwear, the harmony in my mind being replaced by one overwhelming thought, 'why does some people's skin not fit them properly?'

These two were both extremely wrinkled and creased, covered with stretch marks and moles. In some areas their skin was hanging so loose that as they'd shuffled forward the folds and creases had appeared to rearrange themselves into a totally different configuration.

It was one of those situations where I didn't want to look but couldn't help myself, and now I can't get the images out of my head. It was like a perpetual motion 'skin slinky', once it started to move it just kept going.

For the past few hours I've been telling my dear lady she's not helping the situation.

'I've got you under my skin' is not funny.

Sunday 13th January

Day 6 'at Sea' - a bright and sunny day.

There used to be a very popular TV show that claimed 'Animals do the funniest things', the grammar implying nothing else could be funnier.

But I have to totally disagree with that statement because I've yet to see an animal acting as daft as some of the folk on this ship.

From what I've seen there is enough food onboard to 'sink a ship' (if you'll excuse the pun) and it seems there are a number of individuals who feel the cruise company is laying down some sort of a challenge with the 'all you can eat' buffet.

So they're determined that nothing should go to waste, doing their very best to eat their way through several tons of delicious fare.

But in order to attempt this seemingly impossible feat they are forced to spend all morning charging round the decks at a million miles an hour in the hope that they'll burn off most of the calories consumed during breakfast.

(A bit like me on the treadmill)

It also helps to ensure that they don't actually explode during lunch.

This activity is then repeated in the afternoon for the same reasons, but only if they manage to prize themselves off the toilet first, which out of necessity is where they tend to spend a large part of the day.

It's cause and effect theory.

Now I certainly enjoy a stroll around the promenade to treat my lungs to the clean ozone rich air, to feel the fresh sea breeze and salty spray on my face (please leave the room again if you had a little giggle to yourself over that last comment, shame on you.) But since Madeira this healthy pastime has almost become a near death experience for those of us who merely like to amble around at a leisurely pace.

The self proclaimed 'professional foodies' need to expend masses of energy if they don't want to become comatose from hyperglycaemic shock.

They are focused, fast and furious, and woe betide anyone who gets in their way.

My dear lady and I have discovered it's far more entertaining (and safer) to sit at the back of the ship watching the mass of bodies race around. Red in the face and panting heavily they charge at break neck pace around the promenade deck.

The weak are trampled, the slow are tutted and moaned at until they concede room for the bullies to pass. They have to willingly punish themselves in order to abuse their poor overly distended stomachs further with indescribable amounts of grub at every possible opportunity, and trust me there are many, many, many opportunities.

And I'm reminded of a very famous poem. Here is my version.

The Charge of the Cruise Brigade
(Influenced by 'The Charge of the Light Brigade' by Alfred Lord Tennyson)

Twenty laps, twenty laps, twenty laps onward,
All round the decks of this ship
Strode a few hundred.
Forward the Cruise Brigade,
Charged you the food displayed,
Now on the decks parade
Strode those few hundred.

Take heart the Cruise Brigade
First sitting almost laid.
Crew still in shock, amazed
How lunch was plundered.
Theirs not to give reply,
Theirs not to reason why,
Theirs just to make more pie
For a few hundred.

Burgers to the right of them,
Teacakes to the left of them,
Spare ribs to the front of them,
Tempted by custard.
Bombarded with bacon roll,
Boldly they scoffed then stole
Back for more chips with bowl.
Starving few hundred.

Flashed knives and forks they bare,
Flashed as they feasted there.
Stunned all the waiters stare
Greedy few hundred
Straight through the buffet broke
Spurred on by rum and coke,
Sous Chef and Commis choke
Tears greatly numbered.

Then as a savoury treat
Cheese trampled under feet
Cheddar and stilton eat
Crackers out-numbered.
Down to the final plate
Chef is in such a state
Supper club would now be late
Damn you few hundred.

Burgers to the right of them,
Teacakes to the left of them,
Spare ribs behind them,
Where were those hiding?

With so much food in store
Rest there could be no more,
Pride has to win, for sure
Turn back few hundred.

Sound aloud that tea-time bell.
Bravely face this living hell
Till none are left to tell
Of the few hundred.

I'd spent most of the morning on that and my face hurts from laughing at my own silliness.

My dear lady read it and told me I needed to find a more constructive hobby. But I saw her smiling throughout, so she liked it really!

It was another glorious day, so while my dear lady went off to art I'd spent the rest of the afternoon on a sun lounger, watching the back of my eyelids. I'd even taken my shirt off this time and nobody laughed.

I had a weird dream about a lobster, but as I woke up she was singing 'Rock Lobster' by the B52's to me.

I didn't understand the reference until I saw myself in the bathroom mirror when we'd returned to the cabin.

That's going to sting in the morning.

Monday 14th January

Day 7 'at Sea' - a bright and sunny day.

Even brighter in our cabin as I'm glowing like radioactive man.

I'll definitely not be taking my shirt off today, or tomorrow, and probably not the day after either. In fact I'm going to spend the day in the pool, with a t-shirt on.

More later when I've cooled down a bit.

Fortunately, after four hours in the pool, I'm not so sore now. I must also note my thanks to my dear lady for insisting that we bought a dozen tubes of witch hazel gel with us for such an eventuality, it's worked a treat.

But the morning was not without incident.

Basically I'd been standing up to my neck in the cooling water in the corner of the pool when several members of the 'cruise brigade' had turned up. They'd obviously decided that swapping laps of the sweltering promenade deck for lengths in the chilling water was an excellent idea.

Within minutes there were nine huge lumps of hairy maleness thrashing around in a pool the size of a badminton court, all of them trying to swim lengths using various styles. It wasn't long before 'Butterfly' man crashed into 'Underwater Freestyle' man and a fight started.

I say fight but it was just a bit of posturing, name calling and water splashing.

Then security had turned up, two of them, but instead of addressing the conflict in the middle of the pool one of them jumped in and grabbed me under the arms.

"Don't struggle, Sir," he'd instructed, "I've got you."

He then proceeded to drag me towards the steps.

Now I admit my screams were possible quite loud and maybe I shouldn't have tried to drown him. But in my defence his bear-like grip was akin to sandpapering my poor sunburnt chest. I managed to break free from my floundering assailant and made a run for it (in ultra slow motion) with the hairy lumps, distracted from their conflict, cheering on my escape.

It was then that I'd noticed my dear lady yelling at the other official, who was looking rather sheepish.

He'd shouted over to his waterlogged partner who then left in a hurry.

I was free.

Applause and whoops erupted from the hairy lumps and one by one they'd pumped my hand and slapped my back.

Thank goodness that wasn't burnt.

But what had I done? What had just happened?

I was really confused, hoping my dear lady would enlighten me.

I got out of the pool and she helped me remove my t-shirt, lay me down on a sunbed and got out the witch hazel gel.

Apparently, the security officer claimed they'd made a genuine mistake. He'd explained that in their experience the architect of trouble in the pool area doesn't usually stop to get undressed, rather just jumps in as is. Because I had a t-shirt on they assumed I must be the guilty party.

Typical. I was molested for my modesty.

As I lay there smarting, a very loud voice at a nearby table was detailing his own brush with 'the law' in Madeira.

I looked across to see two familiar faces, the male had his hands clasped across a very large belly.

Another couple sitting with them were being regaled with a tale.

Bellyman was wittering on about ordering a

couple of beers in one of the bars. He was saying he'd needed to find a chocolate bar out of his backpack as he was a diabetic and required something sugary after the long walk up the hill. He'd been rummaging through his backpack and had innocently placed a couple of apples and a packet of sandwiches on the table. Next thing he knew this cop was waving his gun around saying they couldn't eat their own food and demanded they leave immediately.

"And he made us pay for the beer and confiscated our sandwiches," his female fraudster added.

"How terrible," the lady listener said. "At least you stayed calm despite being threatened."

"Bloody foreigners," said the Bellyman.

"Aren't we the foreigners?" my dear lady piped up indignantly.

"What?" I thought Bellyman was choking.

"I just thought that as we were in their country, then we're the 'bloody foreigners'."

"What? Who asked you?"

He was a poor judge of character if he thought my dear lady's going to let this one go.

"I know we had an empire once," she continued, "But believe it or not we have to be more tolerant and polite these days."

"What?"

"Actually, I might just have to tell these nice people the truth about that policeman."

"What?"

She turned to the intrigued couple. "He was off-duty, very polite, confiscated nothing and wasn't even armed."

"What?"

My dear lady left it at that.

Except for quietly singing a rendition of Fleetwood Macs 'Little Lies' as she lay back down on her sun bed.

I just had to join in.

So did half the folk around us.

Tuesday 15th January

Day 8 'at Sea' - not a bright and sunny day.

It was a little bit rough over-night and this morning the sky is full of billowing clouds.

I feel another poem coming on, but this one's all my own.

God lifts the water from the sea
To paint his sky majestically
With candy floss of every shape
From smiling face to swinging ape.
Moving, changing every hue
Powerful splendour, beauty too,
Reflecting fire or silver tipped,
Look! Cheeky gnome, and battle ship.
A bird, a bear, or just a ball
Then building, swirling, growing tall
As veiled in grey dark mists surround
With thunder, lightning, raining down.
Uniquely formed each quickly dies,
Cold tears to empty from the skies,
And so my friend don't curse the rain
God clears his sky to start again.

My dear lady thinks that's quite a bit better and likes it a lot.

This afternoon we were experiencing the tail end of a couple of fronts passing to the north of us. With 70mph winds and the sea state described as 'medium to high waves, with spray'. It proved too much for some and they took to their beds.

Unfortunately I was one of them. Even writing makes me feel queasy, so more later, I hope.

By this evening the seas had calmed a little and I feel much better, for which I'm truly grateful. So after a quiet dinner, the restaurant was only half full, my dear lady and I went and sat on the open deck at the back of the ship. The air felt warm and muggy and the sky was blanketed by enormous, dark, angry looking clouds.

As we enjoyed a glass of wine together we were treated to a magnificent lightning display which illuminated the whole of the night sky and inky black sea.

And with each bright flicker of the electrical storm we both greeted its arrival with our own tribute to Queen...'Flash, Ah Ah'.

Even at its nastiest there is a beauty to behold in Mother Nature's performances, but certainly not ours.

Wednesday 16th January

Day 9 'at Sea' - still not a bright and sunny day.

'How much longer?' the cry goes out.

The sea has decided to play rough again today, in fact quite a bit rougher than yesterday, along with 'stair-rod' rain crashing into the decks. Many are refusing to leave their cabins for the duration of the less than perfect weather, so without as many folk milling around, everywhere was lovely and quiet.

But there's a faction of hardened travellers who don't need to escape from this tumble dryer like movement of the ship, in fact they're determined to prove their power of endurance against King Neptune and all his might.

The only problem is they're a grumpy lot and it's not just the conditions outside irritating them, everything does, and they're not going quietly.

The cabins are too hot, the food's too spicy, or the entertainment has been cancelled. I even heard a group complaining that the swimming pools were shut today. Unsurprising really as most of the water has been chucked out by the roll of the ship.

The decks have been closed so that no one gets tossed overboard.

But this force nine is nothing compared to the force twelve they'd experienced last year, nowhere near as bad, and the waiters had continued to serve drinks on the sun-deck.

The happy and serene nature of the first few 'sunny' days out of Madeira has been replaced by an atmosphere of 'stormy' gloom and disapproval.

Nothing escapes their critical attention and nobody is immune from scrutiny.

Now here's the irony.

It's an unmistakable fact that those who complain the most are usually the biggest pains in the universe.

They cough and sneeze without putting up a hand to capture their escaping germs, they refuse to queue, they talk with mouths full of food, they witter on incessantly about themselves and always load their plates with the last of the bananas, even if there are twenty left they'll take all twenty.

So there you have it.

When the passengers are cooped up inside a tin box on a sea day they get completely and utterly bored. It's the only downside of cruising I've discovered so far.

But hey it's not that bad really because it gives me loads of inspiration…just like this.

All my life I've been perfect
And have always been one
To look up to and get good advice.
I'm humble and caring, with generous streak
And I'm honest and truthful and nice.
I'm always on time
And I've never been known
To be grumpy nor glare with distain.
Unbelievably happy whatever life throws
And I've never been heard to complain.

I never jump queues
And I keep my mouth shut
Whether chewing my lunch or some gum.
Never leave the seat up,
Never lewd or unkind
With my comments, and always such fun.
And I'm always polite,
Unlike some I could name,
Highly polished and cultured, so sweet.
I am never too loud
And prefer just to sit,
Never argue or boast to compete.

So as you can see
Good as gold I have been,
The ultimate husband and son.
A model employee,

An incredible friend,
Unbelievably loyal, loved a ton.

So when I go cruising
I feel duty bound
Not to act as my usual self.
It's a must that I let down what's left of my hair,
Leaving manners back home on the shelf.

I must whinge, I must moan
And quite often I do,
After all I'm just here on a break
From my usual life, it's not easy you know
Cause it's so very hard being this fake.
So I'll grunt a 'Good Morning'
Cough and sneeze on your food,
Fuss and moan like I don't give a rat.
You just have to accept that I'm playing a game,
This is not really me,
It's an act.

Because unlike the rest
I've been perfect for years,
This my chance to have oodles of glee.
I'm assuming that everyone's playing this game,
And being a prat, just like me?

I think I'll dedicate it to Bellyman.

My dear lady says I have some very silly ideas.

She also told me I'm starting to go green, then tormented my queasiness with a very loud and raucous performance of "Rock the Boat".

Don't you just hate people who never get sea-sick?

"Don't tip the boat over."

Time to lie down me thinks.

Thursday 17th January

Day10 'at Sea' - calm down, it's calming down.

I was unexpectedly woken this morning with the sun streaming through a crack in the curtains and my dear lady's note perfect rendition of 'What a Difference a Day Makes'.

The sea gods have been appeased and taken pity on this poor Atlantic Virgin.

Sounds like a good name for a travel company.

Assuming it would still be rough today we'd left a card outside our cabin last night requesting a 'Room Service Breakfast' (staying close to the bed, and toilet, was considered to be a sensible idea)

With such a beautiful day in prospect my dear lady decided it would be good for us to enjoy our repast 'al fresco', benefitting from some ozone rich fresh air after we'd spent all day yesterday cooped up inside.

"We might even see some wildlife," she'd added hopefully.

I have to admit 'spotting wildlife' is not an activity I've embraced so far, but it is quite an important part of the trip for my dear lady. Yes I've seen a few birds and even a dolphin or two, but only because she's pointed them out to me I may add.

She's certainly keen, but not as obsessive about it as some are.

There's another hardy group of folk on this trip who regularly spend their sea days scanning the horizon for anything that moves.

They are 'The Watchers'.

I had initially discovered their existence during a walk around the decks on the very first sea day. It was bitterly cold and I'd lasted all of one lap, about five minutes, by which time my face had gone numb. I'd headed for the nearest door to get back into the warmth of the ship and there they were, five of them huddled in the doorway, heads all wrapped in thick woolly scarves with just their eyes showing, which stared unblinkingly out to sea.

At that time I had no idea who or what they were, but enlightenment came swiftly in the guise of a member of the crew who'd been out on deck as well. He too was seeking sanctuary inside and had followed me through the door.

"They're keen," I'd said, "And slightly creepy."

"Who?" he'd enquired. "Oh you mean the Watchers."

"Watchers, why do you call them that?"

He came closer and lowered his voice.

"The clue," he'd said, "Is in the name."

And then he was gone.

For a moment or two I wondered if I'd just stumbled into a Stephen King novel, it all sounded quite sinister, but I was still none the wiser.

Since then my subsequent observations have led me to the following conclusions.

The clue is definitely in the name they've been allotted as they spend countless hours during each and every day just watching the sea.

But what do they see, or more importantly what do they hope to see, if not the sea?

And I believe the answer is...anything interesting.

The keenest 'Watchers' are easy to identify because they're always dressed according to the weather. If it's cold and wet they're swathed in heavy winter coats, waterproof trousers, boots, two scarves, gloves and a woolly hat. On the other hand, if the weather is dry and warm they'll brave the elements by unzipping their jackets a couple of inches and maybe removing one of the scarves, but never both.

If it's hot, hot, hot most folk will strip off and sunbathe, the 'Watchers' just paint sun block on their noses and don a pair of Raybans.

I can only think they dress this way because they prepare for the worst the weather can be and aren't keen to go back to their cabin to change into something more suitable, just in case they miss something.

As a rule they appear to only have two main topics of conversation, which brand of thermal undergarment they're currently wearing, and who saw what, where and when. A tatty moth-eaten notebook in which they record their sightings, in meticulous detail, is hastily produced for each and every encounter, whales, dolphins, birds, ships, land, floating rubbish, in fact pretty much anything, and they validate everything with a large number of photographs.

The cameras they use are monsters, able to photograph the veins on a fly's wing at fifty paces, not that they can travel fifty paces without the use of a wheelbarrow for the camera.

A typical day for them starts when a forward party emerges close to dawn to take up a vantage point, preferably overlooking the bow of the ship. This operative is usually a lone worker taking orders from the more dominant 'Watchers' who are still in bed, exhausted from having done last night's late shift (but nowhere near the bar...honest)

Armed only with a pair of binoculars and a walkie-talkie the look-out will remain statuesque like and in place, whatever the weather, until reinforcements arrive. This occurs either after they've all consumed a warm and hearty breakfast, or a group of playful dolphins are spotted riding the bow wave, then everyone is quickly summoned via the communication devices they all carry.

When a group of 'Watchers' get together the alphas will scrutinise maps and notebooks, talk about currents, sea temperature, isobars and other mysterious things in an attempt to establish their exact whereabouts. This allows them to compare their perceived current position with all the other open water locations they think they may have been to before.

Oh and they argue a lot.

To be fair, this group of naturalists/naturists (my dear lady explained the difference but I've forgotten which is which) are sociable and quite happy to impart their knowledge on any passer-by seeking enlightenment.

I have to say I think it's great to have a hobby, a purpose, an ambition. But with so much to do and take part in during sea days, such dedication to the cause it's definitely not for me.

But out here on our balcony I was about to experience something that maybe, just maybe, gave me a little more insight as to why they do it.

As I'd sat there munching my way through a third croissant a flash of silver streaked across the water right in front of us, then another, and another. Something small, but showing up clearly against the intense blue of the sea, seemed to weave a path across the surface for a distance then disappeared below the surface with a plop.

"Oh," my dear lady squealed with delight. "Flying fish."

I'd stood up so quickly I managed to knock the breakfast tray over. Paddling barefoot in a mixture of orange juice and coffee we'd both leant over the balcony rail, eyes bulging as what seemed like hundreds of silver streaks appeared and then vanished as this unusual species performed a wave ballet for us.

I admit to getting a little bit overexcited, so much so that several of our neighbours came out onto their balconies to see what all the fuss was about.

It was completely mesmerising (the fish, not the neighbours) and I couldn't drag myself away from the rail for fear of missing the next group to display for us.

And all of a sudden I understood why 'The Watchers' do what they do.

Reluctantly I'll have to admit it felt very special to witness a small part of nature going about its day to day business.

Even so, I still think the Watchers are a bit strange and overly obsessive, totally unlike myself.

Okay, I confess I sometimes get a little carried away, but my hobby doesn't leave me cold and wet.

A silver flash against dark blue,
And graceful glide with which they flew
Away from danger, diving deep
Nature's wonders, lithe and sleek.
All swim beneath till needs arise,
Then swiftly taking to the skies

They soar above with fins for wings,
Look! Airborne maestros, splendid things.

In fact my hobby leaves me feeling all warm and fuzzy, especially as I got a big hug and kiss from my dear lady for that one.

Friday 18th January

Day 11 'yet another day at Sea' - but even brighter and sunnier than yesterday.

This will be our last sea day before we reach the beautiful Caribbean island of Barbados, and there won't be another week long stretch of portless days like this until we return back home across the mighty Atlantic in nine weeks time.

For me the sea days have been a bit up and down.

Yes I know that's the ship's natural movement, especially when the wind blows a bit harder.

What I mean is this.

Initially I thought I'd hate the endless views of water with seemingly nothing much to keep me occupied. And of course I'd assumed that the weather would be atrocious, just like it is back in the UK at this time of year.

After all I've watched nearly all of the Titanic movies and I'm positive there was an iceberg in April.

I'd also considered that sharing this small confined space with hundreds of strangers would be horrendous.

Well I've been proved wrong on all counts, and happy to be so.

Having enjoyed some of the best that nature can offer I don't think I've ever been as relaxed and stress-free as I am right now (although I didn't enjoy the bad weather much)

My dear lady too is happy and radiant and it almost feels like we've just started dating again. There has been plenty to occupy my time and I can now accept that doing nothing isn't a crime.

As for the 'strangers', well we're getting to know some of them quite well now and they're very much like ourselves.

They worry about their children, the future and the state of their own health, but mainly they're just trying to enjoy life to the full. Even the ostensibly 'strange' strangers aren't as terrible as maybe I've described them. But they have provided some interesting material for this journal, which I'm enjoying putting together (and long may they...and it continue)

I'm reminded by my dear lady that as the definition of strange is 'unfamiliar and surprising', we too are strange to everyone but ourselves, and even that is in doubt.

This really is turning out to be a voyage of discovery. Maybe hippy Jake was right after all and we all just need to give ourselves some time.

Today was the luncheon for the 'all the way rounders'.

Apparently there are 230 of us who are going all the way round, finishing back in Southampton (I'm not sure some of this lot will last that long, or me for that matter)

They hosted a special lunch for 'we' the special people, which we thoroughly enjoyed.

The champagne and wine flowed like water, and

it's fair to say that as it was free we over indulged, so much so that we had to retire back to the cabin immediately afterwards for a snooze.

My dear lady is now sat out on the balcony getting some fresh air, whilst watching the flying fish and pink elephants chase each other across the water.

I know, I know, there's no such thing as flying fish.

Anyway, back to the luncheon.

We were joined by two other couples we hadn't met before and after the formal introductions our table host, the Food and Beverages Manager Clive, had told us that this would be the first of three special lunches for the 'all-rounders'. Apparently, it gives the officers a chance to get to know their 'exceptionally special' guests. I think by that he meant the ones who'd made a significant contribution to his salary, or maybe they're on the look-out for the trouble makers.

He'd also told us that he selects the guests for his table based on how much they were spending in the bars.

My dear lady kicked me under the table.

Clive must have seen me wince.

"I'm not saying I think you all drink too much," he'd said cheerily. "I just like to be with folk who know how to have a good time."

There appeared to be a lot of kicking going on under the table.

I was thinking Clive must have missed the company's training sessions on tact and discretion.

Thanks to the ladies on the table the conversation quickly turned to more important matters as poor Clive was bombarded by questions, mainly about love, sexual preferences and where does he go on his nights off??

I'd started to chuckle about that one but another well aimed kick stopped me from saying something I'd get told off about later.

Meanwhile the other two men had set about sampling the various glasses of wine on offer, nodding their approval at each other. I just had to join in and catch up.

Service began and we were treated to an exceptionally tasty meal.

Now I'd have to say the food so far has been very good, but this lunch was something else, which demanded my question to our designated officer, "Why can't it be this good all the time?"

I moved my leg just in time to avoid another booting.

Looking a tad uncomfortable by this enquiry Clive's reply had meandered off into the deep dark crevasses of the ship's storage facilities and the limited preparation time available to the galley staff for so many people, and so on.

The waiters quickly came to his rescue, prompted I no doubt by some covert signal. They'd sprung into action refilling glasses and asking if we'd enjoyed our food and would we like desert or cheese and biscuits maybe, or how about an after dinner liqueur?

Offers of food and alcohol always serve to distract the once focussed mind.

Seizing the chance to get back on safe conversational ground, our host announced that we would be loading around seventy tons of food and drink when we reach Barbados, and the same again at one of the Brazilian ports.

Then I get to thinking.

Seventy tons between around a thousand passengers and crew is approximately 156 pounds of food and drink each. That's equivalent to three large sacks of potatoes (I can hear the seams of my trousers tearing as I write this down)

Not forgetting that's only to keep us going for the next two or three weeks then another personally designated 156 pounds per individual will be delivered. I imagine there's going to be a fair number of the 'cruise brigade' being unable to move by the end of the month, and I'll probably be in the same boat.

Silly me, of course I will.

Our only hope is that food is strictly low fat, low in calories or 'gone off', otherwise we don't stand a chance.

On a different matter, Clive was telling us there was an incident on board last night when a heat sensor went off in the forward incinerator plant room. The crew were scrambled to investigate, but fortunately it turned out to be a false alarm.

At the time of the incident the ships company were staging a small pantomime in the theatre and had no time to change as they raced to their designated posts.

The Evacuation Officer, dressed as a pirate, headed for the bridge.

The fire fighting party, led by another pirate sporting a blow-up parrot on his shoulder and supported by Mother Goose and a selection of mythical sea-creatures, headed straight for the danger zone.

The Forward Incident Officer, dressed in a pink tutu and holding his enormous droopy wand (don't ask) had raced to his position on roller skates. Unfortunately he was unable to stop in time, sailed straight past the fire-fighting party and into the plant room where he would surely have perished had there actually been a fire.

Rumour has it that there will be an ongoing investigation into the proceedings as the Captain, raised from his slumbers, raced to the bridge only to discover it was overrun by pirates.

If only someone had the foresight to video this amazing spectacle it would definitely warrant £250 from 'You've Been Framed'.

Where's a bloody photog when you need one?

Anyway, I'm really looking forward to tomorrow.

'Oh we're going to Barbados, in the sunny Caribbean Sea'.

With seventy tons of consumables awaiting our undivided attention it's anyone's guess where we go from there.

By February there will no one left on board with a BMI less than 35.

'Heading further South'

Saturday 19th January

Day 12 'Barbados' - "Land at last," the cry goes out.

We arrived early to find the capital, Bridgetown, bathed in glorious warm sunshine, the sea a beautiful turquoise blue and the unmistakable sound of steel drums drifting across the harbour.

First impressions are that this is a very busy port, with us being the fifth cruise ship to be berthed (and we're the smallest) There are folk of every size and shape spilling down the gangways in droves and meandering along the docks to the terminal building.

The other floating holiday resorts are huge in comparison and I'd started to wonder how they would compare to our tiny little 'home from home'. Then I'd noticed some of the occupants of the closest leviathan looking down on us, literally, and the sudden realisation that there could be so many more 'strange folk' (like myself) to contend with made me glad we're where we are.

We may be small, but we're well informed.

One of the main reasons for the feverous activity here is because this is the 'turnaround' destination for many of the cruise companies 'fly/cruise' holidays. From the vantage point of our balcony we'd observed puddles of people roaming around the quayside looking for the right ship to board. Security were kept busy, with several groups being summarily ejected from the most modern looking vessel only to find themselves trudging up the gangway of an older, rustier version further down the dock.

They didn't look too happy.

Our cabin steward has told us that with such a concentration of opportunities the rival ship's managers seize the chance to attempt crw abductions. Apparently the crew from British based ships are highly sort after by the American market.

I haven't made much comment about the crew so far, but I can understand his remarks because all the staff looking after us are brilliant. Their immaculate customer service skills are well worth trying to purloin.

As this region was originally famous for its pirates and scallywags, I was wondering if there's any chance the photogs could get 'press-ganged' into service. Shame it's a thing of the past and probably illegal anyway, but that didn't stop me from dropping by the gallery before breakfast to warn them of the dangers. I shall pop back later to express my sincere disappointment if they haven't fallen prey to some kind of skulduggery.

After a light breakfast we'd met up with Jeff and Pru on the quayside.

We've been getting on really well with this couple from table one two eight and last night they'd suggested we could team up to share a taxi here to see the island. They're seasoned cruisers and have visited the Caribbean many times, so I'm all for taking advantage of their experience. Not forgetting that Jeff claims to possess an invaluable skill, an essential requirement to survive in this part of the world...haggling for the best price.

In view of his heritage, his claims are not in question.

Once through the port building we were suddenly surrounded by a large, noisy group of drivers, all competing for our attention, and of course our money.

Jeff rounded on the biggest and loudest of the group.

"You!" he demanded in his broad Scottish accent to the man with an even broader neck.

"Give me your best price for Harrisons Caves and a drive around the island until lunch!"

Now I would probably have gone for a much smaller, quieter and less intimidating individual, but looking around I could see Jeff had got it absolutely right. While the other visitors looking for a tour found themselves in an melee of competing drivers, none of the locals seemed keen to stand against 'the big guy' Jeff had picked out.

Genius.

Long before many of the others had chance to finalise a deal, we found ourselves in a large, cool, air conditioned minibus.

Genius again.

Because the driver Jeff had chosen was a big guy it made sense he'd have a big roomy vehicle. I'm learning a lot from our new best friends.

We'd headed off towards the centre of the island with Gus (the driver) happily regaling us with stories of slavery, conflicts through history and general information about himself, his family, his friends and his girlfriends (there seemed to be an awful lot of girlfriends)

I reckon he'd mentioned just about everyone on

the island by the time we'd reached Harrison's Caves. Suffice to say we were having a great time as our convivial host kept us laughing all the way.

I just love caves and this was an incredible underground labyrinth of wonder, well worth the visit, and it was lovely and cool down there.

The majority of the journey through the rock tunnels is made on a train like vehicle, with plenty of stops for photos, and the guides were always recommending the best views. Great couple of hours worth, and did I mention it was lovely and cool as well?

Gus was waiting for us back at the ticket hall and appeared to be chatting up one of the young ladies. By the look on her face our driver, and his antics, were very well known to her. Reluctantly he'd allowed himself to be dragged away and back to his duties.

The continuing drive around the island was a magical mystery tour in itself, with stunning views both out over the Atlantic Ocean to the east and the Caribbean Sea to the west.

All the time Gus chatted away happily. He took us to see a rock, not just any old rock though; this was the most famous of stones on the whole island. When we'd arrived Gus had explained that it had been one hundred percent accurate at forecasting the weather. It was a well worn lump of local stone with the following inscription over it.

If the rock is hot...it's sunny!
If the rock is wet...it's raining!
If the rock is white...it's snowing!
If the rock is missing...it's a hurricane...run!!!

I'd suggested that there obviously hadn't been a hurricane in the area, or this wasn't the original rock.

My dear lady said I was being pedantic, at least that what I think she'd said.

There had been a moment or two of worry as we'd headed back to the port when Gus announced he was taking us to see some real islanders. My dear lady's hand tightened around mine and the look in her eyes suggested worry.

Were we being abducted, held to ransom because Jeff hadn't offered our driver enough cash?

But Jeff and Pru seemed unconcerned, so we'd put all thoughts of kidnap out of our minds...well, nearly all of them.

A short 'dirt-track' drive and we'd found ourselves at Gus's home, an 'off the beaten track' location half way up a tree covered hill surrounded by lush vegetation. With a rum punch in one hand and a coconut bun in the other we'd chatted with Gus's 'momma', and all thoughts of getting back to the ship for lunch were long forgotten.

Momma came across as a really proud lady, keen to tell us how her family had overcome hardship and how her nation had developed. Simple things that we often take for granted are very important to her and her country, it was quite humbling to hear.

After an hour we were all given a big hug and made to promise to come back to Barbados often. I wonder how many times this little scenario played out each time Gus picked up a fare, or were we four of just a privileged few?

Anyway, twenty minutes later Gus had driven us back through Bridgetown and dropped us off back where we'd started the day. We never even quibbled about the extra few dollars he added to the price, despite his earlier arrangement with Jeff. It was well worth the extra to have experienced the real Barbados as an adopted islander.

We were made to feel very welcome.

Back at the port we'd headed to a bar for a couple of 'cold' beers in an effort to ward off the sweltering heat of the afternoon. There was also a chance to sample 'flying fish fingers' and wonder about the differences between those and the standard fish fingers variety.

And the verdict?

Well it may have been the result of a few too many beers, but I have to say they were a whole lot more delicious than that good old bearded sailor's factory processed offerings.

Before we left there was just time for a bit of souvenir hunting (always a good move when slightly inebriated)

I bought a t-shirt with the slogan 'Barbados another hard day in paradise, but someone had to do it' and my dear lady selected a few local watercolour scenes of the island. She said they were quite simple and would like to have a go at copying them.

So that was our very first taste of the Caribbean and I have to say it was very good.

Now we're back on the ship and after a small snooze it's time for dinner and a chance to discover if Jeff and Pru are still talking to us after a day in our company.

One last event of the day to mention and that was about our late evening departure from the harbour.

The Captain had informed us that the sail away from Barbados was well worth witnessing from the open decks, and he'd added that tradition dictates a ship should toot it's horn on leaving to indicate both its thanks to the locals for their hospitality and to bid a fond farewell to the other cruise liners. We were up on deck with many of our fellow travellers enjoying a complementary 'sail away' rum punch and about to discover that size really is everything.

Our little baby ship sounded its little baby ship's hooter. Aah, so sweet.

The answering calls from the bigger ships had several folk dropping their drinks and running for cover. One frail man even suffered mild palpitations.

My dear lady took great delight in singing 'Don't mess with my toot toot'. I think the rum punch was stronger than I'd first thought.

Good job it had been served in plastic cups.

Thanks Barbados, our first time in the Caribbean, we really had a great day and will definitely return if we get the chance.

Hang on a mo, we'll be back in about eight weeks as we'll call here on our way back home.

Silly Sausage.

Sunday 20th January

Day 13 'Grenada' - nice and spicy.

First impressions of Grenada are it doesn't feel quite as vibrant as Barbados. But maybe that's because it's Sunday and everywhere appears to be shut.

Our plan for this morning was to find the perfect Caribbean beach with pristine white sand, have a swim and just relax. We needed to be back at the port for 2pm as we'd booked a tour to hike up Mount

Carmel.

Have we gone completely mad?

It's set to be hot today, very hot, around thirty plus degrees in the shade with the humidity at around eighty percent and we're going to tackle a mountain...Mad or what?

But more about that later.

Once off the ship and through the port we'd had to run another gauntlet of taxi and 'Tour of the Island' drivers, but this time without our table companions to protect us as they'd gone off on a ship's tour.

Jeff had told us that if we didn't want to get a taxi then it was best to say nothing, avoid eye contact and just keep walking. We'd tried our best but the wall of bodies in front of us was impassable.

"We're just having a walk round the town today guys, but thank you," I'd said.

"There's nothing to do" one local shouted, "It's Sunday and the town is closed. Come with me and I'll show you the best sites, and take you to the better towns on the other side of the island."

I could hear the voice but so far hadn't been able to identify its owner.

"Aren't they shut as well?" I'd enquired blind.

I was breaking all of Jeff's rules.

"Probably, but if they are then we can go to my home, share a beer and watch the cricket on TV."

A small man had pushed his way to the front of the throng, amidst jeers from the others he'd grabbed my hand and pumped it vigorously.

"So we have a deal?" he'd said excitedly.

"Better count your fingers now," one of his fellow islanders shouted.

"And you'd better take this my friend." The closest of the others pressed a business card into my other hand. "It'll come in handy when he abandons you for a bar somewhere. Call me anytime."

I took a good look at our potential driver, his bloodshot eyes and the strong beery odour he emitted suggested he was already well into his weekend celebrations. It appeared highly unlikely we'd get a pleasant re-run of yesterday with Gus and Momma, so we'd quickly made excuses about not having much money, which seemed to work, and hurried away towards the small harbour.

Fortunately there were more customers coming through the doors, so he didn't pursue us.

The walk around the harbour was fascinating, with lots of little marine creatures to spot in the shallows of the crystal clear water. There were shoals of blue and yellow stripy fish, black urchins, crabs and even multi-coloured coral forming on dumped concrete blocks.

There were also many other interesting creatures of a none-marine variety floating around the area as well, but we didn't think it would be a good idea to stop and admire those, or take any photos either.

The sun had burnt off all the clouds and we'd definitely be next for a scorching if we didn't keep moving to find some shade quickly. So continuing through a seemingly deserted area and past several makeshift churches with the congregations in full voice, we'd found our way to the Grand Anse Beach, quite by accident.

The clean sand felt warm even through the soles of our walking shoes and the sea looked inviting.

"This will do nicely," my dear lady had

announced with a big grin.

Two beach chairs and a parasol relieved us of $20, and as we'd gratefully settled down in the shade, bottles of ice cold beer started appearing from all corners of the beach.

Some of the locals make a living from a 'fetch and carry service'. For a dollar or two they'll fetch you a sandwich or a burger, maybe a coconut or some fresh fruit.

They never beg, but rather they're happy to work for it, admirable.

Now I'm no great lover of sand and I'll guarantee a small grain of the stuff will never produce a pearl in me, but I loved this beach. This is where the world exists for the islanders. They meet to have fun, swim, party or just try to make a living.

We'd spent an enjoyable couple of hours there, my dear lady and I even braving a swim in the beautiful turquoise sea. I was surprised how strong the currents were in the waves as they landed on the beach. I consider myself a robust chap with a good sense of balance, but I was tossed around like an empty crisp packet as I'd tried to leave the water. I worried my dear lady would surely drown, but she'd had no trouble at all.

As my life had flashed before my eyes she'd stood on the beach tutting loudly.

I must remember in future that just because something looks beautiful and inviting doesn't mean it's not dangerous (a bit like my dear lady)

To avoid a long hot walk back to the ship, we'd taken a twenty minute ride on the water taxi for $4 each. It dropped us right next to the ship leaving me thinking 'what a shame we hadn't discovered this before'. The cooling breeze and salty water spray as we'd bounced over the water was wonderful.

A quick change of clothes and shoes and we were ready for this hike up the mountain to see a waterfall. But the water was already falling on us as the heavens had opened.

We were off to find Mount Carmel, the highest waterfall on the island, which according to the brochure 'is just waiting to be discovered'. But it also shows a picture of the falls, so I'm thinking someone must have already found it.

Our driver and guide, Skipper, was great company and soon had us laughing and joking on the way to our destination, despite many sudden downpours of the wet stuff.

"The path may be a bit damp and slippery," he'd told us.

But boy oh boy he couldn't have been more wrong. It was exceptionally wet and the trail through the forest had turned into a 'mud fest', more slippery than trying to walk on a sheet of glass covered in washing up liquid…in socks.

Normally it's a fifteen minute stroll to the waterfall. Instead we embarked on an hour's ascent up the north face of Everest, but without the use of ropes, crampons or a friendly Sherpa to help out. But everybody worked together and we had some really great fun.

By the time we'd reached the falls, made more imposing by the river swelling weather conditions, we were covered head to toe in caked mud.

But no one had been injured (luckily) nobody was moaning (unbelievably) and everyone was still smiling despite the knowledge that we still had to journey back the same way (really?)

And was it worth the effort?

It certainly was.

The waterfall was impressive for sure, but our own sense of achievement somehow made it seem even more spectacular. This mutual journey of jeopardy had resulted in a certain degree of bonding, sharing water to wash down muddy legs, taking group photos whilst openly laughing and joking with folk we hardly knew before today. Thankfully we'd stopped short of reciprocal grooming.

The route back in some ways was more dangerous because it was mainly downhill. But now we were a team, a well honed and practiced unit experienced in traversing the treacherous muddy slopes of the steepest of mountains...well, more like just sliding down the hill on backsides until someone caught you at the bottom.

Long story short but we all made it back to the minibus in one piece, where another enterprising local armed with a bucket, scrubbing brush and sponge awaited our return. For a dollar each my dear lady and I had our legs washed and boots scrubbed, he was making an excellent job of clearing away the thick mud.

"Can't have you tourists stealing God's best earth," he'd said.

But not everyone in the group was happy to part with their cash, and as they'd trudged past they'd even made jokes about how gullible we were.

"That's just stupid," one guy had laughed at us. "Just wipe it off on the grass over there for free."

"You shouldn't give them money," his female partner had added. "He'll only waste it on weed or drink."

Less than an hour ago I'd helped this guy and his partner across a very muddy stream and prevented her from falling down a steep slippery bank.

With their derogatory comments the camaraderie of the day disappeared, replaced by a rather ugly display of the selfishness of mankind.

Mankind? That's a joke.

I like to keep my journal light-hearted, but this time I really feel the need to record the discontentment I have toward (some of) my fellow man, who never fail at being pathetic and cause such frustration.

It somewhat spoilt the day.

But then I shouldn't feel bad about the things other people say or do, surely their conduct is their problem, not mine.

My dear lady lightened my mood by reminding me that the lady had looked like a fairy on a gob of lard as she'd cavorted through the mud...hilarious.

Back at the port there was just enough time to wander around the town before we sailed.

In the local market we'd bought a few Christmas baubles (bit weird I know) and another t-shirt for me.

More boozy rum punch was brought out for the sail away party along with a very decadent chocolate fountain for all to enjoy.

Stating that I'd looked brave and fearless after our 'Mount Carmel Adventure', my dear lady daubed my cheeks with some of the chocolate from her plate whilst singing a very boozy rendition of 'Mud Glorious Mud'.

Unfortunately another couple who were 'well oiled' saw this happen and decided it looked like a fun game. They proceeded to smear the warm gooey brown stuff all over each other.

The activity quickly snowballed as others joined in, and as we'd left there was a major attempt in progress to break the 'how many marshmallows and Smarties can you stick on your face' world record.

I'm not sure how long it will take the deck crew to scrape up all that mess, I just hope they never find out who started it.

We now have four sea days before we get to our next port, Alter do Chao, five hundred miles up the Amazon.

My growing experience of cruising tells me this could be fun, but at least my boots will have chance to dry out.

Monday 21st January

Day 14 'The Marie Celeste' - almost alive and well.

It appears that the last two days in port has had an effect on everyone because the ship has turned into a ghost boat. Yet the weather is good, so the lack of folk is a bit of a mystery, even the usual 'cruise brigaders' aren't charging around the decks.

Everyone must either have retired to their cabins to recover from some form of over indulgence, or maybe they've decided to remain at one of the beautiful places we've just left.

Dare I even believe that 'press-ganging' actually still happens?

I best not state my preference for anyone's possible demise, but sad to note the photogs are still around.

With just a few hardy customers to look after the staff are at a loose end. Waiters roam the empty restaurant tables, aimlessly wiping away the smeared memory of dribbled custard and ketchup splatters.

In a forlorn attempt to earn a crust of commission, a pack of hungry bar staff mug a lone individual who merely left his cabin in search of a breath of fresh air.

New attempts are made by spa staff to put together an irresistible package certain to entice the unenticable to part with their cash. This is strongly resisted, so abandoning all thoughts of profit, they offer free five minute facials in the atrium. Believing this is just ambush tactics the sceptical travellers still refuse to indulge.

In the corner of a small dingy cupboard disheartened photographers stitch together yet another costume of feathers, believing they will finally beat the masses into submitting themselves to the immortality of a photo shoot.

Meanwhile the lone writer of this journal attempts to carry his musings across a tightrope of silliness suspended over an abyss of stupidity, this time I think he fell off.

Interestingly enough, there was the first in a series of lectures this afternoon about the Amazon, its people and their environment.

Still aching badly from yesterdays' exertions I'd decided to give the gym a miss for today at least, so I was looking for something to keep me occupied while my dear lady was at art class. Quite by accident I'd stumbled into the show lounge where this talk was going on.

Led by a specialist in Amazonian studies, he'd

explained that it was important to dispel many of the myths surrounding this mightiest of rivers.

Firstly he wanted to reassure us that Brazil is a very safe country, the people of the Amazon being particularly friendly.

"However," he'd said, "They are also very poor, so if you walk around with expensive jewellery and cameras on display then you have to accept it may be too much of a temptation for some to resist."

Doesn't sound that friendly to me, but I'll have to admit it was good logical advice.

He'd also suggested that it was probably best not to go out after dark either, as we would almost certainly get lost in unfamiliar surroundings. This would give any local 'intent on mischief' an opportunity too good to miss.

In my day 'intent on mischief' was a label hung on the kids who rang doorbells and scarpered, I'm fairly certain no one ever got mugged.

Next he'd told us that the river was full of piranha, a veracious flesh eating fish with razor sharp teeth.

"But," he'd added, "Movie producers have totally misrepresented them in order to sensationalise a storyline."

Now who would ever have guessed that 'Piranhas in Space' wasn't based on a true story?

"Eating human flesh is a misconception," he'd continued, "As they usually only devour dead carcases and other rubbish that finds its way into the water. It's highly unlikely that anyone paddling or swimming in the river would be attacked. So if you fancy a swim to cool off then do it."

That's all very well, but what about those piranha

'intent on mischief'. Isn't a plump piece of tender tourist flesh a bit too much of a temptation?

Oh and define 'Rubbish'.

He went on to tell us that it's doubtful we'll see or hear anything of the animals as we head up the river. This is because the banks of the river are generally inhabited and the animals have been eaten or driven deep into the forest by their most destructive predator...man.

"So there's no point in worrying about coming face to face with anything dangerous," he'd reassured us. "In fact it's unlikely you'll see any animals at all."

Tomorrows talk is entitled 'Animals of Amazonia'.

I figure it might not be worth going.

The weather has been absolutely glorious, so after lunch my dear lady and I found a nice spot to relax on the sun deck (factor 30 applied of course) and we'd chatted and laughed about the holiday experience so far.

I'm delighted to record she's absolutely loving it.

I know this is a bit of a cliché, but I really feel like we're getting to know each other all over again. Life has always been hectic, for both of us, not only did our careers keep us very busy but there was also the small matter of bringing up two children and building a happy home. We've never fallen out or even drifted apart, but with everything that happened in life we rarely had enough time for each other.

It didn't really change that much when the boys left home for university either. Our work/life balance never seemed to swing in favour of 'life'.

But this trip has facilitated us spending quality time together, sticking up for and looking out for each other. We've laughed more, talked more and my dear lady has even started holding my hand again.

We're only just about getting ourselves into retirement mode, but already I feel there's a vast rekindling of our relationship.

At least I hope so.

Just as I was starting to think this beautiful afternoon had become absolutely perfect, a parrot showed up...all six foot of him. Having sneaked up from behind our sun beds he suddenly jumped up and squawked.

"Watch the birdie," his partner in crime called out as the moth eaten fowl grabbed my dear lady from behind.

She screamed in terror with the shock, reached her arms up and seized hold of the first thing that came to hand. As the camera's shutter clicked away merrily the parrot's head went flying across the lido deck, bounced off a table of drinks and rolled into the pool.

It took many an apology and a complimentary bottle of wine from the photogs to get my dear ladies head out of her hands. I just hope they didn't notice all the smiles and winks she threw in my direction throughout the whole affair.

I really had forgotten what an incredible sense of humour she has, clever girl.

"Cheers me dears."

Tuesday 22nd January

Day 15 'at sea' - a strange meeting and a novel idea!

After a light breakfast I'd headed off for the gym.

I reckoned it was probably time to stop abusing my body with food and alcohol and get back into a more beneficial routine for the sake of my heart.

Probably more to do with a slight concern that my jacket felt a bit snug at dinner last night.

My usual hour of exercise had been completely uneventful until an elderly gentleman arrived just as I was slowing down to finish.

Someone else in the fitness centre before lunch is a novelty. But surprisingly he was in a collar and tie, sported a dark blue double breasted jacket, a panama hat and a pair of brown leather brogues.

This very dapper looking gent nodded a friendly greeting in my direction and proceeded to remove his hat and jacket, hanging them carefully on the rack of dumbbells.

I was intrigued.

I always use the treadmill that gives me the best view of both the sea and the rest of the gym area, so rather than getting off the apparatus, as it had stopped, I'd restarted the belt at a sedentary pace so I could continue watching.

He sat himself down at one of the weight machines, the one where you reach up to grab a pair of handlebars which are pulled down to chest level, followed by a controlled return to the starting position.

He did just that, quite easily in fact as there was only one of the five kilogram weights attached to the lifting mechanism.

After half a dozen repetitions he'd stopped and was looking quizzically at the stack of weights belonging to the apparatus. Pulling the fixing peg out of the top weight he'd moved it all the way to the bottom of the stack and pushed it firmly into the hole of the last one.

Now I've tried out various pieces of the equipment in there and on this particular bit of kit I'd struggled with just six of the weights, he now had all twenty attached, that's 100 kilograms.

I should have said something, but instead I just watched agast as he took a few deep breathes, tightened his grip on the handlebars and pulled.

I'm not sure I've ever seen a face that shade of red before, or the purple tinge that followed as he lifted himself off the seat rather than pulling the bar down.

After a few seconds of frantic midair tugging and grunting he finally gave up and relaxed, or so I'd thought.

To my surprise he tried again, still without success, then again, five times in total all with the same outcome, nothing moved except him.

He'd sat for a moment or two until a more natural pallor had returned, then stood and purposefully strode over to the dumbbell rack to retrieve his belongings. Heading for the exit at a brisk pace he'd nodded and smiled in my direction.

"See you," I called over to him and waved a hand rather limply.

"Same time tomorrow if you fancy," he called back and was gone.

If I fancy, what was that supposed to mean?

Did he see me as a wingman, ready to summon medical assistance when something in his body broke, or was he looking for a witness to his attempts at killing himself?

Now I'll just have to go back tomorrow.

We had another beautiful afternoon of lazing around and soaking up the warmth of the sun. The sea is almost mirror flat and it's impossible to imagine we're floating in the middle of a vast ocean.

It's inevitable that cruising involves a large amount of travel across open water (obviously) and this involves a varying amount of time at sea in order to reach the destination of your choice (can't you tell I'm getting really good at this?)

It's been great to explore the three ports we've visited so far, especially as they're places we've never been to before. The experience has been special.

But the sea days have been special too, an unexpected bonus. To my surprise they've become a very important, and enjoyable, part of this whole cruise experience, for both of us.

We get a chance to relax, or be active, read, write, paint, explore or just sit, as my dear lady often does, watching the ever changing 'motion of the ocean and the sun in the sky' still hoping to catch more than an occasional glimpse of the wildlife as it passes us by.

However, not everyone feels the same way, and for some of our fellow passengers the section of travel between ports is their very own living nightmare.

Whether it's calm or rough it's all the same to them and the slightest wobble of the ship sends them scurrying for anti-seasickness measures. They believe the elements hate them and despise their very presence, while an enraged Neptune boils the sea beneath the boat to exact his revenge.

Such personal rejection (along with the nausea) throws some of the sufferers into a turbulent rage, like maritime werewolves they literally howl and bay at the antics of the sea.

It disturbs them, it hurts their eyes which redden as the mist descends, they desire land and they need it now. But the sea is not perturbed by their ranting and is unable to grant their wish for 'terra firma', so they turn on each other.

Patience is lost and tempers flare as a mere seed of irritation rubs quickly to become a blister of immense rage. As the ship gently rolls with the lazy swell of the ocean it seems that all their negative personal characteristics become enhanced and charge to the surface.

While the normally positive, relaxed individual becomes almost comatose, the irritating git transforms into, well you get the picture.

So with this in mind, I have a solution to deal with these obnoxicants (this is not a real word, but it should be)

It is with great pleasure I give you,

'It's Time to Toss the Tosser'

Good afternoon everybody and welcome to The Cruise Company's new sea day activity 'Toss the Tosser'.

Is there someone on board who you've taken a dislike to because they're particularly obnoxious, odorous or just clearly a waste of space? Then maybe this is just the activity for you. Enjoy consequence free retribution and while away the long hours at sea by ridding the world of one annoying little git.

The rules are simple.

Between 09.00 am and 10.00 am on 'Toss Day' everyone on board gets to cast a vote and the passenger who receives the most votes becomes the designated 'Tosser'.

The 'Tosser' is now allowed 10 minutes to hide somewhere on the ship.

Any 'Tosser' caught leaving the ship during the 'hide time' will automatically forfeit any onboard credit they have and will waive their rights to any later rescue attempt by the crew.

At the end of the 'hide time' the ship's whistle will sound, this will signal the start of the 'Toss' phase of the activity. The remaining passengers now have around one hour to locate the 'Tosser' and 'Toss' him or her from the ship.

Please note that only the designated 'Tosser' (who can be clearly identified by a high visibility waistcoat with beeping and flashing beacons) is eligible for the 'Toss' and anyone caught 'Tossing' none designated persons will be denied access to any of the ships dining rooms for a period of 24 hours.

If at the end of one hour the 'Tosser' has not been located and 'Tossed' they will be allowed to remain in hiding indefinitely until the remaining passengers can no longer identify them as the 'Tosser'

Following a successful 'Toss' the ship's company may 'give a toss' and instigate a rescue of the 'Tosser' but no guarantee is offered and any attempt will be solely at the discretion of Dave, the ship's cat.

No Cruise Company staff are to be included in the vote, search or 'Toss' and any passengers claiming to have mistakenly 'Tossed' the Cruise Director instead of the Tosser will be required to pose for and purchase an entire album of pictures from the ships photographers.

Please note that The Cruise Company accepts no

liability for any injury occurring as a direct result of this activity and passengers taking part do so at their own risk.

We hope you enjoy this new and innovative activity and if you are voted for then maybe next time you go cruising you may consider being a bit more pleasant to your fellow passengers, and a bit less of a 'Tosser'.

My dear lady thinks I've finally lost the plot.

She may be right and she's welcome to cast her vote for me tomorrow, which she probably will do if the song she's singing in the shower is anything to go by.

But wasn't Alice Cooper's song 'I want to be elected' not 'you're going to be ejected'?

Wednesday 23rd January

Day 16 'at sea' - ever the diplomat, on drugs.

Needless to say I couldn't resist the urge to be in the gym this morning and sure enough my dapper gent showed up.

Nothing changed from yesterday, from the clothes he wore to the colour his face turned. Once again the bar of the 'pull down' didn't budge an inch (or even a millimetre if you prefer) and I'm not convinced he's doing his body any favours.

But he did give me the most enormous smile as he left, but then most men usually do that to disguise the pain they're experiencing after such exertion.

I'm still speechless, and apparently he'll see me again tomorrow.

This could be an ongoing saga and I can't wait for the next episode. Even though nothing's really happened I'm hooked, so maybe I should try and find him around the ship to see if I can add some more detail.

More on this tomorrow, possibly.

I think I could do with some instruction when it comes to the matter of tact and diplomacy.

Writing has become an outlet for a previously concealed and unspoken sarcastic sense of humour. But by expressing it in the form of letters and characters I've gained a modicum of self assurance, causing me to verbalise my thoughts aloud on more than one occasion.

It could become a tricky problem and get me into trouble.

For example I was sat in the lounge this morning when one of our fellow guests (female) stopped to say hello.

I'd asked the usual question, "Are you having a good day?"

"Yes thank you," she'd replied, "I've just been for a facial."

Now before anybody gets the wrong idea, she was definitely talking about a treatment in the spa. But I'd struggled with the urge to offer an equally inappropriate reply.

Such as...

"Oh yes you can tell," (this would have been hurtful, so not a good idea).

"Really? You can't tell," (implies that the £70 she'd just spent was wasted).

"You look really good," (could be taken to mean you looked like an old prune before).

"They've enhanced your natural glow," (we both know that's rubbish).

"Next time buy a new dress, at least you can get your money back," (would be too honest).

I'd really had to bite my tongue as all these comments had raced through my head at once. In the end I'd offered a simple, "You look nice."

Which was probably the blandest and worst thing I could have said.

But what would have been an appropriate response to such a loaded question?

I have to admit it's a matter of concern that I'm asking for advice from my journal, like I'm expecting to open up the page tomorrow to discover an answer to the question above.

On a different matter, I've received a note from the Cruise Director this afternoon stating that although he and his entertainment team had had a really good giggle at my new sea day activity, 'Toss the Tosser', he really couldn't see it working as a feasible alternative to deck quoits or table tennis.

He went on to state that initially the Captain had been fully in favour of introducing it into the programme of events and had several candidates lined up for the first 'Toss'. However he hadn't fully read the rules and after discovering his ineligibility to take part had complained about the horrendous amount of paperwork involved, not to mention the cost of search and rescue operations.

He also felt it unfair to place the onus of a rescue on Dave the ship's cat as Dave was already stressed from the excessive ratting duties he's had to carry out recently and any further anxiety may attract some unwanted scrutiny from the RSPCA.

The Cruise Director's note went on to suggest that maybe a revision to the rules would facilitate a change of attitude from the big man at the top, but I should definitely take some time to consider a more 'politically correct' title for the activity.

'Lob the Loser' or 'Pitch the Pest' were just two of the preferred names.

Seems like someone has had far too much time on their hands between shows.

But I'm a little confused as to how they got hold of my idea in the first place. I'm fairly certain no one else has seen it and I only read it to my dear lady once.

I believe there may be a spy in my camp!

The time has come to start taking the medication that should prevent us from contracting Malaria. It's called Doxycycline and right at this moment I'm regretting reading the accompanying leaflet which details all the side effects we could experience.

I think the biggest issue is that we're supposed to avoid sunlight, a bit tricky considering where we are. Having said that we're much better off than most of our fellow passengers because neither of us is on any regular medication.

Not sure if that's down to good living or good fortune.

I got chatting to Jeff and Pru over dinner and they were telling me that their doctor had advised them not to take the anti-malarial drug as it could conflict with all the other medication they're taking for the plethora of health problems they've both got.

Hypertension, hyperlipidemia (whatever that is) angina, arrhythmias, type two diabetes, various 'waterworks' problems and Pru is also asthmatic and anaemic.

"Not forgetting the pain killers for our stiff and creaky joints," Pru had added with a laugh.

Doesn't sound that funny to me.

"Look around you Laddie," said Jeff.

"Can you imagine how many tablets the folk on this ship take each day, just for the chance to stick around for another day or more."

In reality I had no idea.

I'd assumed that everyone was fit and healthy, but then maybe medication is the reason for that.

"If you think about it Laddie you can only go on these long holidays if you're retired. And if you're retired chances are you're old. For some of us things have just stopped working properly."

I have to admit I hadn't thought about it, but now I have and this is what I've come up with.

These tablets keep me going, they lower this and that,
There's a tiny one for water and a larger one for fat.
Three are for my ticker, two to keep me sane.
A puffer helps the breathing, sixteen capsules ease the pain.
There's a daily dose of aspirin so my platelets don't occlude,
And the blue one gives a little lift for when I'm in the mood.
There's a yellow one for weight loss which gives me quite a buzz,
And a pretty shiny pink one, who knows what that one does?
Now my kidneys barely function and my heart beats way too strong,
It's because I'm hypertensive that I have to play along
With this medication buffet, Bendroflumethiazide,
Omeprazole stops heart burn, with Gaviscon on the side.
Colchicine, lorazepam, metformin, just the start,
And a nightly dose of senna plays a most important part.
Simvastatin, cardipine, quinine for cramps at night,
And a hefty block of iron puts anaemia to right.

Now when it comes to pain relief I've tried the blooming lot,
Gabapentin, Tramadol, Codeine, Morphine, Pot!!
And I'm sure a course of HRT would really see me well,
It's the only thing that's missing from this medication hell.
So forgive me if I rattle, because as you may guess
It's the drugs that keep me going, is it really worth it?
YES.

Well thanks to Jeff and Pru for the insight and information, including a gander at their medication case and allowing me to read all the drug info leaflets.

Yes it really is a case, which seems to contain a small high street pharmacy

I had no idea!

My dear lady has been insisting that 'Love is the drug for me'.

That and a whole bottle of Merlot.

Thursday 24ᵗʰ January

Day 17 'at sea' - but entering the Amazon.

"Good Morning. As your long suffering journal my advice with regards to yesterdays question about being tactful to that poor lady who'd spent good money in an effort to look good, is either be extremely honest and say something like 'Why bother, no one's going to look at you anyway', or extremely dishonest with a comment like 'It must have taken them ages to improve your already perfect complexion'.

But be prepared for the consequences either way as neither is right."

Yes, well thanks for that, shame your advice is twenty four hours too late and maybe a little too honest!

Anyway back to reality.

I say reality but my morning visit to the gym has become a touch surreal. Yes my little old gentleman was there again, yes he followed the exact same routine as the previous two days, no he doesn't seem to have suffered any ill effects from his maniacal exertions and no I haven't discovered anything more about him.

I'm sure the personal trainer hasn't seen him yet, she tells anyone off who's not dressed properly and today he was wearing a very snazzy bowtie.

Bizarre or what?

I only tend to 'exercise' on sea days so unfortunately I'm going to miss his antics for a while as we have five full days in port over this next week.

I have to admit to feeling the benefits of my daily exercise, even from my inadequate efforts, so maybe I should make time in the evenings to pop into the gym and keep up the good work.

Or maybe I'm worried I might miss out on seeing what's going on

We turned a corner during the night, left the mighty Atlantic Ocean behind and are now cruising up the mighty River Amazon.

But you can't tell the difference as there is still a mighty lot of water.

In the process we've crossed a line called the Amazon Bar (but no one offered to buy a round)

Apparently this is the area where this mightiest of rivers dumps all the sediment, rocks and vegetation that it picks up on its four thousand mile journey through Brazil. That amounts to three million tons each and every day taken initially from the Andes and deposited in the Atlantic, and all I can think of at this point is WOW.

The scientific community worry about global warming but with worldwide coastal and river erosion on such a massive scale are they missing a point here?

As the rivers eventually cut countries in half and the seas swallow up the edges, surely mankind needs to concentrate its attention on preventing everything disappearing into the sea.

Maybe global warming could actually help the situation by evaporating the water to reveal more of the land that's being moved into the oceans

Just a thought.

But on a lighter (and slightly more sensible) note.

I'm not really sure what I'm expecting from the 'Amazon' part of this holiday. Ever since I booked this trip I felt more comfortable about the visits to the south and west of this continent. But as we're taking the entire round trip we have no choice other than to go with the flow (no pun intended)

From some of the conversations I've had (and overheard) it appears that many of our fellow passengers are just ticking off boxes, and others are just ticking certain boxes again.

Seasoned Cruiser: "Is this your first time up the Amazon?"

Me: "Yes. What about yourself?"

S/C: "Oh this is our forth time don't you know. Fantastic experience what. Are you liking it?"

Me: "Yes it's very interesting, can't wait to get ashore and explore."

S/C: "I don't see why, there's bally well nothing to do."

Me: "I suppose you've seen it all."

S/C: "Oh god no, we've never been ashore here, I told you there's nothing to do so no point."

Me: "Well thanks for the info, bye."

I really hope I'm never this shallow, just visiting a place purely for bragging rights seems a bit pointless.

But then I've bought a t-shirt in every port so far and can't wait to wear them back home to get the neighbours jealous. So what does that say about me?

Since we entered the river there's been a mixture of interest.

Occasionally the banks are so far away there is nothing to see except trees, and when we are closer to the banks there is still mostly nothing to see except bigger trees.

Sections of the river do have people living in small clearings, sometimes as an individual property (I use the term property very loosely) or occasionally in groups of five or more dwellings.

There are always locals in boats, fishing, moving stuff or just messing about on the water and they all wave as we pass by. It would be interesting to know if they're welcoming us to their backyard or gesturing for us to stop polluting their river and bugger off.

Talking of bugs, there's one more feature of this region that we've been given a very serious warning about.

The Bugs.

We're all fully aware that we're in an area rife with yellow fever and malaria, for which most of us are taking tablets to prevent. But the tiny carriers of these diseases, mosquitoes, are apparently the least of our worries, especially whilst we're on the ship. In one of the lectures we were told that Mosquitoes have fairly fragile wings and will rarely cross large stretches of open water as it tends to be too breezy for them to cope.

Even so, the Captain has been on the ship's tannoy this morning to instruct us to avoid going outside as soon as darkness falls.

Vampires?

He also told us that all the entrances and exits to the open decks have been covered with a double layer of fine mesh netting, which under no circumstance should be removed, tied back or damaged.

So what's the problem?

Well it's all about the bugs being attracted to light.

Despite the fact we're huge in comparison to most of the other vessels on the river, we have to remain lit up like a Christmas tree at night so no one accidently bumps into us. So we will literally be the candle all the moths want to fly around, and in this area of the world the moths are more like small fighter planes.

"The outer doors won't be locked for safety reasons," the Captain said. "But I would caution you not to set foot on the open decks from dusk to dawn."

It's definitely sounds like vampires.

"The insects are large and some can deliver a nasty bite. In the mornings any creatures remaining onboard will be removed by a clean-up team. If you see any of them at any time please do not try to pick them up, touch them or even approach them."

Does he mean the clean-up team or insects?

This was intriguing.

At around 8 o'clock this evening my dear lady and I had taken up residence in the library as it overlooks the lido deck, the perfect viewing point. We weren't to be disappointed.

As soon as the sky darkened it seemed to fill up with flying things which started landing all over the illuminated white panels of the ship.

There were huge moths, some as big as a hand. There were black ones, brown ones, red and yellow ones. Then something big hit the window and fell to the floor. It was a huge black beetle with large pincers, spinning around on its back, almost the size of a cricket ball.

Now it's a fact of human nature that no matter what we're told some don't believe it unless they experience it for themselves. As we'd watched, a small group of intrepid explorers were emerging from the door next to the library and out onto the upper deck, quite what they had in mind was hard to determine.

They first stopped to admire and photograph a couple of the large moths on the protective netting, but soon their attention was captured by the spinning black beetle. A foot was duly dispatched in attempt to flick it over onto its legs.

Once righted surely the creature would be grateful.

That would seem to be a definite no because once righted it proceeded to seek retribution against the perceived attacker. Now the small group were in panic mode and trying to get away, but more beetles were hitting the deck and joining in the pursuit.

Fortunately the humans made it back to the safety

of the door unscathed, and disappeared inside, but I reckon they're now wishing they'd listened to the master's warning.

The bombardment of the ship continued and soon the floor, walls and lights disappeared under thousands of insects. As we'd meandered off to dinner with my dear lady singing 'The Ugly Bugs Ball' we could still hear the loud clangs and bangs as many more of the monsters joined the party.

Over dinner talk was all about the bugs, mainly no one could comprehend how many there were on the ship already and how many more there must be left in the forest.

It was great to see the Executive Chef has a sense of humour and tonight's menu included:

Ant(ipasti)

Tossed Beetle(root) Salad

Butterfly Cakes.

Despite the ribbing from Jeff about it being the real thing and we were going to die, my dear lady and I tried all three, and they were delicious.

We decided to head back to the library after dinner.

It seemed very dark outside, until we'd realised that the windows too were now covered with a thick layer of the local bugs.

How many more could there be?

Tomorrow will find us exploring our first port of call on the river, the small town of Alter Do Chao. It should be very interesting, hot and probably bug free.

Friday 25ᵗʰ January

Day 18 'Alter Do Chao' - and it's Burn's Night.

At 8.00am this morning the Captain announced that we'd reached the town of Alter Do Chao and someone had thrown out the anchor. Then he'd asked for volunteers to retrieve it from the bottom of the river as he was pretty certain we'd need it later. He added that he'd considered sending members of the crew, but they'd be hard to replace if they were eaten by the piranha.

Seems he does have a sense of humour after all, but he obviously didn't go to the lecture on piranha.

Anyway today I've had my first experience of tender boats.

A lot of the smaller places we'll visit don't have a big enough dock to berth even this small ship. To get us ashore they lower a few of the life boats (sorry, we're supposed to call them survival craft) which they load up with passengers and head for land. The trip isn't very usually long but, after the stability of a large cruise liner, these tiny craft literally bounce across the water. This is when everyone starts to realise why they're called tenders, particularly affecting the delicate nether regions.

Anyway in small groups we were loaded up into these 'rump bouncers' and duly deposited on the beach, where we're greeted by a vast array of stalls selling local trinkets and souvenirs. To add atmosphere a very enthusiastic band of musicians play traditional music, trying to tempt the new arrivals to part with a few dollars for tips or even to buy their home made CD.

Our friendly Amazonian expert had told us that

this small town is a 'by-product' of the nearby city of Santarem.

There are magnificent, soft sandy beaches here, formed by the river which at this point is a long, slow loop. The rich of Santarem have turned it into the local resort for their bored children to play in during the summer, which in this region lasts a fairly long time.

It's not hard to see why they've chosen this place, but harder to imagine how such a pristine white beach exists on the banks of the Amazon at all. As we stepped off the tender boat straight onto the soft sands, it felt like we'd turned around in the night and headed straight back to the Caribbean.

But Amazonian it definitely is and it's truly magnificent, only the oppressive humidity spoils an almost perfect setting and I'd love to go for a swim to cool off, if not for the possibility of some pesky piranha 'intent on mischief'.

Leaving the beach and heading for the town the first thing to notice is the very marked contrast between the large, razor wired protected, opulent properties of the rich 'out of townies' compared with the local's 'thrown together' tin shacks, which look to be cramped and stifling.

The children run amok while their parents spend their day tending souvenir stalls or providing boat transportation to the main attraction of the area, a long island spit of sand covered with bars and eateries. It seems they basically carve out a living from the antics any visitors prepared to spend cash.

I hope they realise our lot won't. They're all carrying heavy backpacks again.

The town square is surrounded by the usual trappings of tourism, I use the term town square loosely as it's just a dust bowl with a statue, and the trappings of tourism are a few makeshift stalls selling t-shirts, piranha skeletons and hammocks.

Two hurriedly erected bars had been positioned outside someone's house, but with little shade to sit and watch the hustle and bustle of folk going about their business, we'd wandered down to the water front and strolled along the shore for a while.

We'd stopped to watch a group of lads who were unloading a small trailer and carrying its contents, cases of beer, across to the island spit.

Yes, carrying.

The boxes held well above their heads they'd headed into the water and kept going. For some the depth in the middle was too much and heads had disappeared under the surface, but the beer kept moving so all seemed to be okay.

My dear lady give a huge sigh of relief as they'd all made it safely across to the island, but I quickly took her away from the area before the whole process could be repeated. There was still a very large stack of cases on this side of the river.

Back in the town square a tarpaulin cover was being strung up over one of the bars to provide shade, so we'd quickly occupied a wobbly three legged table, ordered two beers and settled in for a bit of 'people watching'.

Now I'd assumed that Alter Do Chao was a regular stopping point for all the Amazon cruises. But maybe I was wrong as it quickly became apparent that on this occasion we were 'the people' being watched.

The locals all seemed to be gathered in groups to observe their visitors, with a lot of pointing and gesturing going on.

The most bizarre thing about this town were the vultures, and I am referring to large, ugly black birds rather than a euphemism for any dodgy individuals bleeding the life out of the locals (although I wouldn't be surprised if both species existed side by side here)

These gigantic birds were perched on the telegraph poles all around the town, watching intently as more and more of the ship's passengers made it to shore. The main question would be 'How many of the weaker ones would make it back?'

By the look in their eyes the scavengers felt it might just be their lucky day.

That probably explains why the locals were watching us as well. Maybe they were taking bets on which one of us would get picked off by the wildlife and were pointing out their favourites.

But make it back we did and we were just in time to see the 'clean-up' team shovelling up masses of bugs into large buckets and tipping them over the side of the ship. There must have been thousands of them.

I am finding the heat and humidity quite draining and a short sleep mid afternoon is often required. This is very much the land of the siesta, and if it isn't it should be, at least that's the excuse I've been using for my dear lady. She has unkindly suggested I'm just getting old and past it.

Anyway, after a short snooze, I took myself off to the gym for an hour, as I'd promised myself. But when my gent didn't show up I'd felt a pang of disappointment.

Back in the cabin my dear lady was already dressed and prepared for Burns Night so I'd quickly showered and eased myself into my dinner suit. I was expecting it to be an even tighter fit than the other night, but was pleasantly surprised to find the jacket fastened nicely.

Now either the exercise is working or spending day after day in a natural sauna is causing me to lose too much fluid.

I really must drink more beer.

Standing together looking in the mirror I just had to tell my dear lady she looked amazing.

"We both look amazing," she'd replied.

That was nice.

Our table companion Jeff, resplendent in his kilt, met us for pre-dinner drinkies and explained what we should expect from this most hallowed of evenings and its festivities.

As a member of his local Burn's Society he'd spoken to the Maître d' about how the proceedings were to be conducted and had been promised a parade of the haggis with a piper, followed by the traditional ceremony of 'The Addressing of the Haggis'.

Jeff had even volunteered to recite the address, but was reassured that everything was 'in hand'.

Unfortunately the whole evening was to be a travesty for Jeff and the wee haggis.

The timings of this most traditional of events went a bit awry. So in order to prevent a re-enactment of some Scottish Rebellion, the members of table one two eight spent the entire night soothing Jeff's mood with copious amounts of whiskey.

The haggis was served as a starter instead of the main course.

Jeff was incensed. "How can we eat the wee beastie before it's been addressed?"

Neeps and tatties soup turned out to be mushroom.

"Bloody edjots," he'd shouted.

Roast Beef and Yorkshire pudding for the main. Jeff refused to eat it.

Cranachan for dessert. Not bad but without the inclusion of oats. Poor Jeff looked so dejected, but the worst was still to come.

The meal concluded with the parade of a rather small and sad looking lump of offal to a pre-recorded accordion accompaniment and not the piper Jeff had been promised. After which one of the entertainment team, who was obviously not Scottish, gave a shortened address then managed to slaughter the defenceless haggis, a whole hour after we'd already consumed it.

At this point Jeff had started fingering the Skean Dhu tucked in his sock, he had a murderous look in his eyes. Fortunately we all knew that it was only a plastic replica as he'd been told he couldn't carry an offensive weapon on board.

But maybe we were all underestimating the damage he could do, even with a bit of plastic.

At least there was a decent single malt to be enjoyed and on this special occasion the purser had obviously been in a very good mood, letting the clientele have doubles at a reasonable price. I was surprised that the more rounds we'd bought the more reasonable the price seemed.

It even placated Jeff, eventually.

There had been a moment of concern when the Maitre d' had been spotted heading toward our table, assumingly to enquire if Jeff had enjoyed the evening. Fortunately Ron had intercepted him and explained it would be for best not to mention the matter...ever.

Afterwards we'd headed as a group (it was the only way we could remain upright) to the Crow's Nest Bar at the top of the ship, and we'd danced (yes, me on a dance floor) to some wonderful Scottish tunes. I can honestly say I've never done the 'Gay Gordons' before and it's probable I'll never do it again.

And so to bed, if only I could remember where I'd left it.

Saturday 26th January

Day 19 'a river day' - has anyone seen my head?

It's official. I hate Robbie Burns.

By 10.30am, and after several cups of strong black coffee, I was almost ready to excuse this famous poets assault on my head, except he was the only one not to buy a round last night and that's totally unforgivable!

But it had been a really good night, and luckily Jeff has almost no recollection of the proceedings.

I'd decided the gym may not be the safest of places for me this morning so went off for a rather wobbly stroll around the decks.

After last night I'd decided that maybe I should take it a bit easier on the drink for a while, but during the Captain's midday report it was announced that today is Australia Day and not wishing to exclude anyone from the party it is also Indian Republic Day.

What better way to celebrate than a lunchtime barbeque with lashings of ice cold Fosters followed by an evening tandori buffet, which wouldn't be complete without a three for the price of two offer on Cobra Beer.

Tomorrow will be Sangria awareness day followed closely by a traditional Amazonian Festival onboard, with a chance to sample some of the twenty six local wines and liqueurs.

I've decided to go back to bed until Rio for the benefit of my livers health.

There was a rather heated altercation at Guest Services this afternoon as a lady occupying a cabin at the rear of the ship and below the lido deck had detailed how she'd been woken in the early hours by what sounded like heavy rainfall. She'd opened her curtains, only to find a crawling mass of huge bugs on her balcony.

Hearing her hysterical screams her husband had jumped out of bed ready to protect his wife, believing an emergency was in progress.

Unfortunately on seeing the writhing pile of creepy crawlies the arachnophobic husband had also started to scream, then fainted, banging his head on a sideboard and gashing his forehead.

Having been treated by the ship's medical team the lady and her bandaged husband were now complaining that the hefty bill they'd been presented with was unreasonable, and were refusing to pay it as his injury hadn't been their fault.

They were claiming that instead of shovelling up the beasties on the rear deck the crew had decided to sweep them off the back of the ship into the water, forgetting of course about the balconies below.

Meanwhile a nurse standing nearby with a wheelchair had insisted the gentleman calm down and take a seat as he'd suffered a serious head injury.

"Not bloody likely," he'd shouted, "I can't afford it."

By the early evening I'd felt steady enough to attempt a splash about in the pool for a bit of exercise. At that time of the day the lido deck is normally deserted as most folks are at, or preparing to go to dinner.

After a few clumsy lengths I'd stopped to catch my breath and noticed someone else had arrived and was disrobing. With his back to me he'd stripped down to his swimwear, took off his panama hat and turned to head for the water.

I'd recognised him instantly. It was the dapper gent from the gym, in a very brief pair of trunks.

I was standing in the deeper end of the pool and had expected him to enter the pool via the steps at the other end. Instead he headed straight to where I was and stood right above me.

"Good evening," he said in his cultured accent.

"Hiya," I'd replied and added, "The water's lovely."

"I can see that. Do you mind if I dive?"

Now that had sounded a bit odd, no make that very odd and I wasn't quite sure what to say in reply.

"Well you're not supposed to because it's not that deep."

"Oh stuff and nonsense to rules," he'd replied.

"Do 'you' mind?" He'd laughed.

"Not at all. Knock yourself out."

I'd meant that as 'go for it', but as he was

probably going to it wasn't the best thing to say.

He'd laughed again, dived in, swam to the far end and then came back and grabbed onto the side of the pool. He was well inside my personal space.

"You weren't in the gym the last two mornings," he'd said.

When I'd explained why he'd held my arm and said, "Oh okay, well I'm Ted and it's so lovely to talk to you properly. I'm here on my own so it will be nice to have a chum I can chat to."

With that he'd set off swimming.

Back in the cabin I told my dear lady the story. She didn't stop laughing for ten minutes, then spent the next half hour singing 'Let's go Outside'.

"He's probably just a bit lonely," I'd insisted.

I really believe she's got Ted's intentions wrong so I'm certainly not going to avoid him just because he's got a little over friendly. I just hope I haven't sent out the wrong signals, but now I'm making assumptions and shouldn't.

Oh well, time for dinner.

Sunday 27th January

Day 20 'Manaus' - a thousand miles in.

An early start for us today as we'd booked a boat tour on the river to see one of the most extraordinary phenomenon in this area, possibly the world.

As it was early morning the temperature wasn't too hot for we pasty skinned folk, but as the morning progressed we knew we'd need to take precautions against sunburn.

But that was just one of a number of concerns as this jaunt up the river would last for five hours and took us into the heart of the rainforest, surrounded by vegetation, water and mosquitoes. For that reason the extra safeguards we'd prepared beforehand were put into action.

Despite the unusual smell, which we were hoping no one would notice, we weren't going anywhere today without our freshly coated insect repellent clothing.

Let's see if any rabid mozzies dared come anywhere near us now.

Manaus, the seventh largest city in Brazil, is situated at the meeting point of two rivers, the Negro and the Solimoes, which combine close by to become the Amazon River.

The water of the Negro River is a rich dark coffee colour, which clearly showed up in the spray as our boat raced through it.

The Solimoes River is described as a white water river, as the mud and silt it carries gives it a very pale creamy colour.

We were off to the location where these two waters meet and when we'd arrived I'd had to admit it was one of the weirdest things I'd ever seen.

Because of the different consistencies and acidic properties of the two rivers they can't properly mix and you literally get what appears to be a speciality coffee with cream floating on the top, but not in a cup obviously, and much, much larger than your average hot beverage.

At this joining point the river is many kilometres wide and this strange spectacle continued as far as the eye could see. As the boat moved through the line where the darker and lighter waters met the colours swirled together, but then separated again.

Then with all the different currents and flow directions it also appeared that the white water was bubbling along the edge of the meeting point in a manner suggesting its excitement to be greeting its new fluid friend. However, the smoother, unexcitable darker water appeared to be acting a tad antisocial.

Really fascinating and totally mesmerising and having tried to describe this wonder I realise I've failed miserably.

After ten minutes or so the boat turned to head further up the river to take us where it was starting to flood into the forest. Passing through several areas where the locals had literally set up floating villages, we saw the structures that the locals called home. They're like large wooden sheds covered with corrugated tin, mounted onto several large tree trunks, allowing them to rise and fall with the water.

Around the main building are smaller, independent floating pontoons such as a 'garden' where things grow in pots and the children play, or one for the dog complete with a small tin roofed kennel. Most importantly there's a toilet, set apart from the main house on its own little floating base, assumingly it has no plumbing.

All are connected together by ropes which also tether everything to the bank.

The only access in and out of these villages is on the water. To get around the village, to shop, or visit friends, or just go for a night out to the local bar, you use a boat.

Our guide told us that from a very young age the children don't get a bike for their birthday, they get a boat instead.

There is absolutely nothing built on the land.

I assume that if the fishing in the area becomes poor or they fancy a change of neighbourhood, then they simply move.

The local drinking establishment is also a large floating structure, complete with a pool table and massive speaker arrays supplying the entire region with music.

For power most of the individual 'dwellings' have their own generators chugging away on one of the floating pontoons, and in some of the larger villages they appear to have either larger communal generators or sub stations supplied by overhead power lines.

That's a very interesting combination of dangers to take into consideration, electricity going into tin shacks, completely surrounded by water. I wonder if they even bother with an earth wire in the plugs?

For us this seemed like poverty on the grandest of scales compared to the standard of life we're fortunate enough to enjoy back home. But for the Amazonian people this is normal, they've lived this way for centuries and they appear content to continue to do so. When they want to eat they catch it, if a bigger house is needed then it's built using the things they have around.

It's quite possible they only realise there's a more materialistic existence out there when this huge white ship sails up their river and spews out its over-sized and over-dressed tourists. These same idiots try their hand at empathy and pontificate ad-nausium about how dreadful things are for these 'poor people' whilst poking the latest Nikon with the longest lens you've ever seen into every nook and cranny they can find.

When the children bring their pet caiman, monkeys and anacondas for these aliens to admire and photograph, they are handed a measly one dollar bill with a flourish, allowing the giver a brief moment of self appreciation for their humanitarian gesture of generosity.

I truly believe only one of the parties in this scenario will walk away from the encounter feeling so much better about their life, despite their lack of luxuries.

There is however a major positive I must mention, as that one dollar bill will actually save a life. It will prevent the child's pet from being invited to take part in a family meal for at least one more day, because instead of the usual phrase 'If you don't work you don't eat' in this part of the world the phrase becomes 'If you don't work you get eaten'.

Needless to say this trip was an eye opener for us, and after the five hours we'd returned to the port, both fascinated and subdued by what we'd witnessed.

We have an overnight stop here in Manaus, but warnings have been re-issued with a vengeance. I'm starting to wonder why there's so many contradictions in the information we're been given. On the one hand we're being told on a regular basis that Brazil is a very safe country, but on the other we've been 'strongly advised' not to go out into the city after dark tonight.

Now for me this means either it's not very safe after all, or we're right about the vampires.

As we're not sure which of these apply we've decided to pack away the garlic, wooden stakes and crosses and head for the bar on the top deck and watch out for dark silhouettes against the sky.

Meantime the crew are off on a midnight caiman hunt in the swamps and mangroves nearby.

I can see the importance of cautioning folk about getting mugged on the streets of an unfamiliar city, but I wonder if it's sensible to let your staff head off into the jungle on a mission to look for something with big teeth and an appetite?

Let's hope they all get back in one piece.

Monday 28th January

Day 21 'Manaus 2' - a town of shoppers.

By the time we'd returned to the port after yesterdays trip on the boats, it was far too hot to venture into the city. It really was one of the most unpleasant temperatures I've ever experienced.

It was much cooler this morning, so we'd set off to explore the city.

Walking out of the port and over the bridge the first part of the city you encounter is the bus station. The buses coming into the station were tightly crammed full of people, and there were just as many waiting to re-board the vehicle for a return journey, loaded down with shopping.

It was complete bedlam, with no etiquette at all. Without waiting for anyone to get off the queues piled on as soon as the doors opened, leaving the poor folk who wanted to get off to fight their way through the masses. I wonder if some of them gave up and hoped the next time they reached the station they'd be nearer to the door.

After you become accustomed to the searing heat

of this region the next thing to assault the senses is the smell, occasionally unpleasant, but always different. It's a grand aromatic cocktail of the sea mixed with wood smoke, cooking food and a million bodies going about their day to day lives.

Manaus is a very busy city and there are small, makeshift stalls set up everywhere, on the pavements, in doorways, down alleys and even in the gutters, and they all sell the same stuff. There's just a single narrow area of the pavement for the shoppers to wander down and the rest is crammed full of traders. A food kiosk is followed by an underwear seller, then mobile phone covers, caps, t-shirts, souvenirs and hammocks. Every so often there's an old man sitting on an upturned crate with a tray on his lap, from which he sells SIM cards or carries out mobile phone repairs.

You can walk a hundred yards and suddenly wonder if you're back where you started from because it all looks the same.

The clientele of the little food wagons block the walkways as they grab their snacks and sit to eat them on a strange unmatched mix of rickety chairs strewn all over the place.

The Amazonian equivalent of fast food appears to be lumps of cheese wrapped in a pancake then deep fried on a stick. In fact everything looks deep fried, except for the large quantities of barbequed meat, which looks like chicken, but who knows?

When cooked the offerings are displayed in huge metal trays, which are covered with plastic sheets to keep off the millions of flying pests. As the hungry shoppers arrive and indicate their choice of fare, generous portions are quickly transferred into what looks like recycled take away foil containers and sealed to prevent interlopers.

With all this going on it's easy to forget that there are also the regular shops on the street as well. The staff seem to spend most of their time shooing the eating squatters out of their doorways so potential customers actually get the chance to go in and browse the merchandise.

It sounds like there are heated exchanges going on all the while, but then maybe everyone is shouting just to be heard above the raucous din of so many people.

We'd managed to make our way round to the cathedral by about 11am, where it seemed like half the population of Brazil was having brunch.

There were many more stalls selling cooked and fresh food, along with a whole area devoted to repairing things.

There was a man resoling shoes with old rubber car mats and a pot of glue, another was repairing umbrellas, another was stitching up the seams of a pair of torn trousers.

Nothing is beyond repair.

We'd witnessed something rather unusual when a well dress gent handed an old looking mobile phone to a very unkempt chap who was sitting on the cathedral steps.

He had a tray full of small electronic parts on his lap and as we watched he quickly took the back off the man's devise, undid a couple of tiny screws and removed a small circuit board. Then he'd rummaged around his tray until he found what he was looking for. He had a small gas soldering torch which was quickly employed and within seconds the phone was handed back to its owner who checked it was back to a usable state. With a smile a few Real were handed over and the gent went on his way.

Back home that would never have happened, electronics are pretty much disposable items these days. But here things are different, even for those who appear to have money nothing is wasted.

A lesson for us decadent westerners.

Following the map we'd been given, we eventually found our way to the opera house, a very grand and opulently decorated building. Once inside we'd joined a guided tour which included donning a pair of felt slippers over our shoes in order glide across a beautifully ornate parquet floor without causing any damage.

The side rooms were impressive with huge gilt mirrors and wall coverings, and each of the small balcony areas had a great view of the impressive stage proscenium.

When the tour had finished we were allowed to go back into the auditorium and sit in the stalls while the local orchestra rehearsed for an upcoming concert.

Simply wonderful.

Back outside we'd crossed the square and walked toward an interesting church. But as there was a mass in progress we'd only been able to look inside the vestibule.

And right there, for the first time, we started to recall the warnings about staying safe in a foreign country. There in front of us, standing at the door of the house of God, was a uniformed guard equipped with a very large riot stick and an even bigger gun.

He scowled at the arriving congregation and even

shouted something to one worshipper which didn't sound like 'Hello, how are you this bright and sunny day?'

Now I accept that poverty and danger go hand in hand in many cultures around the world, but I've never, ever, felt threatened in the House of God before. To witness such a blatant suggestion of menace was very disturbing and it felt like we had no other choice than to leave the faithful to their devotions and head back to the safety of the ship.

As I write this I am aware that today has been an experience I shall never forget...fascinating and scary in equal measures, but at no point did we feel threatened.

Despite its somewhat shabby façade, Manaus is one of the most congested, oppressive and claustrophobic places we've ever visited, but at the same time it was truly amazing. The architecture, the culture and the tenacity of the people is truly admirable and despite a lack of luxuries we weren't in any way pestered by beggars or vendors, in fact we'd almost felt anonymous.

The locals appeared to be quite gentle and unassuming, very polite and happy for us to be there as guests. But maybe this is also a place of unseen extremes, the security at the church suggesting some of the folk are far from hospitable. I'm sure no one would believe that the only place we'd felt uneasy today was in a place of worship.

I reckon Manaus is a fantastic place to get a true picture of life and the people of Amazonia and we've had a great visit. But right now I need to replace about a gallon of fluid.

My dear lady's song choice today has been very

apt, 'Hot in the City'.

Oh and we also discovered the real reason why it is not safe to go into the city after dark. Walking the pavements is a treacherous enough affair in daylight.

There are broken slabs which will trip you up or drop you into huge holes below. Gutters at the side of roads are deep enough to break bones if you fall into them, and street lighting appears minimal. So always heed the warnings of the locals and after dark stay at home.

In this city you don't need to be drunk to end up face down in the gutter.

Tuesday 29th January

Day 22 'Parintins' - love me tender.

A very wet day had greeted us as we'd opened the curtains this morning, after all this is a rain forest, a fact that has strangely escaped some of our fellow travellers attention.

Despite being told several times, by several experts, that torrential rain is highly likely (and necessary) in this region, they've been lining up in reception to voice their disappointment at the Captain's decision to sail the ship straight into a storm.

'Was he really out to ruin their holiday?'

According to Ben, the guest services assistant who's been listening to these complaints, we've been really lucky with the weather so far, and the master of the vessel has used all his negotiating powers and influence to fend off the worst of the wet stuff. Sadly there are bigger and more influential people moving into the vicinity at the moment and we've had to go to the back of the queue for now.

Me thinks Ben has a weirder sense of humour than myself, but then it's probably just a mechanism to cope with the stupidity he must encounter on a daily basis.

The ship dropped anchor around a mile from the town and the tenders were readied to receive their passengers.

The main attraction here is a sample performance of the local carnival called Boi Bumba, a very loud and colourful hour of regional music and dance laid on exclusively for the cruise ships.

Question is do they put on the show because we stop here or do we stop here because they put on a show?

According to many of the tourist guides of the area, there's not much to do in Parintins worth a mention, but I suppose that's just their opinion, let's go see for ourselves. Besides which as it's raining we don't have to go through the twenty minute ritual of applying the mossie repellent.

More later.

After several hours ashore our opinion differs dramatically from the tourist guides despite the weather.

There's a very pretty square, a modern cathedral and some interesting architecture, as well as a very nice beach. It's probably not somewhere we'd go for a static holiday, but our day out here was very nice.

Like Manaus the people are welcoming, friendly and talented as it appears most of the town is involved in the Boi Bumba spectacle held at the Bumbodromo.

We were soaked by the time we queued up for the twenty minute tender ride back to the cool dryness of the ship.

Tendering is always a great opportunity to eavesdrop some of the conversations our fellow travellers have. Today was no exception.

"My friend was married, had two children and everything," the lady in front of us was holding court at a very high volume. "Wonderful husband she had too, had a great job and they travelled all over the world."

"That's nice," said her companion, who seemed to be fascinated by her every word.

"Then," the lady bellowed, "She contracted lesbianism and threw away her wonderful life to be with another woman."

"Oh that's such a shame, where did that happen?"

"In Romford of all places. Now her new female partner is pregnant, goodness knows how that happened!"

Priceless.

May I suggest that all happily married ladies should avoid Romford then.

Back on the ship and there was just time for a quick shower and a walk out on the promenade deck before it went dark. Apparently a few minor impact injuries have been inflicted by the bugs around dusk, so the Captain has suggested an earlier curfew.

It was very quiet as most of the other passengers had taken up refuge inside the ship.

However there was one guy wandering around and rummaging through the rubbish bins. We saw him lifting something out and putting it into a carrier bag, but couldn't see what it was.

When we'd walked passed him he tried to hide in a doorway looking very sheepish.

The folk on this ship are getting weirder.

I really wish my dear lady would stop singing the Elvis classic 'Love me Tender'. Today's journey was quite a bit bouncier than the last and she knows I'm in pain.

Wednesday 30th January

Day 23 'Santarem' - pink dolphins v pink people.

We'd set off early this morning for a good walk into the main town of Santarem. It was very warm but not too uncomfortable, and for the first time we'd heard insects crackling and singing away in the surrounding grasslands. Other strange sounds filled the air, suggesting we're quite close to the forest here.

The first place we came across was a huge fish market at the edge of the town. It was perched on stilts and protruded way out into the river, high above the surface of the water. Crossing the walkway to investigate the tables full of strange looking fish we'd noticed there were excited cheers coming from the far end of the building overlooking the river.

Walking over to check out the commotion we'd discovered a couple of the local lads were tying a fish to a long piece of line and throwing it out into the water. As they drew the line back it was being chased by a small pod of pink river dolphins.

For the next ten minutes or so this had continued and we were treated to a rolling and diving display from around six of these playful creatures. They appeared to be quite timid and had only risen to the surface as they'd tried to catch the fish, but because of their colour they were quite easy to spot even when they were deep in the water.

Occasionally one of the dolphins would succeed in catching its quarry and for a dollar from one of the spectators the lads would run off to buy another fish, probably from Mom.

Needless to say I think this was my dear lady's favourite moment of the Amazon so far and things got even better as we'd reluctantly dragged ourselves away from the playing dolphins to continue our walk into town. The river bank here also resembles a sandy beach and is full of boats and their occupants. They're not very big boats, just the brightly painted traditional 'paddle steamer' type vessels that have two open decks with a small cabin underneath.

They were all moored on the gently sloping waters' edge and the occupying family unload what little furniture they possess and appear to set up home on the beach. The children were playing in the sand, swimming in the surf or tormenting a group of large pigs who had worked together to dig deep into the sand, trying to find a cool spot to lie.

Meanwhile, the Moms were producing some interesting concoctions from what looks like makeshift barbeques or fire pits, whilst Dads were busy mending things or re-painting their boat.

Along with these larger vessels there were many small rowing boats littering the beach.

Back in the UK our sea fronts are full of bars, amusement arcades and fish and chip shops, but here it's hardware, animal feed, boat parts and food stalls of every description. For most of the locals the only means of transport is a boat, so the whole frontage was packed with these smaller craft, some just recently parked up and others being loaded with supplies. After rounding up the kids they'd motor off down the river, large hats and umbrellas protecting them from the sun.

We'd soon reached the cathedral which, compared to ones we've visited around Europe, is a simple building with little in the way of paintings, shrines and altars. Instead there is a multitude of fans and air conditioning units stuck to the walls, and from the sweltering humidity we were experiencing they would be essential for survival when the pews were full.

The temperature outside was rising rapidly as well, and although we'd only been out for around two hours, we'd decided it was already time to head back, the heat is really draining. It took us around three quarters of an hour and despite plenty of sun screen we'd arrived back at the ship nicely pink around the edges.

But before we embarked we were able to see how lots of the locals who don't have their own transport get around the region. Flights are rare and expensive, roads none existent, so if they need to travel some distance to the larger cities for any reason they take a boat.

These boats have three open plan decks. On the bottom deck a lot of the space seems to be taken up by cargo destined for the markets of the city. The middle deck, again open plan, is where the passengers live during the trip, sometimes for three days or more, so as each of them arrives they sling an ornate hammock between hooks in the roof. In a space roughly the size of our cabin there are about 12 hammocks and we are told that the passengers will spend most of the journey in their hammock as the space on the rest of the boat is limited. Finally, on the top deck there are showers and an eating area. It's a good job they are a sociable bunch, I would imagine it gets quite cosy at night, not to mention the bugs.

Oh and the difference between Santarem and Alter Do Chao?

Well to be honest we didn't notice much in the way of opulence in Santarem, but to be fair our idea of wealth and theirs are probably not even close. There are a lot of merchants for sure and a lot more people, but the only real difference for me was in Alter Do Chao the pristine beaches weren't littered with boats, people or pigs.

That strange man was sifting through the bins again during our early evening walk.

We must have surprised him in his activities as he'd tried to disappear into a plant room when he'd spotted us coming. Unfortunately for him the door was locked, so he'd had to stand there looking guilty, kicking his feet against the door and whistling.

I wonder if I should to speak to security!

Today was our last stop on the Amazon, and my dear lady has taken to singing 'Rolling on the river' for most of the afternoon.

I hope this isn't some unintentional prediction of an impending storm.

Thursday 31ˢᵗ January

Day 24 'river/sea day' - crossing the line

Well that was the Amazon River and what a

remarkable experience it was, but also a little bit disappointing at the same time.

My dear lady and I have travelled quite a lot over the years, but only to the typically popular, touristy type locations in Western Europe, and we've never really been exposed to the extremes we've witnessed here in Amazonia.

For us it was just one week but for them it's a lifetime. And yet the locals never appeared to be unhappy, or resentful at our presence, we saw no one begging, yet the poverty was obvious.

Very thought provoking, and I feel I should be more appreciative of what we have and remember those who have not.

The disappointment was the lack of wildlife.

It's understandable around the towns and cities, after all who wants to get eaten?

However we were expecting to see and hear more activity going on in the many, many miles of majestic rainforest we passed through on our way along the river. I think we both had this romantic 'glossy picture' image of the Amazon, unfortunately the animals turned out to be rather camera shy.

Ho hum, time to step away from serious and return to my customary crazy world.

It hadn't escaped our attention that as we'd cruised up (but going south) the mighty Amazon River about a week ago we had actually crossed the equator for the first time. Then today, at around 11am, we crossed it again (going north) on our way back to the Atlantic Ocean.

As we pass the Amazon Bar and leave the river behind us tomorrow morning we'll cross it for the third time (going south) on our way to the next port of call, Fortaleza.

This all sounds a little confusing, but apparently it is of vital importance that all travelling seafarers acknowledge and celebrate the precise time of the initial 'Crossing of the Line'.

So for that reason there was ceremony held today at 2pm.

I have to report there has been a certain amount of discontent, particularly from the seasoned cruisers, who have kicked off 'big time' because the ship's company have failed to celebrate 'Crossing the Line' at an appropriate time. They are claiming that this misdemeanour will not have gone unnoticed by the sea-gods who will now be very angry, resulting of course in certain catastrophe at some time to come.

In a letter to the passengers (written on lined paper of course) the Captain has taken the time to explain that having initially dropped a line to the Royal Office outlining all three dates, Neptune's line manager had replied insisting it would only be possible for His Majesty to attend one line crossing.

In-line with current protocols the Royal Party was originally scheduled to attend for the first crossing, but an administrative error had been made and the booking had mistakenly been 'crossed out' in the sea-gods diary.

Despite this being a very busy time they had apologised for the blunder and had us pencilled in for today, and underlined it specially.

The seasoned cruisers are furious.

They believe that the Captain has 'crossed the line' by taking this line, and in truth believe he'd failed in his duties to drop Neptune a line in time to give sufficient notice of our arrival for the first crossing of the line, in-line with normal practice.

Because his negligence has resulted in an unacceptable delay to the 'Crossing the Line' celebrations, they are taking a hard-line approach to the situation and, in line with age old sea faring traditions, have sent the master an email demanding we start all over again.

This would involve 'Uncrossing the Line twice' so we can 'Re-Cross the Line' in the correct manner.

Neptune has refused to co-operate as his engagement diary is full.

Of course the Captain has also refused to bow to their online demands and has further stated that he is 'Drawing a Line' under the whole affair. He'll be very cross if anyone is caught 'Crossing the Line' without his permission and the 'Line Crossers' presence on his ship will be 'on the line' if they continue to cross him.

Anyway the celebrations went ahead, but without the Captain as he had to steer the ship across a line apparently.

The entertainment team ensured there was lots of mess and people getting thrown in the pool, reminiscent of Butlins.

After a few party games and several innuendos later, everybody went to lie down in preparation for this evenings special entertainment programme. This will include Line Dancing in the Curzon Room, What's my Line in the Crow's Nest and a re-run of the Onedin Line on channel five on the TV.

These activities weren't originally on this evening's itinerary but the entertainment team is just doing their best to annoy the Captain.

Meanwhile, my dear lady has been singing 'Hold

the Line' by Toto all day.

(I think I may have got a bit carried away with this)

Anyway, in other matters I didn't go to the gym again this morning and hope Ted doesn't think I'm avoiding him, even though my dear lady thinks I am.

Instead we enjoyed a lazy day by the pool and spent a boozy evening after dinner with the other guys and gals from one two eight.

This cruising lark is really hard work.

Friday 1st February

Day 25 'a sea day' - deep tan crisp and even.

We crossed the equator (going south) again at 09.43hrs today and I'm not making any more comment about it than that, except to add that it was possible to buy an official 'Crossing the Line' certificate to mark the occasion, stating today's date as the official crossing.

Once again the seasoned cruisers were unhappy. with this and boycotted the event as they believe the certificates are invalid.

The Captain has issued a one word statement on the matter, it read 'Tough'.

The photogs were hanging around the ship at the aforementioned time with one of them dressed as a mermaid, ready to capture the now perceived 'non-event' for any individual desperate for proof it actually happened.

I seriously cannot imagine why they'd believe anyone would want to be immortalised standing next to a six foot, hairy-chested mermaid complete with a shell bra, a yellow woollen wig and have to pay for the privilege.

Talking of the photogs, which I try not to do as it only encourages them, there's been an announcement with regards to a 'passenger photographic competition'.

Anyone wishing to enter the contest is allowed to submit up to three pictures which will be judged by the other passengers. A small entry fee will be charged to cover the cost of printing each photograph, which of course has to be wholly the participants own work.

Closing date for submissions will be the 3rd February, and will be put out on display the next day, when passengers can vote for their favourite composition via a simple ballot.

It'll be interesting, and probably controversial, to see what gets submitted and voted for.

Weather conditions have changed quite dramatically as we're no longer subject to the drenching humidity of the rainforest. So today the sun decks are full once again with scantily clad ladies and gents.

The most dedicated, and fortunate, sun-worshippers are now a deep chestnut colour, while the unfortunate ones have retained that freshly boiled lobster appearance. It has to be noted that the more acclimatised each individual has become the skimpier the outfits they strip down to.

Not always a pretty sight.

But many of them are obviously unhappy with the uneven distribution of the melanin (or tortured skin) around their body. There are distinctly lighter patches in normally unexposed places which need to be sorted out, especially among those who'll be leaving the ship when we reach Rio. To this end they lie contorted on their loungers to expose the bits that need a touch more of a touch from heaven sent UVA.

My dear lady and I spent a very unpleasant afternoon trying to avoid any form of visual contact for the benefit of our health.

One lady removed a modest swimsuit to reveal an extremely brief, bright yellow bikini and a lot more 'natural material' besides.

Now I hardly think three small triangles of fabric on two bits of string constitute any reason for a photograph, but her partner did.

I just hope it's not regarded as a potential competition entry.

My dear lady got really agitated, saying she just couldn't get 'Itsy Bitsy Teenie Weanie Yellow Polka Dot Bikini' out of her head.

When it comes to what's going round in my head, I'd prefer it to be the song.

Later in the afternoon I'd taken myself off to the gym, feeling very guilty about my recent lack of exercise. Ted was in there and so was Nadia the instructor.

It seems she's found herself a customer.

Fortaleza tomorrow and once again we've been warned about issues of security in Brazil's cities.

Makes me wonder why they have chosen this country for both the 2014 FIFA World Cup and the 2016 Olympic Games if they have so many concerns about crime.

But then you can get mugged anywhere. There was nearly a punch-up in the laundry room yesterday probably over a small matter (or even a matter of smalls)

Saturday 2nd February

Day 26 'Fortaleza' - hold very tight please.

The first thing we'd noticed on the approach to Fortaleza, the fifth largest city in Brazil with nearly three million residents, is how similar it looked to most other typically modern cities.

Sailing into the bay we could see a large number of high-rise buildings standing side by side all along the sea front, framed by tall misty mountains behind.

Everything looked perfect and we were imagining hotels, cafes and bars serving ice cold beers on the boardwalk. I could just picture the delights of a golden sandy beach running down to the azure blue sea.

Very civilised.

Dangers...what dangers?

Arriving at the port there's obviously a lot of development going on as the city readies itself to meet and greet football fans from all over the world next year.

It all looked very promising so let's get to it.

Which we did.

Now just two hours later and we're back. This is what happened.

There was quite a long bus ride into the city centre today and the local port authority had laid on a bus.

Yes, just the one.

It's quite possible that many of the seven hundred passengers on board took advantage of one of the many organised tours today, but for those of us 'doing our own thing' I reckon some had a considerable wait to get into town.

Fortunately not for us as we'd managed to be one of the first to get ashore and straight onto the bus.

During the journey into town a lovely local lady told us all about the history and development of this diverse community. She'd pointed out several landmarks along the way and told us all about the wonderful architecture in the historic centre and the beautiful beaches and parks.

Unfortunately nothing could be seen from the windows of our coach because both sides of the road were lined with huge, steel fences.

We passed through the area where we'd imagined that idyllic beachfront, only to discover the buildings were mainly apartments for the locals who appear to have dumped all their waste outside on the pavements. In one area the rubbish piles on the other side of the fence were spilling across the coast road and down onto the beach. Some of the buildings were really shabby and there was graffiti everywhere. People were sleeping rough across the pavements on cardboard boxes and small shanty like cabins offer various services from car mechanics to cooked food.

The facade was crumbling.

Eventually we made it into the centre where the bus dropped us right next to a massive open market, which incidentally looked just like one of the sixties multi-storey concrete car parks they're desperate to get rid of back home.

Our friendly guide told us that it's full to the brim with local artisans, cafes and stalls selling regional delicacies.

What happened next was disturbing.

She went on to instruct us that we should only

walk around this market and up to the cathedral which was next to it.

"To wander any farther would be too dangerous," she'd told us.

"How do we get to the theatre," one lady asked, "I hear it's beautiful."

"It is," was the reply.

"But I really must insist you only go where I've said."

Doesn't sound very good really when a local who is paid to promote her city, doesn't!

Anyway we did as we were told, and who wouldn't after that warning. We wandered around the market which was full of stuff we were now totally suspicious of, and then ambled across to the cathedral, which was shut.

I don't think we spent more than half an hour there before we'd headed back to the bus for the dismal return journey to the ship.

Sorry Fortaleza but that's about the measure of it and this was not our opinion, it was yours.

We discovered later the actual dangers of this place as a couple had taken a taxi to the beach and then been mugged as they got out of the car. They believe it was a set up.

So now I get to wondering about Recife and Salvador, the next two stops, which both carry the same attached safety warnings as Fortaleza. Is it worth the risks if we're only likely to be given a similar city experience?

I need to speak to my dear lady.

I would never forgive myself if I knowingly exposed some poor Brazilian teenage mugger to her retributions.

However the day wasn't totally wasted as the waters of the harbour delivered a certain amount of redemption to an otherwise depressing place.

We were treated to over an hour of immense pleasure as we watched groups of dolphins feeding and playing in the water right next to the ship. It was well worth coming here just for that and frankly that's probably all we'll remember.

And as we sailed away from Fortaleza the Captain apologised for the earlier delays with the shuttle bus and hoped it hadn't spoilt our enjoyment of this 'magnificently different city'

If you listened very carefully you could definitely detect a lack of remorse in his voice or maybe it's really hard to sound that genuine when your tongue's firmly wedged in your cheek.

Sunday 3rd February

Day 27 'at sea' - Boobies everywhere.

Sunday at sea and maybe we should take the opportunity to reflect on our thoughts from yesterday and make decisions about tomorrow. Then again, maybe we should just eat and drink too much and sleep the afternoon away.

Fortaleza was definitely not what we'd expected, far from it, and there were several other stories told at breakfast which have darkened our already dim view of the place.

Because we hadn't been able to do much or wander around safely, it didn't feel like we'd visited one of the largest cities of Brazil in order to experience their unmistakable and vibrant culture, more like we'd accepted an invitation for a guided tour around an institution.

First impressions had been good, from the ship it had looked a lot more modern and inviting to us than Manaus, Parantins or Santarem, and yet it was just a facade.

Authentic and seemingly poorer Amazonia felt like the real Brazil, hopefully its people being a more honest reflection of the region and its culture.

And I start to wonder if you pull down the old shanties do you also remove some of the character and identity of its contents, i.e. the people?

It saddens me to think that governments all around the world think their people will be happier and better off if they transport them from traditional to modern. Taking a family off their log boat and putting them in a modern apartment seems like a good idea, but in reality what benefits does it deliver? I wonder if any of them think it's great to have gained a flushing toilet in exchange for their independence,

Enough.

This is too serious a topic for my journal, but for some reason today doesn't feel very funny.

Since leaving the Amazon behind we've been tracked day and night by a flock of birds. They fly alongside the ship and occasionally dive deep into the waters to catch fish.

The 'Watchers' as usual have been the source of all knowledge, informing us that they're Masked Boobies (the birds not the Watchers) and it's fair to say there's been a magnitude of inappropriate jokes about that, mainly at the expense of the 'Watchers'.

They've certainly attracted a great amount of interest from my dear lady, who thinks they look pterodactyl like because of their wing shape and long beak (again I'm referring to the birds)

Later in the afternoon she'd spent a couple of hours watching and photographing them from the promenade deck, during which time I'd left her to it and headed off to the gym.

I've discovered that by taking my exercise later the rest of the day is working out perfectly.

I'm also seeing more of Ted at these later sessions as well. He's spending a lot more time being instructed by Nadia and appears to be improving as she's always patting his back and saying how well he's doing..

He's even dressing more appropriately, although his shorts are a little on the over revealing side of decency.

These later sessions have been better for me because I haven't felt tired after lunch, allowing me to spend more time having fun with my dear lady instead of napping.

Sometimes we've sat observing others, making up silly stories about the secret lives they lead and what secret mission they're involved with on the ship. Other times we've just talked about ourselves, especially about what the future might bring.

Turns out she's nuttier than I am, and sadly I'd forgotten that. But it's been great and she's determined we should get involved with more of the things available on the ship, together.

She's right obviously.

I've agreed to start dance classes after Rio, but I'm holding out on learning to play bridge for now. The tutors scare me more than the 'Watchers'.

After the gym I'd showered and hurried back to

see how my dear lady was getting on.

Heading through the door onto the prom deck I'd literally bumped into the man searching through the bins again. He'd stumbled backward and dropped his carrier bag, but managed to grab hold of a rail to prevent himself from falling.

The bag clattered loudly as it hit the deck, but nothing fell out and I couldn't see what was in there.

"Sorry," I'd said, "Let me help you."

I'd reached to pick up the bag, but before I could he'd yelled at me.

"Leave it, it's mine, get your own."

He snatched up the bag and was gone, not before trying to get in that locked plant room again.

Now I really think I should speak to security.

My dear lady was still enthralled by the Boobies, which were still shadowing the ship. Their numbers had increased and they were flying in formation.

I have to say that some of the pictures she'd taken were very good.

I must remember to find out what the prize is for the photographic competition.

Recife tomorrow, supposedly the Venice of Brazil, hopefully that means they don't have a sixties concrete car park market.

Monday 4th February

Day 28 'Recife' - what a reliefe.

There was a definite touch of apprehension in the air today as we'd set off on the shuttle bus for the centre of the city of Recife (I say a 'touch of apprehension' but I mean a 'very big slap of dread')

Anyway, despite what's been said about the need

for heightened personal awareness here in Brazil, we're trying to keep an open mind. It's important we don't pre-judge anything or anybody and allow each new location the opportunity to prove the self proclaimed experts right or wrong.

After all you can get mugged anywhere, the altercations in the launderette have been intensifying.

The bus journey in was fascinating and the varied architecture suggests that Recife appears to have a lot of history about it. Local carnival preparations are well advanced and around the main streets the appearance is certainly more affluent than effluent.

The shuttle dropped us off at an old prison complex, a cross shaped three tiered building which has been restored and converted into shopping outlets and galleries. Little has been changed about its structure and all the heavy gates and bars are still in place, protecting the central atrium from the four wings of cells.

Each cell, still fronted by a heavy door and containing an inside windows decorated with bars, is now home to a trader and his/her wares. These range from artwork, jewellery, clothing, foodstuffs and of course the obligatory souvenirs no self respecting tourist can live without.

After a quick look round we'd headed off for a walk around the city. At least today no one had warned us not to.

We spotted Pru and Jeff, map in hand, wandering towards the end of the street and as we all appeared to be heading in the same direction, we'd joined forces, setting course for the historic colonial end of the city.

Safety in numbers theory.

Firstly we'd passed through a roadside trading area against the river railings, which mainly consisted of ornamental fish and aquarium paraphernalia for sale.

Each individual fish, ranging from simple goldfish to more exotic black fantails and Dalmatian fish, were housed in small plastic bags filled with water, obviously. Hundreds of these bags were then displayed by clipping them to the railings or a makeshift metal stand.

Now maybe the residents of Recife don't have much room at home and therefore buy a lot of pet fish to entertain their children. Even so, I reckon at the end of each day the vendors take home a huge number of very hot and bothered little animals. There were an extraordinary number of these traders along the route and I don't think I've ever seen so many ornamental fish in one place.

Jeff suggested that we'd got it all wrong and they were really selling a boil in the bag local delicacy.

I'm not too sure Pru was very impressed by his remarks.

There was an unmistakable stench of stagnant swampy river water (or sewage) around this area which was exceptionally unpleasant, so we'd moved on as quickly as the dangerously uneven Brazilian pavements allowed.

There is definitely a consistency in how bad the pavements are in Brazil, but what causes the problem I wonder. Could it have something to do with the pounding feet of carnival maybe?

"Blame it on the Samba." I told my dear lady as she'd nearly tripped up a kerb

That set her off on an hour long rendition of the Jackson's 'Blame it on the Boogie (Samba)' complete with all the actions.

Jeff and Pru looked worried.

Crossing the river over an old bridge was made difficult because the floor was awash with blankets full of things for sale, mostly second or even third hand stuff including shoes, clothes, records, ornaments, toys and the like. Just like a car-boot sale back home, but without the car, hoards of locals were clamouring around trying to negotiate a bargain or two.

Turning right and walking toward a row of ornate houses we'd passed many interesting buildings, some of which had been renovated and some hadn't. With a little imagination it was easy to see how grand they must have appeared back in the nineteenth century when they'd been built.

For the next couple of hours we'd walked across various bridges, visited several churches and parks, took photos of just about anything and everything and generally had a really interesting look around the city.

We'd even wandered into a seemingly poorer area, which was extremely busy with scruffy people going about their business, but at no time had we felt there was any threat to our well being.

There was a heavy presence of military police in certain places, possibly there to protect government buildings or the like. This also may have been sufficient enough to deter any wrong doer from doing wrong!

Again it was a very hot and sunny day and we'd soon felt the need to head back toward the prison, which I'd noticed earlier just happened to be home to a bar serving cold beer.

As we'd enjoyed some refreshment we'd watched some of the tourists from the other ships in port.

Our lot were ambling about the place looking confused but quite at home in jail, and then there were others who looked very clean, ironed and polished.

There must be a posh American liner visiting as well.

So back to the ship and a chance to reflect on our day in this very pleasant and generally safe city, hence today's headline 'what a reliefe'.

It was certainly more like Manaus than Fortaleza, (thank goodness) and it has certainly restored some confidence in Brazil, and maybe increased our aspirations for Salvador and Rio.

A quick snooze and off to the gym.

Ted certainly seemed to be sweating a lot when I'd arrived. Nadia must be giving him a really hard workout.

Tuesday 5th February 2013

Day 29 'at sea' - a mystery is solved.

We'd been told at the start of this holiday that the entertainment team would be holding several events throughout the cruise to raise money for charity, specifically the RNLI.

The first of these events was held today as the cruise director proudly announced the opening of its annual 'Summer Fete'.

The pool deck had been decorated to look like a typical English village green, complete with bunting and balloons. There were also a series of stalls selling all kinds of bric-a-brac (mostly stuff thrown out as useless by the staff and crew) as well as a range of good old fashioned fete games like 'Apple Bobbing', 'Hook a Duck' and 'Guess the Weight of the Cake'.

Shame the beautiful weather had to go and spoil a perfectly good British Summer activity by not raining, but this did allow the catering department to put on a very impressive barbeque.

As well as lots of fun for everyone to take part in, the main aim of the fete was raise money for the RNLI.

The games charged fifty pence to play, and in return points were handed out to the participants, with extra bonus points awarded for completing certain tasks. Ultimately the passenger with the most points at the end of the afternoon would win a seat for him or herself and a partner at the Captain's table that evening, as well as a tour of the bridge.

It was a hot and sunny day, but that didn't deter folks from vigorously 'Splatting the Rat', violently throwing wet sponges at the Deputy Captain and even having a strip of chest hair 'waxed' in a desperate attempt to win fifty bonus points.

It was quite manic but everyone seemed to be having masses of fun.

A lady, who was travelling alone, fought off all competition to secure that most coveted of places in the dining room, and surprisingly she did have her chest waxed, at least she went through the process, but I doubt she was overly hirsute.

To the disappointment of all the gentlemen travelling alone she chose one of the ship's officers to accompany her to dinner and share her good fortunes.

This however caused a rumpus as it was discovered the officer in question was the same one in charge of the 'Chest Waxing' activity.

To be fair, the said officer didn't look entirely delighted at being picked.

Maybe she was quite furry after all.

Immediately following the fete's closing ceremony, they'd conducted the finals of the 'Boat Building' competition. Apparently this is a regular and highly competitive event in the cruise calendar which also transports the winner to the Captain's table for dinner as a reward.

Passengers are challenged to collect items from around the ship in order to build a vessel that would not only be able to float in the pool, but also carry a cargo of six full cans of beer, and withstand a tidal wave.

The rules were simple.

The vessel can only be constructed from items found in areas of the ship designated for passengers.

Contestants are not allowed to use any items or materials bought on board with the specific purpose of gaining an advantage in the challenge.

Contestants are not allowed to dismantle or remove items of ships equipment or infrastructure without the express permission of the Captain (and don't bother to ask, it won't be given)

The cans of beer must be visible at all times and cannot be completely enclosed within the vessel. Any cans falling off the vessel will result in immediate disqualification, even if the vessel continues to float.

The winner will be the owner of the vessel which stays afloat for the longest period of time with all six cans of beer remaining on board.

In the event of any dispute the Cruise Director's decision is final.

Of the nine competitors who'd lined up for the start of the contest, three were immediately disqualified before their construction even touched the water.

The first was prohibited from taking part because he claimed to be the vessel, stating he would drink the six cans of beer and armed with a floatation device would simply lie in the water.

The staff had tried to explain that this wouldn't be possible as they were required to return the 'unopened' beer cans to the Lido Bar at the end of the event. The man had argued that as he was prepared to pay for the beer then he should be allowed to take part. This however was thwarted by a fellow competitor who insisted that by drinking the beer it would mean, of course, that the beer would be 'fully enclosed', a blatant breach of the rules.

And what about the cans, where would they go?

Another applicant was dismissed from the competition when it was discovered his vessel was constructed around the fibreglass hull of a really large radio-controlled boat. The owner had tried to disguise it by attaching two plastic bottles, half a dozen lollypop sticks with string as rigging, and had then painted the whole thing black. He might have got away with it had he not been carrying the radio control unit, with the aerial already extended.

The third competitor to be removed had made a boat using a small Samsonite suitcase. He'd cut out a hole big enough to place the six cans in and had filled the inside of the case with balloons to give extra buoyancy.

Quite ingenious.

But he was informed that he was being disqualified as he'd also broken the rule about 'bringing stuff on board for the purpose etc'.

He'd agreed that he had brought it on board, but argued vehemently that it had clearly been for the purpose of carrying clothes. Only later had he developed the idea to use it for the competition and as a result the case was now unfit for its original purpose.

Unfortunately for him one of the entertainment staff remembered a previous cruise where the same entrant, with the same vessel had offered the same defence when he'd been excluded. On that occasion his appeal had been upheld allowing him to compete and, in fact, win a seat at the Captain's table.

His partner wasn't very unhappy to be told she'd not have the pleasure this time. But to be fair his vessel was a very good floater, and you could still see it bobbing up and down in the sea for quite a long time after she'd thrown it overboard.

The remaining six vessels were all loaded up with beer and placed in the swimming pool.

I have to say it really did look like a couple of them had been designed and constructed in a workshop with high tech materials, rather than trash from around the ship. If I'd been taking part I'd probably demand an explanation as to how certain items had been found on board.

Anyway, on with the show.

Sadly one craft sank immediately on touching the water, so just five were pushed into the middle with a long pole, ready for the tidal wave to be initiated.

This was duly supplied by Gareth, the largest member of the entertainments team, who gamely threw himself in and out of the swimming pool trying to sink the various constructions with a wall of water.

Unfortunately one boat disappeared after being subjected to the full weight of Gareth's rear end and another fell to a volley of stolen fruit from a party of spectators.

Finally, only one remained and was declared the winner. It consisted of a large collection of plastic bottles all taped together to form an intricate structure. It had disappeared under the water several times, but had always returned to the surface with its cargo intact.

The objections started immediately, mainly centred on where the tape to hold it all together had been obtained. Now call me a cynic if you like, but the same could be said of any of the entries from what I could see. I reckon there was a touch of sour grapes going on, especially as the fruit throwers were discovered to be the winner's table companions.

I've heard that staff are looking into one further complaint, but have already stated that the gentleman in question had been banned from entering the contest on a technicality. They are also demanding that he returns the training life raft he'd acquired from a restricted area of the ship.

Despite his insistence that no rules had been broken, they say it was too big for the pool anyway.

Oh, and the owner of the winning boat?

Well would you believe it, it was the strange man we'd seen rummaging through the bins.

At least this solves a mystery and if I see him

around the ship again I must congratulate him for his achievement, and apologise for getting him arrested.

Wednesday 6th February 2013

Day 30 'Salvador de Bahai' - the Golly still exists.

Yet another hot and sunny day greeted our arrival to the city of Salvador, home (I'm led to believe) to the oldest church in Brazil.

There's a very distinctive African based culture here so we're expecting it to have a completely different 'feel' compared to the other Brazilian ports we've visited so far.

This city, the third largest in Brazil, is built on two levels, upper and lower, and there is a lift service to take you to the older and more historic upper level. On this occasion there were two other cruise ships in and we're berthed furthest from the lifts (someone negotiated too hard for a discount on their port fees me thinks) so initially we'd thought that a long hot walk was on the cards.

But Jeff was about to put us right, again.

There's a jewellery company in Brazil who quite often supply complimentary minibuses at each port. They pick you up from the cruise terminal and deposit you right outside their store in the town, which is usually convenient for the main or historic centre.

On reaching the store the driver and 'a couple of his buddies' usher you inside for a look around and a touch of pushy selling. There is absolutely no requirement to buy, they just ask you to take a look around, hoping of course you're the sort of person who now feels obligated and can't say no.

Jeff had suggested we should take advantage of this service as he and Pru had done many times in the past.

"They'll be no match for me, Laddie," he'd guaranteed, "And we'll be out of the store in no time at all."

Even so I reckoned twenty minutes spent in an air conditioned shop was far better than a twenty minutes walk at gas mark 8. And I can't spend what I don't have, can I?

So the four of us had gratefully accepted the invitation for a ride to the upper town square in a very shiny black minibus, accompanied by six other willing participants.

Now I've no idea how many pieces of jewellery they would have to sell to pay for this sleek piece of super cool German machinery with leather reclining seats and a mini-bar, but I can honestly say I'd started to worry.

Surely nobody can offer this kind of service for free.

As Jeff tucked into a can of beer from the fridge, I had visions of signing away the rest of my pension for a diamond the size of a peanut.

What were we doing?

Approached our destination, in the middle of the upper town square, I could see the shop and what looked like a dozen smartly dressed assistants standing at the curb awaiting our arrival.

My whole wallet flashed before my eyes, screaming!

What happened next happened so quickly I'm not quite sure what happened, but happen it did and, as it happens, it happened for the best.

The minibus stopped and one of the assistants opened the sliding door.

Before he could even voice a greeting two very large ladies in traditional costume bustled him out of the way. One grabbed hold of Jeff and Pru and the other grabbed my dear lady and I and almost dragged us out onto the pavement.

"Salvador bids you welcome," our buxom lady laughed and moved us away from the roadside.

Two of the male assistants from the store had followed closely, voicing their protests at our abduction by the ladies, but they'd quickly retreated.

It was highly likely that the other potential customers on the minibus might seize the opportunity and get away in the fracas, and we were a lost cause anyway.

"Now you have a camera, yes?" the lady had asked.

Without a thought I'd produced my compact Lumix from my pocket.

"So you take a picture of me with your beautiful lady." She sounded all pleasant and friendly

I took the picture.

"Now you have a picture with me too."

She sounded all pleasant and friendly

My dear lady and I swapped places and I was all smiles as this strangely hypnotic lady wrapped her arms around me.

"Now you give me five dollars."

She didn't sound all pleasant and friendly, in fact there was a touch of menace in her voice.

Like I'd said, she was a big lady so I wasn't going to argue.

It suddenly came to mind that there are many

scams carried out mainly to discover where the unsuspecting traveller keeps his cash.

Was this one of them?

Fortunately I always keep a few dollar bills in my shirt pocket for such a need.

I counted out five dollar bills.

"Each," she'd said. A slightly sarcastic smile had returned to her face.

I duly complied and she'd thanked us and moved off to find another potential mug to hug.

Jeff wasn't having an easy time of it and for once his negotiating skills were getting him into trouble.

"You give me ten dollars," his lady was demanding.

"Ah get on," Jeff implored, "For one photo? I'll giye five."

"You'll give me ten."

She wasn't going to take no for an answer.

Jeff's pride was at stake and he desperately tried to strike a deal, but ultimately the argument was lost before it had even begun. Reluctantly, and at Pru's insistence, he'd handed over the cash.

My dear lady had pointed over to the shop where another group of cruisers were arriving in a second minibus. This time the store assistants formed a solid barrier the buxom ladies couldn't penetrate, then ushering their quarry into the store everybody had disappeared.

"At least they got us away from the jewellers," she'd offered by way of consolation.

Jeff was inconsolable.

Anyway we'd arrived and, so far, no walking in the blazing sun.

We'd had a good wander round the streets which

were all decorated ready for carnival and we also found a couple of old churches to visit. The oldest church was showing its age but very ornate on the outside. I had to go and find a place to exchange dollars for the local Real as they wouldn't take dollars for the entry fee.

I made a quick tour of the square to find a money changer with a fairish exchange rate, then clutching my strange looking and even stranger smelling cash we were able to enter.

The outside of the church looked quite shabby but the inside was awash with opulence and magnificence with fabulous carvings and gold everywhere.

Any description I could write here couldn't do it justice.

However I will comment on the marked contrast between the rich trappings of the church compared to the poor state of most of the rest of the town and its population. The generous contributions of the people of Salvador appears to have gone unnoticed by the Almighty and he hasn't rewarded their devotion. But then I'm more inclined to believe that in the past some of His representatives had abused their position, maybe?

Probably a bit too serious again, but then without all these beautiful objects to admire tourists would have no reason to visit churches the world over.

Time for a beer.

For a cost of around Eighteen Real (£5) we'd purchased four very cold cans of beer from a makeshift bar in the town square. Then settling down on four very flimsy plastic chairs in the dappled shade cast by the surrounding trees we'd watched the locals going about their business.

Apparently the carnival here is bigger than Rio's and preparations are well under way to transform the main centre of the town into 'Celebration Central'.

There were a handful of guys hanging bunting and banners from lampposts. Using a very rickety ladder, which almost bent double as an exceptionally large gent climbed up it, they'd managed to attach brackets right at the top of the post.

It was one of those 'you know something disastrous is about to happen' moments which you just can't bear to watch, but have to.

Fortunately no one appeared to have been seriously injured and the ambulance arrived very quickly.

Our attention moved to watch a very large group of badly dressed transvestites pass by in a procession, followed by a colourful group of children playing drums and dancing. We weren't quite sure if the party had started or were they just rehearsing?

As we'd finished off the first drinks an older man wearing a very dishevelled jacket rushed over to where we were sat. He'd smiled and held open a large black bag for us to deposit the empties into, presumably he was collecting them to recycle for a little cash.

"Time for another laddie," Jeff had stated and held out his hand in my direction. He'd not changed any money today, so I'd handed over a fifty Real note.

The big Scot wandered off to the bar.

Seeing that there would be more cans available in the not too distant future, the can-collector sat himself down on the ground right next to my dear lady.

Jeff returned with the four beers and a few assorted packets of crisps.

"No idea what the flavours are," he'd said, "Might be a bit of fun finding out though."

Selecting the nearest bag and opening it my dear lady took a sniff. Before she could offer any insight as to the flavour within, the can collector was nudging her elbow and gesturing he was hungry.

Unable to resist such sorrowful eyes she'd handed the packet over.

The contents were gone in an instant, then pointing to the other snacks on the table he'd indicated 'hungry' again. More crisps were offered along with a couple of packets of the ship's ginger nut biscuits my dear lady kept in her bag for emergencies.

He appeared delighted by the gifts and quickly devoured every last crumb, munching away as 'happy as Larry'.

But Larry (as he was now called) was still claiming starvation, but everything had gone.

Jeff stood and held out his hand again.

"Cough up laddie, I'll get him some more."

I'd handed over a note and Jeff turned toward the bar, but Larry had a different idea. Standing up in front of Jeff and held out his hand

"Coof pup lazzie," he'd said, trying to mimic Jeff's accent.

It wasn't threatening at all, he just put on his saddest face and almost started to simper. Jeff handed him the Ten Real note (about £3.50)

Just like Gollum when he'd chewed his 'precious'

from Froddo's finger, he'd jumped for joy and danced around the square like a lottery winner. He shook his new found wealth at the lady in the bar, then disappeared across the square skipping as he went.

My dear lady and Pru declared a halt to the beer and went off for a browse around the stalls down the side streets. Jeff stated he was too hot to go shopping so I'd bought him another beer. I reckon his pride was still smarting from his earlier encounter with a rather large and intimidating lady.

When the girls returned they told us about seeing Larry enjoying something to eat and a beer in the shade on the far side of the square. So it was good to know that our memorable gift had helped him to forget his problems for a short while at least.

They'd also discovered a street full of artists worth a look at, so my dear lady and I set off for a browse with Pru, leaving Jeff to enjoy the rest of his beer in peace. We'd returned about fifteen minutes later to find Jeff chatting with Larry.

"Come look at this Laddie," Jeff called over.

Larry had handed Jeff a wallet inside which was an ID card with the unmistakable image of our new friend. To my surprise the card clearly indicated that Larry was 'The Chief of Police'.

"He used to be," the lady from the bar told us.

With gestures and some interpretation from the lady the former head of law and order in this area indicated he'd got sick and lost his job and his family. With no pension or state benefits to rely on he now lived on the streets and collected metal cans to make enough money to eat.

"That's just terrible," Pru told the lady.

"He was a good man," she said, "We all do what we can for him."

All four of us had witnessed poverty first hand over the past few days, but now it suddenly felt personal. But then what could we do? Our small gift had satisfied his hunger today but what about tomorrow?

Larry took back his card and with a big smile and a heavily accented "Sank you," he'd disappeared across the square, leaving us feeling a little depressed.

But hey ho, life goes on, so we thanked the lady and left for the lift back down.

We had to do the touristy thing and pop into several of the souvenir shops on our way back to the ship. We didn't really want to buy anything, it was more to take advantage of their air conditioning to cool down.

To our surprise, many of the shops were full of black Gollies, each dressed in the same colourful national costume as the ladies we'd met earlier in the day when we'd stepped off the minibus.

As children my dear lady and I used to collect the metal badges offered by a very popular preserves company, but these days the 'Golly' is regarded as offensive.

I have to admit we nearly bought one as a memory of a lovely, eventful day here in Salvador, but realised it might cause us a whole heap of trouble trying to bring it back through British Customs.

Oh well, maybe next time.

So highlights of the day included seeing the oldest church in Brazil...finding the oldest school of medicine in Brazil, founded in the late 1800's, and still training the local medics...seeing a group of children practicing for carnival...browsing the shops and buying a very colourful picture by a local artist...meeting an ex chief of police in the guise of a man we'd named Larry.

So another good day in another good city.

It didn't feel quite as safe as some of the places we'd visited so far, but it was ok, and Larry was definitely a character.

Meeting him was yet another reminder of how fortunate we are to live in the UK.

Probably inspired by a long defunct toy, 'Betcha by golly wow' was my dear lady's choice in the shower tonight, followed closely by 'Zoom' by The Fat Larry Band...he was hardly that though.

Thursday 7th February

Day 31 'at sea' - get packing Argentina.

Amazingly the first leg of this 'Voyage of Discovery' is coming to an end, and for some of our fellow passengers, and table companions, it also signals the end of their journey.

In just two days time we'll be saying our goodbyes to Ron, Nancy, Steve and Louise when we arrive in Rio de Janeiro. Both couples have been fantastic company and we've spent many a happy evening, and an occasional early morning, with them.

I haven't noted our antics together as much as I probably should have, but then things did get a little fuzzy around the edges at times...hic.

Of the seven hundred or so holidaymakers aboard, two hundred and sixty will be leaving the ship and heading home.

Sadly, some of those continuing on to the next part of the cruise have started gloating and the grumpy faces of those departing are made darker by comments about how cold it's going to be back in the UK, especially after the sweltering heat of Brazil.

For the 'going homers' the enjoyment of the long anticipated carnival of Rio will probably turn to carnage in the chaos of not one, but two of the world's busiest airports. Travellers will need to fly from Rio to Sao Paulo first before boarding a flight bound for London.

But they smile and grit their teeth, for they too can be mean of thought.

So they reiterate their prayers for gale force winds to greet the onward seafarers further along their journey (not that they're bitter you understand)

Then as a final thumb of the nose the excuses begin to flow, telling us, and hopefully convincing themselves, that they're really not bothered to be leaving.

So they say things like...

I'm happy now we're leaving, this ship moves way too much,
She corkscrews through the water as the sea starts getting rough.
The foods becoming samey and I've put on lots of weight,
I'm drinking too much G&T, then sleeping in too late.
I've worn this shirt for ages for clean clothes I have not got,
Cause I'm sick to death of laundry rooms, they're always way too hot.
My cabins claustrophobic with a hard and lumpy bed,
Feather pillows wait at home to rest my sea sick head.

*The crew are far too happy. Dining friends have let me
down,*
Their conversation irritates with talk of future towns.
The comedians not funny and the singers sing off key,
The Captain's voice gets on my nerves with each apology.
From Barbados down to Rio, all the way up Amazon,
Now I've done the bits I fancied I can quickly get me gone.
*But now that I am heading home you know you'll miss me
so,*
*You'll have much less fun without me, so please beg me
not to go!!*

Just my take on actual comments only heard for the first time in the past few days. Strangely, no one had mentioned any of these 'issues' before.

I have to add there has been none of this on table one two eight, well not enough to mention, except maybe lines one, two, three, six, seven, twelve, thirteen and fourteen.

Of course it has to be remembered that if two hundred and sixty are leaving then I suppose it's fair to expect the same number will be joining us as our journey continues.

That will also mean four new table companions, a very hard act to follow indeed.

There's been a lot of talk about Argentina lately as the original itinerary for this trip included three Argentinian ports, the capital Buenos Aires, Puerto Madryn and Ushuaia (the town at the end of the world)

However, we've been receiving information from the Captain, who has received information from the cruise company, who have received information from other ships calling in at Buenos Aires, which has highlighted a developing problem.

Namely 'the continuing Argentinian effort to claim ownership of the Falkland Islands'.

Because the British have rightfully refused to even discuss sovereignty of this 'self governing' archipelago, the Argentinian government are determined to ruin the islands economy by seeking to cut off any source of revenue.

They already have an embargo on British (or British linked) commercial shipping from using their ports, which has now been extended by the local unions and politicians to include cruise ships.

In the past year (the thirtieth anniversary of the war) and in the run up to a referendum of the residents of the islands, several cruises berthing in Argentinian ports have been severely disrupted.

British passengers attempting to leave the ship to visit the cities have been intimidated by protesters, and port authorities have delayed departures for many hours whilst seeking a solemn promise from the Captains of the vessels not to visit the Falklands.

Our Captain has announced that, having weighed up the situation, he has made the decision to cancel our visits to all three Argentinian ports in order to prevent any trouble we might be subjected to. He has also stated that he considers our support for the Falklanders is far more important, a sentiment upheld by all.

There's an understandable swell of opinion onboard, nothing new there as we Brits are never short of an opinion or five. But in some cases folk have gone a little too far with their views, even entering into 'ridiculously silly' territory.

The following conversation between two ladies was overheard (names have not been changed as no one deserves anonymity in this instance)

"Hello Jean, not dancing today?"

"I shall never go to the dance classes again Alice, it's outrageous and I'm disgusted."

"Whatever's happened Jean?"

"Well today they were teaching the Argentinian Tango, I think that's disgusting."

"Oh I know, it is a bit raunchy."

"No it's disgusting because of what they did in the Falklands. We should have nothing to do with anything associated with Argentina."

"It's only a dance Jean...they even do it on 'Strictly'."

"That's totally wrong."

"No it's not, I saw that sexy Vincent doing it."

"No, I meant it's not just a dance, it's a sneaky way of making the unacceptable acceptable."

"What is?"

"The Argentinian Tango...oh never mind."

"I'm sure they'll do something different tomorrow."

"I shall never go to their classes again, and I've told them so. Now I'm off to reception to complain about the instructors. They told me they couldn't understand what all the 'argy bargy' was about."

"Ha ha."

"I didn't think it was funny."

"No Jean. Sorry Jean."

"And I'm going to insist they take Argentinian wine off the menu as well. We must make a stand and show them they can't walk all over us."

"Or the grapes."

"Shut up Alice."

This afternoon the Captain informed us that he's managed to secure a couple of extra port visits to replace the ones we're missing out on. Tomorrow we'll be calling at Buzios, a very popular upmarket tourist destination for rich Brazilians.

A mere eighty miles from Rio, this peninsular is blessed with a number of pristine beaches and a pretty village. Apparently there is little else in the way of major tourist attractions to be found, but it is famous for being the favourite haunt of Bridget Bardot.

Sounds inviting, but it's a tender port so let's hope the sea is kind to my bum.

I've continued going to the gym later in the day, usually while my dear lady gets herself ready for dinner. It's so much more convenient at that time and it also means I can still get a bit of exercise on port days without having to miss out on anything (takes me a while but I get it right eventually)

I am finding that after an hour on the treadmill and a quick shower I'm definitely ready to eat.

No, make that starving.

The past couple of nights I can honestly say I've still been quite hungry when we've left the table after dinner (thank goodness for the midnight buffet)

I'd mentioned this to Jeff during our usual pre-dinner cocktails, adding that it hadn't gone unnoticed that his plate always looked a whole lot fuller than mine, even if we'd ordered the same meal.

"That's because I've had a word, Laddie."

He'd laughed and continued, "On the first few nights I'd asked our waiter if he would be kind enough to bring an extra large portion of everything I'd ordered."

"And he did?" I'd asked stupidly.

"Well you've seen it for yourself, and now I don't even have to ask. If it's on the menu they'll bring you whatever you ask for."

I must have looked unconvinced.

"Think about it Laddie, have you ever heard the waiter say that they've run out of anything?"

I shook my head.

"They always prepare enough of each dish on the menu just in case everyone wants the same thing. What do you think they do with the stuff that's left over?"

I had to admit I'd assumed the crew ate it, but Jeff had told me it's not really the kind of food they would normally enjoy, so why would they.

Jeff was right, so I'd decided to take his advice.

Sirloin steak was on tonight's menu with all the usual trimmings. Our waiter never even raised an eyebrow when I'd asked if it were possible to have a double portion.

"No problem at all sir, would you like extra chips and onion rings as well?" he'd offered.

I wish my dear lady wouldn't keep changing the lyrics of great songs because it suits her needs. Queen definitely didn't sing about 'Fat bottomed boys', and there was no need for Jeff and Pru to join in either.

I reckon an hour each day in the gym is not going to be enough to prove them all wrong.

Friday 8th February

Day 32 'Buzios' - just buzz off.

It was quite breezy during the night as our little ship rolled its way down the west coast of South America towards today's port of call, Armacao dos Buzios.

However, by the time my dear lady and I sat

down for breakfast, on the aft deck outside the buffet restaurant, we were safely anchored in the bay and out of the wind.

There was another big cruise liner anchored here as well, a very large one indeed, which was already emptying its passengers into the town via a steady flotilla of little boats.

From our mooring we had a very nice view of a beautiful, wide sandy beach, which at that moment, appeared to be almost empty.

On one side of the bay there was a lush green coastline and on the other distant mountains rose majestically through the mist.

We ate fruit and pastries in silence whilst a few boobies and frigate birds lazily circled above us. The sun was burning off the last few clouds and everything felt warm and peaceful.

We'd sat for a while, enjoying the ambience and debating when to head ashore on the tenders. We could see that the landing stage on the beach was not too far away and the sea in the bay was ripple free and calm, so we'd decided that once the rush for shore had died down we'd head for the tenders and see what this replacement resort could offer.

After all there must be something interesting to see, otherwise why was that larger ship here.

My dear lady wasn't wholly convinced about going ashore though, saying she thought it looked very pretty for sure, but why weren't we booked to visit here in the first place. She reckoned it would be much better to sit in the shade on the ship, enjoying the wonderful views of the land, rather than sitting in the scorching sun on the beach looking at the ship.

She had a point.

We weren't to know that the gods were about to have their say in this matter, and we wouldn't get a chance to choose.

Just over half an hour later we'd finally decided to give Buzios a go and were at the top of the stairway on the outside of the ship which leads down to the pontoon where the tenders were loading.

One of the staff's walkie talkies nearby crackled into life.

"This is the bridge, tender service is suspended. Please escort all passengers on the tenders and stairways back inside and await instructions please."

We trudged back to our seats on the aft deck, to 'await instructions'.

We didn't have to wait long.

"Good morning ladies and gentlemen," the ship's tannoy boomed. "This is the Captain speaking from the navigational bridge. I'm sorry to disturb the peace of this beautiful morning but I have an announcement with regard to our tender operation. For the time being it has been suspended, but we're hoping to get it going again very shortly. As you can see there's already a rather large cruise ship anchored here," (nice to know his eyesight is okay) "And the harbour master has told us that between the two of us we're causing a bit of a blockage for traffic trying to enter the bay. One or two of the larger yachts have actually had to sail around us. We have therefore been asked to move to a different mooring point."

There was a noticeable pause.

"Unfortunately, this will be half a mile further out to sea."

At this point there had been an audible gasp from

the lady on the next table, the type of gasp you hear when a body's been discovered.

"Of course this will mean that the journey to shore will take a little longer, but unfortunately we will have to comply."

An even louder gasp, I think she must have just found out it was murder.

"Once we're at our new anchorage the tender operation will re-commence and we will be lowering an extra craft so that delays are kept to a minimum. Once again my apologies for any inconvenience, thank you."

In the ensuing silence I expected to hear weeping.

Very slowly the ship manoeuvred to its new position, dropped anchor and, true to his word, our skipper quickly got the tender boats lined up. Again my dear lady and I decided to wait a short while as there had appeared to be a mad rush to get ashore (or away from that fiendish murderer, who can tell?)

At least we had the aft deck to ourselves now.

It was still a beautiful day, but now there was a noticeable breeze and the water seemed a little less calm, as did the people who'd suddenly reappeared.

"That's the second time I've been kicked off that life boat," the gasping lady was saying.

Once again an apologetic Captain came on the tannoy to tell us that the harbour master was now saying that the owners of the luxurious properties on the headland were complaining about a large ship in their bay spoiling their view. As the town relied heavily on their wealthy residents it was his job was to make sure they were happy, so he was insisting we had to move again, just a little further out to sea.

We'd both turned to see how the gasping lady

would react this time.

She was actually weeping.

The Captain went on to state that he would like to maintain a good relationship with the port authorities, especially as they had agreed to accommodate us at the last minute. He had no choice but to comply with their request.

You could hear the frustration in his voice, as if Fortaleza had returned to haunt him.

Unfortunately the area we were moved to this time was a long way off the coast and out of the protection of the headland. The winds and currents here were much stronger and because the water was so much deeper the anchors were all but useless.

Ultimately this also meant it was too dangerous to continue tendering, so the operation was suspended, permanently.

That just left the small matter of getting those folk who had managed to get ashore back on board.

It was amazing and a little worrying to see how much the ship struggled to keep position and the returning tenders had to circle for quite a while in rough seas, waiting for enough of a lull in the winds to be able to be secured safely alongside.

Anyway, we didn't manage to get ashore today as certain local attitudes completely overran sense, with reasonable behaviour by a few being buried deeply in the sands of selfishness on the beaches of Buzios.

Do these affluent 'out of towners' actually contribute that much to the local economy?

Well I'm sure the resident vendors, the hard workers of this area, are always happy to welcome the strange and slightly scruffy inhabitants of the cruise ships, especially when they part with a little money in return for a few meagre trinkets (or beers) But I would guess they have little or no influence to bear on any of the decision makers of the town.

And what about the local public officials, do they have any say in the matter? Well maybe they just have to do what the money tells them to do.

So a pretty place on the outside (so we're told) but frankly I'm not sure 'our sort' were really welcome here in the first place.

Tomorrow Rio, supposedly the carnival capital of the world and without question one of the anticipated highlights of this cruise. It's just a shame we're only there for just the one day and we'll be leaving shortly before nightfall.

Sadly we're not going to be able to see much of the big competition parades as these are held in the custom built venue known as the Sambadrome. Tickets are incredibly expensive and were sold out months ago. The main events don't start until the evening anyway.

But there will still be loads to do and we should get to see some of the street parades which should give us a real feel for the amazing Brazilian party atmosphere. We'll be joining thousands of revellers, all dressed in the weirdest, and sometimes briefest, of costumes with brightly dyed hair (that's them, not us) A festival for the eclectic and eccentric.

I wonder if Ted will be joining in.

I'm hoping he's not one of the two hundred and sixty leaving tomorrow.

Tonight will be the last and probably very boozy evening on board for Ron, Nancy, Steve and Louise.

I'm feeling quite emotional about saying goodbye to them.

They have bought a great deal of fun to this first sector of the cruise and Ron will be well remembered for his desire to get us all drunk and up dancing on Burn's night. I'll never be able to hear the 'Gay Gordons' without joining in and remembering such a wonderful night.

I just wish i could remember it.

At first I'd thought Steve a bit stand offish, but we've enjoyed many beers together and he has a very wicked sense of humour. I know we've laughed a lot, I just can't remember why.

The new arrivals have a hard act to follow and we can only hope that they will, at least, try.

My dear lady is just back from the hot tub and is now taking a shower, and after I've finished writing today's entry I'll be off to the gym.

Tonight I'm really praying that my dear lady will refrain from singing 'We'll meet again'.

Oh dear, too late.

'A new batch'

Saturday 9th February

Day 33 'Rio de Janeiro' - wave goodbye, say hello.

We were up on deck very early this morning as we'd been told the sail in past the outlying islands, the mountains, the beachfront and into the harbour is spectacular. It probably was but unfortunately the weather, for the first time, was against us. A dense low mist covered everything and dawn had barely broken.

We passed the airport runway which juts out into the harbour, but under the mist it appeared to be just an extension to the coastline. Bright orange pulsing lights marking the end of the runway diffused to make it look like the water was on fire and the whole place took on a really eerie façade under the veil of swirling vapour.

Sugar Loaf and Corcovado were nowhere to be seen, and like the city's visiting late night party revellers were failing to raise their heads at this early hour.

I don't know whether I'd been expecting drums and samba music at this time of the day, but all was deathly quiet and absolutely still, which didn't seem to fit in with the image running around in my rather sleepy (and slightly hung-over) head.

So we went back to bed for an hour.

We'd booked a four hour tour to take us around the sights of the city and then deposit us at the train station for the long steep haul up Corcovado to meet Christ the Redeemer in all his statuesque glory.

But it wasn't leaving until ten, so we'd enjoyed a leisurely breakfast and watched the mist rise as the sun finally climbed into the sky. Shame we couldn't see much of the surrounding area from where the ship had berthed, as the port is hidden around the corner from the main bay area.

The tour was quite slow at first as many of the main streets had been closed off for the festivities, but once we'd got going we were taken to see a number of the local attractions.

Brazil is heavily influenced by European architecture and Rio is a typical example. They have an almost exact replica of the grand opera house in Paris, L'Opera. Unlike its big brother though it looks a little out of place as the surrounding structures are much more modern.

This is truly a melting pot of cultures, with Spanish, Portuguese, African, Lebanese and Turkish communities (to name but a few)

Our guide, Reggie, gave us a 'potted history' of the city and its inhabitants. But he was most disparaging about recent immigration trends, with many undesirable foreigners relocating to his city in the hope of finding the usual pavements of gold.

Now they litter the streets, lying intoxicated on large discarded cardboard boxes, sleeping the day away and then roaming the streets at night, scavenging whatever they can find like packs of urban foxes.

So Rio is just like any other big city around the world then, but with nicer views and spectacular weather, which incidentally had improved dramatically by the time we'd arrived at Copacabana beach.

Here we were given half an hour to have a wander around, and while the majority headed into the nearest hotel for a drink and toilet stop, my dear lady and I headed down onto the beach, hoping to experience the atmosphere of this legendary area and mingle with the locals.

The locals did not disappoint.

No matter what their age or size they wander the beach front in no more than Speedos or bikinis. Yet no one stares or points, there's no whispering or giggling at the unusually shaped ones, no looks of revulsion at the exceptionally wrinkled old folk either.

All are equal, all are welcome.

Whether they're walking the dog, jogging, cycling or just taking refreshment at one of the many kiosks or street vendors, these people know how to strut their stuff 'big time'. But there is no chance we can mingle and 'blend in' with the locals because frankly our tans are inadequate and even in t-shirts and shorts we're wearing far too many clothes.

Despite being conspicuously out of place tourists, we'd walked with them, at least we could match them on that level.

But this wasn't a beach as we know it, this was a playground for adults who don't want to grow up, and probably never will. They mark pitches in the sand and play games, fly kites, swim to cool down, throw Frisbee and indulge in serious tanning. They stop only for refreshment or to pose and flirt with anyone they like the look of.

This wasn't just like the movies, this was the

movies, and if someone had shouted "Action" I wouldn't have been surprised.

All too soon it was time to move on, but the joyful experience of Copacabana quickly dissipated with all the moaning from the man sitting behind us back on the coach.

"Those drinks were very expensive and the toilets were disgusting."

"Yes dear." His partner sounded disinterested. "We should have gone down to the beach," she'd added, "It looks really interesting."

"Don't be daft woman, they'd have robbed us."

"Just look at all those nice people, they're far too interested in having a good time to bother with us. I want to go to the beach."

"It's too late we're leaving now."

"Later then, we'll have time this afternoon. I want to go to the beach."

"There won't be...Oh my god, look...two men kissing."

"Yes dear I'm looking, and isn't it wonderful. I'll go to the beach on my own then shall I?"

So on to Corcovado and a meeting with Jesus.

It's difficult to find the right words to describe the experience. From getting on the train, the journey up the mountain and finally to stand at the base of one of the biggest tourist attractions in the world was incredible. If nothing else you have to admire the sheer scale of the operation it must have taken to get this huge effigy up the hill and planted firmly to overlook the city.

It was a truly spectacular encounter, only slightly marred by some stubborn cloud cover, which had refused to budge off the mountains all day. But even though we were denied some magnificent views over this great city and Sugar Loaf Mountain, it was well worth the journey. A photograph could never convey the atmosphere of this awesome place and I've been left with a lasting impression which will always be remembered (dementia permitting)

We were treated to some great vistas once we'd descended below the clouds as we'd travelled back down on the train for the return journey to the ship.

After a light snack on board we'd set out again to explore.

Tours are good but sometimes you need to wander the streets to get a true feel for the vibes of the city. Again we've discovered that the sights and smells of big cities are not always palatable. Rio is definitely no exception and seemingly worse during carnival.

Just a few streets away from the port area we found ourselves part of a large crowd watching the tail end of a street parade, of which apparently there are many.

The images we usually see of the Rio Carnival back home are of the elaborate floats, brightly coloured, skimpy costumed, hundreds of participants all wearing the same outfit variety. This would normally involve one of the majorly successful Samba schools and represents just one end of the spectrum.

The street parade we saw today couldn't have been more different.

Yes there were lots of people having a good time, but the floats were a mixture of old lorries decorated with many scraps of coloured materials, painted boards and ribbons. The costumes are pretty without being opulent, probably homemade by the individual wearing it. The band played a mixture of old and tatty instruments and tin cans.

Quite a contrast to the images we usually see, but very good none the less.

Sadly we'd missed most of the parade but we did get up close and personal with a typical group of carnival spectators. There was a palpable buzz, a feeling of excitement and a sense that these folk were having a really good time.

As the tightly packed fancy dress brigade started untangling themselves from the collective we were surprised to see there was no shouting, no pushing and shoving. As they'd meandered off to find another parade, a bar or head back to their hotel to recuperate for later merrymaking, everyone was smiling, laughing and generally enjoying life.

Had we just discovered the real spirit of carnival? Is this what it used to be like before the multinational sponsors hijacked the concept, a fun community event they turned it into a global money making event and confined the best to an exclusive venue the masses could never afford?

But then the parade at the Sambadrome is believed to be one of the world's most spectacular experiences. Shame we'll probably never find out, at least not on this trip.

At sail away we were treated to much clearer twilight views of the sights of the city, as well as a very strong version of Brazil's national drink, caipirinha to welcome aboard the newbies. I think the plan was to get us all plastered in an attempt to promote accord.

The sights were spectacular, with Corcovado all

lit up. With its black base you could actually imagine Christ was floating above the hills (or maybe that was alcohol induced) The surrounding panorama with all its twinkling lights cutting through the descending darkness was almost as magnificent as the better known attractions on display.

Rio is a visual city, as pleasing on the eye as carnival itself.

But the overriding memory of the day and the question still haunting our minds is why did the face of Christ the Redeemer look just like a certain famous footballer, you know, the one who married a Spice Girl.

Was he truly made in His image? I know his fans believe he was.

So a fond farewell to Rio, we've really enjoyed today and I'm sure we would come back for a second visit as there's so much more to see and do.

My dear lady says I only want to come back to walk down the streets wearing nothing more than my new 'rainbow bright' Speedos. I agreed and told her that it would be nice to be able to do that without anyone judging me.

Her reply was so mean I told her she'd been singing Duran Duran's 'Rio' out of tune all day, then headed off for the gym.

Well another question has been answered. Ted didn't get off in Rio.

I was just fifteen minutes into my workout when I heard, "Hello old chum."

He was now dressed in pink leg warmers and headband and a very unforgiving pair of Lycra shorts.

Seeing Ted like that I'm even more convinced

those 'rainbow bright' Speedos of mine need to go in the bin.

We were greeted by our new table companions this evening in the guise of,

Norma and Barry – she said everything, he said nothing, getting off in Lima.

Linda and Mike – very cagey about everything, staying on to Southampton.

Let's hope they fit in, but Jeff is doubtful, probably because the newbies didn't indulge him with a large scotch, which was on offer again tonight.

Anyhow, the first sector has come and gone, all too quickly for my liking, but it has been very enjoyable. Cruising is turning out to be a very pleasant way to take a holiday, seeing lots of different places without all the hassle of unpacking and repacking, or waiting around in airports for hours.

Tomorrow Santos, famous for its coffee as well as being one of the largest commercial ports in Brazil. Its other lesser known claim to fame is as the birthplace of Pele.

'Who?'

After the hustle and bustle of Rio, tomorrows call may be a total contrast, mainly because it's Sunday, and as a staunch Catholic country we're assuming everywhere will be shut. Apparently there are some really nice beaches there as well, so at least it should be a great day out.

Sunday 10th February

Day 34 'Santos' - 'Pele wuz ere'.

Another warm and sunny day greeted us as we'd

sailed into the large harbour at Santos, a city port in the province of Sao Paulo.

The port is extremely busy with lane upon lane of containers as far as the eye can see. There are huge articulated trucks coming and going, all loaded up with crates which are transferred by cranes to the enormous cargo ship berthed right behind us.

The local port authority has kindly organised shuttle buses to take us into the city as there is little to see or do in the port area, and it would be too dangerous, and pointless, for anyone to wander its container lanes in search of souvenirs or a bar.

Like most Brazilian cities there appears to be an old town and a newer area of the city. Usually these two areas sit side by side, but here in Santos the old town is located on the northern shore of a small peninsular, whereas the popular main beaches and attractions are on the southern side, in the modern part of the town. The ship's tour department have organised guided tours of the old historic town in the north, including the coffee museum, but this appears to be rather expensive. The shuttle buses heading south are complimentary, so we cheapskates are heading that way.

This is quite a busy terminal which we were hurried through to board the coaches by very efficient guides. Once outside we were informed that there was a short wait for the next bus, at which one of our fellow travellers, map in hand, approached the guide at the front of our queue and asked,

"Can you show me where the bus is taking us please?"

The guide duly pointed to the southern part of the map, "Here," she'd said, "By the beaches and the shops."

"But we want to go to the old town," the lady protested.

"Why?"

"Because we'd like to see the old buildings and visit the coffee museum."

"Then you'll need to make your own way there."

At this point she was joined by the rest of her friends from the back of the line.

"What's the point of taking us to somewhere we don't want to go?" one of them mutters.

They study the map, whispering and pointing. There a great deal of moaning with an occasional outburst of "Ridiculous."

Meanwhile the other people in line are starting to believe this is some form of tactic to jump the queue and some are starting to voice their objections.

The lady approached the guide again.

"Look, it's obvious that the old town is closer so it would be much quicker to take us there rather than the beach."

"I'm sorry but the bus is only going here," she stabs her finger on the map again.

"I'm sure there's a lot of others who'd like to go to the old town as well," the lady insisted.

"The guide said you need to make your own way," the chap at the head of the queue snapped. "Either that or get to the back where you came from."

The lady threw him a look.

"So which bus do we get?" she asked the guide.

"No bus, only taxi," the guide replied.

"Where are the taxis?"

"Here," the guide stabs the map, pointing directly

at the drop off point by the beaches.

The lady huffs and with her friends storms to the back of the queue, which of course has grown even longer. A close look at the guides face reveals the slight smirk that says it all,

'Bloody Tourists!'

The shuttle bus took around thirty minutes to make it way across the headland to the beaches, and once there my dear lady and I headed off down the promenade for a nice long, leisurely walk. It would seem like the entire population of Santos does just one thing on Sundays, they go to the beach. I'm sure this includes all the taxi drivers in the area as well because apart from the shuttle buses nothing is moving on the roads.

It's quite difficult to describe the scene because there are so many elements to it.

The locals have turned up fully kitted out for a day at the beach. They stream out from the buildings and cross the streets like ants, each sporting nothing more than the skimpiest bathing costumes imaginable, and pushing little trolleys containing everything they need for the day, chairs, parasols, tables, toys for the kids, food etc.

The beach, which must be over 100 metres from promenade to surf, is divided into three orderly sections. The third nearest the town is loaded with vendors of food and drink, whilst the lowest third nearest the sea is just wall to wall people playing in the surf or just walking. Between the vendors and bathers is where the locals make camp, and there are thousands of them, their parasols form a multicoloured continuous band across the entire seven kilometres of beach.

I think this is the largest mass of people in one place I have ever seen. I imagine there are hundreds of thousands of them and just like the beaches of Rio the young and old, large and small all parade together with no prejudice.

The only issue that we perceived was we were being stared at for being over dressed.

No one really seemed to have a problem with that, it was entirely down to us and the culture of judgement we usually experience in the UK.

After the walk we'd bumped into Pru and Jeff who had discovered a mini bus trip which offered a tour to and around the old town for just ten Real each (about £3.50) So we'd climbed aboard and set off to see the sights.

The journey was okay, nice architecture to admire and the cobbled streets of the old town were interesting, but we'd seen everything in fifteen minutes so had got back on the bus to return to the beach. We could now understand why the guide at the port had been surprised that anyone wanted to go there.

Everywhere away from the seafront area was closed and the streets deserted because everybody was at the beach, enjoying a day of rest with the family.

Back at the beachfront we'd pooled our remaining Real and bought two rounds of beer, ice cold and very refreshing. With just two Real left over my dear lady and Pru went off to bargain with a local vendor selling popcorn at three Real a bag. They'd returned with an exceptionally large well haggled reward (we'll have to put the girls in charge of the money more often)

Back on the shuttle we'd slowly made our way back through the town with the locals making tracks for home as well, crossing the road without any care for traffic which one assumes is because usually there isn't any.

Family groups together, all still in their Speedos and bikinis and laughing and chatting as they amble along, and my final thought as we'd passed them was of how folk back in the UK would react to the scenes playing out in front of us.

Wrinkly old leather skinned grandparents, overweight parents, lithesome teenagers and small toddlers, all wearing no more than underwear and walking through the streets after spending a day together as a family. No embarrassment, no hang-ups.

I can't imagine that ever happening, no way.

I was on my own in the gym this evening. There was no sign of Ted, or Nadia for that matter. I hope she hasn't caused him to strain something.

Next stop Montevideo, Uruguay, the home of the gaucho, where men wear leather chaps and ride for days across the savannah.

My dear lady has been riding a 'Horse with no name' all day.

But first two sea days with a new set of people to observe. I'm hoping they'll prove to be as interesting as the last lot.

Monday 11th February

Day 35 'at sea' - that's not strictly dancing.

Last night's dinner was only the second get together with our four new table companions, and already one of them seems determined to dominate proceedings, and is pretty much succeeding.

In an almost non-stop flow of words Norma was very keen to tell us how successful and interesting their life has been. From the moment we'd sat down she'd hardly paused for breath until her first mouthful of prawn cocktail. Then to everyone's dismay she'd immediately resumed her tales with a mouthful of food, liberally spraying fragments of it all over the table.

I'd expected one of us to say something, especially Jeff or Pru, but nobody did. I couldn't work out if we'd kept silent out of politeness or cowardice.

She'd been reasonably chatty last night, but now she'd found her confidence, and an audience.

By the main course she was still going at breakneck pace. We knew all the places they lived, and for how long, and why they'd moved, and all the jobs they'd both been employed in, and for how long, and why they'd left. Not forgetting the names of their children, and how clever and successful they were, and all the places they'd lived, and for how long, and etc etc.

On one occasion, as she'd taken a drink of her wine, Linda had turned to Pru and quickly asked how we'd got on down the Amazon and what was it like?

Pru never got chance to answer.

"We've been twice," Norma interjected, dribbling some wine onto her dress in her haste to relay her experiences.

"It was smelly and hot and the people were filthy and rude. That's why we decided not to join the cruise until Rio. Not worth going really nothing to see or do. Did we tell you we'd been in Rio for over a week before getting on here, and we went on a four day trip to the Iguacu Falls as well? Now that was really worth doing and much better than cruising down the rancid Amazon. We've been round South America several times before and the only bit really worth doing is Rio to Lima. We'll be leaving then and travelling by rail up to Machu Picchu. Barry just loves the trains and there's not much to see or do once you get past Chile. Peru's just a desert. We like to try out all the old railways on our travels, especially the old steam locomotives..."

And that's how the evening had continued.

By the time the cheese and biscuits arrived there was a desperate need for some brain anaesthetic, so I'd ordered four large ports, two for us and the others for Pru and Jeff. Immediately after that Jeff ordered four large single malts, so I'd reminded him the ladies didn't drink whiskey.

"Even if they did Laddie, my need is much greater." He'd quickly downed one followed by the second and then he'd picked up a third.

"Do you mind Laddie?"

I'm starting to worry that table one two eight might lose its appeal.

Today was the first sea day after Rio and it was time to make good on a promise I'd made to my dear lady.

We're going to learn to dance.

There are a couple of ex-professionals offering classes for beginners in the mornings and improvers in the afternoons. So we'd set off this morning to join the beginners, hoping that at least one of the other participating guests would have a terrible sense of coordination, at least enough to deflect the attention away from me.

This morning's lesson was the Waltz, the most popular of the ballroom dances and supposedly one of the easiest to learn (I'm sure it is, but I can disprove any theory)

At first the instructors gave a demonstration of this elegantly smooth classic, then lined us all up to learn the basic steps.

For nearly an hour the group gently rocked backwards and forwards as we'd learnt 'Right forward, side, together, left forward, side together', and for a moment or two things were going well.

As a finale to the lesson we were told to find a space on the floor, concentrate on the rhythm of the music and dance.

"Just have a go," they'd told us. "Don't worry if you're doing it right or wrong."

So everybody did just that.

One couple charged straight across the dance floor so enthusiastically that they forgot to stop when they'd reached the other side. Others managed to bump into just about everything in their attempt to lift the 'Championship Trophy' they'd obviously thought they were competing for.

It was utter carnage, but also very funny.

As for my dear lady, she's absolutely loving it. It's fair to say that she's extremely graceful and agile, but unfortunately has a sense of timing that makes no sense whatsoever. Even worse is she doesn't realise it, but my pride (and toes) are just going to have to suffer for the cause.

Anything to keep her this happy.

And the song for the rest of the day?

Well obviously for her it was 'Dancing Queen' while I silently whistled 'Dancing with tears in my eyes'.

As we were waltzing this morning my dear lady had missed her art class. So she'd gone to the afternoon session instead, leaving me to laze away the afternoon in the sun, which would have been wonderful but for the 'Watchers'.

It had been lovely and quiet on the lido deck for most of the afternoon, but the peace was shattered as 'Watchers' had started to gather nearby.

It would appear their numbers have grown from an initial group of around eight of them to more of a throng of nearly twenty. Most of them are dressed in some form of jungle camouflage clothing, a bit pointless as they stand out a mile on a ship painted white and surrounded by nearly naked people in brightly coloured swimwear.

But it would appear they're being organised.

"Can we settle down please," a voice declared above the growing din. "And we'll get this meeting underway."

Hang on a minute, I know that voice. It was our new table companion, Norma.

I really didn't want to sit through another session of her grating tones, but at the same time I was intrigued at what lengths she would go to in order to be the centre of attention.

For over an hour she'd lorded it over her minions, but unlike table one two eight her audience was spellbound. She organised a committee, issued a suggested rota system, detailed a recording process and introduced a scheme to share information.

I was starting to wonder if she was really interested in wildlife, or total world domination.

There's was just too much to note here, but then her final act of the get together was to issue a set of 'safeguarding' rules for the members.

So it's total world domination after all then.

I'm expecting them to be wearing uniforms and flying their own flag within a matter of days. But I'll not be asking Norma to detail her plans and aspirations for her newly founded organisation over dinner, Jeff would kill me.

I went to the gym as usual this evening and had to turn the lights on when I got there. Once again there was nobody about.

I'm really grateful Norma's interests lie with the 'Watchers' and she's not a fitness fanatic.

Tuesday 12th February

Day 36 'at sea' - no one's dead yet.

I haven't made any comment about last night's meal and I'm not intending to, because when I look back through this in the future I would like to remember the good things about the people we've met and forget their faults.

I admit I may not be able to maintain this stance with regard to a certain individual, but for now I'll bite what's left of my tongue.

Another lovely day outside, but we were off to dance classes again this morning. After a quick recap of the waltz we were treated to some good old fashioned seventies disco music, and the instructors told us to try and recapture some of our uninhibited youth.

"Let yourselves go," they'd said.

"Feel the music flowing and move with it," they'd said.

"Try to impress your partner like the first time you met them," they'd said.

"Can someone go and fetch the doctor for Mr Smart," they'd pleaded.

Turns out that Mr Smart had tried to impress his future wife back in 1963 by doing the splits.

It has started raining this afternoon, so while my dear lady is at art I'm writing up my journal. I'm sitting in the reception area, hoping for some inspiration to show up.

I've discovered something quite unusual and a touch disturbing this morning. Apparently the staff are amazed that we are now over five weeks into this 'Voyage of Discovery' and yet not a single passenger has left this mortal coil to roam pastures new in the afterlife.

The older member of staff behind the desk was telling his younger, and I'm assuming newer, colleague that on average for a long cruise there is normally at least one passenger who checks out permanently every three or four weeks

We have noticed on several occasions that members of the medical team often walk around the ship during the day and have some very subtle ways of checking on the status of snoozing passengers.

Well they may look like they're asleep, but medics are a suspicious lot (or maybe they're hopeful of something to do, who knows)

They're a bit like traffic wardens as they'll walk the same route several times, taking note of any stationary objects, especially those which look a little dishevelled and worn out. If the object in their sights fails to move in the allotted time they'll hang about and take a closer look, trying to see if the tax has expired. They may even phone reception to check up on insurance matters.

If their potential victim is still unmoved, they'll get closer to see if they can hear the engine running, and as a final resort they kick the tyres.

Fortunately, from what I've seen so far, the owners are just hiding on the back seat, and following an apology for the disturbance the guardians hurry away.

Anyway, back to the conversation in reception, and apparently the crew have opened a book on the demise of the first guest.

Not on who, but how!

'Suffering a cardiac arrest after discovering a real bargain in the shops' is favourite at 2/1

'A fatal seizure brought on after being startled by a photog' is a fair price at 3/1, while

'An unnaturally horrific end in the laundry' is worth a gamble at 15/1

From what I've heard that is a real possibility.

'Over exertion in the gym' is at 25/1

The gym will be empty this evening as I intend to reconsider my exercise regime.

'Frying to death on the lido deck' is long at 50/1

This is only because most guests are already acclimatised and no surprises are expected.

There are however excellent odds on 'Being bored to death at dinner' at 100/1

I'm sure they wouldn't offer this price if they knew a certain member of table one two eight, who has recently been voted 'Most Uninteresting Person

Ever' following last night's full and frank rendition of 'I've travelled the world by steam train' followed closely by 'Interesting railway carriage smells around the globe'. (Sorry, I knew my resolve wouldn't last long)

The medical department have been excluded from taking part as it is believed they have access to certain inside information. It is also considered they may try to make a last minute killing (but not literally) by unfairly driving up the odds on 'by natural causes'.

Historically passengers were allowed to join in and place proxy bets through a member of the crew, but following a spate of highly unusual and unexplained deaths on a previous cruise, this privilege has now been withdrawn.

A bit of nonsense I know, and here's a bit more inspired by the topic of dying.

I hope to die a young man's death.
Still in my prime and feeling fine,
Not weak and over toiled.
Just quick and clean, not in between
White sheets, confused and soiled.

I hope to die a brave man's death.
A hero me with city key,
Admired for selfless part.
Senility, please not for me,
That's no way to depart.

I hope I keep my youthful looks.
My manhood straight, still working great,
Not limp and shrivelled bits.
Big ears, big nose, I don't want those,
Nor skin that barely fits.

I want the right to choose my fate.
Don't want a fuss, hop on that bus,
Depart for place unknown.
Heaven? Hell? It's hard to tell,
As long as it's like home.

I know I really ask too much.
And have no say at end of day
The way my life is shoved.
But I'll stand tall and face it all,
Because I know I'm loved.

My dear lady says she quite likes that one and it's prompted a really nice rendition of 'When I'm sixty four'.

It's just a shame she's chosen dancing lessons over joining the choir.

Not wishing to tempt fate, or make anyone a pile of cash in the sweep stake, I didn't go to the gym this evening.

They may clean up tonight though as we're just off to be bored to death at dinner, but apparently the odds have shortened. There's been a late surge of big money placed by a certain pair of waiters we know.

Montevideo tomorrow, I'm starting to wish it were Lima, but really I mustn't do that.

Wednesday 13th February

Day 37 'Montevideo' - we'll 'meat' again.

Uruguay, one of the smallest countries in South America but home to a never ending supply of beef (or so they claim)

Again we're berthed in a very large commercial port and the only thing we can see from the ship is wall to wall containers. We're one of three cruise ships in port today so it could get a bit busy.

We also have an overnight stay here, so part of today's mission was to find somewhere nice to eat this evening, and hopefully sample the delights of some local culture.

My dear lady says that it's highly unlikely I'll find a local beer called culture.

Last night Jeff had asked me if he and Pru could tag along with us today as apparently he gets to drink more beer if he's with me.

What's he trying to say?

So, my dear lady is possibly right about my growing reputation then, but she must never be allowed to find out. I told Jeff they were welcome to spend the day with us on the understanding that he never repeats the bit about 'him getting more beer' ever again.

He agreed, which is great because what he doesn't realise is that I've been using him as an excuse to get more beer since Barbados.

Seems like we're both onto a winner.

There are several walking routes around the city, so with bellies full of breakfast (minute steaks no less) we'd set off. Fighting through a gaggle of taxi and tour operators we made it safely to the port gates and are greeted with our first encounter of this city.

There are no real surprises because it seems just like any other big city port area, a concrete jungle with its pavement cafes, street artists and vendors selling everything from shirts to sweets.

I know, I know, what else was I expecting?

Well again I'm not quite sure, but sometimes the imagination paints a much brighter picture than what the eyes see in reality.

Thoughts of gauchos riding their trusty steeds across the sun-baked savannah had conjured up images of the real Wild West in my mind.

A dusty shanty town with horses tied up next to a wooden water trough. Suddenly a punch is thrown and a body crashes through the 'saloon' window.

Sadly, no.

Instead I had to settle for two kids riding along the pavement on trail bikes delivering pizzas.

Some friendly officials from the tourist office were handing out city maps, which detailed the walking route and highlighted the main attractions. It was suggested that the route set out in the map should be strictly adhered to for our safety.

As we'd set off, this concern for our wellbeing was backed up by a large presence of heavily armed police officers, who were hanging around the area in gangs. It was noticeable that if anyone looking remotely like a tourist tried to walk off the designated route, the officers would block their way and strongly encourage them to reconsider their actions.

Obviously, you weren't allowed to argue.

Parts of the area are a bit scruffy but in general this end of the town appears to be serviced by a large number of street cleaners and kept tidy.

The walking trail starts by the port and at first takes you through a largish area of outdoor stalls and vendors selling souvenirs (what else would you expect to find in a port full of tourists?)

On the far side of this is what looks like an old railway engine or tram shed. This fine building has seen much better days, but has the appearance of an old Victorian construction with beautifully intricate lattice ironwork supporting the outer skin of corrugated steel.

Around the outside are a number of restaurants specialising in barbequed meat dishes and the smoke and smell from the wood burning ovens combine to form an acrid haze which catches at the back of the throat and stings the eyes.

But above all of that is the wonderful aroma of cooking meat, huge slabs of the stuff, not quite a whole beef carcass, but not far off. There are sausages the size of a small rugby ball and enormous quantities of chicken. These grills are also repeated inside the building, along with a whole range of market stalls to browse around.

Through the lingering fog there was another treat in store, an ornate clock right in the middle of the building, again very Victorian, and looking like it hasn't been cleaned since Victoria reigned.

What a treat, but the smoke inside really does start to choke, so it was time to move on.

There have been a number of warnings from the ships medical team not to eat food from street vendors or even some of the more seemingly established restaurants. They'd suggested that they don't adhere to stringent hygiene regulations here in South America like we do back home.

Stuff that, the meat here looks and smells fabulous and I'm not sure any bugs could survive the roaring heat of those barbeques, so we'll definitely be back later.

Hopefully we'll be able to eat outside though.

We'd ambled through the streets of Ciudad Vieja, the old town, and marvelled at the art deco buildings and colonial houses. Passing through a couple of small but perfectly formed plazas, resplendent with statues of the revered founding fathers and lots of trees etc, we continued on to the main area of the city.

When we reached Plaza Constitution, near to the cathedral, we were surprised to see what can only be described as an open-air table top sale.

This was junk on an enormous scale and it would take far too much time to list a fraction of the stuff on offer. There were lots of cracked tableware and rusty old kitchen knickknacks, not to mention old number plates, branding irons, toys, cameras, photographs and even old glasses without the lenses.

We've probably thrown the exact same rubbish out of our houses years ago and yet we meandered from table to table pointing out old familiar items and smiling about the happy memories they bought to mind.

What a sad bunch we must have looked, having travelled ten thousand miles to see the world and we end up in a flea market. But it was great fun and very interesting to see this old and apparently useless stuff being possibly given another lease of life. One man's junk is another man's treasure and all that.

Anyway, onward and upward to Plaza Independencia.

This impressive square is home to the mausoleum of Artigas, a national hero.

It's a very imposing structure with its own dedicated guardians, who incidentally don't like anyone sitting on the monument steps. You're also told 'No pisar el cesped' by hundreds of signs planted in the grass, but we had no idea what it meant so we were careful not to do anything to upset the guardians.

Surrounding the square are some of the more important and impressive building of the city, Palacio Salvo, the Solis Theatre and the Palacio Estevez where the president works.

Unfortunately none of these appear to be open or visitable, so we carry on up the Avenue 18 Julio, the main route through the city.

Next we visited the gaucho museum, full of too many wonderful things to delight, and it was just incredible to see how decoratively they dressed their horses.

After an hour wandering around the exhibits, Jeff could stand it no longer.

"Is it time for beer yet Laddie?" he'd whispered.

Sounds like a great idea.

We headed back towards the cathedral where there were a number of pavement bars around the square which appeared to be quite popular.

We sat ourselves firmly outside one of the bars and with a surprisingly feeble grasp of the Spanish language they speak here we ordered,

"Quadro beers, per favore."

It's amazing how we lazy Brits get away with our ignorance and expect the rest world to speak English, but at least the word beer is usually understood in any language, and thank goodness for fingers, that allows everybody to get drunk anywhere on the planet.

But our server obviously had an idea to teach us the correct phrase.

"Cuatro cervezas por favour," he enunciated slowly.

Like shiny faced school children the four of us repeated it back to him in unison.

All four beers arrived in huge dimpled jugs, so no refinement for the ladies, but it was cold and refreshing as only a good beer can be.

The smile on Jeff's face was enormous (I think mine was too)

At this point a meal of steak and chips arrived at the next table.

There was a silence between us so heavy you could still hear the steak sizzling on the plate. It was really thick and as the juices glistened in the sunlight Jeff wiped a tear from his eye and we all started to drool at the sight and smell of this amazing, once in a lifetime moment.

Even confirmed vegetarian Pru exclaimed, "That looks delicious."

We just had to do it.

We couldn't sit and salivate over someone else's happiness, we had to get our own personal invitation to a sense sensation, not only to smell the wonderful aromas, but to see it as our own and know we were about to taste the flavours, feel the texture, hear our very own sizzle.

Well three of us had to, and for just one moment Pru looked torn, almost in agony as her principles wrestled with her tortured senses.

"Have one if you want," Jeff told her.

He'd turned to us and explained that she wasn't a vegetarian out of conviction, she just didn't like the texture of meat or fish.

"Quite often at home I enjoy a plate of veg and proper meat juice gravy," Pru said, "And I am really tempted, but I'd prefer to know if there's an alternative."

There wasn't a menu as such, but my dear lady had found a small card showing pictures of various sizes of steak and chips.

"Seems you can have anything, as long as it's steak."

Pru beckoned our server. "Let's hope his English is better than my Spanish," she'd said.

"Do you have any dishes without meat?"

"No meat?" he looked uncertain and his broad smile disappeared.

It's quite possible that asking for 'no meat' here is a bit like a slap in the face, or he had absolutely no clue about what Pru was saying.

"Yes, no meat. What have you got without meat in it?"

"No meat?" he'd repeated, looking even more pained.

This is the land of the gaucho, herding his prized beef cattle across the dusty plains as far as the eye can see. Maybe they have no concept (or sympathy) for the needs of those having chosen to abstain from eating the flesh of animals. Along with the injury to his national pride you can imagine the utter turmoil he was suffering.

"Chicken, we have chicken," he'd said.

"No not chicken."

"Not chicken? Hmm how about ham?"

"No sorry, not ham either."

"Not ham? Hmm how about pasta with sauce then?"

"Yes pasta is good, what is in the sauce?"

"Very nice sauce, no meat"

"No meat?"

"Yes, no meat just duck."

"But duck is meat."

"Nooooo....Duck is duck, duck not meat."

"No not duck."

"Not duck? Hmm difficult."

I admit I've just made this conversation appear very straightforward, but in reality it was conducted by four very animated Brits with no grasp of Spanish and a Uruguayan imitating various farmyard animals along with vigorous shaking or nodding of heads.

So the conversation actually went something like this.

"Do you have any dishes without meat?" Pru had asked.

"No meat?" the waiter repeated her words but looked confused.

"I think the word for meat is carne," my dear lady had offered, studying the menu card in her hand. "No carne," she said, shaking her head.

"Ahh, sin carne...mean no meat...entiendo."

"Si...sin carne."

"Bueno," the waiter said and started flapping his arms. "Pollo...err cluck cluck."

"No no," Pru shook her head, "No cluck cluck."

"Sin pollo?" a scratch of the head, a light comes on. "Cerdo...err oink oink."

"No no," Pru shook her head, "No oink oink."

Pasta and sauce was his next offer, but his attempt to make us understand had been without success, so he'd run into the kitchen and returned with a plate of food.

"Sin carne," he'd said, "Muy bien, muy bien."

"No cluck cluck?" Pru asked, wanting to be sure

they'd understood each other.

"Sin cluck cluck." He shook his head.

"No oink oink?"

"Sin oink oink."

Pru held her hands up and shrugged her shoulders. "What's in it then...que?"

"Sin carne, pato, pato...err quack quack."

"No no," Pru shook her head, "Quack quack is carne."

"Noooo...pato no carne, pato es pato." Poor guy he looked worn out.

"No quack quack." Pru emphasised.

"Hmm, dificile,"

Jeff had nudged me and whispered that I should look at the waiter's badge, his name was Manuel.

Then Pru had said just one word, "Pizza?"

Manuel smiled, "Pizza, sin carne, si, si," and raced off to the kitchen.

"You do realise we haven't even ordered those steaks yet Laddie, and I'm ready for another beer. Any other takers?"

Unfortunately Manuel returned with bad news, the pizza oven was broken or the pizza chef was ill, or dead, or some other excuse we didn't understand. But he did say that chef had agreed to make ravioli stuffed with spinach and covered with a creamy mushroom sauce. In reality we hadn't got a clue what he'd said but when her meal arrived that's what Pru got.

She said it was lovely, made better when Jeff allowed her to dip her chips in his meat juice when they'd arrived. The steaks were as good as our imagination had created them. They were melt in the mouth, wonderfully juicy, thick and tender, all washed down with another couple of rounds of beer.

Enough said, so all ended well.

Best of all though was the price, at around twelve US dollars each for a huge juicy steak and chips and the beer was only two dollars a pint.

We'd sat for quite a while enjoying the usual pastime of people watching, and Jeff and I drank a few more beers while the ladies went and had a look around the cathedral.

When we'd finally decided to make a move we headed back towards the port, where the other two left us to go back to the ship. My dear lady and I had another look around the market stalls in the engine shed and bought a couple of t-shirts, a picture by a local artist and some delicious cakes to eat later.

We've discovered a place to eat tonight as well, which is only just over the road from the port. Understandably, Jeff and Pru have decided not to join us after the earlier events. Pru reckons we'd all starve to death trying to sort out something for her to eat.

All in all a very good day and to be fair to this city it felt quite safe. There was certainly none of the usual 'buy my tat' hassle from the vendors and we didn't encounter a single beggar.

We're off to eat then.

Let's see what a night on the town, and tomorrow brings.

Thursday 14th February

Day 38 'Montevideo' - and it's Valentine's Day

Last night's meal was great, maybe a little on the meaty side for my dear lady, but I loved it. Massive chunks of different meats were brought to our table on sword like skewers, where the passador (I think that's what they called him) carved off as much as you wanted. Everything tasted incredible. But it was strange not to have anything other than meat on our plates.

My dear lady had asked if we could get some vegetables or a salad, which seemed to provide a moment of light humour for our server. Eventually we received an enormous bowl of French fries to accompany the mountain of barbequed meat that was attempting to break the legs of our rickety plastic garden table.

And goodness knows how much wine we drank.

It was a fixed price buffet style meal where everything was included, so we just kept going. We'd arrived at seven and left around ten thirty, and it's fair to say that I think we staggered back to the ship, not because we were drunk but because we were both two stone heavier.

I never realised it was possible to suffer palpitations from eating too much meat.

I do now.

I have to say I was really surprised that there weren't more folk off the ship, but the only others we saw were a group of the staff from the onboard shops and spa.

Anyway, today we caught the 'hop on hop off' tourist bus which does a two and half hour tour of the main highlights of the city.

It was a great option as I was still finding it difficult to walk.

It was a very enjoyable trip which took us through some interesting neighbourhoods as well as around the municipal park and past the national football stadium.

The final section of the ride followed the promenade which runs alongside the River Plate, which looked to be a very good walk, except it would be very exposed on a sunny day like today.

Back at the port my dear lady announced she was hungry and suggested we return to yesterday's lunch venue as she'd really enjoyed the food.

She doesn't gorge herself like I do, and although I still felt replete I didn't want to disappoint her.

It was a very pleasant walk and today there was another street market taking place on the approach to the cathedral to browse around.

We sat down at the same table and Manuel came over.

"Hola Senor, Senora," he laughed, "Sin carne, sin carne."

"Hoy no," my dear lady replied, "Dos filetes de carni es dos cervezas por favour."

I hadn't got a clue what she was saying, or how she'd suddenly learnt to speak Spanish.

He laughed again and went back inside.

They say you should never go to the same place twice as this often spoils a good memory. But I reckon that may not always be true, as today the steaks were twice the size and twice as juicy, proving my dear lady's theory that it's appreciated if you at least try to fit in.

And that was the day, as by the time we'd eaten and walked (staggered) back to the ship it was time to depart.

We had a great time in Uruguay and enjoyed a couple of days filled with pleasant surprises. But once again food and drink has proved to be the highlight of the visit.

Next stop the Falkland Islands and the main focus for this trip...penguins.

My dear lady is already getting so excited at the prospect, and to prove it a certain song by the Pointer Sisters was getting a bit of a work out in the bathroom.

Having missed the gym yesterday I felt I should at least make some sort of effort.

I got changed, walked to the stairway, walked up two flights of stairs, got in the lift, went down two floors and returned to our cabin.

That's enough exercise for today, I'm exhausted.

It's Valentines Night and she doesn't know it yet but I've booked a table for the two of us in the select dining restaurant.

She deserves a treat.

I'm just hoping she's feeling a whole lot hungrier than I am.

Friday 15th February 2013

Day 39 'at sea' - sorry George.

I'm never gonna to eat again
Big fat belly feels so bloated
It's not easy to pretend
I know that I'm a fool
Should've known better than to eat a cow
Lobster soup and roasted chicken
So I'm never gonna eat again
The way I did with you

I'd booked last night's meal a couple of weeks

back as a surprise, but I'd failed to notice they were putting on a special menu for Valentines Night.

It was very nice though, all seven courses of it, with a glass of specially selected wine with each course.

There were delicious pre-dinner cocktails and canapés as well.

Oh joy.

Seriously, I couldn't bend down to take off my socks last night, and my dear lady refused any help to get undressed, so she slept in her frock.

She was convinced I'd try and take advantage of her in her 'pleasantly inebriated' state.

I couldn't even say 'advantage' after all that alcohol, let alone take it.

We finally made it out of the cabin at noon and plonked ourselves down on the first two available sun loungers out on deck.

Lying down was definitely going to be the activity of the day.

I summoned up just enough energy to rub sun screen on my dear lady, but frankly my exposed bits just had to burn.

The topic of conversation we heard during the conscious moments of the afternoon was 'Will we be able to land in the Falklands?'

We're still two days away and yet one couple were already cursing the gods for the maelstrom that must surely be waiting for us just around the corner.

Apparently it's all a matter of probability, according to this self proclaimed expert. He was actually saying that so far we've been fortunate with the good weather and calm seas, but there's no such thing as order in the universe, only chaos.

"So the odds are stacked against us and destiny dictates we're due a change of luck," he'd proclaimed.

"Don't be daft. The Captain said in his noon report that everything is set fair and weather conditions are favourable," a lady insisted.

"But he can't guarantee it," the expert said. "And there's one other factor he hasn't taken into account."

"What?" several voices asked at once, including myself.

"Me and the missus."

Oh no, here we go again...another nutter.

But I was still too full to move, so just had to tough it out and subject myself to the coming nonsense.

He'd droned on relentlessly about their previous cruise catastrophes, mentioning all the places they'd been desperate to visit but were denied access by the forces of nature, who on a mere whim had decided to spoil their fun.

"Despite two previous trips to the Falklands, we've never set foot there," expert stated.

"There are those who believe we're cursed," he'd added as a final offering.

There was an obligatory dramatic pause.

"So you reckon there's a force twelve awaiting our arrival then do you?" someone asked.

Hang on a minute, I knew that nicely cultured voice.

"Most probably," was the reply, "It's all about balance."

"You know in days gone by the best way to regain the favour of the gods and establish balance, as you put it, was to sacrifice the person or persons blighted by the bad luck."

It was Ted.

"Don't you see everyone, we need to make these prophets of doom walk the plank or such like."

"Don't be stupid you old fool," the man protested.

"Oh I see," Ted said. "You can say stupid things but I can't. Stop being so negative and get drunk or something, but don't broadcast your rubbish around these lovely folk trying to have a good time on holiday."

He was actually given a round of applause.

I think I might be starting to like him, well maybe I liked him already.

But I have faith we'll get there. I will not be denied even if I have to swim ashore. My dear lady will see her penguins and nothing else matters for now.

Needless to say we did nothing all day, no dancing, no art, no gym and no dinner either. Hopefully by tomorrow my body may have actually forgiven me.

But l doubt it.

Saturday 16th February 2013

Day 40 'at sea' - will we or won't we part two.

It been noticeably colder today and some wimps have started wandering around in jumpers and fleeces.

The 'Watchers' however are on full alert as certain claims have been made about whales by a 'non-watcher'. The same person had also suggested there were Klingons on the starboard side, but so far neither has been officially spotted.

Talk about gullible.

Thankfully we both felt much better today, although it wasn't safe to venture into our bathroom for several hours last night after certain events.

Dance class was uneventful but fun and I feel we're improving, but probably won't be lifting any trophies soon.

To be honest there's nothing special going on.

There's a talk from a high profile ex-politician this afternoon, who is onboard as a guest speaker to promote his new book about his time in Parliament. His wife, who apparently has written a couple of racy novels, is with him and she'll be giving a talk at another time, probably to promote her latest scribbling.

I hope she realises she could end up increasing the workload of the medical team if she stirs up too many suppressed fantasies among the attendees.

Let's not even think about that.

The ship's Theatre Company are also back onboard, although why they left in the first place isn't clear, we certainly never noticed they'd gone.

And there's a 50% off sale in the shops.

Like I said, nothing special going on.

So I've been sitting in my usual place near to the reception area trying to catch snippets of conversations to inspire today's musings, but the only topic of discussion still appears to be 'will we or wont we?'

Who started these rumours?

There's a lady sitting nearby who claims to be a medium. She certainly looks the part in a multicoloured, full length caftan and exceptionally wild hair.

Although, how she manages to walk with all the beads around her neck is anyone's guess.

I overheard her conversation with one of the boutique staff, and she was claiming to have been reliably informed by her spirit guide that maybe we will definitely get ashore if the weather is good, but she's almost probably certain that there's a possibility we won't if we don't, but maybe we might.

Further questioning has revealed the lady's spirit guide used to be a politician so she was asked to submit this message to the onboard speaker for interpretation as he hails from the same profession.

After careful consideration, the once former member of parliament assured anyone prepared to listen that in all probability there's a reasonable possibility that we could consider almost certain achievability of our aspirations, unless of course there's a probability we could not recognise the almost certainty of a non probable possibility.

He then commended this possibility to the house and went for a lie down.

And if you thought that last statement was confusing and a little bit silly you should listen to some of the actual rubbish being spouted.

Watch this space, all will be revealed.

Dinner was a bit awkward tonight.

No, make that awkward for some, but a whole heap of payback for others.

My dear lady and I have been absent from table one two eight for the past three nights and we hadn't really seen much of Jeff and Pru since our lunch together in Montevideo either.

Tonight we'd met up with them for pre-dinner drinkies, to catch up with any news or gossip.

We hadn't been with them long before they'd told us how bad things had become on our table, with a certain person not only dominating conversation but completely taking over everything.

Pru said that two nights ago Norma had insisted that our waiters should bring their main course immediately after the starters, as she and Barry could never get a decent seat in the theatre.

"Everybody always takes too much time eating their meal," she'd said.

But the lads had insisted they couldn't do that because they're not supposed to bring the next course until everyone else on the table had finished and was ready.

She'd actually told them to do as they were told.

"I told her that I wasn't going to rush my meal."

Jeff joined in the story telling, he was obviously seething. "Besides which we'd ordered soup as well, as had Derek and Pat and the other two."

He turned to Pru, "I still can't remember their names. In fact I'm not sure they've ever told us."

"It's Linda and Mike dear, they did tell us on their first night, but they've hardly had chance to speak since."

"We've named her the 'Vinegar Witch', laddie."

"Yes dear, but don't say it so loud."

Pru hushed him. "Anyway, it ended up with the Maitre d coming over at her insistence to instruct our waiters to serve the two of them as they wanted, without any delays."

"Well that's good," my dear lady said, "It means they'll rush off and we can enjoy the rest of the evening in peace."

"If only." Jeff finished his whiskey and ordered another. "Laddie?"

Pru continued the story while Jeff shredded a beer mat.

"Then, last night things got even worse. We were the first to arrive at the table and sat down. When Norma arrived she kicked off big time because we were sitting in her seat, the one she's been in every night since they'd joined the cruise. She wanted it back'."

"I wanted to throttle her there and then, but Pru didn't want a fuss, so we moved further round the table."

"Derek and Pat had tried to explain to Norma that before Rio the members of the table had moved around each night, giving everyone the chance to get to know each other, rather than just talking to same person all the time. Her reply had been a simple 'that doesn't work for me, this is my seat'."

Just then, Derek and Pat had turned up and joined us, and talk turned to what we should do about the 'vinegar-witch'.

I told them there was no point in challenging her, as she probably the type that thrives on confrontation anyway.

"So how about we have some fun and defy her instead," my dear lady asked.

"How?"

"By just being ourselves, rather than what she wants us to be. Let's not descend to her level, but rather get back to having the fun we've shared so far."

With that we'd headed off for dinner, late of

course.

I don't think any one of use could have predicted what would greet us.

Linda and Mike were already at the table but had decided to wait for everybody else to arrive. Norma and Barry were already tucking into their starters, but that wasn't the issue.

Norma put down her cutlery.

"Good evening," she'd said, spitting food everywhere. "After last night's confusion, please take note of the seating arrangements I've made."

She pointed to the little cards neatly standing by each set of cutlery.

Place cards, each with a name neatly displayed.

I could hear Jeff winding up, but I didn't want him to burst.

"Hey Jeff," I called over holding up the card with his name on it. "Can I be you tonight and you can be me."

Jeff quickly got the idea.

"That sounds fun Laddie, but I really fancy being your dear lady instead."

For a minute or so we'd loudly sorted ourselves out. Jeff indeed became my dear lady while she took on the role of Derek, who took my seat. I sat by Pat who had swapped identities with Pru.

We'd just settled down when Linda and Mike asked if they were allowed to join in.

"Absolutely," was the reply, so we'd all stood up and musicless chairs started again.

So they are fun after all, and the rest of the restaurant must have thought us mad, or drunk, or both.

When our waiter had taken my order there was a

very quiet, "Nice one, Sir."

I have to say I didn't notice Norma's reaction, and neither did I care because they'd quickly finished their meal and disappeared without another word.

We, on the other hand had a fabulous evening, and I have to say Linda and Mike are good fun. I'm couldn't be happier that it's the other two getting off in Lima.

One two eight went to the bar after dinner and my dear lady asked the DJ to play 'In my Chair' by Status Quo', followed by 'Move it'.

She's such a wit.

Sunday 17th February

Day 41 'Port Stanley' - don't slate Maggie.

Yay, we made it, take that all you doubters.

A bright crisp morning greeted us as we dropped anchor in the pretty bay around the corner from the harbour.

My dear lady and I had made an effort to be up and about early to enjoy the sail in, then had a leisurely breakfast outside on the aft deck overlooking Port Stanley.

We were one of the first groups off as we'd booked a Bluff Cove tour and it was easy to see my dear lady's excitement as we boarded the tender for the twenty minute ride to this long awaited destination to visit penguins.

Unfortunately our first encounter of this magnificently cute creature was a total anticlimax. As we'd stepped ashore we we're greeted on the pontoon by the 'anything for a photo opportunity' ships photographer, resplendent in a comedy penguin suit, complete with a sparkling red bow tie.

Trust them to cheapen the experience.

Anyway, we boarded our minibus, which took us through the town to a meeting point a few miles out into the countryside. On the way the young local driver explained some of the islands heritage and culture, with many suggestions on how we should spend our time in this magnificent location.

Unsurprisingly, it didn't take him long to get into a bit of 'Argy bashing' with tales of the conflict and its aftermath. It's a serious matter but he managed to keep it light-hearted with stories of cows being blown up by undiscovered mines.

It was all very entertaining, but maybe not for the cows.

The mood in the minibus was buoyant, so by the time we'd reached the changeover point everyone was in high spirits, including my dear lady who was more interested in how long it was going to take to get to Bluff Cove rather than hearing any more tales of exploding cattle.

Waiting for us at the side of the road were a group of well worn Land Rovers, ready to transport us in groups of four using the only route there was to reach our destination, across open land.

As most of the others already seem to be paired up we were left with a couple who'd obviously come prepared for anything. They were dressed in matching waterproof jackets and trousers, big heavy boots with gators and each sported a backpack stuffed, we'd assumed, with all the latest survival gear, maps, food, hot drinks etc.

The finishing touch was identical bobble hats perched on their heads like Walnut Whips, and I'd started to wonder if my dear lady and I had actually come a trifle under prepared.

But the reassurance that everything would be okay came from our broad shouldered driver, dressed only in a t-shirt and pair of shorts.

He'd greeted us with a vice-like hand shake.

"Hey you guys I'm Bear, welcome to the best tour on the island."

His name suited him. Beneath an unkempt bushy beard was a broad grin, which seemed to fade a little as he moved his attention to the 'wilderness explorers'.

"Not sure you'll need all that gear, unless the Argys decide to come back in the next hour or two," he chuckled.

His accent had a light southern hemisphere twang, not as pronounced as South African but a bit lighter than Australian. But it was totally different to the minibus driver's intonation, which sounded like he was from London. Unfortunately one of our party of four had noticed this and posed the question.

"So are you an Aussie?" asked the hapless hiker. "That accent's not local."

"I'm a bloody eighth generation islander mate, my family have been here for nearly two hundred years."

I thought I actually saw his beard bristle.

"Now get in, we need to get going."

The hiker reached for the front passenger door handle, but Bear had other ideas.

"No room for all that kit in the front mate, get in the back and keep it on your lap."

He turned to my dear lady and his smile was back.

"Here," he opened the door, "You and your bloke can sit up front with me, better view."

I made a note not to upset him, for now it appeared we were his favourites.

Setting off we'd quickly left the road, almost sliding sideways down a short steep bank as we'd started lurching quite violently across the rough terrain towards the horizon.

So that's why the brochure had stated this tour was not recommended for people with back or neck problems.

Bear told us his Land Rover would go anywhere, but the ride would get a bit bumpy.

"Especially in the back," he'd called over his shoulder. "Been having a bit of trouble with the rear suspension just lately. Too many people loading her up with unnecessary shit."

I don't think they'd got off on the right foot somehow.

The half hour drive over the peat bog terrain was great fun with non-stop commentary from Bear about the island, his childhood memories of the invasion, the meaning of life and everything else in between. It was informative and highly amusing, as was the continuing sarcasm aimed squarely at our fellow travellers in the back.

"So what have you got in those bags then?" he'd shouted over the Landy's noisy engine. "Because if you don't have a mine detector in there it's probably best you don't go hiking around here."

We were met at Bluff Cove by the penguin wardens and once briefed on what not to do, which included not trying to steal one of the little critters, we'd headed off toward the smell, an unmistakable whiff of rotten fish.

The penguins, mainly Gento with a handful of the large Kings, were gathered in their hundreds around a grassy bank just above the sands of the beach.

It's quite difficult to describe the scene as there was so much going on, but these penguins have much different characteristics from what I can remember of their captive cousins, and they have a lot more room to do their thing.

They pose and strut, sway and interact in exactly the same way as the animators depicted them in 'Happy Feet'. They all seem to have individual personalities, most are shy but some are very inquisitive and one even tried to follow us when we'd walked away.

Down on the beach they were playing in the surf, standing around in groups preening themselves or just posing. We spent a happy hour watching their antics, took lots of photos and then headed for tea and cakes in the 'Sea Cabbage Café' which seemingly only opens for business when there are tourists in town, or should I say 'on the beach'.

It is miles from anywhere after all and more than just off the beaten track.

A look around the neighbouring Bluff Cove museum took a few minutes as it's only the size of a big shed, followed by the acquisition of souvenir postcards for the folk back home.

The time had come to say our goodbyes to the penguins and set off for the drive back to the minibus drop off point.

Hostilities were about to resume with a vengeance.

It's an unmistakable fact that Margaret Thatcher

has a certain reputation here.

There are roads and public buildings named after her, portraits of her are hung around the town and she'd been mentioned a couple of times by both of our drivers, seemingly with respect.

One could assume they liked her...a lot.

But somehow this fact had wandered unmolested through the mind of the idiot in the back of Bear's precious Landy. He might have been trying to make conversation, or maybe he had another agenda. Whatever his motivation he was about to choose the wrong topic.

"I can't understand why you named a road after Maggie Thatcher," he'd chirped. "She bloody well ruined everything she touched."

How stupid can one person be?

Whatever your views of the 'Iron Lady' this was not the place to berate the person who ordered troops to travel several thousand miles across the sea, to fight and potentially die in order to liberate and protect these islands from the Argentinian invasion.

Including the young lad known as Bear.

I literally held my breath as my dear lady tightened her grip on my hand.

"Really?"

Bear's voice had gone up an octave as he suddenly braked.

"You can't understand, then please let me explain."

He swung his large frame out of the Land Rover.

"Out," he'd shouted, as he'd opened the rear door. "You're going to get the opportunity to test out your map reading skills."

"You can't do this, we have a right..."

"Let me give you a friendly piece of advice mate," he'd said calmly as he grabbed the man's backpack and threw it onto the grass.

"Whatever you do, don't go right, you might wander into a minefield."

There was absolutely no point in arguing with this man-mountain, who obviously cared not a jot about the opinions of the passengers he was ejecting from his vehicle.

They got out and we drove off.

Fortunately for them they didn't have to walk after all.

"They'll be picked up by one of the other drivers," Bear told us as we bumped across the terrain.

"You must know I don't do that often," he'd said with a smile at my dear lady.

"I don't blame you after what he said."

"Occasionally we get visitors who think they're being clever or witty and say all sorts of stupid things. They have no respect because they don't bloody well understand what it was like. Even worse, he called me an Aussie. Bloody tourists."

He laughed and started telling us all about the upcoming referendum about the islands remaining a British territory. He reckoned anyone who voted 'no' would probably be sent packing.

Apparently there are a dozen or so Argentinians living on the islands, and they'll definitely be voting to remain.

We were soon back on the minibus for the drive back to Stanley, it was a relief to get out of the bouncy 4x4 and onto the smooth tarmac road.

If none of the folk on the tour had a bad back before, I'm sure some will have one now.

We were driven past the Falklands very own 'boot hill', a collection of single items of footwear left hanging on sticks. There are many stories as to how it came to be, but I liked the one suggesting that if you leave your own boot behind as you depart the islands, you are meant to return.

Back at the harbour and we were ready to go exploring the town, as we needed to build up an appetite for an afternoon tea of local fish and chips, and maybe a beer or two.

Port Stanley's main street is Ross Road, which runs along the harbour front. It's home to the cathedral with its huge whale bone arch, and the white 'clapperboard' style catholic church. There's a post office, town hall, hotel, the Governor's residence and the offices of the local newspaper, which of course is 'The Penguin News.

It is undoubtedly picturesque, impeccably clean and very colourful.

Just off the main street is a school, community centre and sports centre, all occupying one large site. The only vehicles to be seen on the streets are 4x4's and after the trip to Bluff Cove the reason for this is obvious.

There are monuments relating to the conflict, a poignant reminder of the consequences of war for ordinary folk, going about their own business.

The locals were incredibly friendly.

Even the town's old boy, a very fat and lazy fur seal sunning himself on a harbour slipway had given us a well practiced toothy grin as we reached for the camera.

Time for a beer.

We spent an enjoyable if rather cramped hour in The Victory pub as it seemed the entire population of the ship were in there. The fish and chips were great and we just had to indulge in a couple of pints of the local beer 'Rockhopper' which was very good.

After another wander up and down the Ross Road with a visit to see the inside of the cathedral, we'd ended up in the tourist information shop and bought a Falkland Island fleece each for a very reasonable price. They're embroidered with six cute penguins and will certainly afford some serious bragging rights back home.

It was a sad moment when we'd returned to the ship, but we're really grateful that our visit to the Falklands Islands, and it's little dancing critters, has lived up to our every expectation, and more.

As we'd sailed away we carried with us a whole load of new memories, courtesy of the gods who hadn't seen fit to redress the balance of nature after all.

Fortunately we made it to land, but it's true that many don't due to the unpredictable nature of the sea in this remote region.

Did we ever have any doubts?

Of course not, it was meant to be...the Captain had promised.

Monday 18th February

Day 42 'at sea' - fetch my Cape.

What a fantastic day we had yesterday, probably made better by the news last night that Norma and Barry had requested to be moved to first sitting.

Table one two eight was only laid for eight when we'd arrived and the Maitre d had told us that eating so late wasn't suiting their requirements.

Time for more celebrations.

But we didn't waste any time talking about them and we had a lovely evening comparing notes on the different tours we'd all been on in Stanley.

Today has been considerably colder and the sea had decided to remind us that we're heading toward Cape Horn the southernmost tip of Chile's Tierra del Fuego Archipelago.

That hasn't detered my dear lady, who's had a permanent smile on her face since yesterday. She's been going around telling everyone 'Don't worry, be happy'.

Sadly the joy is not being returned as the weather has turned sour, just like many of the faces around the ship.

Now I'm no expert in these matters but I do recall history lessons littered with tales of maritime disasters accredited to wild and unpredictable seas of Cape Horn. I also remember being told that seafarers who survived a trip around The Cape were entitled to wear a gold loop earring as a sign of their bravery.

Anyway, the signs are not good, and half way through this morning's dance class the ship was moving enough for the instructors to finish proceedings early.

By the afternoon there was a ship wide gremlin day in progress and everything seemed to have taken on a persona of mischief. Staff were heard bickering at each other, little bits of the ship were dropping off or not working properly, wind whistled loudly through gaps, loose doors banged out a retreat, and if all that wasn't enough it appears someone is thieving from the boutiques.

At 15.00 hrs the Captain made another apologetic announcement to inform us that we are due to get eight metres of swell off The Cape, with winds in excess of seventy knots. In the interests of comfort and safety he's going to slow the ship down, turn to starboard (hang a right) and make a dash for the Beagle channel and forgo the trip around Cape Horn.

More moans and groans from disgruntled passengers echoed throughout the ship, but in my humble opinion that's much better than listening to the moaning and groaning from disgruntled passengers puking throughout the ship, yak.

Plus I have to ask what is there to see in the middle of the night, surrounded by water?

Maybe the Captain should have announced we'd just passed The Cape instead, then everyone would have been satisfied, who could have proved otherwise.

There'd certainly be nobody out there selling Cape Horn t-shirts or souvenirs.

This whole incident also goes to prove, once again, that most people never listen.

The Captain had detailed in his message that this bad weather system is travelling from the southwest and due to reach the Cape Horn region at about 19.00 hrs this evening, around the same time that we would have arrived in the area, travelling from the other direction.

At the time of his announcement we were still about a hundred miles north of The Cape and the approaching storm, but within minutes there were the usual bunch of experts gazing out of the windows and calling the Captain's decision unnecessarily cautious.

The following comments were actually made.

"Those waves aren't too bad, I've been through much worse." (no doubt in the bath tub)

"They have no spirit of adventure anymore and put safety before what the passengers want." (and long may they continue to do so)

"I live on the coast and I've seen much worse than this back in the English Channel." (probably while watching the evening news from the comfort of your living room)

"These modern captains have no balls." (and if anything went wrong you'd want them served on a silver platter with a large side order of compensation)

I would love to gather all these folk together, put them on a lifeboat (sorry, survival craft) and send them chugging towards The Cape at 19.00 hrs tonight; I think that might sort the idiots from the experts.

Of course the only problem is that because we'll avoid the worst of the weather, the moaners will not be able to experience anything that justifies the Captain's decision.

Poor bloke, he can never win only apologise.

So, all activities have been cancelled, the decks, pools and the gym are shut and for safety reasons they've also closed the boutiques and spa. Even the photogs are nowhere to be seen and the bars have packed away everything that's breakable.

As the ship began to bounce and shudder more, most folk have headed off to their beds for a lie down, believing things probably won't improve until we reach Chile. My dear lady has also gone back to the cabin, seizing the opportunity of a free afternoon to go through the photos we've taken, hoping to find something to paint.

Surprisingly, I'm feeling fine, except maybe a little frustrated there's nothing to do. So I'm sat here in the main bar, on my own, with a pint of beer in a plastic mug, desperately seeking inspiration for something to write. I've enjoyed composing some of the little ditties I've written (I refuse to call them poems because only clever folk write them)

Now I find it quite interesting that whenever I try to think of something to write I can't, and at other times there are good ideas in my head but I can't commit them to paper fast enough.

Surrounded as I am at this moment with all the wonder and power of nature on display, the fragility of life and the resolve of man etc, all I can think of is this.

Where are you inspiration?
You are such a fickle friend.
Sometimes you overwhelm me
With ideas that have no end.
Yet another day you taunt me
And impart so many lies,
Then you promise me an insight
But deliver nothing wise.

Why won't the words come freely?
I am stumped, with no idea.
I implore you Inspiration
Come quick, I'm over here.
Give me mountains not a molehill,
Barren mind is not for me

Reignite imagination
Liberated, running free.
Don't ignore my desperation
On my knees do I implore.
So please help me Inspiration
Come and feed my mind once more.

Well that kept me occupied for a few minutes, now what shall I do?

Hmm, the weather's definitely getting worse, time for a lie down me thinks.

'Turned North'

Tuesday 19th February

Day 43 'at sea' - he was right, you weren't.

Despite the Captain's attempt to outrun the storm and take shelter in the Beagle Channel, it overtook us then played with us just for fun. For some it was a very rough night.

This morning there were some very strange smells around the ship with a few dark damp patches on the carpets.

I'm still surprised at my own resilience though, and my dear lady and I spent a really nice, and queasy free evening with Jeff and Pru. Admittedly we didn't move about the ship much as once we'd settled in the restaurant it was safer to stay put, which we did until quite late.

As an indication of how bad it was and how much the ship was 'rolling' I must note the following.

We were the only four people on table one two eight.

There weren't many others to be seen in the dining room, and most of those who did turn up didn't stay long.

All the wine glasses on the table fell over and smashed, fortunately they were empty.

The waiters replaced the wine glasses with more stable plastic whiskey tumblers, unfortunately these were also empty.

It took three attempts by our waiters to get whole plates of starters to our table.

The Maitre d treated us to a 'complimentary' bottle of wine, saying that if anyone asked we had to say the one we'd bought had fallen over and was smashed.

The waiters refused to serve soup.

We refused to let the waiters serve soup.

The 'complimentary' bottle of wine fell over and was smashed, thank goodness it didn't make too much of a mess, mainly because it was nearly empty.

The Maitre d replaced it.

The waiters brought a whole selection of main courses out on a trolley.

The trolley ended up somewhere over by table fifty one.

Several plates fell off and were smashed.

They were able to successfully deliver the trolley to table one two eight the second time around.

Jeff got smashed and fell over. Nobody replaced him, much to Pru's annoyance.

I still find it hard to understand why the sound of glass or crockery breaking makes everybody cheer.

There was a lot of cheering going on.

At least in all the kerfuffle no one got injured.

I just love that word...kerfuffle.

When my dear lady and I finally got to bed we'd slept quite soundly and didn't wake too often, except when the wind was howling through the gaps in the patio doors.

This morning everyone is reliving the storm and because most of them are suffering from sleep deprivation they are irritated and annoyed. They lay the blame for their woes squarely on the Captain's shoulders, he steers the ship so therefore he's responsible for putting us into the maelstrom.

I actually heard someone say that they had completed this journey on several occasions and the seas had always been much calmer and flatter on the route they'd taken.

"So why had this Captain taken a different course through rougher seas?"

Fool.

I started to think about the damp patches I'd seen around the ship and wondered if these self centred gits had actually run out of their cabins to throw up in the corridors, knowing someone else would have to clear it up and the smell wouldn't pervade their room.

Anyway, we are now cruising through the calmer waters of the Beagle Channel which leads into the Chilean fjords. We've been told to be on the lookout for penguins, seals and dolphins and we should get to see several small glaciers as we pick our way through these narrowing channels on route to Punta Arenas, our first stop in Chile.

Although the wind had died down, outside it's snowing so only the keen (dressed in light summer clothing) and the 'Watchers' (dressed in full winter survival gear) are out and about on the decks.

My dear lady is eager to see the sights but not enthusiastic enough to freeze her bum off, So we've decided to wait around in the library which overlooks the upper decks. The Captain has said he'll make announcements if anything of interest is spotted from the bridge, and the 'Watchers' make so much fuss over a fin in the water we're bound to see them running into position from up here.

In the meantime I've have something on my mind.

Because it was rough yesterday I'd heard quite a few people saying things like 'they wished we could hurry up to get to the next port' or 'they couldn't wait until it warms up a bit' and even 'if we can just get through the next week or so we can start enjoying the holiday again'.

Admittedly these are throw away comments usually made out of frustration that things aren't as the person would wish them to be, but as we get older shouldn't we value every moment, enjoyable or not,

And I get to thinking, isn't it strange how time gets wished away.

As a child I remember being desperate for certain things to happen and would beg the hours and days to pass quickly. I lived for school holidays, birthdays and Christmas, and nearly everything I'd said began "I just can't wait to be.."

Good idea for a song there I think.

But then that was a time in my life when I had time, and plenty of it so I'd thought.

In middle age I was still impatient, to get home from work, for promotion, to go on holiday, for the kids to leave home and even for things to get better.

But again, rarely did I consider any wish for time passing as a waste, and yet 'doesn't time fly' was a phrase I would use repeatedly.

Then suddenly I found myself at a retirement party...my retirement party, at which one of my long time friends and colleagues was saying how he envied me, and that he couldn't wait to retire. He claimed that when he was finally free from the shackles of employment, there would be so much more time for him to enjoy doing the things he loves doing.

But when he finally leaves work then, just like me, he'll have to contend with the knowledge that another phase of his life has gone, and in fact he will actually have less time to do the things he loves doing.

So with the knowledge obtained through age I would suggest we older folk should spread the word and encourage the young to never wish for the future to hurry up, but rather wait for it patiently instead.

I can't wait to share these wise words with the world.

In the meantime, time is marching on. So I think it's time to call time and take time to consider a better use of my time. In time I may learn the value of time, but there will never be enough time as time is always running out.

Hang on.

I think I've just proved that time gathers speed as we age.

It marches on then runs out.

Anyway, with all this talk of time, I feel another ditty coming on.

I remember the time when I just couldn't wait
For that something quite special to come,
Like parties for birthdays with presents galore,
Or a trip to the beach, such good fun.
But the days passed so slowly it took 'way too long'
For the best bits of life to take place.
So I'd wish for the future to come in a flash,
Not knowing this wasn't a race.

I'm four and free quarters, and that's nearly five
And I'll soon be a big boy, you'll see.
But it's ages till Christmas when Santa brings toys
Hurry up through the snow just for me.
Then I'll go off to school in a blazer too big,
Skin my knees playing football, how sad.
The teachers are boring, terms drag on and on,
It's the worst time that I've ever had.

So I want to grow up, be a man like my Dad,
Learn to drive, get a car, have a smoke.
Go to uni, get drunk, find a girlfriend, have sex,
Take a job, buy a house, that's no joke.
I can't wait to get married, can't wait to have kids,
Oh when will they grow up and leave.
Then it's time for a crisis of midlife and so
I'll get tattoos you'll never believe.
Now my job drives me crazy, can't wait to retire,
Spend my pension on things to impress.
And before my poor body decides to wear out
I'm demanding my share of excess.

Time had no meaning back when we were young
There was plenty ahead so it seemed,
But now that I'm here, looking back on my life
It feels like it's all been a dream.

Do you remember the times when you just couldn't wait
For that something quite special to be?
Were you practiced and careful, your time not to waste?
Or were you impatient like me?
Please don't wish time away it'll pass soon enough
Then you'll wonder just where it all went.
Enjoy every moment no matter how dull,

Each second's not owned, merely lent.

Oh well, that passed a bit of time, and still no sighting for my dear lady to enjoy. But we've just seen the deck crew tying down the chairs and sun loungers, looks like we're in for another rough night, and heavy snow has just started falling again.

My dear lady has just started singing...really?

'Let it snow, Let it snow, Let it snow'.

Snow thanks.

Wednesday 20th February

Day 44 'Punta Arenas' - more penguins? Yes please.

It did get quite rough again last night, but only for a short while, so the evening was pretty much uneventful. At one point Jeff and Mike had suggested we should have a snowball fight out on deck, but after their challenge had been accepted they claimed it would only serve to waste valuable drinking time.

So we didn't bother.

My dear lady claimed they were all mouth and no trousers, which Jeff agreed was correct as he was, in fact, wearing his kilt. He then admitted the real reason he'd changed his mind was because he had no desire to feel the icy wind blowing around his sporran, thus furnishing him with his very own 'snowballs'.

This resulted in a very raucous rendition of 'Jeffery where's yer troosers' from the full ensemble of table one two eight.

By this morning the weather had improved, it was still very cold and breezy when we'd arrived at the port of Punta Arenas, but at least it was dry.

Today we were heading off to Otway Sound, hopefully to see more penguins, specifically 'Magellanic Penguins'.

These are smaller burrowing penguins which spend the breeding season (around this time of year) in Chile then head off to the waters of southern Brazil for the rest of the year. Reports coming back from previous participants of this tour suggest this could be a very good experience, so we'd crossed our fingers and got on the coach.

For the first part of the journey we'd travelled along the Pan American Highway, and annoyingly our guide seemed more interested in telling us stories of the 'carnage and mayhem' left behind by a certain TV trio who like cars, rather than tell us about his beautiful country. Their visit had taken place several years previously but was still a major topic of interest for the locals.

Sad times.

Soon we turned off the main tarmac highway and onto what can only be described as a dirt track. But this, we were told, is the main route between the city and its outlying towns.

Staying on this road for nearly an hour was almost as bone jarring as the trip we'd taken in Bear's trusty Landy, except the suspension on the coach wasn't as forgiving and the seats were harder.

Several bits inside the bus fell off, but it was fun listening to some of the usual moans and groans from our fellow travellers.

When we'd finally arrived at the colony we were told that in the last few days most of the penguins had reared their chicks and had either left, or were preparing to leave.

My dear lady smile had quickly disappeared, replaced by a look of angst, all this way and nothing to see.

The warden had added that there were still a few late hatchlings around, but our only chance to see them was if we remained silent and didn't stamp around the boardwalks.

Fat chance of that from our lot off the ship, quiet is usually impossible so silent would take a miracle.

But it wasn't to be a complete disappointment as we would discover.

A long walk across the site bought us to the beach, and from a viewing platform we were able to see a group of two or three hundred Magellans paddling in the surf. It was possible to make out some of the youngsters practicing their swimming techniques in the shallows.

That had certainly cheered my dear lady up and there was a further moment of excitement as we'd walked quietly around the dunes on the boardwalk on our way back to the coach.

We'd deliberately left the beach last and let the chattering hoards go on ahead, hoping this would give us a better chance of an encounter.

Suddenly a penguin had popped up from its burrow, right in front of us, and stood looking around. Desperately trying not to make a sound and slowly reaching for her camera, my dear lady was in raptures. There within touching distance was this fascinating creature, in its natural environment, seemingly happy to share a moment with two large visitors passing by his home.

She managed to take a few pictures and it even

appeared he was posing for her, turning his head and raising its wings.

Unfortunately, a man in front of us had been keen to find out what we were taking an interest in and was heading back our way. The first we knew about this was when he'd hollered to his wife.

"Quick dear, there's one over here."

Not anymore there wasn't, in a flash our obliging Magellan was gone, probably to warn all his mates of the noisy intruders that were heading their way. We spotted a couple in the distance, racing toward the beach, but after that no more were seen.

Ah well, never mind, at least we could look forward to another hour of fun as our bus disintegrated around us on the journey back.

We made a stop at a rhea farm, a large flightless bird which is the South American relative of ostriches and emus. I'm not sure if we'd stopped to see the farm or to give the driver and the guide time to put the bus back together.

Back in the town we'd headed for the central plaza.

Punta Arenas is a very clean and pretty location, with a lot of development going on both in the centre and along the promenade But there doesn't appear to be a great deal else to see or do and because of the time of year there weren't the usual street cafes and bars to sit and watch the world go by.

There's a monument to Magellan in the plaza and a full sized replica of one of his galleons in the Nao Victoria museum, which wasn't easy to find. There's also a very ornate cemetery to visit on the outskirts of town, but other places of interest like the cathedral and the house of Sarah Braun were closed.

The few cafes that were open weren't very big and most of them were full and turning people away.

It started to rain as well so we headed back to the warmth of the ship and a mug of hot chocolate instead of a beer. Very nice but even more fattening than my usual tipple.

Talking of which, I finally managed to get to the gym this evening, after a whole week of 'overindulgence and laziness' as my dear lady put it.

I know she was only teasing but she's right as I've still been asking for a large portion at mealtimes, but haven't been doing anything to burn off all those extra calories.

When I'd arrived Nadia appeared to be in a hurry to leave and as she'd pushed past me to get to the door it looked like she was trying to conceal something near to her chest.

Ted was there, dressed up in what looked like a weightlifters lycra leotard, still trying his hardest to shift those weights on the 'pull down' machine.

"Hello old chum," he'd called over. It was difficult to miss the fact he was wearing a very bright shade of red lipstick, which he seemed to have clumsily smeared all down his chin.

I didn't say anything though and just a minute or two later he'd left, with a cheery wave.

He looked a bit sweaty though, I hope he's not overdoing it.

All in all a lovely day in our first Chilean port.

My dear lady is ecstatic with the photos of 'her' penguin and she's going to have a go at painting him (or her) tomorrow.

So now we have three sea days during which time we're due to visit two very large impressive glaciers as we slowly make our way north, hopefully to warmer climes. On the way we'll be visiting a couple of the larger towns in the heart of the Chilean fjords as well.

Are we having fun or are we having fun?

Thursday 21st February

Day 45 'at sea' - Amelia Glacier.

We've been cruising through the Chilean fjords all day.

We did go dancing this morning, which was good fun because I managed to plait my feet attempting a quickstep, but other than that we'd spent most of the day just sitting on our cabin balcony and enjoying the views.

The scenery is stunning, with either high tree covered mountains or deeply ridged and glacier scared rocky mountains, all tumbling down to the water's edge. The water is almost mill pond flat and various rich shades of blue, and the reflections shimmer as the ship moves slowly along the narrowing valleys.

There is snow on top of the highest mountains today as we're still a fair distance to the south, but the sun is shining brightly and everything was glistening

We've seen a fair number of different species of wildlife including numerous birds, dolphins, seals and ducks.

Around 15.00 hrs this afternoon we cruised slowly up to the first of two major glaciers in this area and spent a good hour admiring the scenery and experiencing the chill winds blowing in our direction from the ice fields.

The Captain kindly rotated the ship through 360 degrees so everyone could get the best views, and of course take lots of photographs.

I'm feeling a little overwhelmed by it all and don't want to cheapen the experience with any of my usually flippant remarks.

This was far from an ordinary or normal day.

Friday 22nd February

Day 46 'at sea' - Pio X Glacier

Today was almost a rerun of yesterday, with bright sunshine on stunning scenery, words alone just couldn't convey the magnificent sights. It's also getting noticeably warmer.

The second glacier was even bigger and bluer than yesterdays and the Chilean pilots managed to get the ship within half a mile of the ice wall, hoping for a carving, but unfortunately nothing big happened, just a few bits broke away.

It was quite strange looking out over the water with chunks of ice floating around us, but with nothing to compare them with they looked small and not at all dangerous.

The Captain gave permission for the photogs to be taken out on one of the ship's Zodiacs to get some pictures of our ship with the glacier behind.

Now we had a comparison, and the tiny craft appeared dwarfed next to some of the enormous lumps of ice.

Apart from ourselves there's absolutely no sign of human life, the scenery is pristine and there aren't any boats or buildings along the shore line to indicate anybody resides in or around the mountains.

Another very enjoyable day even though it appears we did nothing more than sit and watch the world, and an awful lot of ice, go by.

In the evening we'd met up with the others and were treated to a very large gin and tonic, complete with a lump of glacial ice which had been collected by the crew in the Zodiac.

It was difficult to imagine that as we'd watched it melt we were witnessing the reversal of a process that had formed this piece of ice hundreds, if not thousands of years ago.

My dear lady thinks I should compose something as a tribute to the last two days, I fear however I could barely find the words to acknowledge such splendour. That would be a task for some 'clever' person, far more articulate than I and a mere 'ditty'.

There was a little incident worth reporting which once again clearly indicates that some folk don't pay attention to what's going on around them.

The officer of the watch had made the following announcement over the ship's tannoy.

"For exercise, for exercise, for exercise, man overboard starboard side. Rescue boat crew assemble."

He'd then repeated the same message.

Almost immediately after this the Captain had also made an announcement. He'd apologised (as always) for disturbing our afternoon then explained that the crew were required by Maritime Law to practice for certain possible events. As they would be lowering the Zodiac for the photogs (as per earlier note) they would take the opportunity to practice the rescue of someone in the water.

"In a moment or two the crew will be throwing a member of the ships company from the starboard promenade deck and then executing a rescue. But please don't worry," he'd emphasised. "For the purposes of this drill we use a lifelike mannequin. I repeat we use a lifelike mannequin and not a living breathing person."

Sounds to me like they've had trouble in the past.

Now the masses love something to watch, and of course criticise and mock, so a crowd had quickly gathered at the starboard rail. Unfortunately we weren't far enough away from the melee and the masses weren't being very considerate. One gent pushed his way past a couple sitting nearby and bumped the man quite heavily, so an argument flared up.

Meanwhile at the rail someone had started yelling hysterically.

"They've just thrown that poor man over the side."

"It's a dummy," the lady next to her said.

"It's one of the crew I tell you, look he's wearing a uniform and a life jacket."

"That's okay then, he'll float."

Ah well, at least the pool had emptied, so I went for a swim.

Saturday 23rd February

Day 47 'at sea' - all the ladies love a smart arse

So there you are sitting quietly minding your own business and enjoying the warmth of the sun, now it's finally made an effective appearance, when a large shadow blots out the light and a loud voice asks, "Is this seat taken?" referring to the spare chair next to you.

You politely look up from the book you're reading to inform the unknown enquirer that it isn't 'taken' and they are welcome to use it.

They thank you and sit.

With the obstruction now settled next to you the warmth of the sun is immediately restored, and you return to the complex plot of the indulgent murder mystery you were enjoying.

"Isn't the sun wonderful?" the arrival asks just as you're trying to get your head round a new blood stained clue.

You don't wish to be rude so you answer, "Very."

But you also don't want to perpetuate a conversation so you remain with your head down, eager to avoid eye contact, confident he'll take the hint. But unfortunately the one subject this numpty has no knowledge of is the art of reading body language.

"I lived in Bahrain for three years," he announces. "Forty degrees in the shade, day in day out. Relentless it was."

You sigh and look up from your book. Bad move.

"Really? How interesting." Even worse because now you've offered him an opening.

"I use to play golf out there, well they don't really have golf courses, just sand and greens. I was part of the PGA golf tour once you know."

You have nowhere to go and as you glance around at your fellow travellers with a look of 'Please help me' on you face you have to accept that...

You've been hit by...You've been struck by...
'A Cruise Know It All'

Now luckily this didn't actually happened to me today, but rather to the poor unfortunate chap sitting just a few feet away from where I was also enjoying a rare kiss of warmth from the sun.

Everyone in earshot knows that the ambient peace has just come to a very abrupt end, so several folk give up, get up and leave, others (like me) settle in for a bit of entertainment, and I'm not going to be disappointed.

To try to record or even remember the ensuing onslaught meted out on that poor individual, whose only desire when he awoke that morning was to immerse himself in a really good book, would be impossible. To say the least we were transported around the world, played every sport, met every imaginable famous person who had ever lived and spent several fortunes in the process.

Wow, and all that before lunch.

Well here's my tribute to him and the many like him who just excel at ruining someone's day.

You can tell that I'm a smart arse
Have an answer every time,
And I know you'll love my stories
Every anecdote sublime.
You'll be hooked by revelations,
Gripped by every single word.
Laughing at my clever humour
Loud and proud, I must be heard.

And whenever I go cruising
Folk consult me all the time
I know every port in detail

Where to shop, or wine and dine.
And I've always been this handsome
Causing all the girls to swoon,
Don't you know I've been considered
As the next man on the moon.

I can tell you want to be me
That's a fact, I see your face
Because your life would be much richer
If I let you take my place.
I know exactly what you're thinking
That you love me, can't deny.
You hang on every sentence
Every other word being I.

Please don't try, you can't out do me,
Been there, seen it more than most.
Bigger, better, more expensive
'Is that all?' my favourite boast.
You should really do things my way,
Entertainer, champion Brit,
Not to mention greatest lover,
Can't you tell I'm full of s**t.

My dear lady says that if I ever become like this
as I get older I will end up being very lonely.

"At least I'll have you," I'd said.

She headed off to art, never said a word.

"Then at least I'll have Jeff," I'd called after her.

"You couldn't afford me laddie," a familiar voice
came from behind.

Sunday 24th February 2013

Day 48 'Puerto Chacabuco' - a birthday party.

Today we're in Chacabuco, a town in the heart of

the Patagonian region.

It started cloudy and a little chilly here in Chile, but at least it was dry.

We'd booked a trip to take a walk along the river in a nearby National Park to see the famed Old Man's Beard waterfall and finish with a barbeque lunch overlooking a picturesque lake.

The bus ride through the town suggests the local area has fallen on hard times and our guide tells us they are reliant on the growing tourist trade.

We'd spent an hour or so walking in the forest, marvelling at the size and variety of plants and trees, so many interesting things to observe. We were privileged to be accompanied most of the way by some of the local birds who appear to have no fear of humans and were quite happy to scratch for food around our feet.

The forest trees are covered in lichen and there were big round mosses which have no root system but rather take moisture out of the air. When we'd reached the place for lunch the views were literally stunning, and my dear lady took loads of photographs.

I'm truly grateful we own a digital camera, the potential cost of developing pictures we'll probably never look at again would be heart-breaking.

My dear lady says I'm starting to sound like Jeff.

The meal was to be served in a nearby purpose build roundhouse with a huge barbeque pit in the middle. We were welcomed with a glass of pisco sour, a local drink, whilst a group of locals gave us a flavour of Patagonian music and dance.

Large chunks of barbequed lamb were delivered to the table with hot potatoes and raw vegetables, along with copious amounts of fruity Chilean wine to wash it all down.

The meat was served on the bone and my dear lady and I had fun trying to identify which part of the lamb we'd each been given.

More dancing and singing followed, an impromptu performance by a few embarrassing drunks from our party, and then we were entertained again with a display of proper sober dancing from the locals.

It was great, but my dear lady and I decided to leave the party to enjoy a little peace and quiet by the lake.

A really relaxing experience.

By the time we got back to the ship there wasn't time to head into the local town to explore, so we'd sat on a small beach by the harbour and sent a few texts back home to family.

This area is so quiet, so clean and just so perfect. It's difficult to imagine a more ideal place to live, except of course for the lack of a large supermarket, or any form of fast food, or a cinema, or any other entertainment venues for that matter, and definitely no pub selling proper beer. Oh and not forgetting the months of freezing cold weather, the five metres of rain they have every year, no internet services and patchy mobile signal.

Otherwise it's just the ticket.

Back at the dock there was an argument in progress between a local taxi driver and an elderly couple from the ship. The couple were dressed in matching bright red jackets and the man was leaning heavily on two walking sticks.

They were being quite loud and obnoxious,

claiming the driver had accepted their offer of one twenty dollar note for a day long tour of the area.

The driver through an interpreter, the port representative, maintained they'd agreed a one hundred and twenty dollar fare. The port representative was trying his hardest to mediate, but the elderly couple maintained their claim that the driver had shaken hands on a one twenty deal, not one hundred and twenty.

Considering they'd asked for and received a full day tour of the area in a taxi it was certainly clear to us which party was right and which was profiteering.

Sadly, without anyone else on his side the driver had to concede, more probably because he realised they'd scammed him and weren't going to admit it and change their story. He took the proffered twenty dollar note and there wasn't even a tip.

Disgraceful.

In the bar later we'd told the others what we'd witnessed. Pru was convinced she'd seen and overheard a similar fracas between two elderly passengers and a taxi driver in Punta Arenas.

"It's bad enough that many of these locals aren't well off and work hard to put food on the table," she'd said angrily. "But for someone who can afford a cruise like this to knowingly cheat like that...well I hope it all come back and bites them on the bum."

As did we all.

But until then there were more important things to attend to.

It's Jeff's birthday.

They'd tried to keep it a secret but our waiters had 'spilt the beans' last night, and now we were the ones with a secret.

We'd asked the Maitre d to decorate the table with whatever he could get hold of and arrange a couple of bottles of fizz and a cake. They made a really good job as well and the eight of us had a really good night.

Jeff, resplendent in his kilt, sporran and a traditional ghillie shirt, had a massive smile on his face all night, it was a very loud and boozy party.

My dear lady gave him a painting of a group of King Penguins, he liked it, she was happy.

She'd also spent the best part of the night singing her own mash up of 'Dancing with the Captain' and 'Grandma's Party' which of course she changed to ' Dancing with our Jeffery' and 'Jeffery's Party'. I bet Mr Nicolas would be horrified at such liberties.

Happy Birthday Jeff, party on!!

Monday 25th February

Day 49 'Puerto Montt' - waterfall or rapids?

Late nights celebrating birthdays and early mornings on tour really don't go together well.

I have to admit that I remember very little about this morning.

The alarm supposedly woke us early as the tour we'd booked to head off to the Chilean equivalent of 'The Lake District' left before the sun came up.

We were off to visit a 'spectacular' waterfall, and enjoy a cruise on a lake followed by lunch at a lakeside restaurant.

I do remember dressing and heading off for the short tender ride to the harbour, with a faint memory of getting on the bus.

After that my next recollection was waking up on the coach somewhere close to running water, with a very sore head. My dear lady told me that the scenery on the one hour drive to our destination had been spectacular, with snow topped mountains and glorious deep blue lakes.

My dear lady also told me that sleeping had been the better option, as the tour guide had decided to ruin the wonderful views by turning her microphone up to deafening and spouting on for an hour about the barbaric times the country had endured under Pinochet during the 80's and 90's.

Glad I missed it then.

Once we were off the coach, we'd discovered the National Park absolutely rammed with visitors. Those of us expecting to see the 'spectacular' waterfalls the tour brochure had claimed was here, where very disappointed, as it was more like a stretch of rapids.

But it was worth a photograph with a very imposing snow capped mountain for a backdrop. Unfortunately the best viewing places were already crowded, mainly with American tourists who were busy watching and jeering a group of friends out on the river in a boat. The ride advertised a guaranteed thrill, but it looked like the participants had wasted their money because the engines didn't seem to have enough power to even hold the boat stationary against the flow of water, let alone progress up the river.

After thirty minutes we were rushed away for the next part of our tour, the boat ride on a picturesque lake, followed by a lunch of locally produced food.

The drive to the lake was bumpy and then we'd

waited half an hour for the boat to return from its last trip. The sail around the lake was fairly mundane and uncomfortable as the boat was absolutely crammed with folk (there's a bit of a 'busy' theme running through today)

There was a big restaurant on the side of the lake and when we'd got off the boat we thought we'd be walking there. We'd passed by earlier and could see the food looked really good and plentiful.

But it was not to be. Instead it was back on the bus for another thirty minute bumpy ride through the countryside.

Finally we arrived at a 'German' style restaurant at the top of a hill, nowhere near a lake. It was after three in the afternoon and most of us had not eaten for nearly eight hours.

Sadly lunch was as uninteresting as the rest of the day had been. It consisted of dried out salmon with unintentionally crispy vegetables and no sauce.

There was a bit of an argument between our guide and the restaurant owner, possibly about how late we were, and that was the reason for our meal having congealed.

Anyway, back on the coach.

The trip I have to say was very poor in comparison, but was made even worse when the tour guide spent the entire trip back explaining, again at jet engine volume, how expensive it is to live, be educated, or even be ill in Chile.

She'd praised her employers for giving her a job but her thanks went out for the generous gratuities tour guests always donated, which helped her family immensely.

At this point I wanted to enquire about the rather

large amount of gold she was wearing, along with the intertwined duo of C's on her designer handbag and glasses, but the elbow in the ribs from you know who changed my mind.

Alas, she'd then made the fatal mistake of revealing how expensive it had become to employ a nanny for her children. You could definitely hear a large amount of money being returned to wallets.

Back at the port and we still had an hour or so before the last tender to the ship, so my dear lady and I had headed into town for a mooch around the Plaza de Armas (main square) and the nearby cathedral.

It was lovely and we'd started to wish we'd had a day in the town instead of the tour. A quick beer and we headed back to the harbour. We're not sure what was, or had happened but the roads were at a standstill, and the queue of traffic could be seen all the way along the coast road.

The ship was due to sail at 6pm, but many guests hadn't made it back by that time. Assumingly they were stuck in traffic.

By half past six the majority had arrived but a party of four were still missing. The ships tannoy invited those named folk to report to reception, several times, just to check they hadn't managed to sneak on back onboard undetected.

By six forty five they still hadn't shown up, so the shore party had packed everything away and prepared to bring the last tender back.

There's a policy in place about getting back to the ship late, which everyone is warned about at each port. If you're on a tour organised by the onboard excursions team then they will wait for any latecomers. However if passengers are 'doing their own thing' they won't wait and the ship will sail at the advertised departure time.

From the promenade deck we'd watched the last tender cast off from the pontoon and start its journey back.

It hadn't quite cleared the pier when a minibus had raced up to the quayside, flashing its headlights. Four people jumped out and were frantically waving, trying to attract the attention of the tender.

Meanwhile, on the promenade deck the equivalent of 'Rubber-Necking' at an accident was going on. Realising that folk were late hundreds had gathered to discover 'would we' or 'wouldn't we' leave without them.

Speculation was rife and I'd even heard a few wagers being made by the usual motley bunch of self appointed experts.

At worst the latecomers would have to find somewhere to spend the night, then make their own way to the next port of call.

Fortunately for them, someone took pity and ordered the tender to turn around and fetch them.

Ted and a very flushed instructor were in the gym again tonight, well she was when I'd arrived but she'd left in a hurry again. She never seemed to have worked up much of a sweat in the early part of the cruise, maybe she too is worried about putting on a bit of weight.

For some reason Jeff celebrated his birthday again tonight. His excuse was a tale of distant regal connections, claiming anyone with royal blood deserves at least two parties.

I think the whiskey has finally started to warp his

mind, but as there was cake, frankly no one was really that bothered.

Tuesday 26th February

Day 50 'Castro' - not Fidel but Fido.

After the last two days of early starts and long tours, we'd decided to have a quiet amble around the town of Castro, one of the ports the cruise company has arranged to visit in lieu of Argentina.

The weather wasn't at its best so we were just going to play it all by ear as there was little information available on what there is to see and do. It's a tender port as well, so if it does get wet and windy we can hurry back to the ship.

Our usual visiting party of four had grown by two today as we'd stumbled upon Linda and Mike on the quayside as we were leaving the landing stage.

It would prove a very fortuitous encounter.

As we'd reached the port gates my dear lady had spotted a familiar couple. Both wore bright red coats and were chatting to one of the many taxis drivers trying to pick up some business. We were close enough to hear part of the conversation.

"A tour is one hundred dollars," the taxi driver said.

"We'll give you one ten," the elderly lady had replied and held out her hand. "Do we have a deal?"

My dear lady took off in their direction, shouting, "Excuse me, excuse me."

But instead of confronting the couple she'd positioned herself between them and the driver.

"I'm so glad I've found you again," she said. The driver looked totally baffled.

"I owe you ten dollars." My dear lady took a note out of her pocket and held it out to him.

"Here you are...one ten."

"Go away," the lady had shouted. "This is our taxi."

Now the taxi driver was scratching his head, I think his English was limited and he hadn't a clue what was happening.

Then Linda had stepped forward and had spoken to the driver. I haven't a clue what she'd said but it sounded like...

"Mi amigo te esta diciendo que estan enganando, lo ves."

"Will you people just sod off." The lady in the bright red coat was getting quite agitated.

The taxi driver winked at my dear lady. "Si lo vio, gracias," he'd said to Linda.

"What are you saying, stop trying to steal our taxi and go away. We've agreed a price and this is our taxi."

"Yes lady," said the taxi driver. "The price one hundred dollars." He held out his hand.

"We said we'll give you one ten," the lady snapped.

"Nice lady has give me one ten, and tour is one hundred, and you pay before get in car."

We'd left them to it.

There were a few locals offering boat tours to see some of the smaller islands in the area, which sounded quite interesting. But after yesterday evenings incident we didn't fancy taking any chances, so we'd set off to explore this unexpected hillside town.

There was a very steep walk from the port to the

central square, but it wasn't too far and we soon found ourselves outside the rather gaudily painted, corrugated steel clad cathedral. But the outside was no representation of the beauty revealed inside, an all wooden structure with an intricately constructed ceiling and central knave all supported on carved pillars.

The carved statues are very expressive, and a bit over the top as they are clothed in very elaborate and modern garb.

For me it felt a little like Madam Tausauds.

It was truly fascinating to see the amount of care and craftsmanship that must have been involved in the construction though.

A quick wander around the square followed, and we'd visited a couple of artisan markets as well, by which time Jeff and I are keen to find the local hostelry.

But now we have a Linda, who ordered a huge mix of meat and vegetable empanadas for all of us to enjoy, although my dear lady insisted on ordering the beer and pisco sours.

It was all simply delicious.

One more notable feature of this town is the number of dogs lying asleep around the town square, on the streets, in shop doorways, in the markets and even inside the tourist information office, which incidentally was clearly displaying a 'No dogs allowed' sign.

They all looked reasonably clean and well nourished, so who do they belong to?

Another unimportant mystery not to deliberate for long, so back to the ship for a quick hour in the gym, then a chance to ruin all my hard work in the bar with Jeff and Mike afterwards.

Cruising is such hard work sometimes.

Wednesday 27th February

Day 51 'at sea' - let's go shopping.

There are two sea days before we reach Valparaiso, marking the official end of the second leg of this cruise.

Another batch of around two hundred and seventy of our fellow travellers will be leaving the ship and heading home. Of course this also means there'll be an influx of newbies which could be just as interesting.

Anyway, today the weather is okay but it's not really warm enough to sit outside. So after another session of being bumped and barged by the clumsy folk in dance class, I'd taken a seat near to the boutiques (that's posh for shops) as it's always a good spot for a bit of people watching.

I wouldn't say I do this too often, but within minutes one of the waiters brought me a coffee, without being asked, and the boutiques manager came over to have one of our regular chats.

She's a nice young lady and very sociable, spending most of the day standing outside the boutiques offering a pleasant smile and a cheery hello to passersby. But many misinterpret this as a ploy, a way of getting them into her establishment to spend money.

It may well be the case, but I enjoy her company, as well as listening to her moans about stupid passengers. I've been collecting some of her stories for possible use at some point.

I'm amazed at the rubbish she and her staff have

to put up with, and had I not actually witnessed some of the unkindness unleashed in their direction, I would probably find it hard to believe everything she tells me.

But today her mood is exceptionally upbeat.

I know from previous conversations that the shops have struggled on this cruise to hit the targets they've been set. But all that has changed, Amy told me, as yesterday a gentleman had treated his wife to some rather expensive sapphire and diamond jewellery for their fiftieth wedding anniversary.

She didn't go into any detail, but they do have some very nice pieces in store, with prices ranging from several hundreds to well over ten thousand pounds. I'm guessing from her delight that the gems in question had sold nearer to the top of that range than the bottom.

I'd told her that I was really pleased for her, and she'd added that I would also be very pleased 'with' her as she had a surprise for me. When we get to Valparaiso they'll be getting some special 'Made in Chile' goods to sell onboard.

As part of the consignment they're expecting some beautiful little penguin ornaments made from Lapis Lazuli, and knowing about my dear lady's love of penguins she thought I might be interested.

Now there's a quandary.

It's my dear lady's birthday soon as well, and she has her eye on a very nice amethyst ring in the boutique, she's even tried it on for size and it fits perfectly. I'd spoken to Amy about this several days ago and had actually paid for the ring, but she'd agreed to keep it on display so my dear lady doesn't suspect anything.

Amy had a cunning plan.

She says I should buy her one of the lapis penguins for her birthday, which will be a lovely present for her to open in the morning? Then I have to take her past the shop during the day so she sees the ring is still there. Amy will then deliver the gift to the restaurant so I can surprise her in the evening when she least expects it.

Sounds like a good plan.

And now I come to think of it, maybe some folk are right to suspect Amy's friendly patter as just a crafty sales technique after all.

Let's just hope these penguins don't cost a fortune.

As for the things I've overheard, here is just a couple of examples.

The toilets on the ship are very temperamental and passengers are reminded on a daily basis not to put anything down the toilet other than the toilet paper supplied. One lady made a massive fuss today and wanted to speak to the manager.

Her complaint was ranted thus,

"My toilet's blocked with tissues which I bought here yesterday, why would you sell it to me knowing that it won't flush away."

Sounds like an opening for a ditty.

Or maybe not.

"Why don't you sell Chanel perfume," one very irate gentleman asked. "My wife is so angry about this that she's threatening to leave me if I don't get her some. What are you going to do about it?"

And one lady had actually stated that she was offended to see condoms for sale in the shop, especially as they were sitting next to the sore throat remedies, and she'd picked them up by mistake. Her parting remark as she'd stormed out was, "In my day we practiced abstention."

I'm sure I wasn't the only one to think 'One look at you and everyone understands why'.

Tonight was the last formal evening of this sector.

My friend Jeff was not a happy bunny when we'd met up for drinks, firstly because he'd had to admit his weight gain has got to the point where he's had to add a four inch expander to the fastening of his kilt.

But that wasn't then main reason.

Like me Jeff had promised his partner that they would use their time on sea days to learn to dance properly. So far he's managed to sidestep his promise to Pru, but now she's insisting, especially as we're well over half way through the trip, and Jeff needs the exercise before none of his clothes fit.

I don't think my dear lady has helped his cause by telling Pru that it's really good fun.

"You'll have to help me out here, Laddie," he pleaded. "Tell her I'm likely to hurt myself or even worse."

I'm not quite sure what he'd meant by 'even worse', but I told him he should at least show willing and give it a go, then maybe we could concoct a 'get-out' plan together.

We agreed to bide our time, although I have to admit I'm not disliking the lessons as much as I'd thought I would.

As usual the photogs were out in force giving the 'soon to be departing' the last opportunity to be immortalised in their finery. There was a bit of a queue building up for the Captain's farewell party and we saw Norma and Barry posing with the master of the ship. I have to say they both looked very happy and really smart. She in particular looked very richly dressed and bejewelled.

And then there was Ted, looking very dapper in his white tuxedo and bright red dickey bow. He had a very pretty younger lady on his arm as he took his place for a photo with the Captain.

She looked very familiar, but I can't quite place where I'd seen her before.

Thursday 28th February

Day 52 'at sea' - taking liberties, but not bodices.

The weather still hasn't improved a great deal, so our morning had been the normal routine of breakfast and dancing, followed by a bit of dolphin spotting from our sheltered balcony with a nice cup of coffee in hand.

Ah, the simple things.

For many others the day has been stressful and fraught, at least that's how it's sounded.

There were angry words in the buffet earlier as a group of leavers refused to accept that the manager wasn't prepared to organise a 'packed lunch' for their journey home. He'd explained that there would be plenty of all the usual stuff available for them to help themselves to in the morning, but the kitchen wasn't set up to do a 'takeaway' picnic.

I appreciate it's sad to be leaving, but that's no excuse to be discourteous.

Our cabin is on the same deck as the passenger laundrette, a hot and steamy caldron of gossip and confrontation. It gets quite muggy in there as well, but as far as I know no one's actually been mugged.

From eight in the morning till ten at night there's usually a steady stream of folk drifting in and out of this most important of facilities on the ship.

Some folk go on a regular basis, possibly because they've been restricted on the amount of luggage they could bring because of flying. Others, like my dear lady, only go when the need arises.

Which is a little more often than she wishes.

But this isn't just a place to wash your smalls or iron your favourite shirt, no sir, this is a hub of information, the heart of scandal and intrigue. If there's a rumour going round you can bet your grandmothers pension it started in the laundrette.

Now because many of the folk leaving the ship tomorrow don't want any inquisitive customs officers rummaging through their dirty clobber, the six washing machines and driers have been given a thorough work-out over the past two days.

Patience has been worn thin and tempers have flared, as the usually high demand for the machines had escalated.

There were certainly a lot of raised voices in evidence when we'd headed off for breakfast, and it sounded like there was a full scale row in progress when we'd returned from dancing.

One lady had apparently transfered her clean clothes from a washer into a drier, and then headed off for a cup of tea, as the machine would take at least half an hour or so to do its work. She'd returned some time later only to discover her still damp apparel had been removed from the machine and placed neatly in one of the plastic baskets.

She was accusing the lady, whose clothes were now in the same drier, of some heinous crime worthy of a public flogging.

There was some name calling and a bit of pushing had occurred, so security were called to mediate.

To cut a long story short it transpires that the lady in question had taken over two and half hours to drink her cup of tea. A complaint had been made to reception about the machine being unavailable to use as a consequence, so a member of staff had attended to the issue and removed her washing from the drier.

The lady is now demanding compensation from the staff member as her clothes had been folded incorrectly.

This is just one of the many unusual occurrences to happen in the laundrette.

I feel very sorry for the folk whose cabins are close by, as I know one couple have called security on many occasions. There was even an incident a few nights ago when one passenger had entered the facility at five minutes to ten, ignoring notices on each of the washers stating that they shouldn't be loaded any later than nine o'clock. She'd proceeded filled three machines and set them going. When a member of staff had arrived at ten to lock up the lady had refused to budge until she'd finished.

One of the main issues about the laundrette is that items of clothes go missing.

Heading off to do other things while one's clothing tumbles in the machines is not unusual, after all who wants to spend a couple of hours of their holiday cooped up in a stuffy hot room with loads of whinging strangers (exactly why I'm refusing to learn to play bridge)

Most of the time the owners return, eventually,

but occasionally they forget.

It is not uncommon in these circumstances for a nice dress, or shirt, or something else of interest to go missing, never to be seen again.

Earlier in the cruise one couple had insisted that their cabin steward had 'removed' items of clothing from their cabin. Obviously this allegation was taken seriously. The couple were asked for a description of the clothing that was 'missing', the steward was interviewed and his cabin was searched. It transpired that their clothing was found in lost property, having been 'abandoned' in one of the washing machines in the laundrette for two days.

I only hope they did the decent thing and apologised.

After lunch I'd headed back to my seat near to the boutique

The passengers are not the only ones suffering from stress, poor Amy looked distraught and I was soon to find out why.

Over a calming cup of coffee, which didn't really work that well, she'd told me the expensive anniversary gift that had boosted their sales yesterday had been returned this morning for a refund.

They have a 'no quibble' seven day returns policy, which she'd had to honour, despite the fact she knew the lady had worn the jewellery throughout last night's formal event, and had even bought the photograph she'd had taken with the Captain.

Apparently, the lady had claimed that the sapphires didn't compliment her skin tone as they were too blue, a bit like poor Amy's mood.

I never knew folk could be so conniving.

My dear lady says nothing surprises her and I'm a bit too trusting and naive.

She's probably right, but I'm sure she'd said trusting and naive, not vain. She's currently singing a Carly Simon classic in the shower.

Surely she's got that wrong, but who else would she sing about?

Valparaiso tomorrow and another sector done.

Time really is starting to fly.

'Another new batch'

Day 53 'Valparaiso' - what did you say it was made with?

The weather is back to being wonderful again, lovely and warm and not a cloud in the sky.

After a relaxing breakfast we'd headed out of the main port area and into the town to explore.

There were some tours going out today, mainly into the capital Santiago, but as we didn't fancy the two hour drive there and back we'd decided to stay locally. We're on our own today, as the others wanted to travel into Santiago.

We enjoy seeing the sights in the company of Jeff and Pru, and being in a group must afford us a little more protection in some of the places we've been, safety in numbers and all that. But sometimes we each want to do something different and it's good that we can, rather than feel obligated to stick together all the time.

So today is all about us, and probably means a lot less beer.

The city of Valparaiso is built around forty two separate hills, each being a different area and having its own personality. Most of these 'Cerras' are serviced by an ancient funicular, 'ascensor', which carries up to eight people at a time to the viewpoints and residential areas high above the city.

We'd started by heading for Cerro Concepcion, a

neighbourhood close to the harbour. Its narrow streets are awash with colourful architecture and street art, with great views of the city in every direction. The 'ascensor' to reach the top was the first one ever built and really does look, and act, its age.

We could have spent a lot more time here but there's much more to see. So onwards and upwards, well more upwards and downwards and upwards again.

We managed to find Cerro Alegre next, a very picturesque place with lots of little craft places and cafes, then on to Cerro Panteon a little further inland. This time there was no 'ascensor' to take us up the steep incline so we got some well needed exercise.

There are cemeteries to be found here. It's always interesting to see how different cultures treat their 'dear departed', and there's a separate burial ground here for non-Catholics, or Disidentes as they were known.

Fascinating.

Next we'd made our way to the very pretty Victoria Plaza, where the cathedral is located. Unfortunately the sinners (us) were unable to confess or worship today as the House of God was once again shut for business.

The next 'ascensor' we'd discovered close by was out of order, so we ambled aimlessly around the crowded streets, hungry to find more points of interest.

Eventually down a narrow alley and totally unmarked, as well as being blocked from view by a clothing stall, we'd found a very rickety cable car to transport us up to another 'Cerro'. Sadly the name of this one is unknown to me, as all the signage was broken and covered in graffiti.

This must have been one of the highest of the hills though, as the views over the city rooftops to the sea beyond were incredible. As we'd walked the narrow streets we'd found the local church and got chatting to the priest, who incidentally was British, but has been ministering here in Chile for most of his adult life. He showed us around his small church, which is very old, ornate and open, and suggests we look like we could use a cold beer or two, directing us to a nearby bar.

That was a bit weird as I thought the church was more interested in getting us to abstain from the 'demon drink' rather than recommending a particular den of iniquity.

Anyway, if a priest says the beer is good, it would be sinful not to try it out.

We took a seat outside in the courtyard and my dear lady goes into action with her growing grasp of the Spanish language, ordering a pisco sour for herself, a local beer for me and a menu.

"Very good," our waiter said in perfect English and disappeared inside.

On his return he explained that my huge jug of beer is produced locally, and includes a secret flavouring ingredient that's a derivative of the cannabis plant.

For a moment or two his comments didn't register in my simple mind, but once I'd sampled the amber nectar it no longer mattered.

It was really good.

So there we were, enjoying wonderful views over the city of Valparaiso, drinking a class B substance and pisco sour, made I no doubt from some illicitly grown lemons or suchlike. I think we ate some nice food and indulged in another round or two of drinks, but to be honest I can't really remember?

I recall throwing a couple of dollars into the waiter's hat when he joined in with our rousing rendition of the Carpenters 'Top of the World', but then it may have been the local vagrant busker just seizing an opportunity.

Finally we headed back to reality with a return walk to the ship (I may have been floating) via Plaza Sotomayor, another well kept square with a huge monument to 'Los Heros'.

It's certainly been a very warm and draining day, but we've had a great time. Valparaiso seems like a city where you need to spend a few days in order to discover more of its hidden delights, and who knows you may even find out when the cathedral opens!

For now I hear my bed calling, but according to my dear lady 'It's just an illusion'.

Saturday 2nd March

Day 54 'Coquimbo' - something fishy going on.

Last night is still a little bit hazy.

In the afternoon I'd enjoyed a long, dreamy snooze when we'd returned from the city, then set off for our evening meal, missing out the gym obviously.

At one point during dinner I'm sure Jeff and I had been planning to steal a lifebo...survival craft to head back to Valparaiso. Jeff was desperate to try the 'special' beer and I was just desperate.

I had to have another jug of that wonderful amber liquid, but why I'd felt that way is a complete mystery.

Or was it all just a dream?

Today we had a choice.

We could either stay in Coquimbo for a walk up the hill to visit a huge concrete cross, and get mugged, or take a short taxi ride to the nearby town of La Serena, and get mugged.

Good choice.

This was not my opinion, but once again there have been a number of warnings about personal safety as this is a very poverty stricken area. Advice is extensive and suggestions range from not going ashore at all to travelling around naked.

I know that's a bit of an exaggeration, which is not my usual style, but it's not a million miles from the truth either.

The port lecturer suggested that anybody displaying signs of anxiousness about a potential confrontation whilst out and about, would be seen by the career villain as an easy target.

Basically, if you worry about getting mugged, chances are you will be, so don't go.

However, anyone not of a nervous disposition and showing confidence should be left to wander the streets in relative safety...except for the potholes.

It's the same sad old story, bullies and potholes only pick on softies.

Those who decide to 'risk it' are also advised to dress like a local and act like a local, meaning no fancy clothes, jewellery, cameras, mobile phones or even make-up.

Like I said, naked.

We'd set off in our usual group of four, and at the port gates a tourist representative told us to get an official taxi for the half hour journey into La Serena, as there's little to do locally apart from walk to the concrete cross and get mugged...even the locals are at it now.

"There's a better chance of being unmolested in La Serena," the lady had told us.

That didn't sound much better either, but we weren't going to be put off...we have a Jeff.

The taxi looked new and the driver wore a tie, but spoke little English, and as our Spanish is limited to ordering food and drink we'd hoped to be heading in the right direction as we'd raced off down the coast road.

The fare had been agreed at cincuenta (fifty) dollars, which seemed to be a good price for four of us.

We arrived in a lot less than half an hour and our friendly driver beamed a smile as we'd paid him, muttering something quickly in his native tongue which no one understood. But like typical tourists we nodded and said 'Si' and 'Gracias' ad nauseum, so goodness only knows what we were agreeing to.

Will we ever learn?

The ride to La Serena had been fast and a little bit scary, but nowhere near as scary as the beggars we'd encountered outside the church where we were dropped us off. It was a bit like a zombie movie and they were ready to attack, but thankfully we could move faster than they could.

In fact the whole mood of the town felt quite aggressive and no one appeared to be very happy.

Anyway we had a good look around, the town square, the church and a convent, all very quaint and nicely kept. The town was certainly clean and wasn't really portraying the destitute community we'd been led to believe it was.

It was also getting hotter.

Time for a beer.

We found a little street cafe and my dear lady had ordered beers and pisco sours.

It's fair to say that the waitress wasn't the nicest of people either, laughing at our order and mocking my futile attempts at asking where the bano (toilets) were, was just rude.

Although nobody actually threatened us at any point we didn't feel very welcome here. So rather than staying for another drink and something to eat we'd paid the bill and headed off to find a taxi back to Coquimbo.

As we'd walked back to where we'd been dropped off, we were surprised to find the same taxi driver waiting for us.

That was convenient, or more probably that was what he was telling us earlier...'You'll hate it and be back here in an hour, I'll wait'.

And we'd nodded and said 'Si, gracias.'

He must have thought we spoke the language as he'd chatted away merrily all the way back to the port.

And what did we do?

We nodded and said 'Si' ad nauseum.

We were soon back at the port, and it turned out that the fifty dollar fare was actually for the round trip. When Jeff had tried to pay him another fifty he'd refused to take it.

"Has pagado," he'd pushed the money away.

My dear lady grabbed one of the twenty dollar notes and offered it back.

"Propina, gracias," she'd said (I think)

That just goes to prove that no matter what others suggest, the majority of people are honest. We wouldn't have known the price and wouldn't have argued at paying that fare twice, but this driver wouldn't take advantage of his customers.

Faith in human nature restored, for now at least.

The port area seemed to be quite busy now, so my dear lady and I decided to go exploring, but not naked, and not with Jeff and Pru either as they'd decided to head back to cool off.

We wandered along the harbour wall until we came to what appeared to be a fish market. It wasn't just full of stalls selling hundreds of types of freshly caught marine creatures, it was also a place to sit and eat the same at a large number of 'greasy spoon' type cafes.

The 'plaice' was full and the locals were 'clammed' in like 'sardines', their 'sole' intention to eat fish (ok enough of the fishy puns)

The plates of food being eaten looked very strange and the overall smell in the building was not very pleasant at all. We weren't tempted to try it out, and we'd headed off through the stalls and back outside.

Now the smell was worse.

Right against the sea wall there were a lot of tables where men dressed in white overalls, aprons and boots were gutting and filleting fish. Next to this was a small sea inlet where a very large number of brown pelicans and harbour seals were waiting to be fed the leftovers from the day's trading.

The seals were huge, and every time one of the men threw a bucket of scraps over the wall a fight broke out, giving the pelicans enough time to pinch most of the good bits. I've only ever been this close to animals in a zoo, and to be within a few feet of them was quite amazing (and exceptionally pongy)

Many photos were taken, especially when the pelicans had demonstrated their ability steal things out of containers. They'd work in conjunction with the seagulls, who would spear the lids of polystyrene boxes with their beaks and flick them off. Then the pelicans would scoop out as much of the contents as possible before being chased off.

Amazingly they would then share their prize with the seagulls by spitting out several of the smaller fish.

All too soon it was time for us to return to the ship and say goodbye to this supposedly dangerous port.

Despite a mediocre start it had all ended well, it certainly was a very interesting visit.

As we'd sailed away a local band on the dockside played some lively beats, vigorously waving their goodbyes. To be honest they weren't very good, but their instruments looked surprisingly new and expensive, very similar to the one's I've seen the ship's band playing.

Oh and the lady at the port was right about the walk to the concrete cross being dangerous as two tourists were threatened and one man was punched.

The passenger responsible for the fracas has apologised, saying he didn't realise the couple were tourists like himself looking for directions, and the man he'd punched was an undercover policeman trying to warn him there were muggers close by.

He was let off with a warning and banned from

ever returning to the area.

I'd heard that several more passengers went out looking for a policeman, hoping for a similar injunction.

My dear lady's rendition of Elvis Costello's 'Punching a Detective' was quite inspired.

Sunday 3rd March

Day 55 'at sea' – a few tidbits.

There was many a moan this morning about yesterday's port of call, and the lack of anything interesting to do there.

Except punching policemen!

I disagree, but then I like the simple things.

Observing the locals and how they thrive and survive is inspiring.

Beautiful scenery and the creatures of nature make me smile.

Even looking at the architecture of a big city and seeing how it has evolved is fascinating, and I just love to hear about the history, culture, religion and customs.

Difference is what makes things interesting.

Some folk are way too demanding, and unless there are naked bears and dancing women (or is it the other way round?) they'll never be happy.

I doubt Coquimbo will ever be a glitzy or glamorous destination for the excited traveller as there's no zip-lining through the trees, or barrel riding over a waterfall, not even a catamaran trip with snorkelling, stingrays and endless rum punch.

But then if everywhere was the same there wouldn't be any point in going somewhere different...because it wouldn't be.

Embrace diversity, it's never boring.

At midday the 'Officer of the Watch' had made the usual midday announcement from the bridge to let us know the state of the sea (hopefully calm) the state of the sky (hopefully blue and above us) and the state of the ship (hopefully intact and the right way up with excellent views of the sky)

Thankfully 'all is well'.

But it sounded like he'd contracted a bit of a cold and his voice was quite nasal and raspy. Let's hope that today of all days there's no call to 'Abandon Ship' because it will probably sound more like an announcement for 'A Ban on Chips' causing everyone to throw themselves overboard from the sheer disappointment of such a catastrophe.

But then the outcome would be the same, so as he'd said...all is well.

I think most folk would consider our sea days quite mundane, but for us it works well.

It's a routine that has evolved over the weeks and now we feel we're getting the most we can out of this adventure.

We start with a stroll around the open decks before a light breakfast.

I'm being really good now because earlier on I couldn't resist a 'proper' brekkie. I tried, lord knows how I tried, but I was hooked.

I was dishonest as well because when I was with my dear lady I'd have cereal or fruit to appease her concern for my ever widening waist line. But then I'd sneak back later for a full English when she wasn't looking.

The rest of the morning is for dancing.

Unfortunately my dear lady still has issues with rhythm, but she's getting better. I however have issues with remembering steps, I'm getting worse.

I know I look like a right plonker, especially when we head off in different directions at the same time, but I'm not on my own in that department, so who cares.

While my dear lady heads off to painting in the afternoon I'll sit and write up my journal and record anything interesting that happens around the ship.

Like today two gents were chatting about previous cruising experiences over a coffee.

"Been left on your own today then?"

"No, I'm with the wife."

"Where is she then?"

"Oh she'd gone off to one of the talks."

"So have you been on this ship before then?"

"Not really, just the once."

"What's your table like, friendly folk?"

"Not sure. But it's quite amazing because of all the tables in the restaurant we're sitting at the very same one we had last time."

"With the same people as well?"

"I don't think so, but then I'm not good with names and faces."

"Maybe they've moved to a different table for a change."

"Yes, you could be right."

"We're on a big table for eight, how many are on yours?"

"Oh, there were six, but it's only the two of us now."

Later in the afternoon we'll sit out on deck, go for

a swim or laze in the hot-tubs if it's warm and sunny. If not then we'll take part in one of the many quizzes they have onboard, or play scrabble in the bar with a glass of wine.

Then while my dear lady gets herself ready for the evening frivolities I head off to the gym, but not solely for the exercise these days.

It's becoming quite obvious that something is afoot between Ted and Nadia.

It always seems like they've both been expending a fair amount of energy when I arrive, and are really out of breath. They're never more than a foot away from each other and always giggling like kids.

Almost immediately Nadia excuses herself with a cheeky smile in my direction. Very strange that because she rarely acknowledged my existence before. Ted then announces he's off for a shower, winks at me, and is gone.

It's a conundrum.

We've seen quite a bit more of Ted around the ship in the evenings as well, and always with the same very pretty young lady he was with at the Captain's farewell party.

I'm sure I know her.

I'm wondering if Nadia knows her too.

Anyway, the rest of our evening is usually taken up with excessive amounts of indulgence and has always remained my favourite part of every day.

I've recorded this routine as I worry I'm repeating myself often, taking up valuable journal space, and time. On future sea days I'm only going to mention 'stuff' of any notability.

My dear lady says I'm getting a bit too obsessive about my journal and it seems to be taking up more of my time each day.

She's right of course, but I'm really enjoying it.

This prompted another Costello classic 'Every day I write the book', which my dear lady then suggested would be a good idea...think of a good storyline and write a book. At least it might earn us enough money so we can come cruising again.

I love it.

Monday 4th March

Day 56 'Arica' - drier than dry.

Well today was our last stop in Chile and so far I think it's been my favourite country for the wonderful scenery we've enjoyed.

Arica is right on the edge of the Atacama Desert and surrounded by brown, featureless, sandy coloured mountains. Unsurprisingly it's warm, and there's a haze in the air which was just the wind blowing up dust, not sand but dust.

As we'd stepped out onto the balcony to take a look at the city, everything was already covered in a thick layer of the stuff.

We could see a pretty square with market stalls being set out, and there was a huge lump of rock behind that.

Folk have been whinging again. They reckon it's going to be another duff port considering how barren it looks.

"Don't think I'll bother," was a phrase heard several times over breakfast.

First impressions are often wrong though and I just wish people wouldn't prejudge.

Well, the landscape may have looked a bit arid

but it turned out that the locals were anything but.

For a start, as we'd left the ship we were given a gift of a small, colourful pouch, which was obviously handmade and very stereotypically of Chilean design.

It was decorated with a tiny hand carved flute, a little hat and two little woollen pompoms. Inside there was a map of the area and other information flyers of the local attractions.

This item might sound a bit meagre, but it was the very first time we've been 'given' anything of any use at the dockside, or anywhere else for that matter. It will make a great keepsake and a nice memento of our visit.

Once through the port the main town area appears to have been pedestrianised recently. It's very bright and clean with a number of fountains, trees and statues, and a small group of musicians are playing panpipes, giving the whole pleasant vista an authentic feel.

There are stalls selling all sorts of clothing and souvenirs and the vendors were all dressed in traditional costume.

The whole effect was fantastic.

The cathedral was open, and is very ornate with the iron work being designed by Eifel, he of the Paris 'tower' fame.

Our mission was to get to the top of that rock we were looking at earlier.

For the locals this huge lump of rock is of great historical significance and has been declared a national monument, but for the visitor it signifies a challenge.

They've concreted a path to the top, making it

easier to climb to the summit than in days gone by, but it's extremely hot and the heat from the sun even bounces off the bare stone surface to boil you from every directions.

The reward for reaching the summit is most definitely the far reaching views which are stunning.

The town stretches out along the coastline, whilst inland vistas are of miles and miles of a dusty landscape and many more huge bare rocks.

And there's a flag, but this isn't your everyday normal sized flag, this is a proper flag of immense size, declaring loud and proud...This land belongs to Chile.

The cannons that were possibly used to capture Morro Arica (as it's known locally) from the Peruvians are on display nearby along with their own version of 'Cristo' with outstretched arms.

A bit of a 'war and peace' theme going on me thinks.

There's also a museum dedicated to the history of the conflicts of the area, but sadly it was closed. So after about an hour of taking in the breath taking views, it was time to head off on the path back down to the town.

The town centre isn't very big, but surprisingly is very crowded, so we'd had to find refuge in a bar to save us from getting trampled. What more can I say, we enjoyed beer and sandwiches before heading back to the ship for a fond farewell to Chile.

This leg of the trip hasn't disappointed and has mainly lived up to the images I had in my head.

The scenery has been excellent, particularly the fjords and glaciers. Food and drink have been simple but fresh and enjoyable, the people in the main have been very friendly, and we personally haven't experienced any problems.

We've seen plenty of wildlife and as a destination to visit it comes highly recommended and hopefully one day we too will return.

Now onto Peru, home of the ancient Incas.

I've always been fascinated by ancient ruins, my dear lady says she has too.

Cheek.

Tuesday 5th March

Day 57 'at sea' - fifty shades of red.

Time is passing very quickly and it's hard to believe that eight of the twelve weeks have already been and gone, only a third of this adventure is left.

As we're continuing to head north the weather should improve, with the sun hopefully making more of an effort to join us.

And as if by magic we'd meandered out on deck early today to be greeted by a fresh warm morning, with clear blue skies and sunshine.

It was only 8am and there had already been a scramble for the sun loungers.

I know I've mentioned this before, but it still amazes me that despite so many health warnings about over exposing skin to the harmful UV rays of the sun, there are still many who never seem happy unless they are excessively tanned (leave the room if you had any improper thoughts then)

The difference in skin tone between those who joined the ship in Valparaiso and the rest of the passengers is very noticeable, almost resulting in 'us and them' enclaves out on the sun deck.

For the newbies there's some serious catching up to do.

We've never really been a couple who sit out in the sun doing nothing, but on this holiday we've been happy to do just that.

Maybe we're just getting older.

My dear lady said 'speak for yourself'.

Whether it has something to do with the fact that on a ship there's nowhere to go we haven't been to many times before, or something else, but today was so relaxing my dear lady didn't even want to go dancing.

Early in the afternoon we'd headed for the buffet for a light lunch.

As we'd passed through the melee of loungers it has to be said that a fair few folk had underestimated the power of our great yellow sky companion. Several are turning some very interesting shades of angry pink.

Time for a witty ditty.

Here comes the sun,
You folks must run
To grab a spot to lie.
Unbutton shirt,
Hitch up that skirt,
Before it passes by.

But stay it may
For just one day,
So get it while you can.
Don't whinge "It's sore"
Grit teeth much more
Lie down and be a man.

Forget the creams,

Sun blocking means
Delaying darker skin.
Avoid the shade
Let light pervade
Don't stop the ray's way in.

Don't be a prude
All straps remove,
You'll need an even spread.
Just like a spit,
Rotate a bit
To brown from toe to head.

Must stay all day
Not move away,
Raise arms above your head.
Red bingo wings
And other things
Will smart tonight in bed.

But that's the plan,
You'll have a tan
To prove a time well spent.
If pale you stay
While you're away
Then no one knows you went.

On a different note we're in Callao tomorrow, gateway to Lima the capital. I'm not sure if we're missing out on a special trip because I'm being a bit tight fisted.

The tours department have been offering a three day overland excursion to Machu Pichu, one of the greatest historical sites in the world. It would certainly be a once in a lifetime opportunity and undoubtedly an experience to remember for many years to come.

But at over two thousand pounds each I wasn't keen to indulge. That seems more like the cost of a full holiday rather than a three day break.

I would have paid the money happily if my dear lady had wanted to go, but she wasn't bothered, at least that's what she's been telling me.

Later in the afternoon we'd heard a few folk bragging about going on the trip, but predictably they were expounding more about the cost rather than why they'd wanted to go.

It's a lot to spend on one memory...but they say they can afford it.

My dear lady has been suggesting that 'The money isn't too tight to mention'.

But maybe it is, they just like to say otherwise.

Wednesday 6th March

Day 58 'Callao' - chaotic gateway to Lima.

The start of the day was very misty, swirling clouds of white cotton fog covered the city in a shroud, which cleared and then returned intermittently, very strange.

We've been told that the area around the port of Callao is very poor and subsequently dangerous, under no circumstance should we even consider walking around this part of town.

There are tours into Lima, but these had sold out quickly so we were going to have to go with the alternative arrangements.

The port authorities had arranged for shuttle buses to take us to Miraflores, a more affluent and touristy region of area, but it's a forty minute ride away.

The seemingly simple process of transportation turned out to be quite chaotic, not on the part of the authorities, but rather because of the antics of the passengers themselves.

Five buses were waiting at the quayside as the masses had flooded off the ship at around 9.00am. All five busses had set off shortly afterwards, leaving about eighty people still standing on the quayside.

Now we were watching this from the comfort of our balcony, wondering why those who were left behind remained standing around in the blistering heat. We'd all been given enough information and a simple calculation would clearly suggest that it would be at least an hour and a half before the buses returned.

There weren't that many folk left on the ship either, certainly not enough to refill all five coaches for a second time, as at least eight other coaches had taken out organised tours.

We could only imagine it was due to that age old concern of the Brits...they might lose their place in the queue.

With no shade people and tempers started to heat up, we saw many heads shaking and fingers wagging at the poor port representative.

Anyway, we indulged in another cup of tea and sat on our cool balcony watching the trials and tribulations of the forgotten eighty until the coaches had started to return at around 10.50am.

Gathering up our stuff, we'd made our way off the ship and stepped straight onto a waiting bus, which left almost immediately.

There were a lot of hot and irritated people

around today. The forty minute journey wasn't long enough for them to express the horrors of nearly two hours of sheer hell, and you could hear them whinging about it around the town all day.

When we'd arrived at Miraflores we'd considered getting a taxi into the old town of Lima, but apparently there was a demonstration going on there. A small group of pensioners had organised a rally about some unfairness in the way they're treated, but their protest march had apparently escalated into a major incident, as numbers had increased quite unexpectedly.

So that's where all the whiners had gone off the ship.

Riot police and water cannons had been deployed and large parts of the city had been cordoned off and we were advised not to enter the city.

These Peruvian pensioners are a tough bunch then.

With no real choice we'd had to stay and wander around this seemingly newish area. There's a major shopping centre and really modern hotels, with a great deal of construction work going on. For the first time we encountered the usual trappings of a developing tourist area, McDonalds, TGI Fridays, KFC and Burger King (so much choice and other fast food brands were available)

That aside there's a very pretty town square and an old ornate church as well as some really nice looking beaches.

For me the most amazing thing about this place is the fact that the newer area has been built right on the edge of the cliffs, which are fairly sheer faced and about three to four hundred feet high. The whole natural structure looks like loose scree, with plenty of evidence of erosion. A path through the park, running close to the edge of the cliffs has large cracks down the centre. The land has a definite lean towards the fence at the edge, sections of which are also on a very worrying incline.

It will be interesting to see this place in a decade or two, or what's left of it.

Yes, the eateries have some stunning views out to sea from their cliff top terraces, but I'm not sure I'd want to take the chance.

So we'd found an older part of the town and indulged in some retail and culinary therapy before boarding the coach for the journey back to the ship.

Lima and its surrounding districts are definitely a city of extreme contrast, not unlike many of the major cities we've visited so far. There are the rich, and there are the poor, and the forty minute drive from the port demonstrated a region so overrun by people that tin shanties are squeezed in together on any vacant piece of land between the opulent hotels and luxury apartments.

Amazingly both of these dwelling have similar defences, helping to protect the property of the inhabitants. I don't think I've ever seen security measures like I've seen today. Razor wire, broken glass topped concrete and electric fences are everywhere. Even the roughly erected shanties have infrared lighting and night vision cameras. Seeing the condition of the buildings it's hard to imagine the occupiers have that much of value to protect...except maybe themselves.

Each individual ATM had its own armed guard, as did most of the hotels and shops. There were police everywhere in Miraflores, which maybe another good reason to take all the tourists there, keep them together and they can be better protected.

The guide on our coach told us that uncontrolled large influxes of people from the sierras had arrived and wanted to get their share of the luxury and comfort enjoyed by the coastal city dwellers. But there's just not enough work, or money, to go round so they have to do whatever it takes to feed the family. As the gap between the 'have' and 'have not' widens it gets to the point that the latter believe they have the right to take from the former just to survive, and then they take more just because they want to and can.

And I start to think how we moan about similar issues back home.

Maybe our politicians should look closely at how other places around the world have not coped with the unrestricted movement of the people. All may have the right for sure, but it would seem that the results are far from pleasant in the long term.

Anyway, we've had a lovely day here in Lima and as usual we enjoyed sampling the local beer and cuisine. I believe it's also good to see the worst of a culture as well as its best. We really shouldn't travel the globe with our eyes closed just because we might not like what we see.

Best of all today though was a visit to a local travel agent where a window display tells us that a three day, two night trip to Machu Pichu by train is four hundred dollars each, staying in a three star hotel.

I'd been a little envious of the folk heading out to Machu Pichu on the ships organised tour, but would have been heartbroken to discover we'd paid over two thousand pounds each for a tour available locally for a fifth of the price.

My dear lady wouldn't allow me to get a few brochures to leave around the ship for when the others get back, spoil sport.

Thursday 7th March

Day 59 'Salaverry' – all aboard for the Chan Chan Ruins.

Just a half day in this port, and to make the most of our time we'd booked a tour to the Chan Chan ruins and the Dragon Temple, which are described as older and bigger than Machu Pichu. So we're looking forward to a bit of cultural history and ancient archaeology with a wow factor after all.

The weather was excessively hot before we'd even got off the ship but at least the air conditioning on the coach was working well.

The drive through the local area, again a very dry sandy desert region, reveals the fairly basic living standards of the majority of the people. Tin or brick built shanties randomly litter the streets interspersed with modern individual retail units on an industrial scale. Most of the residencies are in various states of completion, but all the properties have identical defences in place like Lima.

Small shops here and there were open, but they have iron gates fastened across the doorway through which purchases are requested and the goods are handed through the bars after payment is made.

Despite this being classed as a desert region, because of the lack of rainfall, the area around

Trujillo is very fertile. They have over fifty rivers that flow down from the Andes to the sea and they've cut irrigation channels around the valleys to form large fields of produce. Sugar cane, asparagus and artichokes are just a few of the abundant crops they grow and export, so we're told they have quite a buoyant economy, but like Lima they are also plagued by an influx of 'inlanders' looking to share in the bounty.

The Chan Chan ruins are vast, covering an enormous area. If I remember correctly what the guide had said, there were nine individual palaces here, each palace built by the new king which then became his mausoleum when he'd died.

The story's were fascinating but the guide explained that as there are no written records from the period, most of the information she was relaying was based purely on interpretation of pictures on pottery, jewellery and fragments of wall plaster.

The main area we were taken to was very interesting, but looked exceptionally neat and well preserved...almost sterile.

Most archaeological sites we've visited in the past have been littered with building debris where walls have fallen, paths crumbled etc, but not here. There isn't a loose stone in sight, not even swept into a pile in the corner.

Everything appears to have been restored, rebuilt almost to completion and it's impossible to see where original stops and modern starts. For me personally this didn't feel like an ancient archaeological site, but rather a reconstruction for the benefit of tourists.

Having said that it is still a very interesting place to visit, the sheer size of the site is astonishing, not to mention its overall standing in the country's history and how advanced that civilisation was regarded.

On to the Dragon Temple, or Gold Temple or Rainbow Temple, its only one place but it seems they can't quite make up their mind what to call it.

Again this is very interesting and appears fairly complete, but after Chan Chan we're not quite sure what is right and what is not right. The views from the top are spectacular though so the short climb was worth it.

In one respect we were glad we only had half a day here as it was so very hot and uncomfortable. Rather than stop in the local town on our return we'd quickly headed back to the wonderfully cool, air conditioned luxury of the ship, not even bothering to head out onto the decks to wave goodbye to Peru.

Phew.

This was definitely the place for a rousing chorus of 'Feelin Hot Hot Hot'.

I'm starting to have a lot of sympathy for lobsters.

Next stop Manta in Ecuador, home of the Panama hat, but why isn't Panama the home of the Panama hat?

Friday 8th March

Day 60 'at sea' – a very special birthday

As we're fast approaching the equator (again) it's no surprise it's getting even hotter.

Today is my dear lady's birthday, and it started in the early hours of the morning as my phone lit up with several text messages from friends and family back home.

As we were awake she'd insisted on opening her

present.

I'd bought her three of the little lapis penguins and Amy had placed each one in a separate ring box and gift wrapped them for me. She loved them, but I thought I caught a slight look of disappointment in her eyes. I'd almost given in and admitted to having got her the ring as well.

A day of secrets and intrigue had begun.

I made sure to walk her past the jewellery boutique several times during the day, but Amy and the staff had nearly given the game away as they'd sang 'Happy Birthday' every time we were in the vicinity.

They weren't the only ones either and by lunchtime I reckon everyone knew what was going on. The waiters sang to her at breakfast, as did the dance instructors and even the art instructor had painted her a lovely picture on a card.

She got a small bouquet of flowers from the Captain and our steward decorated our cabin door with ribbons and balloons. In the evening there were cocktails courtesy of the Executive Purser.

The evening in the restaurant was exceptionally good.

When Amy and the Maitre d had turned up with a gift bag singing 'Happy Birthday' my dear lady got really excited and started hugging everybody.

I think I'm currently very popular.

(Thanks Amy)

She's fast asleep now and has a lovely contented smile on her face.

I sure she's had a lovely day.

Saturday 9ᵗʰ March

Day 61 'Manta' - not made in China...guaranteed.

Just the one stop in Ecuador and it's here in Manta, one of the largest 'tuna processing' ports in the world.

As we'd taken breakfast on the back deck it was really interesting to watch the ships unloading their catch at the port. The quantity of tuna being moved was enormous as huge grab cranes lifted tons of large fish out of the hold and loaded them onto a fleet of lorries. This was still going on later in the day when we'd returned to the ship, and I'd started to understand why there are concerns about creating sustainable sources for the future.

Fortunately the skies have clouded over so at least it a bit cooler.

We were off to Montecristi today, the town where the famous Panama hat is made. Our guide did tell us the story of why this world renown hat bears the name of a different country rather than its own, but to be honest it was so involved with many different theories, I actually fell asleep.

It was something to do with Panama being a centre for trade so the Ecuadorians sent the hats there to be sold, or possibly because the workers who'd built the Panama Canal had worn them, or something similar.

Our guide also explained at length the manufacturing process and the difference between the various 'grades' of hat, which is painstakingly handmade by nimble-fingered workers.

When we'd arrived in the town we could clearly see how labour intensive the process is, with the weavers working eight hours a day in the relentless heat. We'd stood watching for several minutes as many hundreds of individual fibres were deftly organised and woven into the shape of a hat. It was fascinating but I'm positive I wouldn't have the patience to work like that for a day, let alone a lifetime.

The most expensive Panama can cost thousands of dollars and take months to make. These are known as 'superfino', which are usually made to measure and guaranteed for a lifetime. Whereas the ordinary run of the mill 'still very nice but cheap' version is available for a mere twenty dollar note. The weave is a lot coarser so they're easier and quicker to make.

In the middle of these extremes is the 'fino' which comes in anywhere between sixty and two hundred dollars, dependant on the quality and finish of the fibres and we're told that these are the ones being made as we watched.

We're then invited to browse the market which has many fine examples of all the different 'grades' of Panamas, but mainly they sell the popular twenty dollar hats.

Now a quick reckoning and it's quite obvious to us that the workers are poorly paid.

Sadly though there are always sceptics out to ruin the day, convinced that someone is telling 'porky pies' and they suspect that the cheapest ones are really machine made.

Alas, they're not going to stay quiet about their suspicions.

"So where are these made then?" one of the attendees asks holding aloft a bargain hat.

"Right here."

The lady stall owner points at an elderly lady weaving away at the back of the stall in the shade, probably her mother.

"By her," she'd added.

"Yeah," says the loudmouth. "I bet I'll find a 'Made in China' label."

"Not China," the lady shouts, "Here."

The whole market square goes silent, every pair of local eyes turn and stare. The stall holder grabs the hat and furiously points to the inner band.

"Look, says Ecuador hat, not China."

Not content to just upset the locals our idiot is intent on starting a fight.

"Okay," he'd said. Then holding the hat up again he'd addressed the other stall holders. "So this one is twenty dollars, who'll do me one cheaper?"

The rest of us were backing away desperately trying to disassociate ourselves from any connection with this wrecker of inter cultural relationships. There is only one obvious way to restore peace, so we'd all quickly bought a hat, no haggling just try it on and part with money.

I bought four as it's inevitable the boys and girls back home are going to end up with various trinkets from our travels (whether they want them or not)

This seemed like a good time to add goodies to the collection.

My dear lady treated herself to one that was a little more expensive, after all it was her birthday.

Our purchases seem to have appeased the locals and we'd quickly escaped before anybody else could stir up trouble by asking more silly questions.

We had our usual good look around the church and then visited a most elaborate mausoleum overlooking the town of Montecristi. It celebrated the life of one of the countries visionaries, Eloy Delgardo, who I think was responsible for unifying the country and campaigning to ensure all of the people of Ecuador had access to a good education, especially the girls (the guides English was quite jumbled so I might have got this wrong).

They rewarded him by dragging him through the streets, executing him in a most grotesque way and then many years later hailing him as the people's champion and building an entire complex in his honour.

They seem to breed popular revolutionaries in this part of the world.

Back at the port and it's fairly cool out and we still had time to wander into town.

There are some nice beaches for sure, but everywhere smells a little fishy. Even the beer we'd ordered at a small roadside bar came in glasses that were rather marinely pungent.

Ah well at least they were cheap.

Manta wasn't a very interesting port, even if I was rather fascinated by the amount of tuna being shipped ashore, but Montecristi was a different matter. As a tourist attraction the Panama hat and its production was worthy of the visit and the town was very pretty.

'Where ever I lay my hat' and all that.

And that's hat.

Enough of hat already.

Sunday 10th March

Day 62 'at sea' - hats on parade.

Everyone's parading in their new hats; even the Captain has one.

Although it proved to be a bit of a disaster for some as it was quite windy this morning. At least two new hats are currently making their way back to their makers in Ecuador whilst being tested for their waterproof properties and floating ability.

My dear lady has decided she'll keep hers safe until we get home and has refused to take part in this afternoons Panama Hat wearing competition, as she likes to be different.

We're not quite sure what format the 'hat wearing' competition will take, or how the winner will be selected, however the following rules have been circulated.

Anyone is allowed to take part.

Participants must only wear a Panama hat, no other hats are allowed.

No embellishment of the hat is allowed.

Spectators are requested not to attempt 'knocking off' hats by throwing things.

The winner will receive a new Montecristi hat costing twenty dollars.

It's such a shame those folk who had lost their Panamas over the side can't take part, as they're probably the only ones desperate to win.

Why would you want to win something you already have...oh well.

Just after lunch it was announced that due to several complaints of discrimination against other styles of South American hats such as the bombin, cholitas or felt fedora variety, the competition would now be open to anyone sporting a hat.

There was one gent who'd lined up as a

contestant but wasn't wearing a hat. When the entertainment manager had tried to disqualify him his wife 'Fedora' had admitted to having been 'felt' that very afternoon and her man had most defiantly 'felt Fedora'.

The assembled crowd demanded embellishment, which Fedora refused to give in accordance with the rules, as it wasn't allowed.

The gent was still disqualified as he wasn't wearing a 'felt Fedora', but the spectators demanded he be the winner anyway, insisting he needed the hat as they could hear the top of his bald pate sizzling in the sun.

I know, maybe that was a bit of a tall story.

Talking of which, I'm taking my dear lady's advice and have come up with an idea for a story (I'm refusing to call it a book or novel yet as those very often contain a serious amount of words)

They say you should write about things you know, but I'm not sure 'Thirty plus years of designing screw fastenings' is going to appeal to your average reader, and 'How to fail miserably at growing a half decent tomato' would never make it to publication.

Anyway I've managed to make a start and have written a few pages about a theatre manager called Freddie. I say a start but it could be a middle or even an end, but without a clear plan I haven't a clue where it's going (my dear lady says 'probably the bin')

Harsh, but fair.

The main thing is I enjoyed doing it, isn't that the most important reason to do anything?

Watch this space.

Space...now there's an idea...a theatre in space.

Monday 11th March

Day 63 'Panama Canal Transit' - that'll do mule, that'll do.

A long anticipated event for some and although this is technically a sea day as we're not allowed to get off, most of it will be spent passing from the Pacific Ocean to the Atlantic Ocean along a forty eight mile artificial waterway, a manmade masterpiece of engineering.

It's a very hot day as well, so we're grateful our balcony is on the sheltered side of the ship today and we're able to sit and watch the whole transit without burning.

So not a lot to say except it was fascinating to watch the process, with the 'mules' doing the bulk of the work towing ships into place in the locks. With all the technical stuff and machinery it was definitely a day for the 'boys'.

One of the photogs had managed to get permission to get off the ship in order to take pictures as a memento of the day for folk to purchase. There have been many such occasions where they've combined a photo of passengers with a certificate of achievement in an attempt to boost sales. Crossing the equator, rounding Cape Horn and now sailing through the Panama Canal are just a few examples of this practice, and to be fair there are usually a number of folk who indulge.

But it's not for us, so when he was busily trying to capture those of us on our balconies, we kept ducking down each time he pointed his lens in our direction.

He saw it as a bit of a game.

My dear lady in her bikini saw him as a pervert and kept waving him away.

But revenge was soon to be hers.

As he was in a working environment with the 'mules' moving up and down attached by ropes to the ship, he was required to wear reflective clothing and a hard hat. Each time he lifted his camera to his face he'd managed to knock the brim of his hard hat, causing it to fall to the ground. My dear lady took a fair few photos of her own, including a perfect view when he'd bent down and split his trousers.

She's claiming that when they hold the next passenger photographic competition, that one's going in.

We saw a lot of wildlife including an alligator, or it could have been a large caiman, not quite sure which. There were plenty of Frigate birds and a few brown pelicans to be seen, and there was a fair amount of animal sounds coming from the surrounding rainforest.

They're currently building more locks and increasing the size of the channel, so they can accommodate bigger ships, but modern technology and new machinery have replaced the many men with shovels who dug this out by hand just one hundred years ago.

And not a single panama hat in sight.

Tuesday 12th March

Day 64 'Cartagena' - what's not to like?

Well we've arrived in Colombia and security warnings are now a matter of serious consideration.

The harbour and marina are very modern and full of very expensive looking boats. There are two 'Policia' boats, with several heavily armed men, sailing up and down the lines of yachts and cruisers looking in through windows and questioning anyone on board.

I wonder why.

So off we'd set, but initially we'd almost turned back at the port gates as the taxi drivers appear desperate for a fare and are very persistent. There was a lot of invading of my dear lady's personal space until she actually shoved this one chap out of the way and shouted at him that 'we're not looking for a tour'.

That worked, but several had turned back as they didn't enjoy the experience.

At one stage I'm sure one of the drivers had offered me 'an afternoon with his sister' in return for a trip around the city.

I'm not sure who I feel sorry for the most.

The walk into the city along the harbour was very pleasant and only took about fifteen minutes. After the scrum at the port no one else had bothered us and we'd made it into the old town generally unscathed.

It was well worth the effort because it's a very nice place, with the old walled town containing all sorts of architectural and cultural goodies, enough to satisfy most interests for a few hours.

The city was exceptionally busy but we also felt quite safe. The locals in general appeared to be smiley and friendly, except of course for the myriad sellers of tat, and here they do tourist tat on a grand scale.

We had a really good time walking the walls, browsing the converted prison cells for a retail bargain and visiting Plaza Santo Domingo and the Palace of Inquisition to see the sculptures.

Best of all we avoided buying any tat.

There is definitely a sense of money around and about.

The area south of the old town is unquestionably very exclusive, with many new and luxurious condos and large yachts in the harbour. I'm not going to mention the assumed source of the wealth but those 'Policia' were still roaming the harbour.

Very suspicious behaviour!

So that was our last port in South America and I've come away with quite mixed feelings about our visits here. It's been fascinating for sure and we've really had a brilliant time.

We've certainly enjoyed roaming the towns and cities, absorbing the atmosphere and trying out the local cuisine. We're not sure that's been the same for all of our fellow passengers, and the round trip for some has been more about tourism for the sake of a tick box rather than a genuine desire to experience something different.

Some of it will be remembered for a long time, some of it was unremarkable and forgettable, and yet all of it has provoked a reaction, good and bad.

So far it has been a 'voyage of discovery' as personally I've discovered how fortunate I am. Not only because of my dear lady but also the standard of living and convenience I've enjoyed through life.

Apparently, I'm also 'Too sexy for my shirt'.

My dear lady has just finished her fourth cocktail, and now we need to get back to the cabin before her volume increases.

Wednesday 13th March

Day 65 'at sea' - shave and a haircut, two bob...not these days.

My joints are stiff and rusty, old paint's already peeled.
I'm looking fairly shabby with all my faults revealed.
And my undercarriage droops a bit, well, a lot to be quite fair.
My fallen arches need a lift, success in love is rare.
But at least I've had the chance to live a full and active life,
Free from persecution, safe and happy, little strife.
It doesn't matter who I am or what my interests be.
Criticise me all you want, you can't stop me being me.

I'm not quite sure about the inspiration for today's ditty, except that as we'd sipped a very cooling cocktail at the sail away party yesterday evening, I'd made comment about some rust and peeling paint on the side of the ship to my dear lady.

Her reply was intended as a joke I'm sure, but she was right, I am starting to look a bit 'shabby' myself.

Maybe she'd really meant to sing 'I'm not sexy enough for my shirt' instead.

I've always been a little lax as far as the length of my hair is concerned, and I've never enjoyed shaving. So apart from my daily shower, I haven't indulged in any serious 'male grooming' since we left the UK.

Obviously I'm now a little woolly.

So after dancing this morning I'd booked a 'session' with 'Clint' in the spa.

I couldn't just book a haircut, it had to be a whole session.

I'd arrived a few minutes before my allotted time and was told Clint shouldn't be long as he was just finishing off another client.

I should have taken the hint contained in that remark and left there and then.

A few minutes later this large chap with green eye shadow, black lipstick and a bright orange Mohican came flouncing down the passageway. Please god this was 'Clint' and not the client he'd just finished off.

"Felicitations and hi, so glad you've stopped by."

Oh no he thinks he's a poet as well.

He'd pumped my hand with gusto and continued to hold onto it as he'd led me to his room, chatting incessantly. The only phrase I managed to catch as he'd wittered away was that he could tell I was in desperate need of his help.

'I just need a haircut', was the phrase I would use several times over the next fifteen minutes as he'd sat me down to 'discuss' my treatment.

"And a nice close shave," he'd said, as he'd rubbed cream into my hands. "Oh just look at those cuticles."

He couldn't have looked more horrified if I'd pulled a gun on him.

"Your poor nails are so in need of a manicure."

"No, just a haircut please."

"At least a shave as well, tidy you up a bit for the ladies."

He'd put on his best smile, "Or the gents if you prefer."

"I think my friend Jeff doesn't care what I look

like," I'd said without thinking.

"I'm sure Jeffery would love a nice smooth cheek to stroke," was his reply.

Oh dear, now I was in trouble, best come clean, so I'd told Clint that my friends wife had smooth cheeks, he can stroke them.

"Oh you wicked pair," he'd squealed, "Does she know what's going on?"

"Can I just get the haircut, please."

I have to say he made a good job, but sales driven Clint kept up a barrage of recommendations throughout the entire hour it took to cut my hair.

Even as he'd trimmed the fluffy bits on the back of my neck he'd been most insistent that I should get my back waxed.

Definitely just a haircut then.

Parting with thirty pounds for that was painful enough, thank you.

In the gym this evening Ted and Nadia weren't all hot and sweaty for once. Instead they were sat on a bench facing each other with their heads almost touching.

They'd continued whispering and giggling for a few minutes while I started my routine on the treadmill.

Then they'd stood and headed for the door together.

"Hiya'" I'd called over.

"Just off for a shower," came the reply.

Without even thinking I'd spoken my thoughts out loud.

"Together?"

"Oh yes," Nadia beamed. "I need to supervise his warm up and cool down procedure very closely."

'Caribbean again'

Thursday 14th March

Day 66 'Aruba' - Caribbean tinsel town

We've arrived back in the Caribbean and immediately there's a difference in the weather. It's still very hot, but that sticky humidity no longer drenches the body from head to toe in sweat every time you step outside. There's a pleasant breeze cooling everything down a touch, and it doesn't smell like fish for a change.

With ten days touring the islands in this renowned tropical paradise the time has finally come to put our feet up and just chill.

Today we're in Aruba.

Oh my goodness what a place this is.

Aruba appears to be undergoing a huge facelift and is definitely benefitting from its standing as a regular cruise and holiday destination for the masses. With big white hotel buildings, casinos and a mass of 'designer' shopping, this is a thriving island.

And it's literally pristine, like someone had unwrapped it earlier this morning in preparation for our arrival.

We had a wander around the main town of Oranjestad, then followed the boardwalk out of the main centre and along the pretty beaches, which aren't big but appear to be well tended. There are plenty of shady trees so we'd settled ourselves down for a little beach therapy.

What could be better than swimming in the crystal clear waters of paradise?

The answer is swimming in those same waters surrounded by hundreds of little multi-coloured fish. It seemed they were as inquisitive about us as we were with them.

Most amazingly, despite all of the development going on in the area the wildlife hasn't been frightened away and seemed content to wander around with the tourists. We saw lizards, iguana and many shoals of fish, as well as spider crabs and birds going about their business side by side with sun bathers.

A late lunch of clam chowder and paella was very enjoyable, followed by another wander through the back streets of the town. It's all a bit 'Disneyish' if I'm being honest, almost too perfect, but we had a lovely relaxing day.

Thank you Aruba.

Back onboard and the sail away was a lot livelier than of recent.

Now that we're in the Caribbean the entertainment manager has seen fit to employ the services of a local steel drum band, which will be staying with us until we reach Antigua. If tonight's party out on the lido deck was anything to go by, it's going to get a bit raucous, assumingly because of a rejuvenated 'joie de vivre' amongst the passengers rather than the copious amounts of rum punch they were all consuming.

One gent had definitely had his fair share of the complimentary cocktails, and when it came to his turn to shuffle his way under the pole of the impromptu limbo dancing competition, he'd laid down on the floor, crawled under the nearest table and fell asleep.

We'd left shortly after a display of fresh fruit and ice-cream had been tipped into the pool, where poor Ted was seemingly trying to impress the young lady in the band with his 'diving practice'.

She'd certainly laughed a lot when he'd resurfaced with a bunch of grapes balanced on his head.

He's such a charmer, and I was starting to wonder what his secret was. There certainly seemed to be a lot of admirers hanging around.

So it was off to the gym for me and I'd been surprised to see Nadia thrashing away alone on the rowing machine. I think she must have pulled a muscle that had really hurt her because she'd run off crying.

A day at sea tomorrow, then the small island of Tobago and probably another relaxing day like today, but then that's the whole reason for being here.

Friday 15th March

Day 67 'at sea' - where have we been again?

Where has the last two weeks gone?

Since Valparaiso we've certainly done a lot and yet not a lot has happened, especially on the ship.

I'd started to think that the newbies were quite bland in comparison to previous batches, if in fact anybody had actually joined the ship at all

It didn't seem like it.

But now I'm starting to realise why things have been quiet.

South America was undoubtedly very interesting, and as my dear lady and I had considered this would probably be our one and only visit, our subsequent mission had always been to 'get out there and explore', which we did.

The more recent long days of discovering the best of the towns and cities of the west coast had been quite wearing, and along with the constant need to consider various security and health issues surrounding the area, it wasn't at all relaxing.

Seven hundred or so other folk had probably felt the same, and like us sea days and evenings were spent recharging the batteries, mainly inside and out of the frazzling heat.

Even our evenings in the dining room have been unremarkable. Table one two eight is still the same four couples, but we hadn't been as sociable or indulgent of late. There wasn't any fallings out, it was just the way it was.

Derek and Pam had suffered a touch of sun-stroke in Arica, and we hadn't seen them for several days afterwards. Even Jeff and Pru had excused themselves after dinner on several occasions, as they'd had some early morning starts out on a tour.

I think everyone was starting to feel a little jaded.

But after yesterday things are different and from the chatter going on around the ship, most had a really good time in Aruba. Unusually there hasn't been a lot of moaning and it feels like there's a bit more enthusiasm in the air, a renewed interest around the ship, and I have to admit I'm feeling that way too.

The 'Watchers' have happily acquired an extra layer of clothing and are once again observing the horizon from the front of the ship, and the 'Cruise Brigade' have been able to recommence bombing around the decks at an accelerated rate without actually melting.

The whole ship seems busier, livelier and in general it feels like the start of a holiday rather than one that's been going a while.

We'd received an invitation to a tea dance from the instructors, a chance to experience a proper dance environment and show off the moves we've been learning for the past few weeks.

It was held this afternoon in the lounge bar, and we were spoilt with a proper afternoon tea of crustless sandwiches and fancy cakes, whilst being serenaded by the ships band. Once the tables had been cleared we were requested to take the floor for a waltz.

I knew that this was what my dear lady had been waiting for, her romantic vision of the two of us gliding across polished wooden floors the world over was about to become a reality. As I'd stood and offered my hand to help her up, she'd pulled me back down to my seat.

"I think we should wait a bit," she'd said and nodded towards the gathering throng.

Everybody from the beginners and the improvers classes were there, racing to find space on the dance floor.

But the mobile chicanes were out in force.

It was like going to the pictures, or getting on a train where the folk who got on first have occupied the seats at the end of each row, forcing everyone else to clamber over them.

Here in the lounge, those who had reached the

dance floor first, and I'm fairly certain this was a deliberately planned manoeuvre on behalf of the improvers, had formed an impenetrable square barrier around the edge of the floor with the middle left empty.

Some of the beginners had succeeded in pushing through, others gave up and sat down, while a group of determined souls moved a few tables aside and took up a position on the carpet.

Let battle commence.

By the look on some of the faces I had visions of reasonable folk transforming into a bloodthirsty mob.

The beginners needed to prove they were worthy to be in the presence of the improvers, who in turn wished to demonstrate their superiority over those beneath them.

We sat and watched.

Jeff and Pru were in there, somewhere.

We were worried we may never see them again.

It was chaos, of the utter variety.

When the music started the improvers were flamboyant and brassy, while the beginners stuttered and stumbled and just got in the way. What followed can only be described as a bumper car boogie. The weaker beginners were practically hounded from the floor, but a small pocket of them regrouped and charged the stronger lines of the improvers in a show of resistance.

There in the midst was Jeff and his trusty companion Pru. They took on one couple, then two and appeared to be holding their own, but sadly they were vastly outnumbered and their rally was all in vain.

"Well that's me done, Laddie," Jeff said as they'd rejoined us. "Are you no gonna have a bash?"

"Seeing that lot, then no," my dear lady exclaimed. "I always thought dancing was civilised, but they're just a bunch of thugs. Come on I need a proper drink."

She waltz away singing 'Murder on the dance floor'.

She wasn't wrong, Jeff was limping.

At least the afternoon tea was worth making the effort for.

Saturday 16th March

Day 68 'Tobago' - humming all the way.

Tobago is the smaller sister of Trinidad and our first sight of the port area of Scarborough and the town beyond suggests a complete contrast to Aruba. It certainly appears to be a lot less affluent, well to be honest it looks a bit rough!

Once again though 'first impressions and all that'.

As we'd headed out of the port gates we'd joined up with that famous (or infamous) duo and were treated to a tour of the town with Joy, a local guide who has been tasked by the local government to help promote tourism. She took us through the local market, where the delicacies of the region included pig snouts, tails or trotters, cow heels and tongues, not to mention various other exotic sounding bits of animals.

Joy was definitely promoting something at this stage...nausea.

On through the local mall, selling pretty much the same stuff but with less flies, and then we'd found ourselves out in the fresh air (I use the term loosely)

Joy had certainly been well named as she was so enthusiastic about her town. She certainly didn't seem to notice the bad smells emanating from the long line of rubbish bins she'd proudly shown us next, and the smile never changed as she'd told us how little the islanders actually threw away.

She'd opened one of the bins to reveal a mass of animal carcasses stripped bare.

"And this is all processed to make animal feed," she'd said.

Nice.

Next we'd headed into the arboretum where we'd spent a fair amount of time looking at all the different fruit trees and local flora, while Joy gave us a potted history of the town, which was much more interesting and a little less repellent.

Back in the town we (well Jeff) negotiated a fee for a tour of the island with Jerry the taxi driver.

Jerry was quite old and was constantly mumbling about birds, but he'd seemed friendly enough. At first his driving was of a little concern as well because he'd sat with his nose almost pressed against the windscreen as if he was struggling to see. At least he didn't drive very fast, in fact I'm not sure if he got past second gear.

Firstly he took us to the local fort to indulge in the stunning views from the top of the island. My dear lady was serenaded by a guitar playing local thespian trying to impress her enough to earn a few dollars for food, or something more potent perhaps, but he was a very likeable character despite his personal hygiene issues.

Back in the taxi and on to our next stop.

Jerry was still muttering something about seeing the birds but we're not exactly sure why, unless it was some kind of local joke as we'd asked to go Pigeon Point at the far western tip of the island.

But Jerry obviously had other ideas, and after a fifteen minute drive we'd pulled into a small private driveway and parked outside a big old house. We were told that there was an entrance fee of five dollars each. But to see what was still unknown.

Despite a little scepticism, mainly from Jeff as he was being asked to open his wallet again, we were intrigued. So with the money duly handed over, Jerry took us around the side of the house and sat us down in the garden.

This was exceedingly pretty for sure, but what happened next was really unexpected.

A man appears, cuts up a banana and skewers it in the garden boarder with a stick, sprinkles seed around and then gives us each a bowl of mango ice cream (home made of course)

Then he'd struck a bell, and the garden was suddenly transformed into the most stunning aviary. There were at least three or four different varieties of humming birds as well as countless other species, big and small, dining on the offered treats not six feet from where we were sitting. For quite a while they'd remained feeding, totally oblivious, it would seem, to our presence, and we were thoroughly entertained.

It was amazing to see the speed and agility of the tiny humming birds close to and what a very special treat it turned out to be.

Back in Scarborough we'd thanked Jerry for a lovely trip, he'd muttered something about birds but we still didn't have a clue what he was saying. Much to Jeff's relief it was time for an indulgent beer, so a local bar near to the port was chosen.

With chickens, ducks and goats gathered round our table it all felt a bit like 'Old MacDonald' would be found close by. But the beer was good, even if the locals did eye us a little suspiciously as money and a few little packages were passed between themselves.

As we'd headed out of the harbour later on and waved our goodbyes to Tobago, there had been a spectacular sunset. Deep orange and red streaked the skies, with wispy purple coloured clouds hovering on the horizon. It was really stunning and my dear lady wanted a picture, so I'd raced back to the cabin to fetch the camera.

It's hard to explain but when I'd walked into our room my mind had gone completely blank, I hadn't got a clue what I'd come back for.

They say around seven thousand brain cells die each day, and I'd just had a 'top of the stairs' moment where the information I'd needed to complete the task in hand had been contained in newly deceased neurons.

My dear lady says it happens all the time, I just don't remember it.

Here's my take on proceedings.

At the top of the stairs I stand wondering.
Hands on hips, then a scratch of the head,
Attempting to recall a memory
That all of a sudden is dead.

So trying to gain inspiration
Scanning each bedroom door with a sigh,
Whatever it was lured me up here
Has left me confused, high and dry!

Was it something I wanted to look for?
Or a task that I needed to do?
So I pause for a second to ponder,
No, I don't have to go to the loo.

There's no light at the end of this tunnel,
And it won't be alright on the night.
At the top of the stairs just frustration,
With the chance of remembering, slight.

But now a dilemma has started,
To remain, or give up and go down,
If somebody else sent me up here
That'll make me appear such a clown.

At the top of the stairs I'm still standing.
Hands on hips, with a memory that flew,
I was sure it was really important,
But now that I'm here...not a clue.

My dear lady likes it, and has suggested we move into a bungalow if this starts happening on a regular basis.

She sang 'Memory' from Cats all evening, how rude. But as she'd repeated the line 'Memory, all alone in the moonlight' over and over again, I reckon she can't remember the rest.

Oh and the irony of this, well I have to be honest and say that the whole 'camera' incident actually happened two days ago as we'd left Aruba, I've just adapted it for today. I'm hoping my dear lady doesn't find out as she'll never believe that I hadn't really forgotten about it, I was just distracted by all the other stuff going on at the time.

Honestly I was.

Sunday 17th March

Day 69 'Barbados' - again.

We had a busy and interesting day in Barbados when we were here eight weeks ago, so this time we'd decided to find a beach and do very little.

Heading off for the walk into Bridgetown, we'd stopped to buy a few interesting bits and bobs from a local artist. He was a friendly chap and had recommended a place called The Boatyard for a day on the beach, and told us how to get there.

Just a short walk along the harbour front and across the bridge and we found the entrance. For twelve dollars each we got a lounger, parasol, the first drink and a minibus back to the port at the end of the day.

We chose a rum punch.

So that's what a rum punch should taste like.

I can say no more than it was time well spent as we had a great day just 'chillin and sunnin' 'swimmin and drinkin'.

It was such a hard day in paradise, but someone had to do it.

All too soon it was time to leave and despite the availability of a free shuttle service to the port we'd decided to walk back to the ship, mainly because I wanted to shake the sand out of my shorts and the beer induced fuzziness from my head.

Back on the ship and despite the increasing gap between my brain and body I just had to go to the gym. I'm really concerned about Ted and Nadia.

They'd seemed to be getting on so well and yet the last couple of evenings Nadia has been on her own while Ted has continued to 'dive' in the pool.

She's been watching him from the gym windows that overlook the lido deck, obviously distraught.

But tonight I must report a reuniting of the pair and they were snuggling cosily when I'd arrived.

Happy to see Nadia beaming again I excused myself as I didn't want to intrude and spoil everything.

Sacrificing a few moment of torture wasn't a difficult decision.

Monday 18th March

Day 70 'St Lucia' - one Piton or two?

Another glorious day greeted our arrival, so we got Jeff to work his magic on one of the taxi drivers for a tour of the island.

His skills in this department are amazing to watch as he's never embarrassed to start the negotiations very, very, very low, and usually it pays off. Today our potential driver, Tony, had suggested a four to five hour tour of the island for one hundred and eighty dollars. Jeff's counter offer had been a round one hundred.

I really wouldn't be that brave, in fact I probably wouldn't haggle at all and just accept the first price given.

It seemed that Tony could tell Jeff would be no pushover, but at the same time he didn't appear to be offended either. The fare was agreed at one hundred and forty and off we'd set towards Tony's recommended destination of Soufriere, the former capital of the island, built on the floor of the volcano.

He'd promised us a spectacular journey with the

best views of, and from the island and my dear lady had said she would hold him to that or there'd be no tip.

Tony just started laughing.

"Lady, you'll have so much fun today you'll want to leave your man and stay here with Tony."

At least she'd winked at me before replying, "It won't take a lot."

St Lucia is a very up and down island with a rain forest interior.

The drive was quite intense with steep roads zigzagging up the sides of the very large hills. We'd stopped at the top of the first climb for an incredible vista over the capital town of Castries, with our ship looming large in the deep blue waters of the harbour.

This had set the tone for the rest of the journey, with treacherous roads, stunning views and all throughout Tony had delivered a running commentary second to none.

We heard stories about slavery, pirates and hurricanes as the car engine either juddered up an impossible incline or screamed its way down an almost vertical drop. At many of the sharp bends we'd been informed about landslides and collapsed roads in the area, not to mention all the unfortunate deaths they'd caused.

It would have been quite a worry had Tony not been a master storyteller, it was more entertaining than disturbing.

As we'd approached our main destination we were treated to views of the Pitons.

And at this point I've run out of superlatives.

Even the photographs didn't capture a fraction of the wow factor in front of us, the views across the flat volcano floor and onto the rugged peaks of the mountains were absolutely stunning.

Down in Soufriere, the drive through the streets is a whole world of difference away from the wonderful scenery. The centre looks quite scruffy in parts and locals have goods for sale on upturned crates.

"Times are hard," Tony tells us with a smile.

"But we all do what it takes to get by, and there's always the beach."

A little further on we'd stopped at the Diamond Botanical Gardens and for five dollars each we'd had a really enjoyable hour. The gardens are a tranquil haven after the stress of the perilous taxi journey. It's full of flowers, trees and birds which Tony tells us all about.

Surprisingly he'd accompanied us into the gardens as it turns out he's also a very knowledgeable tour guide for many of the islands attractions, as well as being a driver.

What was it he'd said about doing what it takes to get by?

As we'd strolled along the nature trail, each turn of the path revealed another surprise. Once again Tony gave us a running commentary as we toured the gardens, pointing out brightly coloured hummingbirds flitting from flower to flower.

The falls aren't the biggest we've seen, but the colours in rocks are interesting, and there's a distinct smell of vanilla everywhere.

On the trip back to Castries Tony stopped in one of the smaller villages to get some lunch for himself from a local bakery. He treated us to a local delicacy of sweet bread rolls filled with a mixture of coconut, nutmeg and something that tastes like marzipan, really yummy.

He then stopped at a viewpoint overlooking Marigot Bay. Apparently this was where the movie Dr Doolittle was filmed, and I started to wonder where the inspiration for the name Doolittle had come.

There's a very nice bar here too and Tony asked if we would like some refreshments while he has his lunch.

Would we ever pass up the chance to sample the local beer and hospitality?

Would we ever?

Anyway, back on the road and surprisingly the trip back didn't seem quite so treacherous.

It was interesting to see the children coming out of school in the valleys and waving at the vehicles as they drove past. Every so often someone in a van or pick-up truck would stop and the kids would all pile in the back for a lift up to the top of the hill.

This is such a pretty island with truly stunning views, even the multi coloured shanties had looked picturesque from a distance. It's really hard to imagine extreme poverty in a location like this, but driving through a couple of the small fishing villages and the stark reality is all too apparent. There's little work and the residents only survive by fishing to feed their families.

Even in this most idyllic spot with its white sandy beaches, azure blue sky and crystal clear water, all framed by the lush green forest slopes, it feels like there's an emptiness so deep that it's impossible to look the locals in the eye and not experience an overwhelming gratitude for our own good and fortunate existence.

If ever 'grass is greener syndrome' demonstrates that not everything is as it seems, then its right here in the fishing villages of St Lucia.

We've witnessed a lot of poverty on this trip and in most cases the surrounding scenery was as harsh as the life the people lead.

But here on this lush green island the beauty makes you believe things are so much worse, even though they aren't.

This really is a place offering two distinctive emotions, look left and delight in paradise, look right and be troubled by the squalor that lies alongside. But do the locals feel the same way, or is Tony's comment relevant for everyone, 'there's always the beach'.

That's really not for me to decide.

Talking of decisions, I'm pleased to say my dear lady did have a really fun time today, and I know this because she's been singing 'Perfect Day' (again) since we got back. She didn't want to stay in St Lucia because apparently I'm more fun than Tony.

But only just.

Cheek.

Tuesday 19th March

Day 71 'at sea' - excuse me, I'm talking.

When I was fourteen I had a Saturday job working at my uncle's shop, and there was a plaque on the wall which stated:

'The customer is always right'
(Often confused and misguided, but always right)

This little gem of wisdom and the message it was attempting to convey had been very confusing for a young lad like myself, especially as my uncle always maintained that the customer was never right with another plaque which stated:

Rule one - the boss is always right.
Rule two - if the boss is wrong see rule one.

I suppose it would be true to say that as a young teenager in the early seventies I didn't really understand sarcasm.

But back then the British public never used to complain, well, rarely complained.

Stiff upper lip and all that.

My uncle's sign was just a parody, a bit of fun (at the customer's expense of course) but no one really took these wise words too seriously, least of all the customer.

If any punter had actually managed to drum up sufficient courage to stutter an objection about some wrongdoing carried out against them, then more often than not the protest would quickly fizzle out and turn into a humble apology from the very same person who 'didn't wish to be a nuisance or cause any trouble'.

Nowadays there's an ever increasing culture of complaining and mainly about trivial matters. There is too much consideration of self and rarely a thought for the feelings of others, and we're becoming a very egocentric society (if we're not there already)

There's a lady who's been on the ship since Valparaiso and has gained somewhat of a reputation for complaining. She attends reception so often to voice her displeasure about anything and everything that she now bears the nickname 'Sanatogen', as in once a day.

I've overheard her gripes many times and frankly it's sad that she's wasting so much of her holiday on such trivial matters.

I suppose they must be important to her though.

Her main problem appears to be an expectation that she should be getting more than she's paid for. She'd booked a cheap inside cabin near to the back of the ship, but has spent many sessions demanding an upgrade to at least a balcony, with a different reason for each day.

Because of her loyalty status, her age, her inability to walk too far, noise from neighbours, noise from the engines, she likes a drink so needs a room closer to the bars, or closer to the lifts, the steward hates her, her neighbours hate her, her room service food gets cold on its long journey from the galley, her doctor has told her to sleep with a window open, and the list goes on and on.

She's moaned at the photogs for making her look old, the bar staff for adding too much ice to her G&T and her steward for putting towel animals on her bed which had frightened her to death...if only.

A certain member of staff saw an opportunity to play a bit of a prank when the lady had asked her if the crew had living quarters on the ship.

"There's not enough room," was the reply. "At the end of our shift a helicopter picks us up from the back of the ship and takes us home."

Sure enough the next morning the lady was at reception, once again demanding a cabin change, claiming she'd been kept awake all night by the noise of helicopters landing on the back deck.

There can be no doubt that over the years the British have learnt to complain, mainly because they're hoping for some form of compensation.

If there's a genuine reason to object then do so, but if a small issue occurs then maybe we should consider accepting that sometimes mistakes happen, after all we are human, and we all make mistakes.

We should at least be honest and not dramatise a situation just to get our own way, or our money back.

On the ship I've discovered that each and every complaint is duly recorded in a logbook in reception, no matter how trivial.

I like to imagine the scene below decks as the crew gather in the mess for their evening meal. Collecting their food from the galley they take their seats in silence.

Anticipation is rife as one appointed member stands, clears their throat, opens a well used logbook and trying desperately not to burst into hysterics, reads the day's list of complaints.

I've had a really productive day writing some ideas for my book. We've been outside nearly all day as the weather has been 'just right' for lazing around the pool. I sat with my notebook and pen, scribbling ideas while my dear lady kept telling me to stop giggling.

I think she likes some of my ideas though, 'Paperback writer' has been her song choice for today, probably inspired by the steel drum band, who'd entertained the assembled for most of the afternoon with Beatles Melodies.

Wednesday 20th March

Day 72 'Virgin Gorda' - not any more she isn't.

We have four consecutive days in port before heading back across the Atlantic Ocean and today was our ships maiden call to the small island of Virgin Gorda, part of the British Virgin Islands (identified as British, but the Americans bought out Denmark's share some time back)

It's a tender port so as usual we'd waited till the rush for the shore had died down and then set off mid morning to explore.

As we'd tendered in the whole place looked a little worn round the edges, a bit like Tobago, with a port area that hasn't had the lavish attention paid to it as some of its bigger brothers and sisters around the Caribbean.

But looks, as we have discovered on many occasions, can be deceptive and the harbour certainly contains a fair number of large luxury yachts, so maybe the tattered facade is a deliberate ploy to discourage all and sundry from disrupting their peaceful haven.

Too late, we're here.

We hadn't arranged to meet up with the other two today but they're on the same tender, so we'd chatted about plans for the day. There's an area known as 'The Baths' where huge granite boulders lie in piles, forming scenic grottos with sheltered sea pools.

It's about two miles from the port along a fairly flat and easy road, so my dear lady and I were fancying a nice long walk and maybe a little relaxing on one of the deserted beaches afterwards.

Jeff was all in favour of the walk, but as the sun was starting to heat things up Pru wasn't, so they'd decided to get a taxi to the baths and maybe we'd see them there.

Jeff's face was a picture, he never likes spending money.

Anyway we'd left them to their own devices at the port gates and set off along the road.

We'd passed a line of brightly painted pick-up trucks with canvas tent like structures shading the back. These apparently are the local taxis, and a big sign heralds it's a five dollar fare to the baths.

Hopefully that shouldn't upset Jeff too much.

Five minutes or so later they'd passed us, riding on the back of one of the trucks.

"Should have come with us Laddie, I got him down to four dollars each," Jeff had shouted over to us, a huge smile on his face. He still wouldn't have been happy to part with his money, but getting a discount certainly improves his mood.

"We'll see you up there in a bit," my dear lady answered as they'd disappeared round a bend.

We weren't to know we'd see them much sooner than either of us had thought.

We'd continued along the road for another few minutes and as we'd rounded a corner there they were, being helped out of the back of the taxi truck by a local policeman. With blue lights flashing on the patrol car we'd watched as our travelling companions were led away to be bundled into the back of the car.

We'd just had to follow tradition by calling out "Book 'em Danno, with Jeff shouting back, "Bail us out."

The officer looked very stern, maybe they were really in trouble after all.

For one horrible moment we'd seriously thought they'd been arrested as the driver was still talking to an officer at the roadside while our friends were being driven away.

But what had they done?

We found out that many of the truck drivers were operating an unlicensed taxi service and the police were clamping down today. So while the drivers were being 'written up' other officials had transported the tourists to their destination.

Our friends may have wished for different though. If they'd known what awaited them at the beach they would probably have opted for the cells.

The Baths were crowded, very crowded in fact, and it's not a very big beach anyway.

Entrance is three dollars each, but even this hadn't deterred anyone at all. In fact I reckon the entire population of the island was here, along with the world and his proverbial wife, and all of them had brought several friends who were experts at getting in the way of everyone else.

Okay so let's find the rocks.

This is not a difficult task because they're everywhere, on the beach, in the sea and piled up on the side, and they're massive. But the question has to be where did they all come from? The island is fairly flat at this point so they don't seem to have fallen off anything and most of them are so big it's hard to believe someone, or the sea brought them here.

There is a marked route between the boulders which leads to an open sea cave, but it's quite a tight squeeze and sometimes the visitor has to crawl on hands and knees in places.

We'd attempted to complete this fascinating obstacle course for the chance to witness what we'd been told was spectacular. But we'd had to give up, not because we couldn't do it but rather because we were stopped from doing it by other people's actions.

Each narrow passage would open up into a bigger chamber, and as you'd tried to squeeze through the folk in front would just stand up, stop and stare, leaving the rest of us stuck in a crouch while the idiots at the back tried to push through from behind.

It became a real bottleneck, and my dear lady couldn't cope.

So we'd got out, but that in itself was no mean feat.

Anyway, we escaped out of the area eventually and true to form we found a nearby bar called 'Mad Dogs' and sat looking out for the other two just in case.

This was much better, a real piece of heaven compared to the push and shove at 'The Baths'. A quite place with a cold beer overlooking the sea, a fresh breeze and listening to the birds in the trees was truly idyllic.

So why call it 'Mad Dogs'?

Then a group of the locals had turned up, and boy were they loud. Maybe the name of the bar means something after all, still it was very pleasant while it lasted.

Walking back towards the port and we'd turned off down a dirt track and found a very pretty, almost empty beach for a swim.

So it had turned into a great visit after all.

Jeff told us over dinner that he'd got his money back and the police car ride was free. Even better, they'd been let into The Baths for free as a gesture of goodwill.

But seeing the crowds, they too left in a hurry.

Jeff had tried to find another unlicensed ride, but alas to no avail, and he'd had to pay the full $5.

Virgin Gorda was great, although I wasn't too enamoured by the crowds at The Baths. It certainly felt very Caribbean, but without some of the rougher edges we've seen elsewhere, but then we only stayed local to the harbour.

Well worth the visit.

Formal night tonight and once again Ted was there with the very pretty young lady on his arm, and only an hour after he'd gone off to cool down with Nadia.

I hope he's not going to upset her again.

Thursday 21st March

Day 73 'St Kitts' - sail away and a late night

An early start today as we were off on a six hour trip labelled as a 'Nevis Sail Away'. This would be our first ever experience of a typical Caribbean catamaran trip, with wonderful views of the land, snorkelling in the clear waters, sampling typical local cuisine and drinking rum punch until the lights go out.

But no alcohol is allowed until after snorkelling, so the first hour of the trip was very quiet and reserved.

My first experience of snorkelling was great, although I wasn't quite so enamoured with the kit they'd supplied as some of it looked quite suspect with regard to its cleanliness.

But hey ho, give it a go.

I was really surprised about how much you can actually see below the surface, and me and my dear lady had been so intrigued we were the last to return to the boat.

The bar was already open.

Evidently there are a fair few passengers on the ship who are rarely seen in the bars, and quite a lot more who do like to treat themselves to a favourite tipple, but only occasionally.

I can't say for certain that this is because some folk don't like spending money, but it's very noticeable how many more takers there are for the alcoholic drinks at the sail away parties and special events where everything is complimentary.

There's one particular couple on the table next to one two eight who've been on for the whole trip, and have yet to been seen with a bottle of wine or in any of the bars at any other time.

When our table has been a bit raucous they have meted out some severe disapproving looks, tutting their distain at our enjoyment of the grape and grain.

But when the drinks are free, they have them lined up, as many as six or seven each.

This same couple were on today's trip, and as the drinks were complimentary they were not going to be denied their fair share. By the time we'd reached Nevis they were both fairly tiddled.

While hubby was busy 'Dad Dancing' to the party music being played by the DJ, his wife had slurred questions at the young man serving at the bar.

"Is it true what they say about Caribbean men?"

"Depends what you heard lady," was his reply.

"That you're very passionate and sensual."

"Yes we are lady, and very selective also."

"I've heard you like older and experienced women too."

"Not me lady, but my granpapa does."

She just kept on flirting, too muddled to even realise the 'put-downs' he kept delivering.

It was clear he was playing his own game, and continued to put more rum punch in front of her.

When we reached Nevis the boat had draw right up onto the sand and we'd all waded the short distance to the beach. The staff brought the drinks ashore as well and the party continued for a couple of hours.

There were quite a few locals on the beach selling everything from small trinkets to beautifully polished conch shells. At times it got to be quite a nuisance, but in fairness a polite 'no thanks' was enough, and the trader moved on.

One chap had passed us many times trying to sell fresh coconuts.

"Cheaper than Asda ladies and fresher than your man," he'd called in a style typical of island humour.

"Oh for goodness sake," the lady sitting on the next lounger to us had shouted after him, as he'd passed for the umpteenth time.

"Nobody wants your bloody coconuts. Just shut up and go away."

The poor chap was insulted.

"I'm just trying to feed my family lady," he shouted back at her.

My dear lady had quickly stepped in to defuse

the situation.

"I'll have one, how much?"

She'd sorted out five dollars while he'd split the husk open for her, and with a polite 'thank you' he went on his way declaring, "Coconuts, cheaper than Asda, guaranteed to put a smile on the crabbiest of faces...except one."

My dear lady then turned to the complainant next to her, "It's really very nice, would you like to try some."

She's always a one to wind others up, but I don't think she'd expected the lady to accept.

"Thank you dear, very kind of you."

She took a huge piece of the white flesh.

"They really are my favourite and so much better when they're fresh," she'd said.

Oh the chutzpah.

On the way back we were treated to a buffet of jerk chicken, ribs, rice and peas, with lots of fruits and salads. It was quite spicy but delicious.

The 'only drink when it's free' couple missed the food as they'd fallen asleep on the netting at the front of the boat.

She was certainly turning an interesting shade of pink.

There were quite a few of the 'Watchers' on the trip as well, understandable as they like to stay as close to the water as possible.

On the way back they'd fallen out. A few of them were trying to assert a little one-upmanship on the others by claiming they'd seen a 'hawksbill' turtle. But of course the counter argument of 'that's not possible' from the rest of them was hailed as a moment of sour grapes, with strong undertones of possessing a 'Well if I didn't see it then it wasn't there' attitude.

A notebook had been grabbed and various scribblings and crossings out were made, but that was as bad as it got.

Back at the port and for a change we didn't go for a beer, at least not straight away.

What can I say other than it's a very enjoyable place to explore.

Independence square, the cathedral and the Anglican church were all interesting, if a little plain, but it was fun just watching the locals going about their business...very slowly.

Because it's not far to our next port, St Maarten, the Captain has arranged for us to stay in port tonight until midnight. There's a local band on board and a special local menu for this evenings meal.

But we're not going to miss the chance to go ashore and spend the evening in town.

We'd asked at the local tourist information and they'd recommended a place on Sandown Road. It was easy to find and we'd enjoyed some amazing goat water, like a curry, the tradition dish of St Kitts, while soaking up the unmistakably hospitable atmosphere.

A great day, and the Caribbean is quickly proving why it's such a favourite holiday destination.

My dear lady's smile has never been bigger and every song she knows with the word paradise (Phil, Coldplay and Guns N Roses no less) has been sung today.

Well pleased.

Friday 22nd March

Day 74 'St Maarten' - a drive and another late night

Pru wanted to go shopping today as this is supposed to be a very good port for jewellers. She's after a memento of the holiday and despite Jeff's best attempts to dissuade her she wasn't going to be put off.

But that was for later, first we were heading off on an unexpected adventure.

We've enjoyed this part of the trip so much that my dear lady and I have been discussing the prospect of coming back to this beautiful part of the world at some point. So I'd wanted to see what driving in the Caribbean is like, and to that end we've hired a car today. We've only got it for a couple of hours but it hasn't cost a lot, so we're just off for a drive around the island.

Okay, so the first problem was it's a left hand drive, this I'd never done before.

At the first gear change I'd managed to put the clutch down but instead of changing gear I'd opened the window. The solution was to put Jeff in the passenger seat to change gear for me.

I never realised how hard it is to drive a 'leftie' car, I would have thought it better if everyone else around the world changed to the proper side.

Only joking.

We did have a great time though and it was really worth it for some of the views around the island.

But the conclusion for this experiment was that it's probably better to get a taxi, certainly a lot less stressful. The roads are good but the locals drive like it's a formula one racetrack.

Back at the port and we hopped on the water taxi to head over to the main town area Philipsburg.

I couldn't count how many jewellery shops there were, all displaying the same 'bling' in almost identical windows. How they can survive together in the same place and make money is a mystery for my simple brain. There are literally hundreds of them, all desperate for your business, all modern and lit up like a stage, all offering free gifts and cold beer, and not surprisingly they're all empty.

Step into these emporia at your peril if you are weak minded, they contain seriously good sales staff that basically super glue themselves onto your shoulder and never leave you alone until you've parted with large wads of cash.

Of course they'll start high by offering you diamonds worth thousands, but they'll quickly move on to more reasonably priced articles if you don't exhibit the traits of a potentially wealthy client.

Everything is at least forty or fifty percent cheaper than the ticket price, and if you manage to put the right expression on your face then even that 'special' price can be adjusted to a 'very very special, only for you, once in a lifetime price'.

Finally, if you're really brave, stubborn or genuinely not interested, you'll arrive at the ultimate 'my boss will kill me for this price, which frankly you'd be mad not to accept'.

And that's how it was today.

"I am in fact mad" I'd explained to one salesman.

"How so?"

"Because no one in their right mind would enter a shop like this having neither the intent to buy nor the money to do so. Who would do such a thing?"

"So why did you come in then?"

"Because we're here with them," I'd said pointing over at Jeff and Pru. "And unfortunately that means subjecting myself to hassle from the likes of you when I could be enjoying a beer in a nice cool bar somewhere."

"I can get you a beer," he'd offered.

"Okay, but I'm still not buying anything."

"Surely your lovely lady is worth spoiling, I have the perfect thing."

"Oh I'm not his wife," my dear lady joined in the protest. "I'm just his sister."

Clever girl.

After three more jewellers and several more offers we couldn't refuse, we'd made our apologies to Jeff and Pru and told them we'd meet up in the bar by the water taxi when they were done.

We had a really nice amble through the streets and found ourselves at the end of the town overlooking the salt pans. With the mountains as a backdrop it was really pretty.

The architecture of the last few stops has been quite similar with brightly painted wooden houses lining the roads, which in most cases are narrow and roughly surfaced.

Anyway, an hour or so later and it was that time of the day again, so back into the main square for a beer and a bit of people watching. Jeff and Pru eventually showed up, but she hadn't found anything that she'd liked, at a price Jeff liked.

It was interesting to hear some of the conversations going on around us as several groups had appeared to have taken part in a popular contest.

'How many free gifts and beers can you scam in a

day without buying anything.'

One couple were bragging that they'd managed to acquire three silver charms and had enjoyed at least six beers apiece in two hours.

Now I'm wondering why I always feel bad about walking out of a shop or market without buying something.

I'm not sure I could knowingly take a freebie in the sure knowledge I wasn't going to buy anything, but then if they're offering why not.

Some folk must have bought a fair few souvenirs during this trip to take home as the water taxi to the port was awash with familiar faces carrying an assortment of new luggage. When we'd got to the embarkation gate there was a massive queue to get back on the ship, as security were asking to search all baggage.

"It's empty," the guy just in front of us was saying.

Now there's a face I haven't seen in a while, it was 'Bellyman'.

The official had explained that he still needed to have a look.

Bellyman held it by the straps and shook it vigorously, "Did you hear that?" he'd asked, "Not a sound. Why? because it's empty."

"You're holding up the line sir, put the case on my table and open it, or my colleagues will." Two huge man mountains standing nearby threw their shoulders back.

Even I was getting suspicious at this point.

He had little choice but to comply.

"Can you open it now, please sir," the official had asked, tapping the combination lock.

Bellyman had mumbled something to which the officer had replied, "Sorry?"

"I can't," he'd shouted. "I was messing with it in the bar and I've locked it somehow and can't remember the code. Happy now?"

The smile on the officials face indicated he was happy, but not yet finished. He'd reached under his counter and produced a screwdriver. Before the passenger could voice any objection he'd snapped off the lock and opened the case for a quick rummage.

"Thank you sir, you may go now."

Don't you just love to watch a deserved comeuppance in progress?

After a shower and a short nap we were back in the town as it was another late sailing. Not quite as good as St Kitts, but the bar we ate at was very lively and the staff were exceptionally friendly.

On a slightly gloomy note, tomorrow is our last stop before the long journey back across the Atlantic. I thought by this stage we'd both be glad to be heading home, but that's not the case at all.

Sad times indeed.

Saturday 23rd March

Day 75 'Antigua' - Nelson's gaff.

So we've reached the penultimate port of the cruise and our last stop in the Caribbean.

We've also discovered that John Lyons aka George Toolan from a 'Touch of Frost' is on the ship as a guest speaker, and rumour has it there's also a 'Goodie' and a 'Nolan Sister' ready to keep us royally entertained on the trip back home.

But first, let's have a quick look at Antigua.

We've only had one plan in mind for Antigua since we joined the ship in Southampton as friends had told us to head straight for Nelson's Dockyard for a lobster lunch at the Copper and Lumber Hotel.

Jeff and Pru were interested in this as well, so we'd headed off from the port and set Jeff on a taxi driver.

Today he'd picked (on) Kenny who at first seemed a little moody and subdued, a sure sign Jeff had really tightened the screws on the fare.

But he'd quickly perked up and was soon laughing and joking his way to a good tip.

It's almost impossible on any of the islands for the humble tourist to be able to get a taxi for just a specific journey, they all want to give you a tour.

So today's deal with Kenny was he would give us a tour of the island, take us to the dockyard, wait for as long as we wanted and then return us to the port, all for one hundred dollars.

How could we refuse?

We had a really good day, probably one of the best, and as we'd sat eating lobster and drinking beer in the central courtyard of the 'Copper and Lumber' the sun had shone a little brighter and the sea appeared a little bluer.

Home seemed a long way away, in both directions, and it wasn't easy to accept that the time has finally come to exchange this glorious weather for a cold and wet UK.

But on a happier note, I'm excited about the journey back as it'll afford me loads of time to concentrate on this book I'm getting obsessed about writing.

So as we leave the Caribbean I'm definitely

feeling more positive about the future, my future, our future.

I said ten weeks ago that this holiday would be a journey of discovery, and now I've discovered that a new adventure should start each and every day. But it doesn't have to be a frenzied dash into the unknown, in fact adventures can be anything from the emotional exploration of imagination to cooking dinner.

If nothing else I want to take back a lesson learned from the laid back attitude of the islanders here in the Caribbean...'no worries'.

Ode for the restless

Life is not a race for running,
No one wins a medal gold,
And the faster that we run it
Well, the quicker we'll get old.
Think of time as always moving
Flying by or marching on,
Stamping sixty beats a minute
Never pausing, quickly gone.

Never caring if you're famous,
Not a jot if you're well heeled.
Treating everyone as equals
Time convicts, with no appeal.
And you can wish to hold this moment
But it doesn't hang about.
Just remember, time's still passing,
In the end it runs right out.

So, come sit and mull things over
Take the weight off, rest awhile.
Please relax and take it easy,

Slow life down, attempt a smile.
Maybe tarry for a moment,
Afore ye go enjoy a dram,
Ponder long, consider wisely
The fragility of man.

Squander not a single second
Make the best of every day,
Don't glance back, look only forward
No regrets and no dismay
For the time we may have squandered
Worry not just where it went,
Value life for what it gives you,
Every moment wisely spent.

I'd say that the Caribbean has been great and can't wait to return, but then maybe I should take my own advice and have a little patience.

And so to the gym, something else I need to concentrate on while I can as I don't suppose I'll be very motivated back in the cold UK.

My dear lady is already asking how much it'll cost to stay on the ship for another couple of months and won't stop singing 'Let's go round again'.

What have I started?

'On our way home'

Day 76 'at sea' - or maybe that's just a rumour.

I reckon cruise ships are one of the greatest places in the whole of the civilised world for rumours, which range from the simply obvious to the incredibly ridiculous.

They've been going on all the time since we left Southampton, but there seems to have been a crescendo of some of the more bizarre ideas as each of the different sectors approached its conclusion.

Early on there were the stories about certain individuals among the passengers and their status or occupation, with at least ten millionaires, four brain surgeons and an ex SAS officer acting undercover, to name but a few.

We were also supposed to be blessed with the presence of a world famous and well respected fashion designer, a recently retired Preston North End footballer and Paul Daniels. It turned out that the designer was just an eccentric with strangely coloured hair and very little fashion sense, and the footballer had played for North Preston Grammar, his school team back in fifties.

The stories about Paul Daniels however were true, he was on the ship earlier on but every time anyone approached him he'd disappeared.

His shows were actually very good, but he wasn't as popular as the lovely Debbie McGee, the passengers seems to like her a lot, but Paul 'not a lot'.

Again, just kidding.

And so for some of the more ridiculous rumours.

At one point the ship had a crack in the hull, the crew were working to rule and a whole organised gang of passengers had been arrested for nicking stuff from the shops (now that one I could believe)

The weather was going to stop us getting out of Rio, a lightning strike on the ship had confused the radar in the Panama Canal and we were heading in the wrong direction, and don't forget the gods were going to sink us before the Falklands.

A member of the crew had been bitten by a caiman, someone was suing because of a splinter and rum had actually been discovered in the complimentary punch served during the sail away parties (now that's just silly)

Anyway the latest rumours about a Goodie and a Nolan Sister have diminished, but I can say without fear of contradiction that John Lyons is definitely onboard.

There's nothing more embarrassing than suggesting to a popular TV star that you just love the show he's in, and then proving you haven't watched it.

Which is just what I did.

I'd seen all of the early series of 'Frost', and I was disappointed to learn some time ago that they weren't going to make any more episodes. But trust me to put my foot well and truly in it, complete with smelly sock and hobnail boot.

"It must be great to work alongside such a beloved actor like David," I'd said to Mr Lyons when he'd asked if he could share our table in the bar this evening.

"Indeed it is. He's such a comic even when the cameras are off."

I had a question burning in my head, a chance to pay tribute to his own acting skills and maybe ingratiate myself a little (nothing like sucking up to a star)

"When Morse finished," I'd said. "They bought back his sidekick Lewis for his own successful series. Is there any chance George Toolan might be the next great British crime buster? It would be great."

I can't be sure, but I thought I'd heard my dear lady sigh.

"It would be great," John agreed. "But a bit difficult really."

"Why?"

"Because he's dead," my dear lady, Jeff and Pru all shouted together.

I wasn't sure whether to run away or what, but my response came quickly.

"Yeah, but so was Bobby Ewing, and that didn't stop the writers bringing him back."

Maybe I should have run away instead.

Fortunately, it appeared that I was forgiven for this foe par as John stayed chatting with us until dinner. I have to say he's a really nice 'bloke' and the TV people have got it all wrong and missed out on a fantastic opportunity by killing off George.

'Duellin Toolan' would have been a sensational hit.

I didn't know Mary J Blige had a song called 'Mr Wrong', but thanks to my dear lady I do now.

Monday 25th March

Day 77 'at sea' - Sammi Sunbed.

Only the second day of the Transatlantic trip home and already there have been quite a number of arguments among the assembled and the grumpy 'on our way home' monster is starting to raise its head.

Fortunately there hasn't been any full blown 'toe to toe' rows yet, just a few little niggles and the odd spat or two have taken place. There's definitely a smattering of Victor Meldrew type attitudes around, ready to deliver a terse 'You can't do that' or a less than polite 'Do you mind' turn of phrase.

And what have the miscreants who are attracting these remarks done to deserve a verbal tongue lashing?

Have they barged through an orderly queue to reach the last of the tea cakes?

No.

Did they shout obscenities throughout the show company's moving rendition of 'Bring Him Home'?

No (but frankly they should have done)

Were they caught rummaging through Mrs Smiths racy underwear in the laundrette?

Oh come on, have you seen Mrs Smith?

The main cause of these disputes has been space, or more importantly, how someone has positioned, or is positioning themselves within a space.

Just like any resort with a swimming pool the whole lido deck is neatly lined with closely packed chairs and sun loungers each morning, ready to receive the sun worshippers. The early birds, intent on grabbing the best position, proceed to clear some personal space around their chosen spot by shoving the surrounding furniture away.

Like a long line of shopping trolleys the loungers scrape across the wooden deck until the one at the end hits something fixed and halts any further progress.

Now their chosen spot has to be arranged properly with regard to many outside factors, there may even be a touch of Feng Shui going on.

Loungers are turned to face the sun, but any breeze or drifting funnel smoke has to be taken into consideration, along with ensuring there's enough room for making adjustments to ensure an even tan as the day progresses. A small table is obtained for the storage of drinks and other accoutrements.

This ritual is repeated by everyone present resulting in random puddles of occupied loungers arranged identically around the pool, with the rest in a cluttered heap up one corner of the deck, resembling a traffic jam on the M25.

Now as the morning continues, more and more of the bronzed gods arrive for a session of tanning (steady now) and this is when the territorial fights break out. The late arrivals carefully untangle a piece of the discarded furniture and attempt to drag it into a free space.

But those already in position have made sure the space around them isn't quite big enough to accommodate the newcomers, and certainly not in pairs. The best open spots are taken and no one wants to be around the edge as its half in shade.

Negotiations start, with the arrivals trying to persuade several sets of residents to 'shuffle up' a bit, but a reasonable response is not forthcoming.

Of course, it's not the established occupants who

are being inconsiderate, oh no, that would be a preposterous suggestion. Possession as we all know is not only nine tenths of the law, it also allows the possessor of the said space to be an evil selfish bastard as well.

So this is how all the trouble starts, and never seems to end.

Anyway, this afternoon the two of us had managed to find a table overlooking the melee, so we'd settled down with a nice cold bottle of rose to enjoy the drama.

After we'd opened the second bottle, my dear lady had suggested that 'a sun bed's lot is not a happy one' (yes she was singing it to that well know tune from Pirates of Penzance) and she demanded I write one of my ditties in recognition of the sterling work they do, and the perils they face on a daily basis.

Okay, here goes, but remember I've been indulging in the grape as well.

"My name is Sammi Sun-Bed I'm a happy little chap,
My legs all new and shiny, but I'm really in a flap,
This morning someone placed me on this cruise ships lido deck
Now I'm looking all around me and I'm thinking 'flipping heck'
There are rows and rows just like me, but oh no, for goodness sake
They're all grey and shabby, there has been a big mistake.
My name is Sammi Sun-Bed, I'm brand spanking new & clean
Not sagging or discoloured, I'm the best you've ever seen.
I was made to go to St Moritz to laze upon a yacht,
But it seems as though I'm stuck right here, with this disgusting lot."

'Hey young Sammi please be nice', the other's beds replied,
'We were once all pristine fresh, until we came outside.
But just you wait and see what great delights you have in store,
When you've been abused by this lot you'll be crying out for sure'.
"Oh I only want a nice girl her size no more than eight
No children armed with crayons or fatties with a plate.
Only folk who've had a shower and smelling fresh and sweet
I don't want brown disgusting goo all stuck upon my seat."
The others laughed and pointed as the customers arrived,
'Look! here you are young Sammi, try this one out for size'.
A man was getting nearer and our Sammi felt quite shocked
The man was in tight bathing trunks, with shoes and woolly socks.
No no cried Sammi desperately, this really isn't fair
He's twice the size of Wembley, with greasy matted hair.
And they call those budgie smugglers but they're hardly cover alls
What the hell's that hanging out, please god it's not his...cabin key."
Sammi felt that he was breaking, there was nothing he could do,
His only hope at end of day was someone came with glue
To fix the damage now being caused by one almighty lump,
His feet all wedged in Sammi's straps, who was this careless chump?
He could hear his rivets groaning, new legs splayed out of square.
Poor old Sammi Sun-Bed now wished he'd been a chair.

Take that Wordsworth and Poe, what do you

know?

Cummings and Plath, you're having a laugh.

Keats and Bukowski...oh forget it.

Tuesday 26th March

Day 78 'at sea' - weirdoes weirdoes everywhere, with not a drop to drink.

For us, this holiday has been one of the best, but also one of the strangest for no other reason than the inescapable proximity of other people.

Unlike a hotel surrounded by acres of countryside or the like, a ship offers limited space, and it has to be said that at times it's been hard to escape from the weirdoes.

Of which I accept I am one...to a degree.

This isn't a continuing reference to the antisocial behaviour mentioned yesterday, but rather about the opposite end of the spectrum, as there are other folk who actually crave the company of others and want to make friends. You know you're in for some of their unwanted attention when, despite there being no one else in sight, they ask if the seat next to you is occupied.

Thinking about it now, maybe the sun lounger pushers have a valid point after all!

Now I can't be rude, it's not in my nature (but hopefully I'll learn otherwise someday) so I've never refused a request or sent anyone away.

But then inevitably the incomer will spoil a peaceful day by wittering on about something, either complaining, or bragging, or just wanting to offer their opinions to anyone who'll listen.

One particular 'all the way round' couple have been known to clear a deck of its occupants in minutes as once they get an ear to bend they'll go on and on about how unlucky they are and how badly they've been treated by all and sundry.

It's just an annoying drone at a time you're trying to relax.

My dear lady says if it was a wasp she'd kill it.

Still as I've said often, it wouldn't do for us all to be the same.

I was watching the couple in question this morning and at the same time my dear lady had been humming 'Hero' (I doubt it was a reference to me)

So that tune was lodged in my head and I have to offer this to go with the melody:

There are weirdoes
When you look around this ship,
You don't have to search too far
They'll come and find you.
They're all over,
If you wander to the bar,
In the restaurant, or tour
They will be there.

It's a long cruise
If you take this trip alone
Someone reaches out a hand
For you to hold.
Then you face them,
And you realise with fear
That a weirdos sitting near
You can't escape.

Well that was a bit of fun, if not a bit silly.

I hadn't seen Ted around the ship for a while, and he's not been in the gym for the past few days either.

But then today he'd walked past us and I'd called

him back to ask what he'd been up to.

"This and that, my boy," he said with a broad grin on his face.

"And how's your pretty young friend keeping?" my dear lady had asked.

She's only ever seen Ted escorting the young lady to dinner.

"I bet she's sad to be going home after such a lovely holiday," she'd added.

"Oh, I thought you knew she works here on the ship, your man here sees her often enough as she's the gym instructor, Nadia."

So that's why she looked so familiar, but what a difference with her hair down, out of lycra and all dressed up.

"Then I bet she'll miss you when you leave the ship in Southampton."

"Not at all, the Captain married us yesterday and I'm staying on with her."

"Well congratulations, we hope you'll be very happy."

"I will be now," he'd said with a real glint in his eye. "I've been on my own forever, and just when you think that's the way it'll always be, life delivers the one surprise you really weren't expecting, certainly not at my age."

He shook my hand, "Nice to have met you both," he'd said and started to wander off. "But I won't be seeing you in the gym anymore lad. I'm getting plenty of exercise, so no need."

He winked and was gone, a definite spring in his step.

I wonder if he ever managed to pull that bar down.

Don't suppose it matters now.

Wednesday 27th March

Day 79 'at sea' - a challenge.

'We are all different' is absolutely true, and long may it continue to be so.

I'm starting to realise that people are an inspiration, the silly things they do and the unbelievable things they say fascinates me.

Bizarre has grabbed my attention and promotes curiosity, and that in turn arouses emotions and encourages the imagination.

For the past three months I have benefited from the antics of my fellow travellers to fill my journal with nonsense, a process I have really enjoyed.

I don't mean to belittle anyone when I write, but rather remind myself that's not the way I would want to be seen, now or in the future.

When I'm critical of someone I only want it to be because they have been cruel or dishonest to the detriment of others.

My dear lady has actually stated she likes my silly ditties, but after the last two bits of nonsense she wanted me to try my hand at being serious.

Okay, I'm up for it.

In Plain Sight

The eyes that I look through
Have seen so much
From the unmatchable beauty of each season
To the heartless acts of destructive man
These are the same eyes that saw
My first day at school

All those years ago, crying when left alone
Eyes blurred and reddened, confused
At twenty one they looked down the aisle
Toward the one
Whose eyes had caught my eye, captivated
To want to see her always
Clearer than a photo put away in a drawer
To be forgotten
My eyes hold the memory of seeing my children
Enter this world, and my parents leave
And as they focus they reveal what's important
Everything they show
Affects the way I feel, and I shut my eyes tight
To see clearly again

I'm not sure if she liked it or not, she hasn't been able to tell me without crying.

It's all about the eyes.

Thursday 28th March

Day 80 'at sea' - well I'm impressed.

I went for a stroll this morning but my way was blocked by a group of the 'Watchers' who were comparing their new 'babies' in the middle of the promenade deck. Well I say babies but I mean cameras, which are actually the size of a small child. They cradle them like they would a human baby, lovingly caressing the telephoto lens and drooling over pixels, which of course are mega.

The main drawback to these monsters is that they are only able to take pictures of objects smaller than a microbe and at least five miles away. Owing to the sheer weight of their equipment they can't hold it steady for any longer than 1/250th of a second at

800ASA with the f:stop set at 4.

I have no idea what I just said but it sounded right.

Anyway I eventually persuaded them to let me pass without too much more damage to my sanity, or thankfully their babies, and I'd left them comparing close-ups of a wave.

I didn't bother to go round twice.

I spent the rest of the day putting together some ideas for 'the book' and the storyline is really starting to take shape. I've mapped out some characters and a basic synopsis, so I'm well impressed with myself.

My main couple have been trying to start a family for a while without success so she's persuaded him to go to see their doctor.

I'm absolutely chuffed with the way things are building.

Trouble is I'd completely lost track of time and before I realised how late it was my dear lady was hurrying me up to get ready for dinner. I've had no time for my journal so will just have to add a couple of musings before heading off to bed.

How about this for a vicious circle.

We all want convenience but that costs money, so we work longer hours to earn more money to enjoy more convenience. But it's only because we work longer hours that we need more convenience.

Therefore, work less & save money

Oh and a special thought for the day.

Exercise increases heart rate and blood pressure.
Drinking beer increases heart rate and blood pressure.
So drinking beer is exercise.

I can't just let it go at that, so here's a little ditty.

'ditty'

Friday 29th March

Day 81 'at sea' - Good Friday, yes it was thank you.

Apparently we developed a 'slight' problem with one of the onboard generators during the night and the Captain has been on the tannoy this morning to apologise, again.

He had to slow the ship down to conserve energy while the problem is fixed, but this means we're likely to arrive late in Ponta Delgada, resulting in less time for the visit. As a gesture of goodwill the master has arranged for thirty pounds to be credited to each cabins onboard account and hopes that will appease the masses and prevent them from revolting.

Too late.

I mean what do people expect, oh they just annoy me with their inane rantings.

Tomorrow will be our last stop of the trip, and despite his earlier statement the Captain had announced this afternoon that the generator has been fixed and we've managed to make up time.

We won't be that late docking after all.

He's not getting his money back.

Oh well, time to finish another little bit of nonsense I've been working on. It's taken a while and is loosely inspired by hearing about all the stuff folks have bought on their way round. It's called...

THE TWELVE DAYS OF CRUISING

MADEIRA - At the first port of this odyssey my true love bought for me

A Blandys' Madeira wine

I love Madeira wine, so was really happy with this gift from my sexy 'True-Love' and we can share it on our balcony as we cross the Atlantic.

BARBADOS - At the second port of this odyssey my true love bought for me

Two Barbadian t-shirts

And a Blandys' Madeira wine

A t-shirt always comes in handy so a good choice, and we've been at sea six days so another bottle of Madeira to replace the empty one brilliant.

I'm such a lucky lad to have such a wonderful 'True-Love'.

GRENADA - At the third port of this odyssey my true love bought for me

Three spicy nutmegs

Two Barbadian t-shirts

And a Blandys' Madeira wine

Well okay, Grenada is a spice island so it's an appropriate gift. But more Barbadian t-shirts are a bit of a mystery. Still the Blandys' will come in handy for those balmy nights sailing down the Amazon with my 'True-Love'.

ALTER do CHAO - At the fourth port of this odyssey my true love bought for me

Four stuffed piranha

Three spicy nutmegs

Two Barbadian t-shirts

And a Blandys' Madeira wine

The piranha were a bit of a surprise, those teeth are bloody sharp. The nice nurse in the medical centre says the stitches will need to come out in five days, and added I wouldn't bleed so much if I drank less alcohol. At least I was able to use one of the Barbadian t-shirts as a tourniquet, how clever of you to make provision my 'True-love'. Not sure where all those nutmegs went in the confusion though.

MANAUS - At the fifth port of this odyssey my true love bought for me
Five swinging hammocks
Four stuffed piranha
Three spicy nutmegs
Two Barbadian t-shirts
And a Blandys' Madeira wine

The hammocks are really colourful, but why do I need five, or even one for that matter as there's a perfectly good bed in our cabin. But I found the lost nutmegs and like marbles they don't break when you tread on them. The nice nurse has given me some gel for the bruising and a few extra glasses of Madeira should help.

PARINTINS - At the sixth port of this odyssey my true love bought for me
Six Bui Bumba dancers
Five swinging hammocks
Four stuffed piranha
Three spicy nutmegs
Two Barbadian t-shirts
And a Blandys' Madeira wine

Wow, six Bui Bumba dancers, what an unusual gift. At least they'll have somewhere to sleep tonight after setting up the hammocks in the cabin. Around midday they started building a fire on the balcony and were eying up the piranha, so I had them change into Barbadian t-shirts as a disguise and sent them one at a time to the buffet for a curry instead. Hiding the piranha is a dangerous business, maybe I should have been more carefully when I pushed the drawer shut with my bum.

So another trip to the medical centre for a few more stitches from the nice nurse, who has a really gently touch. But why have you moved out of our cabin my 'True-Love'? I know it's getting crowded and a bit smelly, but please come back.

SANTEREM - At the seventh port of this odyssey my true love bought for me
Seven river dolphins
Six Bui Bumba dancers
Five swinging hammocks
Four stuffed piranha
Three spicy nutmegs
Two Barbadian t-shirts
And a Blandys' Madeira wine

Dolphins, live pink river dolphins...really?

You little scamp my 'True-Love', you're having a bit of fun with me I can tell.

The Bui Bumbas kept me up all night drumming, and now there are twelve of the bastards what a bloody racket they make. I've suggested it would be a good idea if they leave at the next port but they say they're too comfy and too well fed to cooperate.

The dolphins are taking turns in the shower, so the bathroom is permanently occupied, and the injury to my backside has gone septic. The nice nurse has given me some antibiotics after telling me that sucking out the poison was unnecessary and unethical. I've begged my 'True-Love' to stop with the generous gifts, but everything has been pre-booked through the cruise company's special gift service and has to run its course. She's also refusing to let me share her new cabin as apparently I smell of fish. But she must miss me because her new cabin smells strongly of my aftershave, it's always been her favourite.

RECIFE - *At the eighth port of this odyssey my true love bought for me*
Eight bags of goldfish
Seven river dolphins
Six Bui Bumba dancers
Five swinging hammocks
Four stuffed piranha
Three spicy nutmegs
Two Barbadian t-shirts
And a Blandys' Madeira wine

Thank goodness my 'True-love' missed out gifts from Fortaleza, that port was s**t!

More bloody fish though, but at least the dolphins have something to eat now. All fourteen of them got quite moody this morning, clicking and whistling their disapproval of their cramped conditions in the bathroom. So the Bui Bumbas kindly offered to lower them over the side of the ship in the hammocks for a swim in the sea. But a fight broke out when they accidently dropped one of the dolphin on a fire they'd built on the balcony. Threats were made and some very unpleasant fishist comments were hurled around, so the dolphins returned to the bathroom and locked the door. I phoned my 'True-Love' in her new cabin today to ask if we could have lunch together, but her nice cabin steward answered, so I presume she was out. He sounded really breathless, probably from vacuuming the carpets.

The very nice nurse took out some of my stitches today and gave me a smile.

SALVADOR de BAHAI - At the ninth port of this odyssey my true love bought for me
  Nine voodoo dollies
  Eight bags of goldfish
  Seven river dolphins
  Six Bui Bumba dancers
  Five swinging hammocks
  Four stuffed piranha
  Three spicy nutmegs
  Two Barbadian t-shirts
  And a Blandys' Madeira wine

At last a useful gift, thank you my 'True-Love'.

I dressed all nine voodoo dollies in Bui Bumba style and threatened to stick pins in and throw them over the side of the ship unless all twenty four dancing drummers promised to leave the ship at the next port. They agreed and kindly lowered and released all of the dolphins back into the sea as well. They'll take all of the t-shirts, hammocks and stuffed piranhas with them so I can start with a clean slate in Rio, if not a clean cabin. Hopefully I can put things right for my 'True-Love' to move back in with me. I've had a word with the ship's security and to my relief they've informed me there are no more scheduled deliveries to be made. Finally my injuries are healing and the very nice nurse says I should make a full recovery once the course of injections is finished. For the first time since Grenada I feel good, and at last the nightmare is over.

RIO de JANERO - At the tenth port of this odyssey my true love bought for me
  Ten Redeemer Statues
  Nine voodoo dollies
  Eight bags of goldfish

Seven river dolphins
Six Bui Bumba dancers
Five swinging hammocks
Four stuffed piranha
Three spicy nutmegs
Two Barbadian t-shirts
And a Blandys' Madeira wine

Why my 'True-Love' why?

Apparently security lied to me so as not to spoil the surprise. The very nice nurse has told me not to worry too much, and promised to continue to help me through this difficult time. I'm going to pray to the Redeemer via these newly delivered effigies to give me guidance, show me the light and bless my nice nurse.

MONTEVIDEO - At the eleventh port of this odyssey my true love bought for me
Eleven Tango Dancers
Ten Redeemer Statues
Nine voodoo dollies
Eight bags of goldfish
Seven river dolphins
Six Bui Bumba dancers
Five swinging hammocks
Four stuffed piranha
Three spicy nutmegs
Two Barbadian t-shirts
And a Blandys' Madeira wine

Bloody Tango Dancers, now there's a f*****g novelty. Come on my 'True-Love' surely you can do better than that. This is the home of the gaucho so why no horses or cows to deposit more s**t in my room? My cabin's completely trashed anyway so I've taken refuge in the medical centre with the remaining bottle of Madeira. Even my nice nurse laughed at your unimaginative gift, and held my hand a lot and stroked my head, so kind.

THE FALKLAND ISLANDS - At the twelfth port of this odyssey my true love bought for me
Twelve Gento Penguins
Eleven Tango Dancers
Ten Redeemer Statues
Nine voodoo dollies
Eight bags of goldfish
Seven river dolphins
Six Bui Bumba dancers
Five swinging hammocks
Four stuffed piranha
Three spicy nutmegs
Two Barbadian t-shirts
And a Blandys' Madeira wine

Ok my so called sodding 'True-Love' you win.
The projectile defecating penguins are the final straw you b***h. You're dumped, you hear me, you're gone, finished. And I'll tell you something else you tramp, the nice nurse likes me and is looking after me and makes me feel good about myself, so there.
We have so much in common, in fact we even wear the same aftershave!

Well I'm glad I got that out of my system as it's been nagging at my brain for the last few days. I'm just relieved the original version stopped at twelve.

<u>Saturday 30th March</u>

Day 82 'Ponta Delgada'
There's something special about approaching

land from the open sea. Initially there is no more than the faintest of lines on the horizon, like a veil of mist on the edge of the world. As it grows the mist becomes a grey shadow with just the suggestion of form. But then it starts to look more like land, with silhouettes of mountains and trees rising out of the sea slowly and majestically.

It's a wonderful sight, and you catch your breath in anticipation of things to come, a new place, a new culture full of interesting sights, sounds and smells. Your imagination runs amok with the desire to set foot on dry land, to experience all that this mysterious place has to offer.

Then some git with a squeaky voice calls out to let you and everyone else within earshot know that he's disgusted by the price of orange juice in the bar.

Yes, thanks for that mate.

There was a bit of drizzle in the air today so we'd watched the mid-morning 'sail in' from the comfort of the upper bar. This same guy had been moaning for ages about the cost of everything on the ship, and how much profit they must be making out of him.

He was also bragging that this was his eighth world cruise, so maybe he's right.

Anyway, I'm reminded to ask the Captain about introducing 'Toss the Tosser' for the last few days, as I'm sure he too will have a list of potential participants.

Ponta Delgada was really nice, apart from the weather, and it was a shame we only had a few hours to stretch our legs and have a cup of really decadent hot chocolate.

We were wondering if some of our lot had developed a bit of a death wish, as there had been quite a queue to hire a Segway to explore the town.

That was fun to watch, but not so much for those who fell off...often.

I didn't realise some folk considered killing themselves was better than going back home.

My dear lady was singing 'Here comes the rain again' in the shower as I'd left the cabin to spend another lonely session in the gym.

I'm going to send a letter to the cruise company when we get home, I mean why would anyone spend their holiday in the gym?

Sunday 31st March

Day 83 'at sea' - Easter Sunday tips.

With reference to my earlier comments about rumours, there's a tale being distributed about some members of the crew receiving in excess of two thousand dollars in gratuities each month.

Ah, so it's that time again.

At the end of each leg there's an opportunity to reward the waiters and stewards who have looked after us so well by tipping them. I've been told that this has been part of cruise etiquette for all time, and still forms a large part of the overall staff remuneration. In comparison to the cost of the cruise it's a very small amount and although it's not compulsory, it's expected, unless of course you haven't been happy with the service.

Now I understand that for us Brits tipping is always a bit of a hot topic because it's not a culture we're generally used to, but come on meanies, you know the situation and you should factor the cost in with the holiday.

I'm so disappointed to hear passengers scheming on how they'll get out of paying their gratuities.

One couple has stated that they'd seen their waiter ashore at one of the ports, and as he had the latest iphone and was shopping for an expensive watch, then he's obviously paid far too much and wouldn't need their hard earned cash.

Others have criticised the efforts of the staff, claiming to be unhappy with the service they've received as the reason to avoid parting with the cash they deserve, yet in each port the same folk will pay ten bucks for a tatty t-shirt.

Shame on you.

It's customary to give gratuities on the final evening on board, but it was noticeable at the end of each of the other sectors how many of those who were leaving didn't show up in the restaurant. I no doubt the same will happen on Tuesday, as some folk will go to any length to save a bob or two.

Next there be some poor soul claiming that they won't be paying their gratuities owing to the heavy loses they've suffered at the gaming tables, or that they need to be careful with the pennies because they've just booked another two cruises.

Oh too late, I heard both of those excuses last night.

Maybe it's time to start a new rumour, folk who don't pay their gratuities are going to be put on an international 'tight wads' register and are likely to be banned admission into any of the bars or restaurants on any cruise ship in the future.

I am truly amazed by some of the excuses...but somehow I'm not surprised...and my dear lady wonders why I increasingly declare 'I hate people!'

Well some of them.

For now I'm off to the laundrette, I have a rumour to start.

Monday 1st April

Day 84 'at sea' - what a fool.

The weather has been very mixed today and the captain has suggested that things may get a little rough over the next couple of days (let the rumours of impending doom begin)

But it appeared that no one believed him as it's April Fools Day, and as the skipper had taken his usual stroll around the ship he'd been greeted by a barrage of 'Nice try Captain, you can't fool us'.

I'm really starting to hope it isn't a prank, and considering where we are and where we're going my money's on the Captain getting the last laugh.

It's been really funny watching the sun worshippers trying to catch the last vestige of the big yellow ball in the sky on the odd few occasions it's poked its head out from behind the clouds. They race for the loungers, stripping off to reveal as much skin as they dare, then collapse in a heap with arms spread wide to maximise their exposure, only to be disappointed by an immediate appearance of a dark cloud and shower of rain, which promptly sends them scurrying for cover.

But the weather is just playing 'peek a boo' and the fine rain stops almost as soon as they make it back inside, and once again the sun comes out. So they attempt to return, only to be spotted once again, that devious precipitation waiting just long enough for them to bare all and relax. Such fun it has with them.

Anyway, enough silliness.

On second thoughts, there's always room for silliness, but I couldn't possibly say where the inspiration for this came from.

Silent Gassings
Why can't women fart like men?
It really isn't fair,
To not announce to those around
There's methane in the air.
A man will trump with dignity,
His head held high with pride.
Embarrassed not by loud retort
To be identified.

Now fuss-less knack the ladies have
Techniques that never fail,
With covert wind that barely moves
A mark on Beaufort scale.

But lack of sound just covers up
Foul breath released, and if
The lady be a beauty
More odorous the whiff.

They'll pass it off and blame the dog,
Or point toward their man.
He's had a chicken balti,
Several pints and keema nan.

But let's just look at facts here,
From Queen to bears in wood,
To save us all exploding
Venting gas is good.

So come on girls, when passing wind

Allow your light to shine,
Give a hearty farty thrump,
And holler, "That one's mine."

Sorry ladies.

Tuesday 2nd April

Day 85 'at sea' - but not for much longer.

Well the packing is all done and we're not far from the Isle of Wight approach, so as I also need to pack my journal away this will be a short entry.

Then we'll be off to say our goodbyes, especially to Jeff and Pru.

It has, without doubt, been fun (most of the time), frustrating (some of the time) but it's also fair to say that our journey was made a little bit more special thanks to the people we've met purely on the whim of the Maitre D when he'd allocated places on table one two eight.

Strange, because somehow I'm not sure we'd be this compatible back home, but with a common purpose it has worked. I doubt there's a future for any of the associations we've made because of the distance we live away from each other, but it was very good while it lasted.

And finally, a question has to be answered...was this the voyage of discovery we were promised?

The answer is a resounding yes, in many ways both geographically and personally, especially as I'm rediscovering many of the wonderful things that I'd stupidly forgotten about my dear lady.

So thank you South America, we had a blast.

'Amazon and Atacama Amazed'

'Caribbean and Columbia Charmed'

'Penguins and Panamas Perfect'

Hang on a minute...Penguins and Panamas?
Now there's an idea.

Acknowledgements

Jamie Gray would like to give his thanks to everyone he bored to death with his relentless and unreasonable demands to read excerpts from this manuscript, as well as those he bullied into agreeing he's a fantastic and witty writer.

Specifically he wishes to show his gratitude to his family who have resisted the urge to have him committed long enough for him to complete this demanding project.

He also wishes to personally thank you the reader for persevering to this furthest point and hopes the nightmares will end soon.

His wife should receive the greatest proportion of his gratitude though, as not only did she tolerate the afore mentioned 85 unbroken nights in his company, but has had to repeatedly relive those 85 nights for the past three years. Jamie has promised her another long holiday now this project is finished.

His wife is keeping her options open.

Disclaimer

The author has described the ports visited in relation to the activities he and his wife participated in, and is his own opinion. This does not constitute an official overview of any of the locations or what is or isn't available. Costs quoted may have changed

36353514R00220

Printed in Great Britain
by Amazon